NO GODS WEST of HERE

BOOKS BY HANNA GAARD

MYTHCYCLE

No Gods West of Here

No Saints Left Standing (January 2027)

A MYTHCYCLE NOVEL

NO GODS WEST of HERE

HANNA GAARD

No Gods West of Here
A Mythcycle Novel

Paperback ISBN: 979-8-9949780-0-9
Ebook ISBN: 979-8-9949780-1-6

Library of Congress Control Number: 2026917350

Published in Astoria, Oregon USA by the author in 2026.

With gratitude for bad decisions
that teach us what we want & deserve.

♥

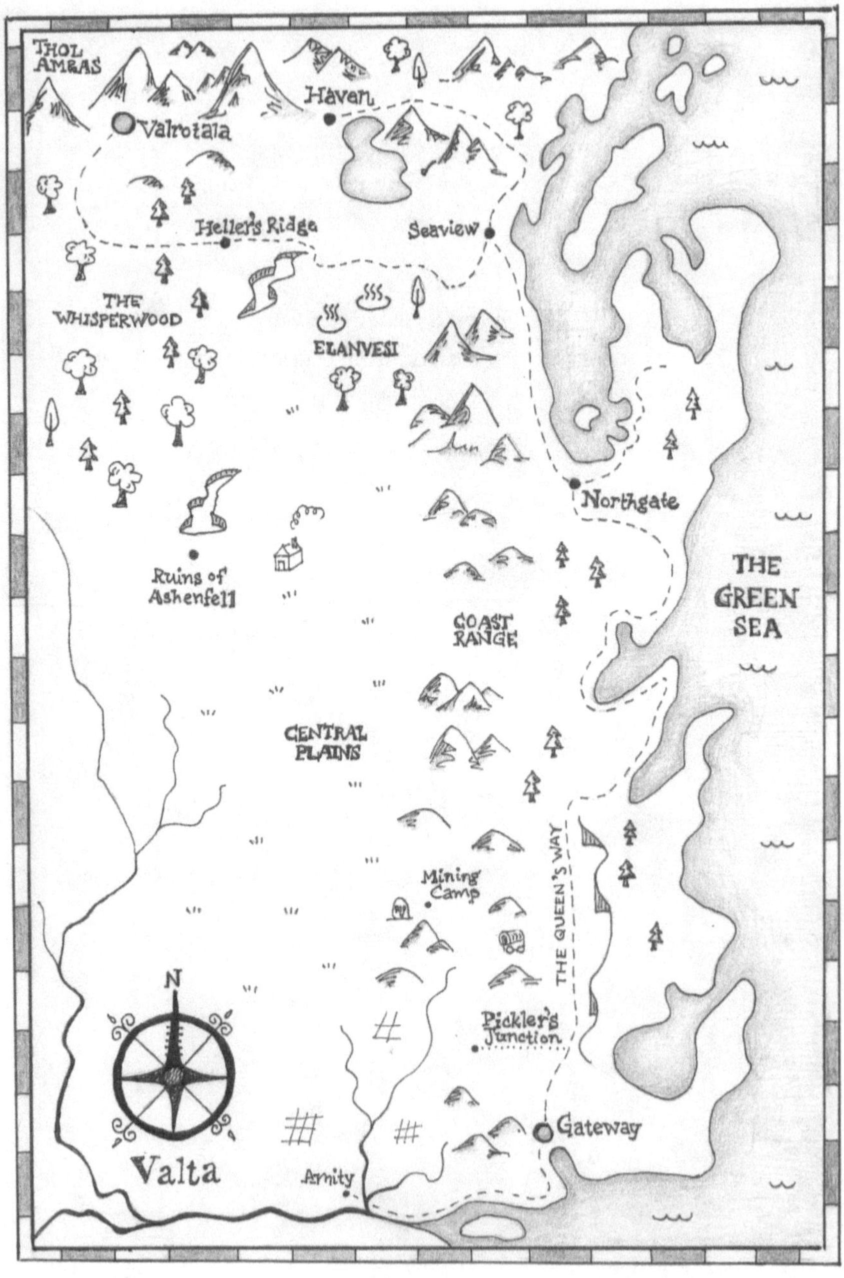
THOL AMRAS
Haven
Valrotala
Heller's Ridge
Seaview
THE WHISPERWOOD
ELANVESI
Northgate
Ruins of Ashenfell
THE GREEN SEA
COAST RANGE
CENTRAL PLAINS
Mining Camp
THE QUEEN'S WAY
N
Pickler's Junction
Gateway
Valta
Amity

AUTHOR'S NOTE

No Gods West of Here is an adult romantic fantasy that contains language and themes intended for mature audiences.

This book includes strong language, violence against people and animals, gun violence, murder, blood and gore, depictions of sex acts, grief, trauma, historical accounts of slavery and genocide, colonization and its impact, attempted sexual assault, and a dubious consent scenario involving coercion and deception. One scene involves the death of young animals (this occurs off-page).

A complete list of content warnings is available at:

www.hannagaard.com/content-warnings

ACT I

NO CLEAN CHOICES

1

THE BODYGUARD NO ONE ASKED FOR

TALIA

I came to Valta looking for a faerie story. I found a monster.

— T. SALAREN, PRIVATE NOTES, 401 AC

On the third day at sea, Talia returned to find her cabin door ajar, which was impossible. She *knew* she'd locked it. She nudged the door with her toe and froze.

A man sat in her desk chair, elbows braced on his knees. The journal—*that* journal—lay open in one hand. His fingers hovered over the ancient text, a lattice of white scars across his knuckles. So he wasn't a scholar then.

At least he couldn't read it. Only a handful of people understood the dead language, and she taught most of them.

Her fingers gripped the doorframe, and she straightened her glasses before forcing herself to step inside.

"Excuse me." She had to swallow to get the words out. "This is my cabin."

He looked up with a flat expression, as if she were the one out of place. His eyes were pale gray, not even a color. How strange.

"You should've locked the door." He glanced back down at the page.

He has to be baiting me. She bit back a sharp response and stepped farther into the room. His shoulders curled forward, just a little, shifting to cradle the book in both hands.

She stopped mid-step. "Who are you?"

"Riven Valros. I'm to escort you to Gateway." He still acted like he was reading.

She closed her eyes and exhaled slowly. *Right*—so she hadn't gotten away after all. Her family just made her leash longer and brought in this hulking stranger to hold it.

"You really shouldn't have that," she tried.

"Neither should you." He closed the journal, making no move to relinquish it.

Her chest tightened. She *shouldn't* have it. She needed to get it back, but she couldn't call for help. Anyone who came would see the journal, and that little book could destroy her career.

The ship lurched. She pitched forward, grabbing the edge of the desk to steady herself. Riven stood in one smooth motion and caught her shoulder, feet planted wide against the tilt. The scent of cedar washed over her, clean and biting.

He cradled the journal gently in his other hand, like he knew what it was worth. Like he knew how to handle precious things. Heat rushed to her cheeks, thoroughly unwelcome, but he wasn't looking at her face. He was looking down at her arm.

"Where's your partner?" He picked up her hand and tipped it to the side, making the delicate silver engagement bracelet spin around her wrist.

"We were—I didn't—" The words hurt. "It's over." *Turns out, getting on a ship to cross the world without telling your fiancé first will do that.*

His hand paused there, wrapped around hers. She waited for the usual rush.

Nothing came.

Skin to skin contact always brought emotion with it. An echo of whatever the person felt. This man gave her nothing. If he cared at all, she wouldn't know.

He released her and, finally, set the journal in her hand. He moved past her to the door and paused with one hand on the frame. She caught herself noticing the strain of fabric across his shoulders. The blue silk was elegant, incongruous with his scarred hands.

"*Turvamei,* scholar," he said.

Safe journey.

A formal farewell in flawless Starscript. How did a hired blade know that phrase?

"*Teiti varlo tiesi.*" The counter-greeting slipped out before she could stop herself.

And the stars light your way.

He gave a small nod. "Lock your door, boss. You're a long way from the capital. Out here, if folks want something, they take it."

The door clicked shut.

She lunged forward, her hands shaking so badly it took two tries to turn the lock.

Just what I needed. A bodyguard I never asked for. She never thought of comebacks in time.

She sank into the empty chair, too shaken to climb to her bunk. Her grandmother knew exactly where she was, which meant Holloway would too. How long until they sent someone to bring her home?

She hugged the journal to her chest. The leather was still warm from Riven's touch.

She needed to complete her research, but that was going to be harder now with Riven Valros watching her every move, especially if he spoke Starscript and picked locks.

Talia sighed. *This is going to be a very long voyage.*

Sure enough, Riven was in the dining salon the next morning. In the library when she retreated to read. When she found him perched against the deck rail in the afternoon sun gazing at the horizon as if he wasn't there waiting for her, she'd had enough.

"This is ridiculous. What could you possibly report back to my grandmother? 'Still on a boat'?"

The wind was brisk, tugging curls out of her braid. She fought to look serious while clawing them back out of her face.

"Who said I'm reporting back?" was all he said. It was an infuriating thing to do, answering a question with a question. She decided to ignore him from there on out.

Riven didn't seem to care when she glared or gave him the silent treatment. He just matched her silence as he trailed her around the ship. Days passed that way. The standoff was ridiculous, but she wasn't going to be the one to break it.

Since she couldn't study the journal during the day, she'd taken to interviewing prospectors instead. Twenty years since Valta was discovered, eighteen since the first flux claim, and the relic rush was in full swing. Half the Lower City seemed to be crammed into steerage. That's where she was, mid-conversation with a fortune-seeking clerk, when a loud boom rocked the ship.

Her stomach lurched, and she reached to catch herself on a pile of crates, which slipped under her hands. Riven was beside her before she saw him move. He reached down and helped her to her feet.

"You seem to fall a lot."

Talia had no idea if he was joking or not. She hadn't seen him smile once.

"It's not me, it's the ship," she said, brushing herself off. "What happened?"

A shout went up from the passageway. A group of prospectors was crowded together, and the first mate elbowed through.

Instead of pulling back, Talia pressed forward for a better view. The crowd parted, and a man was carried out on a stretcher. A tan arm hung over the edge, veins black as ink spreading under the skin. Talia pressed herself against the wall to let them by, and when she did, a small round stone fell off the stretcher.

It rolled to her feet; she picked it up. The moment her skin touched it, energy surged through her. Emotions hit her in rapid succession. Panic. Then euphoria. Then something vast and hollow, like falling. Stabbing pain shot through her arm.

Riven's large hand closed around her wrist. "Drop it."

She held on. He yanked her back, and her shoulder slammed

into his chest. The stone slipped from her grip and hit the wood floor. He kicked it away, sending it skidding under a crate.

"We should get abovedeck." His tone didn't invite her to argue.

"What happened to that man's arm?" She was so shaken, she forgot that she wasn't speaking to him.

"You've never seen burnout." He seemed almost surprised.

"Obviously not. That was a flux stone, right? What did it do to him?" She hated admitting when she didn't have an answer, but she needed to know. "What's burnout?"

Riven glanced at her hand, then back at her face. He hesitated, like he wasn't sure how much to say.

"When you channel too much flux," he said, "it can hurt you. Or kill you."

She didn't know what that meant, but a term flashed in her memory. *Flux channeling*. She'd seen it in one place only: Vael's journal. The heretical one she had in her satchel at that moment.

"What does that mean, to channel flux?" *Say more, you infuriating man.*

"What do you call it?" he asked. "Burning flux?" Not an answer.

Prospectors clawed flux from the earth, then lamps and furnaces burned it for fuel. A *person* couldn't burn flux. The verb didn't make sense, and she'd never seen anything like the damage on that man's arm. Could that have happened to her too? But Riven had gone quiet again. Done being helpful, apparently. This was exactly why she was supposed to be ignoring him.

Her palm was tingling. The sensation was fainter now but still noticeable. She went back to the dining salon and played a solitary card game while he hovered in the corner.

Later that evening when she was finally alone in her cabin, Talia cracked open the journal. She knew the exact page.

Stars and fucking moons, this voyage was meant to be our salvation, but this continent will be our grave. Flux channeling was the foundation of civilization. Now we are surrounded by mortals, and we grow more like them by the day. Disgusting.

The journal had been written by a god, Vael, the Divine Navigator, but it didn't read like scripture. This was one of the tamer passages. Laced with profanity and scenes of debauchery, it made all thirteen gods out to be frauds and petty assholes. That was heresy, even if it was true.

Vael called channeling "the foundation of civilization," but she'd never heard of it. And yet a hired blade recognized the word?

Nothing about Riven Valros made sense.

And now that he knew she had Vael's journal, her life was in his hands.

2

WELCOME TO GATEWAY

TALIA

Within ten years, flux had made people rich beyond reason and transformed backwaters like Gateway into true cities. Few questioned where it came from or what it cost. There was simply too much money to be made.

— *THE FOUND CONTINENT: COMMERCE AND COLONIZATION IN VALTA*, ALDER PELL, 411 AC

The smell hit her first, a mix of sawdust, brine, and bodies. Beneath it, the metallic tang of flux generators working overtime. Dockhands shouted, cranes groaned, children darted through the crowd with open hands. Gateway struck Talia as the sort of place where anyone could show up with a new name and an interesting story, and no one would care if either was true. A city for fresh starts.

She ran down the gangplank. Seventeen days on that cramped ship had left her itching to move. Holloway would track her down eventually. He always did. But if she slipped into this crowd, maybe she could be someone new first. Just for a little while.

The gangplank flexed under her feet, and she looked back to see Riven with a valise in each hand. She hopped down onto the dock and gasped when the press of bodies didn't make space for her. An elbow dug into her side. Someone's shoulder slammed into hers. Hands tugged at her jacket, and she pulled her battered leather satchel to her chest, curling her fingers around the buckle.

"Spare a coin, miss?" A pair of dark eyes stared up at her from beneath a pile of curls. It was a child, their tiny fingers outstretched.

Before she could answer, Riven shouldered past and dropped her luggage with a crash. The child's eyes went big, and they melted back into the street.

He stood out on the crowded pier. A head taller than Talia, who was taller than most men. Broad as a doorframe. His unusually fair hair—very pale blond, like his beard—was tied back, his expression unreadable.

"Stay close." The crowd broke around him, and suddenly she could breathe. "This isn't Vaelis."

Perfect. He was already treating her like a child. But technically, wasn't she his employer? She forced a smile.

"Thank you for the escort," she said, reaching for the tone her grandmother used with staff. "I'll manage from here. You can go."

"No," he said simply. "Do you have the address?"

He held out a hand. She hesitated, then fished the fellowship acceptance letter out of her satchel. His eyes fell to the page. She took one step back, watching his face as he read. She took another step back, but his eyes stayed fixed on the paper.

A gap opened between a man with a wide-brimmed hat and some kind of blue-robed priest. *I'll find a way to collect my luggage later*, she decided as she slipped between them into the crowd.

The docks had crowded her, but the street swallowed her whole. Bodies pressed in, reeking of sweat. Mud sucked at her boots. A crane swung overhead, gears sputtering as it strained under its load. She wrestled a notebook and pencil out of her satchel, jotting in the margin: *flux power everywhere!*

She made it maybe twenty paces before a hand landed heavy on her shoulder.

"Nice try, boss."

Riven towered over her as he plucked the notebook from her fingers, marked the page, and snapped it shut. He steered her out of the current of bodies and handcarts and into a narrow corridor between a warehouse and a flux transformer. It hummed so loud her teeth buzzed.

"I'm perfectly capable—"

"Of getting yourself crushed. I can see that." He handed back the notebook. "Consortium is at Fourth and Fuller. Let's go."

She wasn't sure what to say. She'd barely left the Upper City before this voyage. Could she even find the address on her own?

"Where's my luggage?"

His hand found the small of her back. "I sent it on ahead. Stay close."

They pushed into the next street, and Gateway shifted into new colors and shapes, like the turn of a kaleidoscope. Half-finished buildings climbed between colorful market stalls and teetering stacks of crates. In one storefront display, clear bowls overflowed with blue crystals that appeared to be charged with flux.

Wooden poles rose up at regular intervals with wires strung between them, and atop each pole was some kind of lantern. Back home, flux was rationed. Here, it lit every street corner.

She wanted to look at the window display, but movement yanked her attention back to the square. A massive wooden cart careened into view, an iron cage strapped to the top. As the cage rocked and tipped, a metallic groan echoed from the vehicle.

The crowd shifted like a wave, and voices rose to shouts, solidified into warnings. Talia pushed forward instead of back, craning her neck to see what was inside. The crowd peeled apart, and something pressed against the cage bars.

Her first impression was of a giant insect. Mirrored eyes caught every flicker of light. Mandibles clacked like misfiring gears. The spined neck led to a catlike body with a long, whiplike tail. Veins under its hide pulsed with blue light. *Insect, panther, monster*. Words slid through her mind, but none of them fit.

Riven's arm locked around her waist, and he hauled her back, her bootheels dragging lines in the dirt. The cart roared into the space she'd just been standing, so close her skirts whipped sideways. The world seemed to slow as the cage passed in front of her face. The mirrored eyes locked on hers, and Talia saw herself reflected as it saw her. Small and vulnerable. Prey.

A keening scream tore out from behind clashing mandibles,

rolling into a pattern that sounded almost like words. The creature hurled its full body against the bars. Once. Twice. Three times. Metal whined under the strain.

The bars held. The wooden cart beneath it wasn't so strong, and it folded. Wheels buckled. The axle snapped, and the cage slid back off the broken platform, slamming into hard-packed dirt with enough force to crack the door open.

The monster flattened itself between the bars and scrambled to its feet.

A scream climbed Talia's throat, but she pressed her lips together so only a strangled hum came out. Riven stepped between her and the chaos. She wasn't a small person, but he lifted her from the waist and spun her away from the street as if she weighed nothing. He set her back down behind a wall of crates and pressed cold metal into her palm—a gold-plated revolver with Starscript etched along the barrel. Undoubtedly a relic. In her panic, Talia's only thought was how pretty it was.

"Stay here," he said, voice calm. "Use this only if you must. Do not run. The *ruthopanth* will chase."

Ruthopanth. She didn't know that word. Was it Starscript? A few Starscript roots could fit. *Rothma* meant "shadow" or "darkness." *Ruthei* meant "untamed" or "wild."

Her brain chased the puzzle as she crouched behind the crates. Language made logical sense, even when the world around her didn't. She had heard rumors of monsters in Valta, but this was something else—

Then Riven drew his swords, and she gasped out loud, losing her train of thought. He held two long blades made of some kind of silver metal, with crystalline cores that pulsed blue. As the blades cleared their sheaths, they hummed low like a swarm of bees.

He moved too fast to follow. The monster lunged, and Riven was already sidestepping, lowering a blade to catch it in the side. Dark fluid seeped from the wound, and it recoiled with a howl. The flux street lamps overhead flickered to life, guttered, flared blue sparks, and shattered, like they'd been overloaded.

The square had largely emptied, but not everyone had made it out. The cart's driver lay pinned in the wreckage.

The wounded creature circled once, darted in, and yanked him out with its mandibles. Flipping its head, it tore the man apart. Bits of bone and flesh sprayed.

That's when she noticed the children huddled behind a market stall.

Where are the enforcers? Is anybody coming?

Her gaze locked on the children, a girl clutching two smaller boys. The monster hadn't noticed them yet, but it only had to turn.

It's just me. Curse all the gods.

She raised the revolver and pulled back on the trigger. It clicked harmlessly, and she screamed in frustration.

Riven had circled behind the ruined cart. Now he stepped back into view, engaging the *ruthopanth*. His silk shirt was torn. Blood and ichor ran down one arm, red and black, but his steps were even. *He's fine, right? He has to be okay.*

She couldn't work the gun, and there was no clean shot now. She dropped the relic and edged closer to the children, flinching as broken glass crunched under her boots.

A generator behind the monster sizzled, blue sparks cascading from damaged coils. It didn't look so different from the flux conduits at her grandmother's manor. Shouldn't the principles be the same? If she could just close the circuit, maybe she could get it to overload like the street lamps had.

She reached down and grabbed a piece of shredded lamppost. It felt like metal in her hand. *Let's hope it's conductive.* She lifted it and threw as hard as she could.

The shard twisted through the air before striking the generator, and energy exploded outward in a crackling arc of blue light. She grinned. *Definitely conductive.* A curved bolt struck the monster squarely in the side once, then twice. The veins under its skin flickered, too, like it was part flux itself. *Now that's interesting.* The creature's howl sounded like metal on metal, and its head thrashed as it backed away from the generator.

Riven took the opening. He crossed both blades in front of his body, pointing down, and plunged them into the monster's neck, nearly severing its head. The *ruthopanth* convulsed and went still.

He paused over the body, exhaled, and tipped his head to each side, cracking his neck. He wiped each blade on the creature's corpse, smearing black ichor on its ruined hide like he'd done it a hundred times. Maybe she shouldn't have been so eager to shake him off. She took a steadying breath and approached him.

"You killed it," Talia said, feeling ridiculous as the words slipped out. *Obviously he killed it.*

"You helped." His face was splattered with blood and flux dust, but underneath the mess, he was looking at her differently. Brackets around his mouth hinted at a smile.

Was that a compliment?

A bell clanged somewhere nearby. The noise echoed through the empty streets and faded. The children emerged from their hiding place, glanced around, and took off running.

"What's that bell about?" Riven called after them.

"Curfew, mister," the girl yelled back, not stopping. "Best get inside." The kids slipped down an alley and were gone.

The square stood at the intersection of four streets, and down each of them lights blinked out as doors and shutters slammed.

Talia picked up the revolver from where she'd dropped it in the dirt, sliding it into her satchel as she walked up to Riven's side. The sun had fallen without her noticing; the streetlights were blown out, windows going dark. She shivered, rubbing her arms.

"We need to get off this street." Riven's voice rumbled, all hints of a smile gone.

They cut across the square, weaving through the wreckage of broken carts and spilled fruit. A squeak drew her attention up to a sign swinging on rusted chains: *Rooms by the hour.* The building leaned sideways against its neighbor, paint flaking, windows pulsing with strange greenish light.

Riven tugged the door open, gesturing for her to go ahead.

The bell tolled again, and Talia flinched.

"This place? Really?" she whispered. Her hands still shook. Blood and mud spotted her skirt, and the revolver weighed heavy in her satchel, still unfired.

"Safer inside than out."

Talia had barely stepped over the threshold when the door slammed shut behind them, cutting off the bells mid-clang. Heat and noise engulfed her, and sweat prickled her skin. On the walls, blue flux lamps buzzed inside green glass bottles, casting everything in sickly turquoise. Smoke twirled in the air, smelling burned and sour. She coughed.

Riven pressed in behind her, pinned between the closed door and her frozen form. She mumbled an apology and stepped farther into the room. A jerky movement caught her eye to the right. A flash of skin. A woman was straddling someone's lap in a corner booth, dress pooled around her hips, a man's fingers clutching her bare thighs.

Talia's gaze jerked away and landed on a raised platform. A dancer moved with nothing above her waist but jewelry and sweat, coins glinting at her feet. Against the far wall, a man knelt between a woman's skirts. Suddenly she saw all of it, every corner, every booth. *This isn't an inn.*

An emotion—*lust*—slammed into her chest, thick and suffocating. It wasn't hers. Desire so raw it burned her fingertips. Anger spiked through her ribs. Fear coiled in her stomach, metallic and cold. Every emotion in the room crashed through her body, one after the other, tangled and relentless.

She couldn't breathe. Couldn't sort her own feelings from the onslaught.

Her gift for empathy had only ever been triggered through physical touch, one person at a time. This, whatever this was, was radiating off the entire room like heat from stoked coals.

"Boss?" Riven's voice came from somewhere far away.

The room spun. Her knees gave out. By every god, what was happening?

3

THE LEASH

DAWN

Green cloaks GO HOME (in boxes)

— PAINTED ON A DOCKHOUSE WALL, GATEWAY

Dawn didn't pick her targets anymore. Just killed what she was pointed at, same as any weapon. That's why she was under a table, cheek pressed to a sticky floor. Someone was getting railed on the other side of a too-thin wall, judging by the rusty whine of old mattress coils. She would have picked a nicer brothel, herself. This one smelled like old gin and cheap perfume. Like it'd quit trying.

The *savuthe* smoke tugged at her. The flash of skin under skirts teased. *Not yet,* she told herself. *Work first. Fuck later.*

The squeaking quit. Not a minute later, a door swung open and her target strutted out with his shirt buttoned crooked. *Good for him. At least he got one last tumble.* He was younger than she expected. A haversack hung over his shoulder.

Dawn waited a beat after the door closed and then slid to her feet, shadow-quiet. Only her necklace of trophies clinked faintly. She adjusted her hat to tuck the pink ends of her hair under the brim. Most folks in this town knew her on sight, and the hair was a dead giveaway.

The man paused in the alley to light a pipe. A flame flared behind his curled hand before her knife sliced into his throat. Blood surged warm and thick over her wrist. She eased him down quietly, a practiced motion.

His pockets gave up a few coins, a sealed packet, a ring fat with sapphires. She slipped it all into her jacket. The haversack had fallen open when he dropped, and papers spilled in the dust along with a green cloak, unfolding as it slipped to the ground.

Dawn froze. She held up the cloak. Three silver pins glinted at the collar. Not just an enforcer. An enforcer captain.

"Fuck."

Always before, Lore had sent her after corrupt merchants, gang leaders, maybe an ex-lover or two. Enforcers were Pentarchy military police. That shit should be off-limits.

She stuffed the cloak back in the bag with the papers. She'd killed plenty of assholes, but this crossed a line. Dawn had her own secrets. She didn't need this kind of heat.

She wiped the blade on the dead man's shirt. Slipped down the alley. Walked fast, but not too fast.

She fucking hated this job.

Dawn rounded a corner and nearly ran into Lorry Jones pissing on a wall. He grinned and waggled his cock at her. *Jackass.* Didn't need to see that. Didn't need him to place her here either.

Patrol lamps flashed at the end of the block. She palmed her knife, considered her options, and knocked into Lorry. He grunted, but he didn't seem to notice that Dawn slipped the bloody knife into his pocket as she passed.

When she reached the end of the alley, she tipped her hat forward and shouted at the patrol. "If you're looking for the captain, he was talking to that guy!"

The soldiers pivoted toward Lorry. Dawn kept on going. *Poor bastard should've stayed home.* She refused to feel bad. A choice between a drunk criminal and her own skin? That was easy math.

Starfall Sanctuary sat on the western edge of Gateway, where half-built chaos gave way to rocky foothills. The compound walls were real stone. The city would grow up around them and fall to rot long before those walls crumbled.

Inside, gardens ran in neat rows with enough food to feed a

small army. Children darted between the cabbages. Their laughter made Dawn smile. A flux generator hummed smooth and steady. Blue-robed acolytes shuffled through the complex.

Her jaw tightened. The prophet had built all this. Lore Tavis, with his slick speeches and borrowed gods, made his own church when the old one wouldn't ordain him. He bent rules and bodies to his will. And damn him, it worked. The pantries were full. The lights stayed on. Lore and his gospel of the "new gods" had done what the Pentarchy and their army of enforcers never could. Starfall was a good place to live.

As much as she hated the man, he took care of his people. Hard not to respect that. But for tonight, hate would do just fine.

Lore's chambers were at the end of a hall. Her boots clicked as she stalked down it, threw the door open without knocking. Ancient fae relics glittered behind him like stars trapped in glass. Dawn didn't kneel. Didn't kiss his hand. She saw herself to his desk and slung the haversack onto it with a thud.

"You knew he was Pentarchy."

The asshole didn't miss a beat. "Of course I knew." He reached into the bag, drew out the green cloak, let it spill across his desk. "Captain Heron Valence. Second-in-command of the Gateway garrison. He's been ramping up patrols."

"Killing one of them brings the rest of them out. Like hornets. You sent me in there blind."

"I sent you in there to do your job." He pushed the cloak to the side. Pulled out a thick envelope. "Which you did. Efficiently, as always."

He opened the envelope, and his eyebrows rose. "Deployment orders. Troop escalation schedule." He looked up. "The Pentarchy wants to occupy the continent."

She didn't give a shit.

"You lied to me."

"No." He stood and moved around the desk. Stopped close enough she could smell amber and smoke on him. "If I'd told you the target was an enforcer, would you have refused me?"

"Guess not."

"Then it makes no difference." His voice went smooth. Always did before he asked for something. "Just one more thing."

And there it is. Dawn needed a drink, but there was no use fighting it. "What's that?"

"A scholar from Sovana came in on a clipper ship this morning." He tapped the deployment orders. "The Pentarchy is tracking her."

Dawn sighed. "Someone thinks she's special."

"It would seem so."

"You want the girl or what she knows?"

"Both."

He held out a hand, and she paused before taking it. His fingers lingered, his thumb tracing her knuckles. That familiar drain tugged at her, like standing too close to a flux conduit. She didn't flinch, just let him have it.

The man was a leech.

He dismissed her with a smile. Dawn breathed easier as soon as the door closed behind her.

Colt found her in the courtyard. The boy was all mud and smiles.

"Show me your teeth," he demanded.

She crouched to his level. Her fluxborn-tooth necklace clinked as she lifted it. He touched each tooth like treasure.

"What's this one?"

"*Lontherivio*. A squid as big as a carriage. Saw it bite a man in half."

His eyes went wide, and his innocent grin did something funny in her chest. She'd spent her life killing every fluxborn monster that crawled this world. Was damn good at it too. And now? Trapped. Leashed. Running errands for a man who pulled her strings and smiled while he did it.

Weeks since she'd strung a new tooth on her necklace. Weeks since she'd felt the rush of a clean kill.

"Is it true they used to be people?" Colt asked eagerly. "Before they made the true gods mad and got stuck as monsters?"

Where the fuck did he hear that? Dawn held in her choicest words for the kid's sake, but she wasn't going anywhere close to that story. Lore's made-up gods had nothing to do with it.

"Adults will tell all kinds of lies if it gets you to behave," she said. "My advice is, don't listen."

Colt nodded seriously, and his small fingers rested on the teeth like they were relics. "When you get more," he whispered, "can you make me a necklace too?"

Dawn swallowed. "Sure, kid."

A lie. When she broke Lore's leash, she was never coming back.

A metallic screech cut through the courtyard, followed by screams and feet hitting dirt. It was coming from the east. The market. She could smell blood in the air and something else, sharp and wrong. Fluxborn. In Gateway.

Dawn was on her feet before she registered moving. The gates stood open. "Get the kids inside!" She grabbed the nearest acolyte. "You, close the damn gates."

Colt tugged her jacket. "What is it?"

"I'll handle it." She forced calm into her voice. "You're safe."

The blue robes ushered children inside. Dawn stood alone, every scream prickling over her skin. It killed her to stand here, but someone had to guard the gates.

After some time the din faded. Someone else must've gotten the kill. Then the curfew bell rang. A deep ugly note rolled over the city. Dawn stopped to listen.

"Curfew?" she muttered. "Since when?"

Gateway didn't ring bells. Gateway drank and gambled and whored straight through to firstlight. A curfew bell meant the enforcers were cracking down. Putting order where it didn't belong.

Lore must have known this would happen when he gave her that job. What was his game?

She wasn't going anywhere tonight. Come morning, she'd head to the market, see what was left. Maybe find whoever got the kill and buy them a drink.

4

ONLY ONE BED

TALIA

No one comes to Gateway for the accommodations. The services, on the other hand, are exceptionally popular.

— "LETTERS TO SOVANA," *THE GATEWAY GAZETTE,*
VOL. 2, NO. 8, 397 AC

The crowd pressed in, bodies packed tight, teeth glowing in greenish light. Her grandmother would faint if she knew Talia had set foot in a place like this. Gods, she hoped Riven wouldn't tell her.

His hand found her shoulder. "Keep moving," he said quietly.

Riven's touch grounded her, and she forced herself to move up toward the bar. The bartender had shoulders like an ox and one eye clouded white. Her glare snagged on Talia's lace collar and Riven's blades.

"Curfew's on," she said flatly. "Doors stay shut till firstlight."

"We'll need a room," Riven said. "Till firstlight is fine."

"Only got one." The woman fished a key from her apron. "Big enough if you don't mind sharing." She glanced between them. "You want supper too? There's stew."

Riven set coin on the bar. "Yep. Stew as well."

He claimed a corner table where he pressed his back to the wall and watched the door. Talia sank into a chair across from his.

Stew arrived in chipped ceramic bowls. She picked up her spoon and let the gray, mud-thick mess slide back down before taking a bite. It was hot and rich, spiced with something that burned.

She blinked. "This is actually good."

Riven's mouth quirked. Then the fiddler launched into a new song, and the whole tavern roared. Talia focused on her bowl. Her hands shook, emotions pressing in from every direction.

Every direction except Riven. He ate methodically, back to the wall, eyes tracking the room. His presence was a blank space in the swirl. She breathed it in.

"You all right?" His voice was low, meant only for her.

"Fine." The lie came automatically. She was always expected to be fine, so she always said she was. "What was that out there? You called it a *ruthopanth*?"

"Ah." He paused and took a bite, chewing slowly. Then he said, "That's one flavor of fluxborn, mutant monsters. Strange to see one in town." He shook his head. "Eat. Then we'll head up."

"I can handle—"

"Not a question, boss. Been a long day."

She wanted to argue, to insist she could manage, but she honestly just wanted to disappear.

"Is this normal? In Valta?" She kept her voice low.

"Pretty much." He took another bite, still scanning the room. "Folks who might die tomorrow like to remember they're alive."

"That's grim."

He shrugged. "Meet a few more fluxborn, you might change your mind." He stood, dropping coins on the table. "Let's go. You've seen enough of Gateway's finest."

He cut a path through the crowd, and she followed in his wake. When they reached the stairwell, the pressure eased. Fewer people standing around, more room to breathe.

The music fell behind them as they climbed, but the walls grew thinner, and other sounds filtered through. Rhythmic thumping, a woman crying out. The entire building seemed to throb, and Talia felt her face burn.

At the landing, she nearly walked into a couple before her mind caught up. The woman was bent over the railing, skirts hiked up. The man stood behind her, trousers around his ass, thrusting into her with an urgent, offbeat rhythm.

Their pleasure hit Talia low in the gut. Her breath caught in her throat, and she couldn't move, couldn't look away, couldn't escape the urgency, the heat, the building pressure—

Riven's hand closed around her elbow. "Eyes up, boss."

He pulled her past the couple, his body shielding her from them. The couple didn't stop; they didn't even seem to notice. The wet slapping noises chased her up the stairs.

"I didn't mean to look—" she started.

"Kind of hard to miss it."

At the top of the stairs, the hallway tilted, or maybe her balance was off. Riven unlocked the last door and pushed it open. There was one window, grimy with dust. One chair. One washbasin. One bed.

Talia's stomach dropped. The bartender said that, didn't she? *Big enough if you don't mind sharing.* It hadn't fully registered. The room was smaller than her closet back in Vaelis. The bed took up most of it—a double mattress. No couch. Barely room to stand.

Riven cleared his throat behind her, and she stepped into the room, pulling to the side to let him pass. He went to the window first, testing the latch. Checked the lock on the door, frowned, and dragged a small table across to brace it. His swords went on the chair, hilts facing out.

He moved like a priest performing a ritual, each movement deliberate, automatic. It would have never occurred to Talia to check the room like that.

"You do this every night?" Maybe it was a strange question, but she was too curious to hold it in.

"Only when I plan to wake up again." He stripped off his jacket and hung it by the door, then perched at the end of the bed. "You still have the gun?"

She pulled the pretty revolver out of her satchel and handed it to him. The room felt even smaller now with his knees taking up half the floor space. She crossed to the washbasin, rolling up her sleeves before splashing her face and scrubbing her hands. Blue flux dust dissolved off her skin, clouding the water.

"That's interesting." She rubbed the flux-infused water between two fingers, and it felt almost oily.

"Don't drink it." His voice rumbled in the small space.

Did he think she was that reckless? She dried her hands on her ruined skirts and turned.

Riven sat at the end of the bed, elbows on his knees, cleaning the revolver with methodical focus. The room seemed to shrink around him, those broad shoulders blocking her view of the door, the scent of cedar and steel radiating from his skin. Every time he exhaled, it felt like she breathed him in.

There was nowhere for her to sit except beside him, on the bed they would share. She hesitated. She'd always been able to sense what people wanted before they asked. With him, she had nothing.

The whole evening pressed in at once: the violence, the public sex, the surge of emotions. Her body still hummed with echoes of the couple on the stairs, and a line of sweat traced a path down her lower back. She would have to take her dress off. The hoop skirt was in ruins, and it wasn't as though she could sleep in it.

She looked at Riven again. What did he expect? That was the thing—she had no idea, and not knowing made her feel lightheaded. She didn't want to wait for him to ask. It was easier just to offer. Get it over with. She moved closer to the bed, her fingers twisting in the blanket.

"You've done a lot for me today," she said carefully. "I don't like being in anyone's debt."

He glanced up but didn't say a word. He just watched her fidget.

"So, if there's anything you want..." She forced herself to meet his eyes. "I could repay you."

The words hit the air all wrong. Even without reading his emotions, she heard it, like a sour chord. Riven went very still. Something dark flickered in his expression, and his gaze dropped to her hands.

"You're shaking."

She looked down. She was. When she looked back up, those gray eyes glared back.

"If you think that's what I want. Or what I expect." His voice was quiet in a dangerous way. "You're wrong."

"I just thought—"

"You thought I brought you up here to fuck you." The words came out low and hard. "You think you owe me that?"

Heat flooded through her, shame and fear and a flicker of that strange secondhand desire. His gaze traveled down her body, like he was considering it. Then something shuttered in his face, and he looked away.

"I don't take scared girls to bed. And I sure as hell don't touch children I'm paid to protect."

The word landed like a slap. *Children.*

"I'm not a child. I'm twenty-six."

He shook his head, and a hint of a smile touched his mouth. "Go to sleep, boss. Your virtue is safe with me."

Her virtue? It wasn't like she'd never been with a man before... but no. She wasn't about to get into that with him.

He turned away, checking his weapons one last time. Then the flux lamp clicked off and the room sank into half dark, blue light leaking through the shutters. She had to lean on the wall to pull off her boots and skirts, fingers clumsy with humiliation. She slid her glasses off and folded them next to the sink, then she crawled onto the bed from the bottom. The mattress dipped where he lay on top of the coverlet, fully clothed.

The space between them smelled spicy, like warm cedarwood. She pressed herself against the cool plaster wall, but her body wouldn't settle. Every nerve buzzed with borrowed heat and mortification. She was acutely aware of him, every whisper of fabric shifting, the sound of his breathing, the warmth radiating off his body.

But the emotional static that had crackled in her mind all evening was gone.

She reached out, fingertips brushing his arm. Warm skin, steady pulse. No fear, no anger, no emotions at all. Just silence. She focused on his breathing until sleep pulled her under too.

A BROKEN PROMISE

VAELIS • 16 YEARS AGO

The map on the schoolroom wall was wrong. It ended at the Green Sea, as if the world stopped there, but Talent knew better. Ships had crossed it for the first time four years ago. The Lost Continent was a real place full of ancient fae cities and magical forests, treasures and monsters. All just a sunset away.

Master Tide droned on, reciting cities she'd memorized years ago. Vaelis, their home, the capital of Sovana. Holbrook Span, where Cordon and Holloway's family owned factories. Vesipor, the famous shipyard up the coast. She glared at the teacher. She knew all this already. Why insist on describing places she'd already been?

Talent folded her lesson paper into a tiny boat and set it drifting across her desk. Cordon caught it without looking up. He smiled at her, quick and secret, both dimples flashing.

A moment later he tipped the sand shaker, spilled the ink pot, and shouted, "Master Tide! The map!"

While the man flapped over his ruined parchment, four children slipped out the door and into the sun. The rose garden became their harbor, the fountain their sea. They fashioned a sail from a stolen tablecloth and a mast from two broom handles.

Holloway tied the knots, tongue between his teeth. When he finished, he looked up at his older brother for approval.

"Good work, soldier," Cordon said, and the boy beamed.

Cordon declared himself captain.

"I'll be navigator," Talent said quickly.

Cordon barely looked at her. "That's a good job for you."

"What about me?" Little Merit tugged Talent's sleeve.

Talent started to answer, but Cordon was faster. "You're our dragon. A friendly one who eats bad people."

Merit bared her teeth. "Rawr!" She pounced on Holloway, who fell laughing and let her win.

Cordon grinned, sunlight sparkling in his hair. Talent focused on her map. Dragons weren't part of this story, but no one had asked the navigator. She traced coastlines in stolen chalk—Sovana on one side, Valta on the other. Each mark felt like a promise. She'd chart the way, like a real explorer.

When hunger found them, Cordon raided the kitchens and came back with warm buttermilk biscuits. Holloway complained about breaking the rules, but he ate his in three bites. Cordon gave two to Merit and the last one to Talent. Merit tore her extra biscuit in half and offered to share. Her little sister made it impossible to stay annoyed. They collapsed in the grass, full and warm in the late-afternoon sunlight.

"Let's go to the Lost Continent someday," Merit said. "For real."

Cordon propped himself on an elbow. "I can pay for everything, once I'm head of the Sennett household. We'll need a proper ship."

"I'll be an explorer by then," Talent said. "I'll get us there."

"And I'll—" Holloway began.

"You'll keep the girls safe," Cordon said, clapping his shoulder.

Holloway nodded, solemn now. He was always a good soldier.

"We should all promise," he said, "so it's real."

They stacked their hands. Talent pressed hers into the middle, between Cordon's and Merit's.

"We swear to explore the Lost Continent," they chorused, calling on the gods like they'd been taught. "May Thyss the Oathkeeper bind this promise."

For a heartbeat, the garden held still, and everything was sunlight and laughter and the smell of crushed grass. Then time moved again, and the spell broke. Each child would chase adventure in their own way.

But not together. And not all of them would see the journey's end.

5

LIKE A CHILD

TALIA

Both versions of the story agree on this premise: love freed Elanwei from the shackles of duty. For one day, she was no one's daughter, no one's prize, no one's burden. The traditions diverge on what happens next.

— *THE LOST FAE PRINCESS: A FAERIE STORY WITH TWO ENDINGS*, TALENT SALAREN, 398 AC

Talia woke to sunlight and near silence. No bells, no monsters, not a hint of sound through the thin walls. She lay in bed, taking in the low creak of timbers settling and the steady hum of a single blue fly bumping against the windowpane.

It had taken a moment to remember where she was. Riven's side of the bed was empty, although the pillow held a dent where his head had been. She wondered if he'd left, but then she smiled. Most likely not.

She should go straight to the Consortium. That's what yesterday's Talia would have done. But she felt different today, on her own, with a whole new city to explore. She took her time pulling on her tattered hoop skirt and lacing her boots.

She washed her face and slipped her glasses back on, appraising herself in the looking glass as she tugged her auburn hair into a thick braid. Her once-bronze skin had grown paler after so much time in her office. It made the freckles stand out on her nose.

You're finally here, she told herself.

Downstairs, the tavern floor was sticky. Dust motes floated in the sunbeams. The bartender was slumped over the bar, snoring into her arm. Riven leaned against the wall by the door, half in shadow, half in sun. He was holding a mug of something warm, steam curling from the surface.

He glanced up when she approached, then kicked off the wall and pushed the mug toward her. The taste was bitter, but it woke her up.

"Sleep well?" he asked.

"Like a child." She grinned back, daring him to get the joke.

He almost smiled. At least, something softened around his eyes. She'd take it.

"Good enough," he murmured.

She pushed through the door into the street, and he followed. The sun glared, but the air was so clean it tasted like ice. The scene of last night's violence looked washed and new.

Riven stood at her shoulder, scanning the rooftops. "Should we get you to work?"

"They don't know exactly when I'm due to arrive," she said. "They won't miss me yet."

He shot her a glance she couldn't read. "Where to then, boss?"

"I need..." She glanced at her bloodstained dress. "A replacement for this. And"—she took a breath—"I'd like to see the city."

Riven waited, looking down at her as if he knew she had more to say.

"Actually," she added more quietly, "I was hoping to explore on my own."

She'd thought he was going to argue, but he seemed to be considering it.

"I'm not helpless," she added.

"Didn't say you were." He drew the revolver from a holster at his side, checked it, handed it to her. "Safety's here. Don't point it at anything you don't want dead."

Their fingers brushed as she took it. Still no emotional signal.

"Don't do anything I wouldn't do." He stepped back. "Meet back here at highsun."

He was letting her go? Just like that? A small, bright pleasure unfurled in her chest at the idea of spending a day alone. She couldn't think of a single time she'd skipped school or work.

"What will you do?" she asked.

"Scout for rooms. I'm guessing you might prefer your own bed. Maybe a desk, if you're lucky."

She had to admit, a desk would be nice.

She gave an awkward wave, then she turned and started walking. The city was waking up now, alive with hammering, shouting, the scrape of saws on new timber. Smoke curled up from chimneys and cook fires. A woman with a baby on her hip haggled over bread. Two boys raced by, kicking up blue flux dust that shimmered in the light.

She stopped in the middle of the street, letting people flow around her. No one here knew her name, let alone what she was running from. The laugh that escaped was half sob, unsteady and hers. It felt like something cracking open inside her. She was twenty-six years old, and for the first time in her life, no one was telling her who to be.

She hitched her satchel higher—journal, revolver, everything she needed—and turned toward the market, toward the shop where she'd seen those glowing crystals in the window.

She hadn't lied, but she hadn't told Riven the whole truth. She did need a new dress, but first, she had a mystery to solve. Flux was everywhere here, and it was acting strange. She was going to find out why.

6

ALL KINDS OF PREDATORS

DAWN

Don't go chasing dead dirt.

— FRONTIER VERNACULAR, ORIGIN UNKNOWN

Dawn crouched by the water pump, *savuthe* smoke curling from her lips. Someone had scrubbed the square before firstlight, but they missed some spots. She could smell it. Under the blood and flux dust, a hint of vinegar. Sharp and wrong.

The sheriff's report said one dead, but Sheriff Elm was a poor excuse for a lawman. She counted three stains in the dust. She'd bet anything, three bodies had fallen. So two missing. Plus the professional cleanup job? She didn't like it.

She flicked the *savuthe* twist away and scanned the square. Old Brim and his boy Timber were replacing busted boards like any other morning. Merchants restocked their wares. Folks stepped around bloodstains without looking down. A whole damn city pretending they hadn't seen a thing.

That's when she spotted the girl. Fresh off a boat in a blood-splattered hoop skirt, heeled kid boots, flashy silver brooch. She wasn't beautiful, exactly, but Dawn was drawn to her. She had the same coloring as most folks in Sovana, reddish brown hair pulled back in a braid. Dark eyes that darted around like the world was brand new. Her old-fashioned spectacles kept sliding down her nose. Clearly well-off. No prospector, that one. Definitely not a working girl. Had to be Lore's scholar. Easy mark for any predator.

Damn. Dawn wanted to keep looking into what went down last night. But Lore would be pissed if she let this one slip. Dawn watched the girl head into Brindle's flux shop. Not a minute later, Flint Jones ambled in after her. *Speaking of predators.*

"Fuck's sake," Dawn muttered, heading in after them.

Flint wasn't half as clueless as his brothers, which made him twice as dangerous. Any luck, he wouldn't know it was her that got Lorry arrested last night. He was likely to hang for it.

The air inside the shop was warm and metallic. Shelves loomed over her as soon as she walked in. Straight ahead, across from the door, was a narrow counter with a register and a door to a back room. The rest of the shop was a maze of shelves packed with crystal bowls, shards in jars, bits of bone wired with copper. The whole place pulsed, like a trapped heartbeat.

Flint stood a few shelves over from the counter, broad shoulders blocking half the aisle. Hat low. Hands in pockets. Watching the scholar. Dawn knew what a hunt looked like. The girl paused at a display of crystal fragments.

Flint made his move.

"Ever seen flux crystals before, sweetheart?" he asked as he sidled up behind her, voice soft and low.

The girl, clueless, smiled at him.

"Not quite like this. Flux is highly regulated in Sovana. Do these form naturally?"

Dawn slipped into the aisle next to them, pretending to study a jar of cracked relics. She didn't step in. Not yet.

"These little ones?" he said. "Sure. Mines near town are all stripped, though, so these get dug up farther west. Dangerous work, you know. Folks die for crystals like this."

He leaned in as she bent to look. Dawn smelled a shift in the air, musky with lust and something mean. That set of shelves ran clear to the back wall. Girl didn't know she was cornered yet, but she'd find out soon.

"How do they get used?" she heard the girl ask. "Do you burn them, like in Sovana, or can you channel with them?"

Dawn went still.

Channel. That specific word. Not *use* or *power*. Sick climbed in her throat, and she swallowed hard. Someone must have taught her that word. But who? Anyone who knew about flux channeling was long dead.

Flint edged closer, voice dropping low. "Girl like you asking smart questions. Let me show you something special. Private stock."

He gestured toward the back room. "Come on. It's just through here."

The girl hesitated, glanced at the exit. Flint shifted his weight, blocking the aisle.

"Unless you don't have coin?" His smile went sharp. "That a problem, sweetheart? I'm sure we can work something out."

He ran a finger, real slow, up the side of her arm. She tried to step around him. He moved with her. Still smiling. *That's enough of that.* Dawn moved around the end of the shelf and stepped up behind him.

"Morning, Flint." Dawn didn't bother hiding her smirk.

He went stiff. His slow smile was all teeth as he turned. "Dawn. Didn't see you there."

"No? You distracted by something?" She bared her teeth right back.

The girl blinked between them, but Dawn didn't look her way. Flint was getting pissed off, she could smell it on him. *Good. Be mad.*

"Hey, professor," Dawn said, speaking to Talia while she kept staring Flint down. "Find somewhere else to shop."

Flint's nostrils flared. "The fuck you think you're doing?"

His weight shifted before he took a swing. Dawn ducked, slammed her elbow into his gut, then brought the butt of one revolver across his jaw. Bone cracked. He crashed into a display and blue light skittered across the floor. The scholar yelped.

"Now would be a good time to run," Dawn said all casual, brushing crystal shards off her shoulder.

The girl didn't need to be told twice. She bolted for the door.

Flint got his feet under him and spat blood, grinning through it. "You just fucked up, Dawn. Do you know who that girl is? What she's worth?"

She shoved the barrel under his chin. "Stay away from her."

"Why? Lore Tavis want her for his weird sex cult?" His eyes glittered. "Cuz I can share."

Aw, fuck. What'd he have to go and do that for? Most folks in this town knew better than to insult Lore out loud. If this bastard didn't shut up, Lore would put him down, and she didn't need two brothers dead back-to-back. It was bad luck. Her finger tightened on the trigger. She kept the first chamber empty around town, but this asshole didn't know that.

Click.

Flint flinched hard.

"Next time, it's loaded," she said. "Stay away from the girl. Stay the fuck away from me."

She stalked out of the shop, and his laughter followed her out, wet and ragged. "This ain't over, sweetheart."

Outside, Dawn lit a fresh twist of *savuthe*. It couldn't be a coincidence the scholar had asked about channeling the day after a fluxborn attack. She had to be mixed up in it somehow.

Someone was caging fluxborn and wanted it buried, and someone had set Flint on the same girl Lore wanted safe. None of it added up. She fucking hated puzzles.

She took another drag and started walking. Lore's scholar was alive for today, but it was going to be some work to keep her that way. *Great.* Just what Dawn didn't need.

7

PAPER CUTS

TALIA

The durative suffix is easy to overlook, but 'ammentella' *does not mean* 'to take.' *It means* 'to keep drawing, continuously,' *presumably from a source with ample supply.*

— T. SALAREN, FIELD NOTES, 401 AC

Talia hadn't told Riven about the flux shop, and she didn't plan to. It was over, she'd survived, and she'd prefer to move on.

While she was out shopping, Riven had found them new rooms at a place called the Flux & Fiddle. Hers had a wooden desk, an armchair, and a window that looked out on the harbor. She hardly slept that night, watching the light move across the ceiling, rehearsing what she'd say when she finally shared her work.

She rose early and pulled on a new white blouse and long forest green skirt, then braided and rebraided her hair until her curls stopped sneaking out. Her hands shook when she tied the ribbon. She squeezed her fists until they steadied, slung her satchel over her shoulder, and stepped out.

Riven leaned against the doorframe, arms crossed, like he'd been there awhile. "Morning, boss."

She felt a rush of relief that surprised her. "You don't have to escort me, you know," she said, even as she smiled.

"Promised I would." He kicked off the wall and fell in beside her.

Gateway was quiet at this hour. White fog clung to the wood-planked streets. Each step stirred up blue dust that swirled in the air and sparkled on her boots. Details caught her eye, like the Starscript glyphs embedded in signs. She wanted to stop and study everything, but instead she kept a mental list for later. Riven drew her attention to different things; he steered her clear of puddles where dust had gelled into mud and gave a wide berth to a wagon with a sagging wheel. By the time they reached the Consortium office, the city was fully awake.

Talia squared her shoulders and pushed inside. *This is it.* A wide desk fronted the room, and the clerk looked up when the door opened.

"I know I'm early." She couldn't hold back her grin. "My name is Talent Salaren. I'm here for the research fellowship."

"Salaren." The clerk repeated her name in a strange way, like he was trying to figure out where he'd heard it. She almost cut in to explain who her grandmother was when he continued, "Yes, your luggage arrived yesterday. I'm Webb. I can show you down."

He led her down a switchback staircase into a narrow basement. The space was cramped and cool. A handful of desks sagged under stacks of books and papers, illuminated by wavering flux lamps and a strip of thin windows near the ceiling. Her valises were stacked in the corner.

A massive map covered one wall—Sovana rendered in familiar detail, while across the Green Sea, Valta was only a jagged coastline and a big patch of white. Someone needed to fill in that space. She could do it; she was sure of it.

She set her satchel down on the first open desk and waited for Webb to leave before she sat and pulled out her notebook. She'd spent hours outlining the theory she'd drawn from Vael's journal. She wanted to be able to explain it without looking at her notes.

Flux is a consumable resource, scarce and dwindling in Sovana. However, early sources (see: Vael's journal) suggest a different way of drawing on flux was once prevalent. He describes cities, transit, domestic tools, all sustained by flux with no indication of scarcity.

The language itself diverges from modern terminology. There is no mention of flux extraction in Starscript; no mining, no refining. Instead, flux is consistently associated with *ammentaa* *(to draw from, as one draws water from a well). In nearly every instance the verb appears with the durative suffix* *-ella:* *ammentella* *(to channel), suggesting an ongoing process.*

Throughout Vael's journal, flux is framed as a sustainable system—more akin to tending crops than burning fuel. If this was achieved through technology, it was pervasive enough to shape the language around it. Evidence would likely present itself in cities or ruins of sufficient age (approx. 400 to 600 years).

This was why she'd kept Vael's journal, despite the risk of being caught with it. If self-sustaining flux was possible, and if she could figure out how it had worked, it would change the world. The rebellion in Vaelis was growing; blood was being spilled in the streets over flux rationing. Vael's journal hinted at an answer, but she needed access to fae ruins to decode it.

Footsteps echoed on the stairs, and she flipped her notebook closed. Two men filed in.

"You're the Salaren girl," the taller one said.

A round-faced man pushed past him. "Wait, Talent Salaren? I've read all your essays! The way you traced Starscript verb evolution from—"

"Later, Peat," the tall one snapped. He looked at Talia. "That's my desk."

He cocked his head, expecting her to move. Talia's jaw tightened. She'd gotten here first. But her grandmother's voice whispered in her head: *Don't make a scene on your first day*.

She gathered her notebook and stood. *No, of course I don't mind, don't mention it, my work isn't going to change the world or anything*, she thought bitterly as she stepped aside.

Peat smiled apologetically, wringing his hands. "Sorry about Nadir. He's not at his best in the morning. You can work here."

He showed her to a desk shoved beneath a sputtering flux lamp. His cheeks flushed pink as he moved papers off the chair.

"It's fine." Talia forced a smile. "I've worked with difficult scholars before."

Peat brightened. "I really did enjoy the one where you cross-referenced faerie stories and religious texts—"

"Peat!" Nadir barked from across the room. "Leave her alone."

Peat's face fell, and he shuffled quickly back to his own desk. Talia wanted to call after him, tell him she didn't mind. But the words stuck. She never knew how to do this part—making friends, the easy back-and-forth of small talk. So she took her new seat, opened her notebook, and pretended to read.

Some time passed before she heard another set of feet on the stairs. An older man emerged. He wore a trim gray suit, and he walked directly to Talia's desk.

"Miss Salaren?" He didn't wait for her reply. "I am Emmer Hendricks, the chief researcher here at the Independent Scholars Consortium. I am well acquainted with your grandmother, the esteemed Marionette Salaren."

He ducked his head at her grandmother's name like a nervous pigeon. Talia wanted to laugh, but she kept her face flat.

"It's an honor to be here," she said, keeping her voice low and level. "I'm looking forward to advancing my research into Starscript sigils and—"

"Now about that. This is not that kind of fellowship. That is, we will have to see about the research topics."

"I see." Talia didn't understand what that meant, but she knew well enough not to challenge an authority figure in his own office. "Well, I'm here. Where should I start?"

Emmer frowned and waved Peat over. He came with a stack of expedition logs. "These need to be copied for the archives in Haven," Emmer said brusquely before stalking away to a large desk in the corner.

Was this what *not that kind of fellowship* meant? Was she a note-taker? Talia glanced at her notebook full of hypotheses, work she could complete only by studying real relics in the field. She'd get there. She dipped her pen and got started.

The first reports seemed routine—supply lists, relic catalogs. Many sections were redacted. There weren't many words; she copied them quickly. The dates were recent, within the past few months, which was encouraging. Expeditions must be going out regularly.

She flipped to a section with no redactions and stopped.

Site Fourteen: Excavation suspended after full crew loss. Equipment recovered, heavily damaged.

She stared. Read it again. Flipped ahead.

Team Seven: No contact for three weeks, presumed lost.

Her hands moved through the stack. There were more. Whole expeditions gone. Crews torn apart by "aggressive local fauna."

She approached Emmer's desk with one of the logs. "These reports, the casualties. They seem extreme."

"You were asked to transcribe, not analyze." He didn't look up. "These are sensitive reports. Can I trust you to keep that in mind?"

"Don't you think it's worth discussing?"

"Not with you."

Her hands curled into fists. She wanted to tell him she was the preeminent Starscript scholar in the *whole world*, that she'd translated texts he couldn't even read, that she'd been awarded a research fellowship here, not a secretary position.

Instead, she went back to her desk and bent her head over the pages. She worked in silence for the rest of the day, copying records until her hand cramped. When the light from the windows started to dim, Emmer stood and walked out without a word. Nadir followed. At least Peat gave her an apologetic wave.

She waited until they were gone to trudge up the stairs. The lock clicked behind her as she stepped out onto the street, where Riven waited, leaning against the building. She had assumed he'd be gone, but after a day so full of disappointments, it was nice to see him. She wondered what he'd done while she was inside. Did he have friends in Gateway? Family?

"How did it go?" he asked.

"Fine," she lied. Always fine.

The Flux & Fiddle was quiet that evening. They passed through the saloon, nodding to Velvet—the outspoken owner who also tended the bar—and climbed the back stairs to a narrow hallway with a half dozen rooms. Talia's was just at the top of the stairs, and Riven was closer to the shared washroom at the far end.

When they reached her door, she mumbled good night and slipped inside, locking it behind her. Then she pulled out the expedition report. The one she'd slipped into her satchel when Emmer wasn't looking. Her pulse hammered as she opened her notebook to a fresh page.

She began to copy. Every word. Every detail about the crew that had vanished. If there were patterns, she'd find them. For the first time all day, she felt like herself again.

Dangerous curiosity. That's what her grandmother had called it. Talia had never thought of herself as dangerous before, but maybe her grandmother knew her better than she thought.

8

A NIGHT OUT ON THE TOWN

TALIA

In the Gateway saloon, wranglers and clerks share a whiskey bottle with merchants and landowners. Whether this is civilization or the absence of it remains a matter of debate.

— *COLLECTED DISPATCHES FROM THE WESTERN TERRITORIES*, CASH BRENTHAVEN, 399 AC

The second day at the Consortium passed much like the first. On the third day, she stayed late to clear out the stack of field reports. She was the last person out of the office, and when she left, her desk was empty. She was excited to tackle more meaningful work.

It was a little surprising that she hadn't heard from Holloway yet. She'd assumed he would write as soon as he found her goodbye note. She considered breaking the silence first, but what would she say? She was sorry she'd left without saying goodbye, and she assumed the wedding was off? That she'd nearly been killed by a bug monster on her first day? Every time she pulled out her stationery she stopped and put it back. Better to wait until she did something worth writing about.

That wouldn't be today. Riven was waiting to escort her, as he had every morning and evening so far, and she was glowing from their conversation when she stepped into the basement. Then she saw her desk. A new pile of field reports looked ready to tip over. Easily twice as many files as she'd already cleared out.

Talia took a deep breath, gathering her courage, and walked over to Emmer's desk. "When do field assignments happen?"

He looked up and sighed. "Fieldwork goes to senior fellows first. Six months, sometimes longer." His gaze flicked over her. "People die out there. You are in no way prepared."

Six months. Sometimes longer.

"Of course." She fought to keep her voice steady.

She let her hand lightly brush his. Disdain prickled under her fingers. Not concern or respect. Just annoyance. *So that's how he really feels.*

Her smile didn't crack until she turned away. She made it back to her desk before she let out a slow breath. She had more reports to copy. Other people's fieldwork to transcribe. Her mind replayed the interaction, picking apart her delivery.

Peat must have noticed she was spiraling. "It's not you," he said. "He's like this with everyone."

She doubted it. Emmer seemed to take special delight in shutting her down.

Peat cleared his throat. "You know, a few of us are going to the Broken Wheel tonight after work. Just for a drink. You should come."

She hesitated. She would have said no a month ago, but she was supposed to be on an adventure.

"I'll think about it," she said, offering a smile.

The stack of files hardly seemed to shrink as the day dragged on. Emmer left for lunch and didn't come back, then Nadir and Peat headed out around lowsun. When Talia found herself transcribing the same sentence for the third time in a row, she decided she could leave early too. Her feet felt heavy on the stairs.

Riven was waiting outside, leaning against the wall with his arms crossed, even though she was early. Did he seriously just wait there all day? He straightened when she came around the corner.

"How'd it go?"

"Fine. Busy day."

"Any progress on the journal?" He gestured at her satchel.

She bristled and glanced back over her shoulder. She kept forgetting he knew. "Some."

He nodded and started walking ahead. She was stuck. No closer to understanding the redacted field reports. No closer to cracking the journal's secrets. Riven was her only real friend, and she hardly knew him. Without thinking, she reached out and caught his arm. He froze, eyes dropping to where her fingers pressed against his sleeve. She let go.

"Can I ask you something?"

He nodded.

"When we first met, back on the ship," she said slowly, "you spoke Starscript."

"Starscript?" His lips quirked. "That's a rare skill."

"If you did know anything about the journal, or flux, or how channeling works—"

He cut her off. "Do not trust anyone with those questions, especially not me."

She almost never asked for help so directly, but she'd grown comfortable with Riven. His dismissal hit harder than she expected, and she fought to keep her expression neutral.

She was tired of being stonewalled—first by Emmer, now by Riven too. She stepped back and felt herself withdrawing, then stopped. No. She wasn't just giving up. Not today.

Her pulse was racing when she said, "I'm going out tonight."

"Where are we going?"

"*I* am going," she said, "out with some colleagues. To the Broken Wheel. It's a bar."

His eyes narrowed. "Boss—"

"I'll be back by curfew." She met his eyes. "You were only hired to get me here, right? So you're not actually my bodyguard, and I'm not asking permission. I'm telling you my plans."

She held her hands behind her back to keep from fidgeting. She wanted to look confident and capable. He studied her.

"Keep the revolver on you," he said finally.

Her hand went to her satchel, feeling the weight of it. "Got it."

"And if anything happens—"

"I'll be fine." She wasn't sure it was true, but she needed this. Needed to make one choice for herself.

He gave her a dark look, but he stepped aside. She walked past him, heart hammering, a smile taking over her face. She was going out drinking in a frontier saloon.

The Broken Wheel was delightfully chaotic. Stepping through the double swinging doors, she nearly sneezed at the sudden bite of sawdust and *savuthe* smoke. Every table was packed with every manner of folks—prospectors, wranglers, fishermen, clerks—all mixing together under the gaudy antler chandeliers. The jangly noise of bad piano playing barely cut through the roar of overlapping conversations.

She hovered in the doorway until she spotted Peat, Nadir, and Webb, who'd claimed a spot in the back. They waved her over and their warmth seemed genuine.

"You made it!" Peat pushed a chair out with his foot. "I was sure *maybe* meant *no*."

She sat, hanging her satchel over the back of the chair. Peat ordered a round of whiskey, and when he handed her the glass, the brush of his fingers carried good humor and joy. The whiskey burned down her throat, but it left a sweet aftertaste. To her left, Nadir laughed and winked at her. He looked so different here, leaning back a little in his chair. Almost like a normal person.

"So," Webb said, leaning forward with a crooked grin. He was about her age, but the brush of freckles across his nose made him look younger. "One week down. What's the verdict?"

Talia set her glass on the table. "It was...educational."

Nadir snorted. "Those sound like proper Vaelis manners talking. You know, I had to copy field reports for eight weeks straight when I got here. Absolute waste of time."

Webb raised his glass. "To Emmer Hendricks, crusher of hopes and slayer of dreams."

Talia laughed. They drank and warmth spread through her chest. Was she making friends?

"Cards?" Webb asked, flashing a deck from his coat pocket. "Gateway Fives. Loser buys the next round."

Nadir leaned over to whisper dramatically in her ear. "He cheats."

"I play to win," Webb shot back.

Webb shuffled and snapped the deck, then dealt. The rules were easy. Easier still for Talia to track the cards. By the third hand, Talia was winning without trying.

"You're suspiciously good at this," Webb said, squinting over the fan of cards in his hand.

"Beginner's luck," she answered, biting her lower lip.

"Sure," Nadir murmured. "I think you cheat too."

"So everyone in the world is cheating now?" Webb asked. "Seems more likely you're bad at cards."

Nadir made a vulgar gesture, and Peat choked on his drink.

Webb dealt another hand, and the night loosened around her. She hadn't realized how much she missed this—talk that wasn't cautious, friends who didn't hover, the simple joy of winning something that didn't matter.

"You're trouble, Salaren," Webb said, tossing in his last coins.

Is he flirting? She let a finger brush his wrist as she reached for her cards. His emotions rushed through, curiosity and attraction braided together. *Oh, he is.*

A small, steady glow built in her chest. Maybe she'd been approaching this wrong. She was so fixated on mysteries about the past, but what if she let herself relax and just experience her own life for once? The work would still be there tomorrow.

"That seems like an exaggeration," she said, trying not to grin.

She was still smiling when the shooting broke out.

The first gunshots cracked like books dropped flat. The crowded tavern froze. Then chairs scraped, and people scrambled to take cover under the tables.

A wave of cold dread crashed into Talia from around the room.

A prickling surge of panic crawled up her legs. Her hand found her satchel, and she was walking across the room before she fully registered the choice. The revolver was heavy and cold in her grip.

Time moved strange and slow as she scanned the room. Two bodies lay crumpled near the front door, blood pooling dark as ink across the floorboards. Across the room, near the bar, a sweaty man had one arm locked around a woman's throat and a smoking gun pressed to her temple. A stocky bald man was facing them with his back to Talia. He alone hadn't taken shelter, and there was something off about his relaxed posture in the middle of a shoot-out.

The bald man turned his head to light a smoke. She knew him. It was the man who'd cornered her in the flux shop. Flint, was it? And the woman being held, that was Dawn, the wild pink-haired woman who'd punched him. The room was frozen. The silence roared in her ears, and the moment felt too familiar, this quiet before violence.

She was back in the market square. The cage tilting, the *ruthopanth* breaking free. Standing there helpless while people died.

Not again. She couldn't do this again.

Something hot and reckless was flowing through her. She stepped through the wreckage of chairs, spilled drinks, bodies pressed to the floor. She leveled the revolver. The bald man was so focused on Dawn, he didn't notice until the barrel touched the back of his skull.

Talia reached around and locked her other arm around the man's throat, mirroring the way Dawn was being held. "Let her go."

9

AMBUSH AT THE BROKEN WHEEL

DAWN

Gods give us life. Guns make it equal.

— FRONTIER VERNACULAR, ORIGIN UNKNOWN

Dawn shoved through the swinging doors of the Broken Wheel and scanned the room. Counted exits. Let her eyes adjust. She spotted the scholar at a corner table, laughing with three soft-looking men. Still alive after a week. Lore should be pleased.

A low whistle drew her attention. Flint Jones again. Bastard had his back against a wall, hat low, smiling like he'd already decided who'd die tonight. That meant there'd be—sure enough, two of his boys posted near the door, ready to cut off her exit.

Shit.

She could've left then, but she crossed to the bar instead. Ordered a whiskey, just to hold. Flint drifted closer, easy as ever, the smell of smoke and rot rolling off him.

"Hey there, sweetheart," he said all casual. "Babysitting again?"

"Walk away, Flint."

He tilted his head toward the scholar's table. "She's a pretty thing. You sure you don't want to let me have her?"

"What the fuck is your problem? I said walk away."

"I saw her first," he said. "And I want a bite."

He nodded at his guys, casual-like, but Dawn was ready. Her revolver was in her hand just as quick. The first boy standing by the door never cleared his holster. One shot to the chest, and he was down. The second got his gun up. Dawn put one through his throat. Two clean shots clear across the room.

Folks hit the floor as soon as the gunshots rang, chairs crashing. Dawn glanced over at the girl—and an arm clamped across her windpipe. Birdy. The other fucking Jones brother. *Fuck.* Bastard must've come through the kitchen.

He twisted her wrist, and pain shot up her arm. Her gun hit the floor. Flint scooped it up and handed it to Birdy, who pressed the hot barrel to her head.

"Evening, Dawn," he breathed.

Her eyes darted between each exit: front door, balcony, kitchen, windows. Every way out was useless with her own gun jammed in her face. His sweat stank worse than his breath. Sour and rank, rolling off him in waves.

Dawn kept her eyes half lidded, like she was bored. She could take Birdy's head off before he blinked. Tear out his throat, at a minimum. It'd be messy, and she still might take a bullet.

"Oh, honey." Birdy chuckled as he followed her gaze to the windows. "You wouldn't make it halfway."

What a dick. She was pretty fucking tempted to tear his head off.

The gun clicked under Birdy's thumb.

Dawn's skin prickled. Heat wanted to pour from her hands. Turn these fools to ash. *Not here*, she told herself. The Jones brothers were not worth it.

Another click answered across the room. Her eyes slid sideways.

Huh. Didn't see that coming.

Lore's little scholar, the one who'd frozen at the flux shop, had an arm locked around Flint's neck, a relic of a revolver jammed against his skull. Chin high, eyes flaring. She smelled like fear and adrenaline tangled together. Holding the gun wrong. But fuck if the girl didn't commit to the bluff.

"Let her go," the girl said slowly, voice steadier than her hands.

"You shoot, I shoot," Birdy barked, spit flecking Dawn's cheek. Birdy yanked Dawn's arm tighter. *Oh, this man wants to lose some body parts.*

"Ow," Dawn snarled, mostly for the show of it. She let heat creep into her voice. "You really want me angry?"

Flint's eyes darted between the girl and Dawn. The math had changed now that he had a gun to his own head. Sweat beaded on his scalp as his situation sank in. The girl pressed the barrel in harder. She had spirit.

"Just let her go, Bird," Flint croaked. "This ain't worth dying over."

Birdy eyed their boys piled at the door. *Friends of his? A pity.*

The girl's chin lifted. "Drop the gun. Let her walk out. Your boss can follow."

Birdy muttered curses, grip slipping. The second his fingers twitched loose, Dawn twisted free, cracked an elbow into his ribs, and put a table between them. The girl shoved Flint hard and stepped back, revolver still up.

The whole room exhaled.

"You bitch," Birdy spat at Dawn.

Bitch? She hadn't even scratched him yet.

Dawn rolled her shoulders. That girl had stepped up and saved Dawn's life when she could've run. Maybe the scholar wasn't completely useless.

She winked at the girl. "Not bad, professor. First rodeo's always the roughest."

The tavern slowly came to life around them. Folks worked together to right an overturned table. The girl's friends checked on her, then made themselves scarce.

Sheriff never showed, and neither did the enforcers. Local garrison had been a bit of a mess since that captain got killed. She didn't want to deal with it herself, so she let Flint and Birdy slink off.

Then Dawn bought the girl a whiskey. Stars knew she'd earned it.

The scholar's hands shook around the glass. She introduced herself as Talent Salaren and paused after the name, like Dawn should know it.

"Talia, actually," she said, cheeks going red. "Only my grandmother calls me Talent."

"Dawn." She studied the scholar over her glass. "So, what was it? You brave or reckless back there?"

"Both, probably." Talia's laugh was shaky but honest.

Dawn grinned. She liked the honest ones.

"Hell of a bluff." Dawn threw back her whiskey and tapped her glass for another.

"Was it that obvious?"

"If you'd pulled that trigger, you'd've lost that thumb." Dawn grinned. "But Flint didn't know that, so no harm."

Talia took a bigger sip of whiskey and looked down at her thumb. *Kid has spine under all that polish.* Dawn leaned back in her chair.

"So, what's a fancy scholar like you doing in this shithole anyway?"

"Research. I want to study the ruins here—Starscript inscriptions, flux technologies—"

"Can you read that shit?"

Talia blinked. "Starscript? Yes. Fluently. I teach courses, actually, at the Lyceum back in Vaelis."

Dawn's grin widened. *Perfect.* Lore needed a translator. Dawn hadn't exactly told him she couldn't read. And here was a real-life professor, desperate enough to be in Gateway and reckless enough to pull a gun she couldn't use.

Just then both saloon doors crashed into the wall. A hulking figure filled the doorframe, chest heaving like he'd run hard. Gray eyes swept the room and locked on their table, and Dawn's stomach dropped. *What the fuck is he doing in Gateway?*

Dawn shot to her feet, but he was already moving. He crossed the tavern in seconds, dropped into a crouch next to Talia's chair.

"Are you hurt?" His voice came out rough. Controlled, but barely.

"I'm fine." Talia blinked at him. "How did you—"

"I heard about trouble at the Broken Wheel." His eyes swept over her before he exhaled sharply.

Then he noticed Dawn. His eyes met hers, and an emotion

flashed. Fear? Grief? He shut it down and his face went clear, like weather moving through.

"It's Dawn now," she said quickly, before he could use her old name.

"Dawn." He said it, testing, like it didn't fit in his mouth.

"Oh!" Talia seemed oblivious to the tension. "How rude of me. Riven, this is Dawn. Dawn, Riven. He was my bodyguard for a little while, but now he's—" She trailed off like she didn't actually know.

He stood slowly, keeping his eyes on Dawn. "We know each other."

"Hey there...Riven." Dawn stumbled on his name too. "Didn't know you were still taking bodyguard gigs."

He flinched. She enjoyed that. Okay, she could work with this.

"You missed the show," Dawn said, flashing her best smile. The one that showed the dimple on her chin. "Our professor just won a shoot-out with some local lowlifes."

Riven's head snapped back to Talia, and Dawn grinned as the muscles rippled along his jaw. She'd forgotten how fun it was to bait him.

"You did what?"

"I thought that revolver looked familiar. You should have taught her how to shoot it." Dawn handed him her whiskey. "Here. You look like you need this more than I do."

Now his mouth twitched between a grin and a grimace. Almost proud—Dawn wagered—and scared shitless. "You do not understand. You could have been killed."

"I understand that I wasn't." Talia's chin lifted.

He made a low frustrated sound. Dawn almost felt bad. Hard enough work keeping this girl alive. Dawn's offer was about to make that job even harder.

"So, you're in town to study relics?" Dawn tapped the table with her fingers, itching for her drink back.

Talia nodded. "Yes, I am. Or at least, I was."

Dawn cocked her head to the side. This was a trick she'd learned watching Lore, using silence to draw out a story. Riven leaned in, too, like he didn't know what she'd say. *Interesting.*

"It's just, I thought I'd be able to study real ruins," Talia said, looking down at the table and fidgeting with the neckline of her dress. Dawn gave her another beat, but Talia didn't fill the quiet this time.

"Well, if you'd like," Dawn said, "I do know some people with those kinds of connections. I could make an introduction."

Riven's glare burned a hole through her, but she ignored him. If Talia wanted to dig up every cursed relic in this graveyard of a continent, that was her right. This prick wanted to play bodyguard? He could damn well do his job this time.

Talia bit her lip, then nodded. "If you don't mind. It can't hurt to make connections."

"Smart." Dawn grinned, snatching her glass back from Riven and downing the last bit. He glared at her some more.

"Are you ready to go?" Riven asked Talia. "It's getting late."

Dawn nodded. "Get some sleep, professor. You deserve it. Just let me know when you're ready for that intro."

Talia seemed to stumble as she gathered her satchel, bumping into Dawn's arm. Riven's hand found her shoulder, steering her toward the door. He didn't look back.

Dawn took another sip and watched the doors swing close. She didn't often read people wrong, but Talia was hard to pin down. Too timid to voice any opinion. No survival instinct at all. But she stepped up when it mattered. Girl was braver than she had any right to be.

Shame that Lore would chew her up. Dawn knew she'd be sacrificing Talia if she made that introduction. But she didn't have a choice. She needed Lore to fulfill his end of their deal more than she cared about some brave, reckless scholar. Dawn sighed and signaled the barkeep for another round.

10

UNEXPECTED FIELDWORK

TALIA

Your research fellow Talent Salaren is not dangerous. However, intelligence reports place her in contact with rebel sympathizers, and she may be at risk. We have her under surveillance, but I recommend limiting her access to field assignments until further notice.

— RECONSTRUCTED CORRESPONDENCE, H. SENNETT TO E. HENDRICKS, 401 AC

There was no way Talia was taking Dawn up on that introduction. She'd scanned Dawn's emotions before they left the Broken Wheel and picked up some real guilt, deep and complicated. Talia didn't trust it. Now when she saw Dawn around town, she crossed the street to avoid her.

She would just push forward with the Consortium. Two more weeks passed, filled with the same slow drudgery, but she didn't know what else to do.

She was dropping a ledger off at Webb's desk when a flash of red caught her eye. A thin envelope lay half buried under requisition forms. It looked like official Pentarchy stationery and had *URGENT* stamped across the top. The return address was printed in precise block letters: *HOLLOWAY SENNETT.*

It wasn't addressed to her. Opening it was probably illegal and certainly unethical. But her childhood best friend's name was right there. She tugged at the engagement band that still circled her wrist—his bracelet—and tore open the seal.

There weren't many words, but they cut: *We have her under surveillance...I recommend limiting her access to field assignments...*

She closed her eyes and fought to stay calm. Holloway had never hidden his disapproval of her work, but seeing it in his own handwriting made it real. This was nothing short of sabotage. If anyone saw this letter, her fellowship was over. Forget six months, she'd never make it into the field.

She glanced at the staircase. It was empty.

He hadn't written to her. He'd sent this directly to Emmer. If Holloway trusted her so little, if he believed for a second that she might side with the rebels, her loyalty was spent. She flipped back the glass shield from the flux lamp on Webb's desk, slipped the edge of the letter into the open flame, and watched it catch.

Wax hissed as the paper curled and blackened. She fed it in slowly with shaking hands.

"I'll show you not dangerous," she muttered to herself.

Flux burned clean—no ash, no smoke—but consumed fuel slowly. The bit of paper was still sizzling when a shadow fell over her.

"What are you doing?" Riven stood in the doorway. His eyes flicked from the lamp to her face. Then, quietly, he said, "Walk with me."

She hesitated, letting the last bit of paper disintegrate between her fingers in the cool burn of the flux flame.

"Now, boss." The soft edge on the nickname was gone.

She shoved the lamp lid closed, grabbed her satchel, and followed him. Where was he taking her?

Sunlight hit her like a slap as soon as she stepped out onto the street. Gateway buzzed, too loud, too crowded, like any other day. Emotions pressed in on her: annoyance, hunger, impatience. She breathed through it like she'd been practicing.

"For a renowned scholar, that was reckless," Riven said finally, walking ahead of her.

Her pulse was racing. Why did he care? He already knew enough of her secrets to ruin her life if he cared to.

"What did you see?" The question came out thin.

He slowed to let her catch up, and his hand found the small of her back.

"You don't understand the danger you're in." His voice was low. His index finger was tapping her back in time with their steps. "This is not a classroom. Bad things happen out here."

Is that a warning or a threat? Gods, she wished she could read him.

"Where are we going?" she asked.

"You didn't cross the sea to copy reports in a basement."

He angled them down a side street, away from the main flow of traffic. Buildings thinned, and wood planks gave way to packed dirt. The city walls loomed ahead, a patchwork of wood and stone. The guards barely glanced at them as they passed through the gate. Outside, the world opened into rolling hills, distant ridgelines, ruins half buried in golden grass.

After about twenty minutes of walking, Riven led her up a small hill to a cluster of weathered stone formations. There were ancient walls of varying heights, wind whistling through the gaps.

"What is this place?" Talia breathed.

"An old watchtower. Real ruins."

An archway rose from the rubble, its upper curve intact enough to hold a ring of glyphs. The script spiraled, worn but readable. Her mind translated almost automatically, a simple welcome.

His eyes followed her as she moved deeper into the fallen structure. The site had been picked over, but two lovers' initials carved into the inner wall made her smile. Graffiti was timeless. She was reaching out to touch it when Riven's hand closed over her wrist.

"Listen," he breathed.

Then she heard it too. A screech of wagon wheels, men's voices pitched low, leather creaking. Without a word, Riven pulled her farther behind the half-collapsed wall.

His chest pressed warm against her back. She could feel every weapon he carried, the dual blades bracketing her hips. His hand spread across her ribs, steadying her, but since she couldn't read his emotions, the contact just felt solid, like a wall.

She could see the road below through a narrow gap in the rubble, and a wagon rolled into view. A reinforced cage was strapped to the top of it, just like in the market, and there was something inside of it. This creature looked almost like a lion, but it had feathers. A gryphon.

"Is the sedative holding?" a male voice called out, surprisingly clear over the distance.

The man came into view, and Talia jerked back in surprise. She recognized the brown canvas uniform, the bulky supply pack slung over his shoulder. That was Consortium field gear. A second man approached him wearing a distinctive green cloak.

"Should be good for now," the enforcer answered. "We need to be farther from town when it wears off."

"Lost Mat last week trying to net one of these," the Consortium scholar said. "Took his arm clean off."

"Could've been worse. Hydra poisoned three men in Unit Eighteen." Another green-cloak came into view, adjusting something on the cage. "At least this one's going down easy."

A wave of dizziness hit her, and she pressed her eyes closed. That was the field report she had in her room. Unit Eighteen. She remembered the three fatalities, but there was no mention of a hydra.

"Nothing about this is easy." This fourth voice rang sharp, authoritative. "We've got our orders, let's move."

It was bizarre, scholars and military officers hauling a monster down the road. They circled the wagon, checking straps and tightening restraints with the bored efficiency of routine.

The gryphon's head swung toward the hill, and its golden eyes locked on the gap where Talia and Riven hid. Suddenly it screamed, a sound like tearing metal and breaking glass. Riven pulled her tighter against his chest. The men below cursed and jabbed prods through slats, pumping some kind of sedative into its neck.

"It smells something up there."

She felt like she was choking. Tears stung her eyes. Her muscles locked into place as she hyperventilated, and a halo of black edged her vision.

"Easy," Riven breathed against her ear. "I'm right here."

The gryphon's movements slowed, and she felt her own body relax. She'd felt its terror—primal and absolute. Her empathy had never worked over that kind of distance, and it had definitely never picked up an animal's emotions.

Wheels creaked, and the voices started to fade. Riven didn't relax his grip until the wagon blurred into a smudge on the road. When he finally stepped back, her legs wobbled. She steadied herself against the wall, and his hand hovered near her elbow, ready to catch her.

"Why are there so many monsters in cages?" she asked, shaking out her hands. "Is that a normal thing here?"

"No." Riven looked grim. "Not normal."

"Those were enforcers and Consortium scholars together." Talia felt like she needed to list the facts out loud. She needed to hear him agree that she wasn't making it up. "They mentioned Unit Eighteen. That unit was assigned to fieldwork. They should have been out there conducting research, not—" She gestured at the empty road.

Riven just nodded.

"Emmer told me that fieldwork was too dangerous for me." Her voice rose. She was angry, she realized. "But they're not *doing* fieldwork. They're doing something with these monsters."

"What will you do now?"

She felt the anger simmering in her chest. She had taken a real risk coming to Valta. She'd disobeyed her grandmother, broken her engagement, and held on to that heretical journal. Now she was running out of time to make it worthwhile. It was only a matter of time before Holloway sent another letter or even tracked her down himself.

She couldn't keep hoping things would change on their own. She'd rather make a risky choice than be left with no choice at all.

"I guess I'm going to ask Dawn for that introduction."

FIRST REBELLION

VAELIS • 12 YEARS AGO

Talent's first true rebellion took place in church. The Grand Cathedral's vast sanctuary shimmered with sunlight filtered through thirteen stained glass gods. Talent and Cordon's engagement had just been formalized, and they'd been seated together.

The high priest related the entire foundation myth. Talent had heard the story of how the Divine Navigator led the Twelve across the Green Sea so many times, she could recite it by heart. Then an invocation for each god, thirteen times over, kneel and rise. Her knees ached, but she didn't complain.

"Vael the Navigator, guide our ships. Meren the Lastlight, keep our hearts aflame..."

Talent mouthed the words, but Cordon did not. He traced a pattern on the polished wood pew with his thumbnail, humming under his breath.

"Stop that," she murmured.

He leaned close. She smelled the wax in his hair. "If the gods are so powerful, why do they need so much flattery?"

"Because they deserve it," she whispered.

His mouth curved. "What about me?" He reached down, catching her hand. "We're betrothed now, so I deserve it more. Come on, I'll show you something better than prayers."

Before she could refuse, he pulled her up the side aisle. Holloway whisper-hissed for them to get back in the pew, but they slipped through a half-open door into a narrow stairwell. Cordon's laugh bounced off the stone walls.

The stairs led to a hidden alcove above the choir loft. Through a lattice screen they could see the congregation below, hundreds of bowed heads, the high priest's robes hiding his feet, like he was levitating.

Cordon climbed up onto the rail, swinging one leg into open air. "All this," he said, flicking his fingers toward the cathedral, "built for an overblown faerie story."

"You shouldn't say things like that."

"Why not?" Something flashed in his blue eyes. He never looked at her like this when others were around. "You don't believe the gods are real, do you?"

"I do." But her voice wavered.

"Come on, you're the smart one," he teased. "You really think magical beings with the power of creation and shadow and death are watching over us? If you had that kind of power, is that what you'd do with it?"

The gods were stitched into the seams of her life—prayers at dawn, blessings before dinner, gratitudes before bed. Yes, she'd noticed the similarities between the faerie stories she adored and the religious parables, but she'd never said so out loud.

"The gods might not be physical beings," she said, fidgeting with the hem of her dress, "but the stories reflect a deeper truth."

He brushed a curl behind her ear, and she jolted at his touch.

"See?" He spoke under his breath, so she had to lean in to hear. "I knew you were smart. Tell me more about that."

Below them, the choir sang a gentle hymn, voices drifting up like smoke.

She tilted her head into his hand. "Well, I think actions and choices are real. If the gods' words shape your choices, doesn't that make *them* real?"

"No, that makes them a myth." He looked down at her, thoughtful. "You're real. Right here in this moment. Don't you feel it?" He placed a hand on her heart, which was thrumming out of control. "The gods, not so much. I want to hear you say it. Tell me the gods are a myth."

"Why?" Her voice was barely a whisper.

"Because you always follow the rules, just like my brother." One finger slid down her breastbone. "But the rules don't apply to us."

Her face was on fire. She wanted to hear him say again how smart she was.

"The gods are a myth," she whispered.

Dimples flashed in his cheeks. Then he cupped her jaw and leaned forward—

"Tally, are you here?" Holloway's voice echoed up the stairs, and they jerked apart.

Her best friend stood in the doorway, cheeks blotched red like he'd run up the stairs. He looked at Cordon, then at her. He never frowned, but he was frowning now.

"You're going to miss the closing prayer," he mumbled. "Come back down now and no one will get in trouble."

"Well, we wouldn't want to get in trouble," Cordon said with a grin.

Then he winked at her. *Winked.* As if this was all a big joke. As if she hadn't just forsworn the gods for him. Talent hesitated, waiting for thunder. For divine fury. For any sign the gods had heard her blasphemy. It never happened.

Holloway ushered them back down the stairs, and they slipped back into their pews, and the service carried on. Neither gods nor grown-ups punished them. She had to wonder, after all that. Were the gods even listening?

11

THE GATEWAY PROPHET

TALIA

The most dangerous man on the frontier is not the outlaw or the enforcer. It is the preacher. He does not need to lie. He pushes on the broken promises that hurt most, the ones you feel but can't quite name. It's a wonder anyone resists.

— *COLLECTED DISPATCHES FROM THE WESTERN TERRITORIES*, CASH BRENTHAVEN, 399 AC

Dawn just grinned when Talia asked for the introduction. She said it'd taken her long enough, as if Talia was always going to come around. They arranged to meet at the Flux & Fiddle, and Dawn would lead them to some place called Starfall Sanctuary.

As they made their way across town, Talia picked up a strange tension between Dawn and Riven, like there was something unspoken between them. They had similar coloring, unusually fair skin and lighter-colored hair. At least, she assumed Dawn's hair looked blond under the pink. They didn't seem like siblings. She couldn't figure it out.

The place, Starfall Sanctuary, came out of nowhere. They turned a corner to thick stone walls and a grand-looking metal gate. It felt like a different city inside. The air was easier to breathe. Acolytes in blue robes moved in small groups, reclined on benches, spoke in low voices. A circle of children listened to a story in the courtyard. Contentment hummed under her skin like a sustained note at the end of a pleasant song.

The Lyceum back in Vaelis had promised community built on shared knowledge, and delivered politics and backbiting instead. This place looked like it kept its promise. She had an absurd impulse to pull a blue cloak over her head and dissolve into the crowd.

"Ah, you're here."

She turned. The man approaching was striking in a way that scattered her thoughts, which was inconvenient, because she needed those.

He had dark hair curling to his shoulders and hazel eyes flecked with gold. He wore a well-made coat, simple, with a silver pendant at his throat shaped like a seven-pointed star. He moved with unhurried confidence, and when he got close enough, she caught the faint scent of amber and smoke.

"Talent Salaren." His voice shaped her name with a perfect Vaelish lilt as he extended his hand. "I'm Lore Tavis. Welcome to Starfall Sanctuary."

"It's an honor to meet you." She smiled, trying to place him and failing. Tavis wasn't a surname she'd heard in high society.

"The pleasure is entirely mine." He released her hand slowly, nodding at Dawn and Riven before turning his full attention back to her. "You're in Gateway to work with the Consortium?"

"Yes," she said carefully.

"What a waste." Then he gestured toward a larger building ahead. "Come. I have a rather unique relic that I'd like your help with."

He'd dismissed the Consortium and sought her expertise all in the same breath. A laugh slipped out before Talia could suppress it. He walked beside her on the gravel path, not ahead. Close enough she caught the smoky scent again. They were about the same height. Riven's steady footsteps kept pace behind them.

The doors of the building were carved with flowing Starscript that made her fingers itch for her notebook. Dawn stood guard outside. Riven paused, then followed them in.

It was a library. Inside, shelves stretched toward a vaulted ceiling. The spines were well creased and free of dust. A working archive to rival the Lyceum.

"Welcome to our collection," Lore said quietly beside her. "We rescue texts and artifacts the Pentarchy considers too dangerous." He let her take it in for a moment. Then, "But I'm getting ahead of myself. There's something I want your opinion on."

She shivered. The Pentarchy had a long memory and little patience with people who crossed them. But the relic on the table pulled her attention before she could dwell on the threat.

It was a delicate metal ring. Glyphs curled across the curving surface. The conjugation was unusual, but the suffix caught her eye —*ella*. She turned it carefully in her hand.

"Most would translate this as *tribute* or *offering*," she said. "But the durative suffix makes it continuous. So, not *offering* exactly." She traced the curves. "Closer to *lifelong devotion*."

When she looked up, Lore was watching her. She couldn't tell what he was thinking without touching him, and she wasn't about to do that.

"Devotion," he echoed slowly, tasting the word. "I like that."

He leaned close as he reached past her.

"What about this one?" He placed it beside the first, a piece of slate with blue veins twisting through it. "How would you interpret this glyph?"

The symbols seemed to shimmer under the flux lamp. Her pulse quickened. The same looping suffix in a more familiar context: *flux ammentella*. Flux channeling.

"This one I know." She leaned closer, forgetting everything else. "This verb suggests flux is being consumed but not burned."

He leaned in too. "The civilization that inhabited this continent before maintained an organic system for generating flux," he said. "They called the process channeling. You've seen this term before?"

Her breath caught. Lore knew about channeling, and he knew how it had worked. She'd been struggling with these questions alone for so long. She had so many questions. What did he mean, *organic system*?

"Yes, I know it. I reconstructed the word myself. I didn't know if it was a real process or a metaphor, but that's the subject of my research. How to make flux power sustainable, renewable—"

"Accessible to everyone." He finished her sentence, and when his shoulder touched hers, she didn't pull away. Instead, she sifted quickly through his emotions—passion, and something that felt uncomfortably like her own excitement mirrored back.

"You seem excited by this," he said. The gold flecks in his eyes flared, and she had the strangest feeling that he knew what she'd just done. "Most people grow nervous when they realize how revolutionary this could be."

"It changes everything." The words spilled out, and she took a breath to slow herself. "No more burning through relics for power. No more rolling blackouts in the Lower City."

"Did you spend much time in the Lower City when you lived in Vaelis?" He sounded skeptical.

"No, not much," she conceded. "But the people who live there freeze in winter. There's not enough power to go around, and it shouldn't have to be that way."

"No, it shouldn't." He was quiet for a moment. "You want your discoveries to help people. Not just advance theory."

"Of course I do." How was it a question?

"The Consortium won't help you do that."

Her throat tightened. That might be true, but it sounded awful when he put it so bluntly.

"I know. They won't even let me into the field for six months." She tried her best to keep her tone casual, but she knew she must sound bitter.

"Six months." He shook his head. Stepped closer. "And even then, will you be able to pursue your theories on channeling? Or will they simply let your research—"

"Get buried in a vault," she finished.

"It sounds like you're caught between the path you were told to want and what you actually care about."

How could he possibly understand her so well? It was like he could read her mind. She pushed the questions aside. It felt good to be seen, and she didn't want to ruin it by overthinking.

"I am mounting an expedition to Valrotala," he said, slowly, like he was thinking through a new idea. "The old fluxlines run across the continent. There will be many opportunities to study channeling sites, and I could use someone with your skills."

Riven cleared his throat. "Have you been to the fallen fae capital?"

Talia looked between the two of them. The city of Valrotala was legendary. She'd heard stories that it was here on this continent, but she hadn't really believed them.

"As far as the gates," Lore answered curtly. Then he turned back to face Talia. "And yes, if you're wondering. It is a real place."

Riven's brows were pinched together. He opened his mouth, but Talia jumped in. "When do you expect to leave?"

A smile flickered across Lore's face, there and gone. "Two weeks."

Two weeks. She could be out of the Consortium basement doing real work in two weeks.

"I would love that—" The words slipped out, but then she stopped herself.

Something nagged at her, something she was missing. He'd mentioned danger earlier. And the Pentarchy.

"You're not affiliated with the Consortium," she said slowly. "Or the Lyceum. But this must take significant funding." She gestured around the room.

"It does," he said, holding eye contact. She tried not to blink first. "I'm fortunate to have people who believe in what we're trying to accomplish."

"But not the Pentarchy."

"No." A faint smile. "Not the Pentarchy."

There was an edge to his voice that made his smile feel sharp too. She was close to naming something he found amusing. She just didn't know what.

"How controversial is this work, exactly?" she asked.

His eyes flashed, and he was quiet for a moment. Considering his words, maybe.

"The thing is," he said finally, "I should tell you this before you decide. It's only fair."

There must have been a draft, because suddenly she felt cold all over. "Tell me what?"

"Just, the Pentarchy considers this work more than controversial."

"You're a rebel sympathizer." The first phrase that entered her head was the line from Holloway's letter.

"No." He spoke calmly, gently, watching her face. "I lead them, Talent. The rebellion operates out of Starfall."

Talia stared at him. Her mouth felt dry. Holloway had said she was under surveillance. What if he found out she was meeting with the *leader of the rebellion*? Joining Lore's expedition would make every baseless suspicion Holloway had of her true. Just staying in this room gave him reason not to trust her. *Gods.* Had she already crossed a line?

She forced herself to breathe slowly. The Consortium was burying her work, she reminded herself, and she'd already crossed a line months ago. She'd kept the journal. That's what had started all of this.

"Can we talk outside?" Riven cut in.

Heat flared in her chest. She knew he didn't trust her judgement, but she could feel Lore's eyes on both of them. Couldn't he treat her like an adult just this once?

"We're talking about this now," she snapped. "If you have something to say, say it."

His jaw worked. Finally, he said, "That place was abandoned for a reason. You follow him there, there's no clean way out."

"He's right to be concerned," Lore said from behind her. His voice was gentle, unbearably reasonable. "It is dangerous. The ruins are unstable. There are frequent fluxborn attacks. And yes, the Pentarchy might retaliate."

What they were talking about, it was so much worse than keeping the journal. She'd seen people at all levels of society hanged for associating with rebels. Even Holloway couldn't save her if this went wrong.

"If you want your work to matter—" Lore's eyes held hers. "If you want to ever help those people in the Lower City, this is your chance. Staying with the Consortium will only hold you back."

She believed her research could change the world. Even more now that she knew flux channeling was real. It hurt to imagine giving that up. But associating with rebels would destroy everything else in her life. If she did this, she could never go home again. Not safely.

"I need time to think."

"Of course. Though I will remind you, we leave in two weeks. After that..." He spread his hands. "I cannot help."

Two weeks. To choose between her life's work and her duty to her family. He moved toward her, closing the distance she'd put between them.

"Come back another day," he said quietly. "You can have private access to the collection. No interruptions. I'll show you what I've learned about channeling."

He extended his hand. She wondered if this was a trap, some way to get her to agree to join him. But when she took it, all she felt was genuine curiosity and respect buzzing harmlessly against her palm.

"I'll consider it."

"I hope you will." A smile broke across his face, drawing a single dimple on his left cheek. "It would be such a waste to see your talents buried."

She didn't fully register leaving. Cold air hit her face, and Riven was saying something about a task he needed to see to. She waved him off without fully listening.

Dawn fell into step behind her as she followed the path back to the front gates. She turned toward the market, then froze. A flash of green—enforcer patrol. She turned to the river instead.

Channeling was real. And she'd been right; it could change everything. But joining Lore would make Holloway right. Would he feel vindicated by that? Or would some part of him—the boy who'd believed in her—be disappointed?

She had two weeks to decide. Stay with the Consortium, safe in a basement with her work buried next to her. Or associate herself with the rebellion. Either way, she was running out of time.

If she joined Lore, she risked everything. If she stayed, she might never make it into the field. If she ran—where could she go? She already knew how Holloway felt. Little chance her grandmother would be more charitable.

Every option branched into more options. So she did what she always did when a choice truly mattered. She pushed it down and kept walking.

12

FAIR WARNING

DAWN

Flux channeling requires a power source. The mechanism seems related to the elein *mating bond, of which we know little. With the beasts gone feral it is hard to test, but I may have located an uncorrupted source.*

— LORE TAVIS, *ON THE NATURE OF FLUX*, UNPUBLISHED

Dawn first met Lore three years ago, and she'd sized him up all wrong. Too pretty. Too polished. A city boy playing rebel hero while real people bled. Then he'd said what he'd said.

"Your mate, Ehrue. She's alive."

Her knife was at his throat. "Don't you fucking dare."

Nobody knew she'd had a mate. Nobody knew Ehrue's name.

"The true gods speak to me," Lore continued, unfazed by the blade. "They have many voices. Hers is one."

"Bullshit."

But his eyes held hers, steady in his own belief. "You used to trace the scars on her shoulder while she slept. Three lines." He paused. Let it land. "For the three children she dreamed of. You counted them like prayer beads when the nightmares came."

Lucky guess, she told herself. Con artists had all kinds of tricks. He probably paid someone to dig up her history.

But her hands shook. Nobody was alive to tell her story. She'd spent years mourning until she was numb. More years hunting the fluxborn monsters that took her mate. This pretty bastard shouldn't know any of it.

He still might be lying. She knew that, and it didn't matter. If there was even a chance Ehrue was alive—even the smallest fucking chance—Dawn would do anything. She wanted it to be true so bad, she closed the trap herself.

Three years later, she was still waiting to reunite with her lost love. Still running fucking errands for Lore. So when Talia walked out of Starfall, Dawn recognized the look in the girl's eyes. That dazed, desperate hope.

Lore had a new target now. Dawn had delivered her. *Fuck that.*

The girl was walking fast, taking one random turn after another.

"Come on, professor," Dawn said. "You look like you could use a distraction."

"I'm fine." Her voice was distant.

"Sure, you are. That's why you're walking in circles." Dawn caught Talia's elbow and steered her south, toward the distant sound of whooping and laughter. "Let me guess. Lore wants you to come with us."

Talia stopped walking. "I haven't decided—"

"He doesn't exactly take no for an answer." Dawn had more she could say about that. "Question is whether you follow without looking or open your eyes."

She'd brought this city girl to Lore's doorstep. Least she could do was give her some tools to survive it.

"Come with me," Dawn said. "I've got something that might cheer you up."

The breaking corral sat outside the south edge of Gateway, where grassland met construction. A crowd gathered as wranglers worked wild horses, all dust and skill and sweat. Talia was staring.

"Nice, right?" Dawn grinned as a wrangler dismounted with a bow-legged swagger. "But that's for later. Right now, you're gonna learn how to ride."

Cannon was exactly what this town needed more of: grizzled, competent, honest as a slap. He ran the corral and stabled horses for folks in town. Dawn explained she needed an easy mount for a city girl.

"She ever been on a horse?" He sounded skeptical, and rightly so.

"Sidesaddle park ponies, I'd wager."

He snorted and pulled Jonquil from the paddock, a patient bay mare shaped like a barrel. What followed went exactly as bad as Dawn expected.

Talia mounted with confidence. Squeezed with her calves instead of her thighs. Jonquil took three steps, and the girl slid sideways and hit the dirt.

Dawn offered a hand. "You good?"

Talia took it, jaw set. "Again."

"Stop thinking so hard," Dawn called on the next circuit. "Feel what she's doing. Move with her."

She tried, failed, ate dirt again—and again, and again, each time a little angrier, a little more determined. Dawn watched with growing respect. City girl had some steel under those skirts.

"Loosen your shoulders. You're fighting her."

"I'll fall."

"You're already falling. Might as well relax while you do it."

Talia shot her a look, but she tried. Loosened her death grip. Let her hips move with the horse instead of against her.

Dawn whistled. "There it is. She's riding."

Talia's face lit up. Beautiful, Dawn thought. Not the cleaned-up city version. This girl here, all flushed and fierce with a shit-eating grin. Strands of hair escaping her braid, dress hiked up to her knees.

"Not bad, professor." Dawn swung down from her mare, Brimstone, a fiery girl she'd raised from a foal. "You're almost ready to walk that horse real slow into the wilderness."

Cannon gave Talia an approving nod when they brought the horses in. "Nice work out there. You can come by and ride her any time."

Wranglers stripped off their shirts at the trough, splashing cold water over their necks and faces. Dawn hauled Talia over to watch from the fence.

"Best part of the day," Dawn said with a chuckle, tipping her head at the display of muscled, dusty humanity.

"You're shameless," Talia said. Her cheeks were flushed, but she kept glancing over.

"Damn right." Dawn pulled out her flask and took a pull. "That's the difference between you and me, professor. I don't pretend I'm not looking."

She offered the flask. Talia took a cautious sip and coughed.

"So. We need to talk about Lore," Dawn said.

Talia's eyebrows came together. She frowned. "What about him?"

"Let me put it this way," Dawn said, turning her knees to look right at the girl. "You know in the old stories, when someone offers you everything you want? There's always a price. That's how it is with Lore."

"That seems dramatic—"

"You're gonna tell me he didn't say exactly what you wanted to hear in there?"

The girl took that in for a minute. She bit her lower lip when she was thinking, Dawn noticed. "He did tell me something. A breakthrough, really, in my research."

"I'm sure he did." Dawn took the flask back. Took a long pull. "That's what he does. Finds what you want and hooks you."

"Wait, you invited me there."

"I know." It sat heavy in Dawn's chest. "I shouldn't have. I thought—" She stopped. What had she thought? She'd thought they needed a translator to crack the gate at Valrotala, that's what.

She'd been selfish. And after watching Talia eat dirt all afternoon, she was feeling some way about it. Not quite guilty—Dawn didn't do guilt—but she didn't like it.

"Look." Dawn's voice dropped. "I want you to come. I do. Just keep your wits. Don't let him—" She dug for the right words. "Don't let Lore charm you."

"I'm a little hard to charm," Talia said. But the way she said it, defensive and quick, carried its own message. The girl was halfway gone already.

"What you need is perspective." Dawn nodded at the trough where the wranglers were finishing up. "You could pick any of those boys. Or girls."

Talia sounded like she was choking. "Dawn!"

"What are you worried about?" Dawn leaned closer. "You're not in Vaelis anymore. Out here, you can write your own damn story."

Dawn watched a redhead laugh, her head thrown back, throat on display. The woman caught her looking and shot her a wink. *That's worth following up on.*

Talia stared into the flask. Flustered. Chewing her lip again. Was any of this landing? Or was the girl too trained and timid to make her own way?

Fuck it. She'd just say it straight.

"I mean it," Dawn said, dropping her teasing tone. "Whatever you do, don't let anyone else write your story for you. Not Lore, not your people back home, not me or that bodyguard." She waited until Talia met her eyes. "You deserve to choose for yourself."

They started back toward the main part of town. Stars were coming out, one at a time. The sky was going purple, like a bruise.

"How long have you been working for Lore?" Talia asked quietly.

Dawn's hand found the necklace at her throat. She ran her fingers over the point of a tooth, worn smooth. *Three years now. Damn, it feels like forever.* A lick of flame curled up Dawn's throat, and she swallowed her anger back down.

"Long enough."

13

OLD FRIENDS

TALIA

The Pentarchy enforcement corps brought order to the western territories. What it displaced to do so—the informal codes, the frontier courts, the uneasy truces between religious and secular factions—was largely lost. No one who valued what came before had the power to write history.

— *ON ORDER AND ITS DISCONTENTS*, CREST ALDAINE, 405 AC

The door to the Flux & Fiddle might as well have been a portal. Outside, big skies and unbroken horses. Inside, raw humanity. Talia stepped from cool autumn lastlight into the clash of piano and roar of a crowd. Sweat and dust glued her blouse to her back, and all she wanted was a cold bath.

She scanned the room for the fastest path to the back stairs, but white-blond hair caught her attention. Riven sat at the end of the bar, back to the wall, watching the door. His eyes locked on her.

Don't let anyone write your story for you.

It wasn't bad advice; she just wasn't interested in some random wrangler. Did she want *him*? She laughed at the thought, but her heart fluttered when he nodded. She didn't have a whole plan, but she figured she could start by buying him a drink. Apologize for snapping at him back at Starfall.

She started toward the bar, tilting her shoulders to squeeze through the press of people. She was almost there, just past the first table, when the door creaked open.

"Tally!"

She stopped. Only one person would use that nickname. She turned, her stomach twisting.

Holloway Sennett stood in the doorway, backlit by blue flux streetlights. Black uniform, perfectly pressed. Green cloak with three silver pins. Slowly, he set a small suitcase and his harp case onto the floor and straightened back up. His eyes never left her face.

Her hands and feet prickled, and she felt dizzy. He must be here to arrest her. He must know about the rebels. The journal.

He was smiling that same crooked smile that used to dissolve her anger. Her childhood best friend. The man she'd been engaged to. He was here in Gateway, crossing through the saloon, angling through the crowd to get to her. Now his smile was breaking into a full grin. When he reached her, he slipped his hands under hers and squeezed.

All his emotions hit her. Joy came through first—bright, sharp, spreading up her arms. Relief next, cool in her chest. Then desire, sparkling and familiar. She couldn't breathe. She wanted to pull away, but it felt like everyone was watching.

"I looked everywhere," he was saying. "The docks, the Consortium offices—"

"What are you doing in Gateway?" Her voice came out thin.

"I was reassigned." Joy kept crackling through his touch, like static. "There was a captain position open." He kept squeezing her hands. "And I missed you."

Her chest felt tight. He wasn't here to arrest her. Knowing Holloway, he would do everything he could to keep her safe. It didn't feel so different.

Velvet materialized beside them. Talia had never seen the owner of the Flux & Fiddle look so flushed and flustered. She was tending bar tonight, and it was packed.

"Talia! Who's this handsome thing?" Her hands grazed Holloway's arm.

"Holloway, this is Velvet Fawkes." They were jostled together by the crowd. "Velvet, this is—"

"Her fiancé." Holloway's smile widened, and he extended a hand.

Technically true. She'd never said yes. But then, she'd never said no. And she was still wearing his bracelet.

Velvet shrieked. "Everyone! Talia is engaged!"

The saloon erupted into cheers, and glasses crashed together. Talia looked back over her shoulder. Riven was still at the bar staring at her. His jaw went tight, and he set his glass down hard.

Velvet ushered them to a corner booth, taking Talia by the shoulders and jostling her through the crowd and into a cushioned chair. Holloway settled beside her, too close.

"First round is on the house!" Velvet came back with a tray of amber liquid. "*Liethi.* Gateway's finest."

Dawn showed up, sliding into the booth across from them. "So, you're the fiancé she forgot to mention."

News traveled fast, apparently.

"Holloway Sennett." He shook her hand. "Are you one of Tally's friends?"

"I'm *Tally's* riding coach." Dawn's grin sharpened. "Working on loosening her up. Maybe you can help me out?"

Talia groaned. She picked up a drink and started sipping before anyone could toast. The *liethi* burned deep in her chest, like whiskey but hotter.

The redheaded wrangler from the corral joined them, and she introduced herself as Ruby. It was more than crowded now. Holloway's hand felt for hers under the table, but she reached for another drink.

Holloway stood. "Let me buy the next round. It's the least I can do for showing up uninvited."

When he returned, Cannon was there and already grumbling. "Damn enforcers everywhere. No offense, but Gateway used to be a free place."

Dawn piled on. "The Pentarchy aren't too popular here, I'm afraid. How'd you end up with a green cloak anyway?"

"Trust me, I know," Holloway said easily. "Enforcers can be real pricks. Present company included." That got a round of laughs. "I guess I thought I could help people." He looked at his drink. "Fix the system from the inside."

"Sorry to say, it ain't fixed." Dawn looked at him thoughtfully.

"No, ma'am." He met her eyes. "These days, I'm just trying to do the least harm I can."

Dawn nodded. Lifted her glass. "To the least harm."

They drank.

Talia watched them warm to him. She should have been charmed, too, but she could feel Riven's eyes on her every time Holloway touched her arm.

The Flux & Fiddle was one of the classier saloons in town. She'd never seen it this rowdy. But word had gotten out about an engagement party, and *liethi* was flowing. Someone had pushed the tables back from the fireplace, and a growing crowd was dancing. A glass shattered somewhere to wild applause. The flux lamps pulsed brighter with each beat.

"Dance with me," Holloway said, grabbing Talia's hand and tugging her onto her feet.

His hand spread across her back, warm through the fabric of her blouse. His affection rushed through her, spreading up from her waist. It was too much. She couldn't catch her breath.

Over Holloway's shoulder, she saw Riven. Still in the corner. Watching her spin. Watching her lean on Holloway's arm. Velvet tried to tug him onto the floor, but he waved her off. The song kept playing. The room spun, and not just from dancing.

"I need—" She tried to pull away and stumbled.

Then Dawn was there, supporting her. "My turn."

Dawn was shorter than Talia, but she had no trouble holding her up. Dawn's emotions were sharp, controlled—a constant sweep for danger, brief sparks of joy. She smelled like leather and something sweet. Like burned sugar.

"Your eyes are glazing over, professor. You in there?" Dawn sounded concerned. *That's not very Dawn-like.*

"I'm fine."

Holloway was dancing with Velvet now. It wasn't any formal dance Talia had ever seen. They were spinning each other by the elbow, and everyone was cheering. Having fun.

Riven was still in the corner. His eyes flashed and he leaned forward. Her body responded, heat coiling low in her stomach. Dawn spun her around. Held her at arm's length and noted where she was staring.

"Shit, that's not a good idea. Let's get you some water."

The piano had stopped. Holloway was moving toward the front of the room. When had he gotten up? He pulled a chair closer to the fire, and the crowd quieted.

Then he opened his battered instrument case. A rosewood harp gleamed in the firelight, its edges worn smooth by years of handling. He paused to tune it, head bent, the motion precise and unhurried. He settled it against his shoulder and started to play.

Conversations died. The crowd froze. Dancers shuffled to the edge of the room, glasses held midair as the entire saloon held its breath.

The melody thrummed in Talia's bones. It was their song. He'd written the music, and she wrote the lyrics. The Divine Navigator leading the Twelve across the Green Sea was an old story. The foundation myth was usually about creation and hope, but this version wove in the bittersweet theme of the home they'd left behind. She knew every note before he played it.

They looked not back at the fading shore.

They broke the ships for timber,
Raised their city beam by beam
Spoke words they had to borrow.

Revered as gods, their tears are salt,
Their dreams trail out behind them.
The tongue they borrowed has no word
For what they have abandoned.

So, raise your cup for the home they lost
The books they could not carry,
Who built new life from the bones of the crossing
For just one more tomorrow.

She'd written those words in the dark months after Cordon died, and she hadn't heard them in years. The room had gone still with shared emotion—that peculiar sharp-edged awareness of being alive that follows gutting loss. For once, the feelings she absorbed from the crowd were the same ones she felt. Perfectly balanced. The pressure in her chest eased.

There was just one wrong note. Holloway's love for her ricocheted through the room, and it carried a message: *Come home. Be safe. Let me protect you.* When the last note trailed into silence, everyone was clapping.

"That was something Tally and I made together," Holloway said. "We used to dream about charting the stars and exploring the world, just like the Divine Navigator." He looked at her. "You made it here. I'm so proud of you."

In the corner, Riven's chair scraped. He dropped a stack of coins on the table with a jarring clatter that echoed through the quiet room. Talia tried to catch his eye, but he didn't look back.

The party was winding down. Cannon had long since left. Dawn and Ruby stumbled out together, and Holloway was slumped over the table. Talia helped him stand. His arm settled heavy across her shoulders. She didn't know where else to take him except up to her room. They climbed the stairs together, and after struggling his way through the door, he collapsed into the armchair.

"Who is he?" Holloway asked, leaning back and closing his eyes.

"Who?" She worked his boots off his feet and then brought a blanket over from the bed.

"You know." He waved his hand. "Beardy bun head."

She barked a laugh. "What did you just say?"

"That big man in the corner, with the bun and the beard. He was staring at you all night." His words were slurring badly.

Her face warmed. "Oh. I'm pretty sure he hates me."

"No one could hate you, Tally." Holloway was fading. "You're so smart and beautiful. And tall. And smart."

She laughed again. "You're drunk. We can talk in the morning."

"But you like him. Does he make you happy?"

"He makes me feel like I'm my own person," she said. He wouldn't remember this in the morning. "Not just Marionette Salaren's heir."

"And I make you feel safe."

"Go to sleep, Holloway."

He tried to say something else, but the words didn't come together. He just fell asleep.

That's when she noticed her desk. By the gods. She had papers everywhere, half-translated Starscript, piles of notes from the journal. She slid everything into the drawer, turned the key, and slipped it into her pocket.

Holloway stirred in the chair. The man who'd crossed an ocean for her. At one point, he had been her best friend. Her safe space. He could destroy her career if he saw half the notes that had just been sitting on her desk. It would be too risky to join Lore's expedition now that Holloway was here. She climbed into bed, and the key dug into her hip.

WALTZING WITH GHOSTS

VAELIS • 10 YEARS AGO

The practice room smelled like rosin dust. Afternoon light striped the floorboards. Someone had polished the mirrors so carefully that the windows' reflection looked real, a second city caught in the glass.

Two people missing now. Cordon dead. Merit—no one knew where Merit was. Just gone.

And Talent stood there, still breathing. The tilted mirrors showed her three times over. None of the reflections looked quite right.

"Begin with a simple waltz step," said Madame Cross. "Posture, please."

Talent's slippers carried her to the edge of the marked center square and stopped. Cordon used to spin her here until both of them were breathless, collapsing in a tangle of laughter.

She could not step into that square.

"Miss Salaren?" The metronome clicked. "One, two, three."

"I can't," Talent said. It came out small.

A figure stepped onto the floor. Holloway bowed slightly to Madame. The look he gave her carried more authority than a raised voice.

"Let me take it from here," he said.

Madame pursed her lips. "We are already behind."

"Then we can't waste any more time." He held her gaze until she stepped back, gathered her things, and left. He was only fifteen, a year younger than her, but people listened to him.

He crossed the room. He looked impeccable—neat waistcoat,

precise knot at his throat. The only thing out of place was his hair, a cascade of golden curls that followed no instructions.

He offered a hand. "May I?"

She took it. "I hate this room."

"I know." His voice was quiet. "So do I."

He placed her right hand on his shoulder; his left found the small of her back. They stood like that for a breath.

"One," he murmured. "Two. Three."

He stepped back, and she followed. Her left foot dragged where it should have lifted. He shifted his weight, turned the mistake into a pivot.

"Look here," he said gently. "At me. It's easier that way."

"I can't do this." Her voice cracked.

"I'm right here." His thumb brushed her knuckles once, then twice. "We'll get through it together."

She made the mistake of glancing toward the mirror. Cordon looked back—his face pale and wrong, the way it had been when they pulled him from the river.

She stopped hard, breath catching. "I keep seeing him."

Holloway didn't tell her she was crazy. He held her hand steady. "Breathe with me."

They moved again. She stepped on his foot. He didn't wince, just guided her through the turn as if that was the step all along.

"I must look ridiculous," she said softly.

"You look brave."

The room slid past: window, mirror, empty chair, door. She made mistakes. He covered them. Each time, she leaned harder on his shoulder.

He hummed under his breath, and she followed the sound. The pressure in her chest eased, just a little. She felt safe within the circle of his arms. By the final figure, her feet had remembered. When the dance ended, they stood in the center of the square, hands still joined, breathing matched.

A sob caught in her throat. Holloway pulled her close, and she rested her forehead against his shoulder.

"I don't know how to do this," she said. "Without Cordon. Without Merit."

Her fault. All her fault. If Holloway knew what she'd done, he wouldn't be holding her like this. He'd push her away.

"We'll figure it out together," he said quietly.

"We're the heirs now. Everyone's watching us. Expecting us to be perfect." She didn't even know how to get up in the morning. How was Holloway so steady?

"We'll make them proud." His arms tightened around her.

She nodded against his shoulder. Tucked his words away like gifts. She wasn't watching his reflection in the mirror. If she had been, she might have seen it sway, just a little, as the weight of her grief pulled him off-balance.

14

BLANK MAPS

TALIA

Beyond the boundary stones, special field protocols apply. Scholars are reminded that all materials recovered in restricted zones, including maps and field notes, are subject to Pentarchy review.

— INDEPENDENT SCHOLARS CONSORTIUM, FIELD OPERATIONS DIRECTIVE 7, 399 AC

She swung her legs over the edge of her thin mattress and nearly kicked Holloway in the head.

Two days of this.

He hadn't done anything wrong. He'd brought her breakfast as she nursed a hangover. Kept quiet while she read. He even volunteered to sleep on the floor. Incredibly, annoyingly thoughtful—and constantly there.

The journal stayed locked away. The key stayed in her pocket.

She dressed quietly and slipped out before he awoke.

Outside, the sky was a flat gray as she made the walk alone. All the magic seemed to have leeched out of the streets. She wondered if she should buy a proper coat. Winter wasn't far off.

The Consortium basement was dim and airless. The lamp above her desk buzzed and spat. That horrible lamp, this tiny desk. Why did she feel like a child in time-out?

Her chair squealed against the floor as she pushed it back. A narrow hall at the end of the room led to the archives.

"That area is for senior scholars." Nadir didn't even look up as she stepped in that direction.

Something in her snapped.

"I don't know if you caught my name when I arrived," she said, forcing her voice to stay level. "Salaren. Talent Salaren, from Vaelis. My family funds a good portion of the Consortium's research."

Now he looked up.

She smiled. "I'm seeing those maps."

Nadir scowled, but he didn't stop her.

She opened the door to the tiny room and nearly jumped out of her skin when she saw a figure sitting in the almost-dark. *Who the...*

Riven turned. So that's why he hadn't walked over with her. He was already here.

A map lay unrolled across the table. Another half folded. A drawer stood slightly ajar.

He'd been at this awhile.

"Wait." She stepped into the room, the door clicking shut behind her. "What *are* you doing here?"

He just turned and started clearing off the table before she could see what he was reading. "Well, boss, what are we looking for?"

She hated how he never answered her questions.

"Um, maps," she said, gesturing at the shelves. "I'm getting out of Gateway."

He looked at her sharply. "Sure that's a good idea?"

"I'm not waiting anymore. I didn't come here for this."

He stood and reached past her, pulled a map from the shelves, and dropped it onto the table. It landed with a thud and started to unroll on its own.

"Where?"

She blinked. "What?"

"Where are you going?" He stepped back, giving her space. "Show me."

It wasn't a suggestion. Fine, if that's what he wanted.

She leaned over the map, tracing the coastline with her finger. Gateway sat on the eastern edge of the continent. Roads branched north and west.

She pointed, a little too quickly.

"Here. I'll go north on this road, then follow it this way."

He stepped in beside her, close enough she could feel the heat off him. His hand came down over hers—gently, with just enough pressure to redirect her finger.

"Here? Three expeditions went this way." His finger tapped the parchment, on a small notation. "None came back."

Her stomach twisted. She'd seen those reports.

"That doesn't mean I can't—"

He clicked his tongue, interrupting her, and moved her hand again.

Another note. "Two ended here."

"I'll ask Holloway to come, then." She said it without thinking.

It was the wrong thing to say. Riven's face drew into a scowl.

"You'd be guessing and calling it a plan." He yanked another map off the shelf and slammed it onto the table. "Good way to die."

There was the coastline again, Gateway, the roads and the rivers. But in the middle of this map—just blank parchment.

"Nothing," she murmured.

He was next to her now, looking over her shoulder. His cedar scent was everywhere. He traced his finger along the wide river that made its way inland past Gateway and up to the Thol Amras mountains.

"You think so?" He was staring down at that blank space like he could see through it.

She pushed the map away. So this was all there was. The great Consortium archive. It looked like a child had started coloring in a book and given up halfway through.

"Tell me then," she said. "What's out there? Why can't I trust Holloway?"

He didn't answer. He looked at her steadily, then he reached down and picked up two of the maps, rolling them tightly and slipping them into his jacket.

"What are you—"

He stepped out of the room before she could finish. She took a step to follow and the door clicked shut, loud in the small space.

Had he just stolen those maps? No. He was trying to get a rise out of her. Her fingers clenched around the brittle edges of the parchment until it crinkled.

She thought about Lore's library—dangerous, yes, but full of knowledge. She'd bet those blue-robed acolytes kept immaculate records. She'd like to see their maps.

When she returned to her room that evening, there was an envelope waiting on her desk. Heavy paper, elegant handwriting. No seal, but it didn't look like Holloway had touched it. *Thank the gods.*

Starfall Sanctuary, inner gardens.
Tomorrow at lastlight. Come alone. —L

She tucked the note into the drawer with the journal. She'd meet with Lore tomorrow.

15

FRIENDS THAT SLAY TOGETHER STAY TOGETHER

DAWN

Authorized transfer: Pickler's Junction holding facility to [REDACTED] via The Queen's Way. Eight (8) specimens, sedated and contained, two to a cage. These specimens are valued assets. Loss is unacceptable.

— PENTARCHY ENFORCEMENT CORPS WEST,
TRANSFER ORDER 44, 401 AC

Riven was in a mood. You knew someone long enough, you could tell. His jaw was always tight. He never said much. But tonight, he was—Dawn didn't know how else to put it—moody.

It was his idea to be out here too. He'd taken some maps from Talia's office, said this was the route they were taking the fluxborn.

They were crouched on a rocky ridge above the Queen's Way, a couple hours north of town. The night smelled like rain, and Riven smelled like horse. Dawn's calf was starting to cramp. She was ready to call it off when he lifted a hand. One round lantern came over the horizon. Then another. Then a line of them, bobbing into view.

"That's not one wagon," Dawn said.

Riven didn't look surprised. "Nope. It's four, at least."

"Shit." One wagon would be fun. Four wagons might get messy.

"Good thing we're good at this." Riven's smile showed teeth.

The wagons matched Riven's description. Wide, low-set wooden frames with metal cages strapped on. The vinegar stink of fluxborn was hard to miss. Riven's hand touched her shoulder, a warning. She was growling.

"I'm with you," he said, "but we need a plan."

There were at least a dozen guards down there, best she could count in the shifting lantern light. The wagon-cage contraptions were better lit, clustered together near the back of the procession. The numbers weren't great, but they'd handled worse.

"Hit in front of the wagons," Dawn said. "Split the line."

Riven nodded. Then he launched himself into the darkness. It was a decent drop. Dawn waited a full beat before she heard his boots hit the ground. A guard started to shout, but it ended in a gurgle. She listened as blades whistled through the air and made contact with metal and flesh. The scent of blood carried on the wind.

Dawn fired from the ridge until someone shouted to douse the lanterns. That killed her line of sight. The burn of powder and gun smoke filled her lungs. She reloaded both revolvers before dropping down herself.

The impact shot pain up her shins, but she ran for the cages. Slammed her revolver into one guard's jaw, felt bone give, shot him in the chest. Paused to take stock. A couple of the wagons were burning. Smoke everywhere. Shouts and howls echoed strangely in the haze.

Riven stalked through the smoke, crouched, then vaulted on top of a cage. Rifle fire flashed from three different angles. Dawn's heart jumped—*what the fuck*—but he was already cutting into the roof. He gripped the top edge of the cage and threw his weight. The whole thing crashed over.

Two huge direcats lunged out of the busted cage, started tearing into the soldiers. *Good idea. Let the fluxborn do some work.* More figures appeared through the smoke. She put rounds into anyone who tried to get the fluxborn under control.

The convoy held longer than it should've. These were trained soldiers. They tried to regroup, but Dawn pulled a flux fuse from her vest and threw it under the last wagon. Pink and green flames licked up the sides, and the fluxborn inside howled as they burned.

The fight died fast after that. When the dust settled, they had two prisoners left alive. One of them had a broken leg, and Riven held the other at sword point.

"You talk, you live," Dawn said, looking between the two of them. "I don't need two of you."

She grabbed the one who could walk, dropped him on his knees. He didn't break till she turned away.

"Haven! The cages were going to Haven—"

The other guard snarled at him to shut up so Dawn shot him.

"You win," she said. "Keep talking."

He babbled about delivery times and handlers' names, nothing else useful. She shot him too. He hadn't won anything.

Dawn told herself it was part of the job. She'd put plenty of men in the ground. But her hands shook after. Riven didn't say a word.

It was a long walk back to where they'd tied the horses. Dawn's shoulder was bleeding bad. Took a bullet, apparently. She'd live. She checked Riven up and down. Not a scratch. She'd be damned if he sulked the whole way back too.

"So, what's your plan?" she asked. "Talia's got her own personal enforcer captain now. You gonna say something?"

"What would I say?" His voice was flat. "She's engaged. I'm just watching her back."

She'd never known Riven to be jealous. Something else was going on. "She's paying for that?"

He didn't answer right away. When he did, his voice was careful. "In a way."

"Don't do that half-answer thing with me," Dawn snapped. "What is the job?"

He flinched. "I'm keeping an eye on her. For her family."

"Wait, you're spying on her?"

"She can't go with Lore," he growled. "That man is dangerous, and she trusts too easily."

"Yeah, exactly, she trusts *you*. Have you seen the way she looks at you?"

"I told her not to trust me." He paused. "It was a mistake. I need to put an end to it."

"But there's a contract, right?" she asked. He just grunted. "You'd break a contract? That's—fuck, that's not nothing."

He ran a hand through his hair. "Not the first time."

Dawn blew out a breath. Sure, there was one time he'd gone against his word in his entire fucking life. He'd broken his oath for her. Look how *that* had gone.

The rain had started. Soon she was drenched through. Shivering. Mud pulled on her boots with every step. Every time she closed her eyes, rifles flashed behind her eyelids. She was a long way from bed.

"You catch where that crew was headed?" she asked, switching gears.

"Haven."

She'd heard the same thing. Was hoping to be wrong.

"It's a military outpost," she offered. "Pentarchy. Way up north."

He just grunted.

"We'll go that way to Valrotala," she said. "I can take out the rest of the fluxborn then. If that's where they're at."

"You're really doing that? Going *there*?"

She couldn't come up with anything better to say than the truth. "Lore has a lead on Ehrue."

It hurt to say her name out loud. Dawn wondered, not for the first time, if she was alive at all. Even if she was, how much would Lore ask for before he delivered?

"Truly?" Riven knew how much that meant.

"Yep." She breathed out long and slow. "You should come too. It'll be fun. Old times and all that."

He huffed through his nose. Gruff and unimpressed as ever. Then he reached out and took her hand. Squeezed it.

"I'm sorry, Thauni."

Hearing her true name brought a rush of grief she didn't have a place for. She pictured Ehrue's face. Memories burned in her throat, where tears might once have been. She squeezed his hand back. Tighter than she meant to.

"Yeah. Me too."

16

THINGS LEFT UNSAID

TALIA

It was fae custom to bind a bodyguard to their ward with liturgical Starscript inscribed on the skin, and physical intimacy was encouraged to 'bind heart and flesh.' The story does not distinguish between love freely given and Althen's role as an oathsworn protector. It is possible the lovers themselves didn't either.

— *THE LOST FAE PRINCESS: A FAERIE STORY WITH TWO ENDINGS*, T. SALAREN, 398 AC

Talia was sitting at her desk in the dark, the glow of the street lamps from the window barely bright enough to write by. The curfew bells had long since sounded, trapping her inside. She tapped her pen against her notebook and looked over at Holloway. He slept like a dead man, flat on his back. Boots in a straight line next to the bed.

He *wasn't* dead. If he was, he wouldn't be breathing quite so loudly. She gave up on being productive and stood, slipped on her shawl and boots.

As soon as she lifted the window latch, cold air hit her face. Frost caught in her eyelashes, but the rainstorm had cleared. A drainpipe ran down beside her dormer window, and she gripped it for leverage as she climbed. She was breathing hard when she reached the flat part of the roof.

Gateway was beautiful from above. Streets glowed blue like little rivers. Wooden structures leaned against each other, covered in scaffolds. Cutters and galleys and smaller fishing boats rocked at anchor in the harbor. The gentle splashing reminded her of home.

She filled her lungs with cold air, held it, and let it go. Then she opened her notebook across her knees. The wind lifted the pages as she sketched the jagged line of Valta's coast from memory.

"You don't care for your desk?" Riven's voice rumbled.

She spun, nearly slipping on the ledge. He stood near the back of the roof like a gargoyle, collar turned up against the wind.

She pressed a hand to her chest. "Gods, you scared me."

"I apologize." He stepped closer. "May I join you?"

She waved a hand at the space next to her. "What are you doing up here?"

"Rough night."

A trace of gunpowder clung to him, faint but unmistakable. He'd been involved in something violent, then. None of her business.

He nodded toward her notebook. "Working on a map?"

"Trying to. A little hard, given what I have to work with."

"A little hard from a rooftop in Gateway. It's all out there." He gestured at the dark hills in the distance.

His arms flexed, braced around his knees. Whatever altercation he'd gotten into, she imagined he came out on top. She looked away and listened to the boats, and quiet settled between them.

"How do you know Dawn?" she asked, finally. She hadn't been able to figure that out. The two of them couldn't be more different.

"We grew up together. Poor kids, big egos. Kept each other's secrets. Hard to get rid of someone after that."

She glanced at him sideways. "You have a big ego?"

"When I want something."

Her eyes darted away from his face, to the sky, to the sea, back out at the city. "Is that how you ended up in Gateway?"

He didn't answer right away. "You could say that."

The quiet flowed back in like a tide as the damp roof and chilly wind worked its way through her shawl. Riven must have noticed because he rose and dropped his coat over her shoulders, quick and practical. The canvas was heavy, still warm from his body.

"Holloway." Her friend's name sounded foreign on Riven's tongue. "He is a childhood friend, too, yes? Congratulations."

"I'm not marrying Holloway." The words rushed out. "I mean yes—technically we are engaged, but I didn't—" She stopped. Why did words always fail her when they came out of her mouth? This was why she preferred writing. She tried again. "I didn't want you to find out that way."

"But it's the truth." His expression was unreadable in the moonlight.

"Not exactly." Her throat was tight. "It's...not a happy story."

"You don't have to tell it."

She almost didn't, but it came out anyway. Maybe she'd been holding it in for too long. "I was promised when I was fourteen. But it wasn't—" She stopped and tried to slow her breathing. *In and out.* "Holloway and I were just friends. I was engaged to his brother."

An image of the river flashed in her mind, lanterns floating across the surface. A mother's wail echoing over the water. Her eyes stung, and she blinked hard.

"Cordon died ten years ago." The words felt hollow. She couldn't explain it, didn't fully understand herself how it happened. Just that Cordon was gone, and it was her fault.

"I see," Riven said quietly.

Her throat closed. Maybe someday she could say it better, when the truth didn't feel like it was choking her.

Silence crept back in, and he didn't even try to fill it. She focused on the distant sound of rigging ticking in the harbor below, the gentle crush of waves under the docks. The same sounds, the same sea, echoed in her grandmother's study.

"A few months ago, our families announced that Holloway and I would be engaged." She looked at the horizon, fighting not to watch his reaction. She'd give anything to read his emotions.

Riven finally spoke. "That's why you came to Gateway."

"I didn't say no. I didn't say yes. I just ran. Took the fellowship and left." She waited for him to call her a coward, but he didn't say anything. "I've been hiding here. Pretending the decision wasn't waiting for me. And then he showed up, and it was announced like that, and everyone was cheering, and I—" Her throat tightened. "I froze. Again."

"You didn't want to hurt your friend."

"That's not—" She stopped. "I never want to hurt anyone. But I always do."

She looked over and Riven was watching her intently. Like he could see the shape of what she wasn't saying, even if he couldn't make out the details. She felt certain, without knowing why, that he'd lost people too.

The moonlight flattened shapes and colors to planes and shadows. He looked almost like a statue in profile when he nodded toward the horizon.

"This isn't a faerie story, boss." His voice was steady, but his hand tightened on his knee. "You don't know what's out there."

"That sounds like something Holloway would say." She pulled away and immediately noticed the cold. He frowned.

"I won't stop you. Just—be careful. You can't trust Lore." The words came out sharp and a little rushed.

A little late for that. She was sick of vague warnings that came without evidence. She was meeting Lore tomorrow, and she couldn't cancel based on nothing.

Riven was just telling her what to do, as if that was enough. How could she make up her own mind when nobody trusted her with information?

"Then explain it. Why should I trust you?"

He stilled. Then shook his head once, like she'd missed something obvious. "You should go in."

It was not unkind, but it was final. She wanted to scream—the conversation was over. She didn't even know what she'd wanted, just that she wasn't satisfied.

"Goodnight, Riven."

He locked eyes with her. "Goodnight, boss."

The coat slipped down her arms as she turned, and he tucked it back over her shoulders. She made it back to the windowsill without slipping. When she looked back, he was still there, a dark outline against the stars.

Inside, Holloway stirred, but he never stopped snoring. She closed the window softly and returned to her desk. Her fingers shook as she picked up her pen.

I'm tired of being careful. I'm done waiting for someone else to give me permission, because no one is going to. I want to see what's out there, and I'll do it on purpose. Not because I ran away.

I wonder if he would go with me?

She stopped and stared at the last line. The ink bled into the page, and she blotted it quickly, folded the note, and locked it away with the journal and her notebook. The key made a small click.

She switched off the lamp, and the room plunged into darkness. Across the room, Holloway slept. Breathing loud and steady. Boots still in a line. Ever the soldier, even asleep.

She pulled Riven's coat around her shoulders and let herself drift, the scent of cedar and gunpowder grounding her.

17

SWEET ROT

DAWN

Flux burnout kills. There are no degrees of burnout and no recoveries on record. Exposure therapy may reverse the process, but there's no ethical way to test the hypothesis.

— LORE TAVIS, *ON THE NATURE OF FLUX*, UNPUBLISHED

Blood dried stiff on Dawn's sleeves, gunpowder caked in her hair. Every time she blinked, she saw flashes of violence. Fluxborn burning. Bodies in mud.

She couldn't go back to the Fiddle like this. Couldn't sit under bright lamps and pretend to be human.

She needed the noise to stop.

Lore had things for this.

She'd brought the horses back to Cannon's, brushed them, curried them. Got them fed. Now Starfall's stone walls glowed gold in the firstlight. Her boots crunched on gravel as she passed through the gates.

Lore's people met her. Eased the coat off her bleeding shoulder. Led her to a basin of honey-scented water. Warm hands washed the blood from her arms. They pressed honey wine into her palm. Thick and golden. It burned down her throat and dulled the screaming in her head.

When the cup emptied, it was full again.

"You've done enough," a girl said. "Rest a little."

By the time they guided her down the corridor toward lamplight and cushions, her body had gone pleasantly heavy. Her bare feet left faint wet prints on the stone.

She woke hours later to colored light on her eyelids. When she opened her eyes, stained glass threw green and amber shapes on the ceiling. Her head was thick, her mouth sticky-sweet. Another full cup waited by her hand, and it went down easier this time.

Music and voices drifted from the main hall. Fiddles and low laughter. Dawn slid off the divan and padded toward the sound.

The hall was full of bodies. Half dressed, sprawled across cushions, wrapped in each other. Moans, laughter, the smell of sex and honey wine. Lore's Rest Day ritual. *Remember the sweetness you fight for.* Not prayers. Not offerings. Just oblivion.

A woman with dark curly hair and glazed-over eyes tugged at her robe. Dawn stepped over her reaching hands. She needed to speak with Lore more than she needed release. She kept going. Took another swig of too-sweet wine before pushing the door open.

She expected more chaos, but Lore's chambers were draped in shadows. No incense, no bodies. Just books and dust and a low-burning fire. Lore sat alone at his desk. Sleeves rolled up, robe half open at the chest. His dark hair was loose, falling into his face as he bent over a page.

He looked up as the door shut. Smiled.

"Don't you look like hell," he said with a nod to her wounded shoulder. She grinned. He was best when he didn't twist words.

"You're missing your own party." She jerked a thumb back at the hall. "Thought you'd be out there, blessing the faithful with your gods-fearing cock."

He chuckled. "Rest Day is for their enjoyment, not mine." His pen tapped on the paper. "But don't tell. 'Prophet with ledgers' doesn't inspire quite the same devotion."

"So it's all an act?"

"Not all." He tilted the cup in his hand, watching the gold liquid slide. "Life is painful, and my people work hard. They deserve release. If calling it sacred takes away their hesitation, then that's what it is."

"But you don't believe any of that shit?" Dawn pressed.

"Sex is a tool," he said. "Just like any other tool. No more holy than this glass of wine."

She'd seen him on Rest Day before, accepting those acolytes' devotion just fine. She always figured he enjoyed it.

"Pretty sure you're doing it wrong," she muttered.

"This isn't what you came here for." He eyed her coldly, bored with her judgment.

"Right," she sighed, sinking into an empty chair. "I tracked the fluxborn. Enforcers are shipping them west like fucking livestock."

She told him what she'd seen: the variety of fluxborn, the cages, the convoy bound for Haven. Lore listened without interrupting. When she finished, he sat still and closed his eyes. His eyelids fluttered as his focus slid somewhere else.

"Yes," Lore said softly. "I see it. This is not the true gods' work. It is men reaching for a power they don't understand."

"I have to stop it," Dawn said. Her throat felt scraped raw.

"We will," Lore agreed. "You've brought me the last key. We can depart soon."

"Well, that's not ominous as fuck." She hated when he slipped into prophet mode mid-sentence.

"The scholar," he clarified. "She is the one we need to open the gates of Valrotala."

"Talia?" The girl's name slurred a little on her tongue. "I don't think she'll join us."

"She hasn't chosen me yet," he said softly. His eyes fixed on Dawn. "But she will."

His tone didn't sit right. "Are you threatening her?"

"She's the threat," he said. "Did you know her grandmother is the chancellor of Vaelis? Marionette Salaren sits on the Council of Five, Pentarchy leadership. The girl will inherit more wealth and power than you or I could stack in ten lifetimes."

"You hate her?" Dawn had no idea he'd known so much about Talia. But then, he knew all kinds of things.

"I hate what she represents," he corrected. "I hate that a thousand children froze in the Lower City while she grew up with a warm bed and tutors and fancy books. I hate that I have to use the tools of the people who broke this world to mend it." He sighed. "But I don't hate her. I don't get that luxury. She's a resource. Resources are meant to be used."

"Does she get a say?" Dawn asked. "Or is she a shiny trinket for your gods? What? Tie her to a rock and throw her in the sea?"

His head tipped to the side. "I'll give her a choice," he said at last. "And I'll make sure her other choices aren't worth pursuing."

What a load of crap. "You and the Pentarchy. You're both the same monster."

"The difference is I feed my people." He didn't sound defensive at all. Just matter-of-fact. "And I don't lie about the price I'll pay for their safety."

The honey on her teeth felt sticky now, sour in the back of her throat. She pushed to her feet, backing toward the door. "You keep telling yourself that."

"You'll see," Lore called after her in that same calm voice. "When she takes my path, you'll understand why it was necessary."

The midday sun caught her full in the face as she stepped outside. For a moment, Starfall looked perfect again—bees in the lavender, children reciting lessons, the smell of baking bread.

Then a teacher said, "Truth without obedience is chaos."

The children echoed the words, steady as a heartbeat.

Dawn crossed the square. She saw scribes copying Lore's sermons word for word, quills scratching in perfect unison. At the bakery, a man lifted a loaf from the oven and smiled up at Lore's sigil above the door.

He was everywhere. She walked faster. Farther out, the air cooled. The cloying scent faded from her hair. Lore wasn't a monster. It'd be easier if he was. He was a shepherd who cared for his flock and culled it with the same brand of love.

Dawn broke into a run, putting distance between herself and Starfall's walls. She'd tell Riven tonight. They could warn Talia together, before Lore boxed her in completely.

18

TERMS OF POWER

TALIA

I'm sending someone your way: the Salaren heir. Signs of latent affinity and fluent in Starscript—exactly what you need. When you receive this, she will be on the next clipper. Move quickly. Someone with her gift and her name, properly aligned, will open doors.

— INTERCEPTED CORRESPONDENCE, W TO LORE TAVIS, 401 AC

Lore's garden lay nestled behind its own wall in the far corner of the Starfall compound. Starscript twirled around the gate. Talia touched the cool stone arch and took a deep breath before stepping in. This was a choice she wouldn't be able to take back.

Fruit trees formed alcoves around stone benches. The low wall cut off the sound and view of the rest of the world.

Lore was standing by a fountain at the center of the space. He'd shed his formal coat and the pendant. With his dark hair loose around his shoulders, he looked almost vulnerable. When he saw her, a smile broke over his beautiful face.

"You came," he said, and there was surprise in his voice.

He led her to a narrow bench under a pear tree. A few fruits were still scattered on the ground. She sat carefully, folding her hands on her lap. The stillness, the warble of the fountain, the wall—they might have been alone in the world.

"You seem troubled," he said, his gold-flecked eyes studying her face as if she were a text. "What's wrong?"

She bit her lip, then exhaled.

"I went back to the Consortium." She glanced at the fountain, the rotten pears at their feet. "They don't even have maps. Not complete ones. They lock away the knowledge they do have. There are so many rules, I can't even ask questions."

Lore let the words settle, let the silence stretch until she fidgeted with her skirt. "You're doing something interesting."

"What?" It wasn't what she was expecting to hear.

He was staring straight at her with those dark, gold-flecked eyes. She tried to hold his gaze, but she glanced away first.

"You're very good at telling me how the Consortium handles knowledge," he said. "But not how it feels to be trapped by it."

She *did* feel trapped. "Are you reading me?"

"I'm listening to you. There's a difference." He paused. "Though I had a suspicion when we met. Today confirms it."

Heat climbed her neck. "Confirms what?"

"That you have an affinity for reading emotions," he said. He was half smiling, and that one dimple flashed. "And that you lean on it when you feel exposed. You're sitting exactly far enough away to avoid brushing my hand, but I imagine you'll test my intentions soon enough."

The shock of his words hit so hard she felt weightless. She had never, *never*, heard her ability named out loud, let alone had someone trace her actions back to it.

He reached into his coat and drew out a milky crystal. It flashed in the last of the sunlight. "Would you let me show you something?"

She leaned in closer. The crystal seemed to pulse with warmth, and she couldn't hold back her curiosity. "I've never seen anything like that. What does it do?"

"It helps clarify what's already there. It will amplify your natural gift." He smiled. "It would be easier to show you."

He held his hand out, the crystal resting in his upturned palm. "This only works if you let me in. Would you allow that?"

She hesitated, looking down at his open hand. It sounded dangerously intimate.

"What exactly do I need to do?"

"Feel what I'm feeling. Let me feel what you're feeling." His eyes held hers. "I think you'll enjoy it."

Her curiosity won. Slowly, she slipped her fingers over the crystal in his open palm.

His skin was soft and warm, calloused only where a pen might rest. The crystal grew warm between their joined hands, and his emotional state came into focus as shapes and colors. Something about the stone gave visual structure to what she sensed.

"What am I feeling?" he asked softly.

"Confidence," she said immediately, surprised by how clear the impression was. "And curiosity. You want to see what I can do."

"Good. What else?" His finger traced circles on the back of her hand.

She concentrated, letting herself sink deeper. His emotions had a structure to them. Layered, and surprisingly deep.

"Loneliness. Despite all your followers, you feel alone."

His grip tightened slightly, and she felt a ripple of surprise before her perception snapped back to the surface.

"What about you?" he asked. "What are you feeling?"

She turned inward.

"Nervous energy, mostly. I'm afraid I'm making the same mistake again. Being naive."

He was very still except for the finger still tracing gentle patterns on her hand. The crystal pulsed between them, and she felt a burst of static as he considered what to say next.

"Tell me what would reassure you about my intentions."

Her breath caught. "I'm not exactly sure. Maybe if you valued me, even when I don't say what you want to hear?"

"Reasonable. Would you like to know what I value about you?"

Her heart hammered. "Sure?"

"We don't know each other well yet, but I'll tell you what I see," he said. "I see courage enough to challenge me. I see compassion for your bodyguard even when he opposed you. Integrity. You left everything comfortable behind in Vaelis." His eyes never left hers. "These things reflect who you are. Not what you can do for me."

No one had ever complimented her so precisely before. She wanted to believe him so badly it was frightening.

"How can I know if that's real?" she whispered.

"You can't."

Through the crystal, only calm sincerity. No sign of deception. But there was something else—a hint of unease. He tugged her hand gently, pulling her attention back when her gaze drifted.

"What is it?" she asked, barely breathing the words.

He looked like he didn't want to say what came next, pressing his lips together. "There *is* something else you should know. About your bodyguard."

Her stomach dropped. "What about him?"

He hesitated again and let out a small sigh. "Our meeting in the library. It was just the three of us. By evening, the Pentarchy had patrols near my gates. Someone in that room informed them we had met."

She squeezed the crystal. "No." The word came out sharp. "Riven wouldn't do that—"

He cut her off. "Someone who was in that room told the Pentarchy what we discussed. I don't believe that it was you." Lore's sympathy flowed through the crystal.

"You're mistaken." But her voice wavered.

"Can I ask, has he warned you to stay away from me?"

You can't trust Lore. Riven hadn't exactly been subtle on the rooftop last night.

"He's protected me. He gave me a gun. Took me out to study ruins. He wouldn't do those things if he didn't care."

"Of course he would." Lore's voice was pitched low, somewhere between a murmur and a growl. "That's how surveillance works. Earn the subject's trust, stay close. I suspect that you haven't spent many days without his company."

That was true too. Riven was at her door every morning. He waited outside the Consortium, even when she worked late.

"His loyalty is to his employer." Lore pressed her hand between both of his, giving it a small squeeze. "I'm sorry. I know you've grown close."

Close. Riven knew about the journal. She'd told him about Cordon. She really had no secrets left. He followed her everywhere.

It fits. Gods, it fits.

She struggled not to spiral. Lore could be lying. Or Riven could be lying. She couldn't think through all the implications now.

"Dawn would have told me." Her voice came out shrill. She knew she sounded desperate.

"Dawn's loyalties are divided." Lore wasn't letting go.

Talia's stomach felt tight. The cloying smell of rotten fruit was everywhere, making her dizzy. Back in the corral Dawn had told Talia not to rely on anyone. Including Lore. Including Riven. Had Dawn tried to warn her?

"How do I know who to believe?"

He squeezed her hand again, and earnest sympathy sparkled up her arm. He hurt for her at the same time his suggestions hurt her.

"Only ever trust yourself, Talent. But consider I'm not the one pretending to be neutral. I am very biased. Come with us." He was speaking intensely. "Finish the work. My people will protect you from the Pentarchy."

"Tell me what we'll face if I go." She refused to simply agree.

"Direct questions. I like that." He smiled, and his teeth were perfectly white. "It will be dangerous, of course. The deep continent holds magics you'd associate with faerie stories: haunted forests, enchanted hot springs. The fluxborn roam freely beyond the boundary stones. Pentarchy patrols won't hesitate to eliminate threats. Some of us may not return."

"I'm not much of a fighter. You still want me to come?"

"I want you to choose to come." He released her hand. "What would help you make that choice?"

She flexed her fingers. They felt strangely empty. "What is the expedition's purpose?"

"The official purpose is to unlock the secrets of flux channeling for the rebellion's benefit. To ensure that knowledge doesn't fall into your family's hands. Or the Consortium's. Or anyone else who would use it to maintain the current order."

"And the unofficial purpose?"

He looked genuinely pleased that she'd asked. "Valrotala holds answers I've been seeking for years about the nature of power."

It wasn't a complete answer, but it didn't sound like a lie.

"I'd be trusting you with my life."

"You would have to, yes."

She studied his face in the fading light, weighing everything he was offering against everything she knew. The challenge, the intellectual partnership, the promise of meaningful work—it was everything she'd hoped to find in Valta.

At the same time, Lore had his own agenda. He was trying to manipulate her emotions. She could feel it sinking in.

He was isolating her. Cutting her off from Riven, from Dawn. He would make himself her only ally if she let him, but she didn't know how to fight back.

Everything he said had the ring of truth, but the crystal couldn't reveal lies. It only showed feelings. Lore was sincere in his convictions, but that was all she could know.

"What if there was another way?" The words slipped out before she'd fully formed the thought.

His teeth vanished. "What do you mean?"

"What if I don't formally join you at Starfall, but I don't go with the Consortium either. I could publish under my own name." She talked faster as she filled in the idea. "You would get access to my findings; you can use them however you like. I get to keep authorship under my name, and I can continue with my research after."

It was the exact right answer. An elegant way out of being controlled by either side.

"No." The word cracked in the air like a whip.

The crystal shattered in Lore's fist. Blood welled between his fingers. He was standing over her, looming, and she could feel his sudden rage like physical heat, pulsing from his body. She scrambled to stand up, but he caught her wrist. It wasn't hard enough to hurt, just hard enough to keep her from leaving.

"I will not beg for scraps from the Salaren family." He spoke through his teeth. "I have worked too hard, for too long, to compromise on this."

Her pulse hammered. She tried to pull her wrist free, but his grip tightened.

Then he stopped—released her quickly, like she'd burned him. Stepped back. Bright blood trailed in thin lines down his wrist. He opened his fist and let the crushed crystal fall. The shards hit the stone with small, perfect chimes. When he lifted his head again, his expression was smooth, composed. Only his ragged breathing betrayed his emotion.

"I apologize," he said softly. "You need to understand what's at stake. This isn't something that can be done halfway. The Pentarchy will destroy you before they let you operate independently. You don't have that choice."

Her pulse roared in her ears, and she tasted blood. She must have bitten her tongue.

"I need time to think," she managed. The words scraped out thin and high. She needed to get away from here.

"Of course." His smile was small and perfectly polite. "Consider what independence truly means. How alone you'd be on that path."

She stumbled back a step. Then another. He was already turning away from her, stooping to collect the shards, the tiny glassy tinks following her like bells. The sound chased her through the garden gate and across the compound.

She didn't remember the walk back, just fragments: the streetlamps flickering on, a passing cart, someone laughing. Every sound hit her nerves wrong. Her hands were shaking so badly when she reached the Flux & Fiddle, she had to use both hands to move the door latch. She wanted to scrub the amber scent from her skin, to anchor herself in anything that wasn't him.

She stumbled up the stairs. The only light in the hall came from under her own door, and she scrambled for it.

19

COMFORT, OR SOMETHING LIKE IT

TALIA

Holloway Sennett was, by every account, exactly the man he appeared to be. If events had played out differently, that might have been enough.

— *SONS OF THE PENTARCHY: A BIOGRAPHICAL RECORD*, 443 AC

Talia closed the door and pressed her back against it, gasping for breath. She was home. She was safe. The sound of crystal shattering still hung in her ears. She could taste blood on her tongue. The rest was a blur.

Her pulse thundered in her ears. The air felt too thin to breathe properly. Holloway stirred on his cot, and suddenly he was on his feet and the lamp was flickering on. His hair was mussed with sleep, but his eyes were alert and scanning her for damage.

"Tally, what happened? What's wrong?"

Her throat worked, but nothing came out. He took one step toward her and stopped, reading what he could from her face. Carefully, he reached for the bottle of whiskey on the desk.

"Come, sit," he said gently.

She sank onto the edge of the bed, and the mattress dipped under her. He walked back to the desk and poured whiskey into two chipped cups. His fingers brushed hers when he passed her one.

She felt his concern through the contact, steady and uncomplicated. She took a sip. The heat of the whiskey slid down, loosening the knot behind her ribs. For a second she thought she might cry, but her eyes stayed dry. Only a little choking sound escaped.

"Hey," Holloway said, low and calm. A voice for skittish horses. "What happened out there?"

She tried to talk, but the words stayed stuck. She swallowed more whiskey, and that didn't help. She leaned back into the saggy mattress and forced herself to breathe.

"I don't know who to trust," she said when she got some air back.

Holloway's jaw flexed. He reached out slowly and brushed a strand of hair from her face, his fingers trailing earnest affection where they grazed her skin.

"You can always trust me."

She stared at his face, this classically handsome enforcer captain. Square jaw, deep smile lines, dark golden curls tumbling over his forehead. The boy she'd known was still in there, reshaped by wind and work. His neck and shoulders were thicker, broader.

"You changed," she said quietly.

"So did you." His mouth tipped, the ghost of a smile. "You're more alive here. You never smiled so much in Vaelis." His gaze flicked to her mouth, then back to her eyes. "I like this version of you."

She leaned into him, and a day's worth of stubble scraped her temple. She remembered how he used to follow her when they were children, just to make sure she was okay. Safe. Holloway had always made her feel safe. He slid one hand behind her neck, slipping his fingers into her hair.

"Tally." He was the only person left in the world who called her that.

She knew it wasn't fair to him, but she reached for his free hand and pulled him in. His mouth met hers, and he made a small sound of surprise. Then he reached up to grip her jaw and kissed her back so eagerly their teeth clicked. She tasted whiskey on his tongue.

He explored her mouth, then relaxed and let her press back into him. It was a rhythm that almost worked, but she felt the mismatch. He kissed her like a promise. She kissed him for comfort. It wasn't the same thing.

For a few heartbeats it was enough. His chest felt solid beneath her hands, his fingers laced through her hair. When they broke apart, breathing hard, he pressed his forehead to hers.

"I missed you," he said breathlessly.

"I missed you too." The admission surprised her because it felt true. She did miss something about this, even if it was just being wanted.

He pulled back enough to meet her eyes, a crooked smile playing at his mouth. It only took him a second to scan her face, and he saw what wasn't there. He knew her too well.

He looked away. Then he blinked hard and smiled, that old Holloway grin that made everything feel lighter. He shifted back to where the bed met the wall, giving her space.

"It's okay." His smile seemed genuine, if a little sad. "We don't have to."

Talia should feel bad, but all she felt was relief. She scooched off the bed and crossed the room. The whiskey bottle made a small, friendly glug as she refilled his cup, then hers.

"So, what happened tonight?" he asked, gently.

She sat back down and drew her knees up to her chest. Where should she start? She couldn't tell Holloway she'd met with Lore.

"Someone suggested that Riven's loyalties aren't with me."

Holloway's expression changed almost imperceptibly, but she knew him. He'd gone very still, and his casual disinterest seemed forced.

"Do you think it's true?"

"I don't know," she admitted. "It's possible. Sometimes he looks at me like...there's something there. But I don't know him that well, and Marionette hired him first." The two of them always referred to her grandmother by her first name.

Holloway looked down at his whiskey and took some time sipping it.

"What do you think of him?" she asked finally.

His fingers tightened around the cup. "If Marionette hired him, he'd have to honor that contract. The scope could easily extend beyond protection."

"That's not what I asked." She heard the sharpness in her own voice and winced.

"No," he said calmly. "You asked what I think of him." He sighed and tipped his head back against the wall. "I think he's dangerous. This isn't a faerie story. Men who live by oaths and swords, they hurt people for a living."

"That's not fair," she said before she could help herself. "You don't know him."

"I know the type." His tone stayed level. He wasn't giving her this. "And I know you. You want to see the good in people. You always have."

"I'm so sick of people telling me what they think I am, and what I shouldn't do." She almost whispered it, but of course he heard.

He held her gaze. Then he nodded. "You're right. I'm here for you, Tally. Whatever you need, just ask."

Something in her chest spasmed. He didn't know what he was offering. Didn't know how involved she was with Lore and the rebels. He couldn't give her unconditional support, not really.

He walked over to the washstand, wet a cloth, wrung it out, and came back.

"You're shaking," he said. "May I?"

She hadn't noticed the tremor in her hands, but suddenly she felt dizzy. He touched the damp cloth to her wrists, then her throat. The coolness spread outward. He traced down her collarbone, rested his palm there. It steadied her more than the whiskey.

"Better?" he asked.

She swallowed. "A little."

He sat again, closer this time, their knees almost touching. He took her empty cup, set it aside, and shifted so his shoulder brushed hers.

She let herself lean on him. She wasn't leaning toward Holloway so much as away from Lore, and she hated herself for it.

She closed her eyes. The image that rose uninvited wasn't

Holloway's face. It was a different man, with gray eyes. She eased away just a bit, and Holloway frowned.

"Let me hold you," he said quietly. "Please. I need—" He stopped. "Just for tonight."

How could she say no? She nodded. He kissed her forehead and pulled her glasses off her face. Then he stood to click the lamp off.

He let her have the blanket, tucking it around her before settling beside her in the narrow bed. He pulled her close, careful, like she might break. They kept their clothes on. She had a feeling it wasn't what he really wanted, but it was the best she had to offer.

The room's edges softened, and outside, the city muttered to itself. A dog howled from far away.

"Tally?" Holloway's voice was muffled in the pillow. She'd thought he was asleep.

"Yes?"

"You don't have to tell me everything." He paused. "But you don't have to shoulder everything alone either."

"Okay," she said, though she didn't see how that could be true.

She lay awake, watching the streetlamps flicker across the ceiling. Holloway's breath was light and warm against the back of her neck.

She wasn't sure she could trust Riven.

Lore had terrified her.

And here, in Holloway's arms, she felt safe—and utterly alone.

THE STARSCRIPT ARCHIVE

VAELIS • 9 YEARS AGO

Talent studied religiously and prayed just as hard. She could recite the thirteen gratitudes in her sleep. She tried to take up as little space as possible, to anticipate what others wanted before they asked. When she got this right, her grandmother's hand would rest on her shoulder, and she'd murmur "my steady light." Talent lived for that praise.

She arrived at the Lyceum bright eyed and eager to impress. Her roommate, Marina Devais, called her "the governess" within a week. One night at dinner, Marina held court, drawing all eyes to herself. When talk turned to scandals, her attention found Talent.

"You were engaged once, Salaren. Cordon Sennett, right?" Marina's voice turned syrup-sweet. "So sad. Imagine being so dull a man would rather drown than marry you."

Laughter bloomed. A boy choked on his wine.

Talent's fingers tightened around her fork. The memory was there—the balcony, the river, a mother's scream—but she pushed it down. She pressed her lips together in a pleasant-enough smile.

"Imagine being so desperate for attention you'd mock a dead boy to get it," Talent said through her teeth.

The laughter faltered. She stood, pushed back her chair, and walked out.

She didn't have a destination in mind, but it started raining as she walked past the library, so she went in. It was almost empty inside. No one whispered her family name as she passed deeper into the shelves. No one looked at her at all. She was just a girl with a book, the same as anyone. Slowly, she unfurled her shoulders to her full height.

The next day she returned, and the next, until the library became a habit, then a refuge. One day, she found a slim book half hidden behind the ledgers. Its title, nearly rubbed away, read *Tales of the First Age*. She hesitated, wary of childish things, but curiosity got the best of her.

The stories smelled like happy memories, parchment paper and dust and old ink. The warrior who loved a sparrow. The dragon who couldn't fly. They weren't gentle stories, but they were real—not in fact but in feeling. She fell asleep at the table that night and woke with pages imprinted on her cheek.

She started searching for older texts—following footnotes, chasing references. One evening, following a draft of cold air through the north stacks, she found a door that shouldn't have been there.

The latch was stiff, and the books behind it were older than the Lyceum itself. Cobwebs draped the shelves. These weren't bound in leather. These were older—wood boards tied with cord, pages thick as fabric. When she opened one, the spine cracked.

The script inside meant nothing at first. Swirls and dots, lines that curved like water. Dried ink raised under her fingertip. Someone had written this. Someone had meant for it to be read.

The text became her obsession. She copied symbols on spare parchment, teaching herself their rhythm. Curves became familiar. Patterns emerged. Slowly, meaning glimmered through.

A name: *Vael*. A place: *Valrotala*.

These weren't fantasies. They were chronicles. Real people, real histories, recorded in a language no one alive could read. No one except her.

Her reality cracked in half. On one side, the faith she'd grown up with. In that version, Vael was a god who led their people to salvation across the sea. Thyss was his trusted right hand, the arbiter of truth and justice.

On the other side of the rupture, these books. The characters had the same names as the gods, but they were people with lives and families and flaws. She was especially drawn to the story of Thyss and his brother Althen, fierce guardians who spent their lives protecting the people they loved. When the Lost Continent sunk into the sea, Thyss held a place on the boats for his brother, but he didn't make it out.

That story pulled tight in her chest, the particular grief of doing everything right and still losing. It was just a myth, but it rang true. She thought she'd outgrown faith and wonder, but they found her again in that dusty corner of the library. The stories took her hand, and they led her home.

The rest of the world couldn't hurt her there.

20

ONE LAST JOB

DAWN

If you can't find love, take a lover.
If you can't find a lover, have a drink.
One night isn't forever,
But it's longer than you'd think.

— DRINKING SONG, VALTA, ORIGIN UNKNOWN

Dawn had been pacing since firstlight, muttering at the walls. She kept running her hands through her short hair, and the pink ends were sticking in all directions.

"Don't join the expedition. Lore is using you." Too direct. Talia would ask questions that Dawn couldn't answer.

"The ruins are dangerous. You're not ready." The girl would dig in her heels at that, just to prove her wrong.

"I was wrong about him." Dawn would look foolish for bringing her to Lore in the first place.

She checked her revolvers for the third time. Still loaded.

Years mourning Ehrue. Years of Lore's promises. And now—when Valrotala was finally in reach—her damned conscience decided to bite her. It was infuriating.

After she slept off the honey wine, she went straight to Riven. Told him what Lore had said. When he calmed down, they went to warn Talia together. But by then she'd stepped out for the evening. After that, it was too late.

Dawn didn't know what it was Lore said, but Talia spent a full day locked in her room. When she came out, she wouldn't say shit.

Riven tried to talk to her. That didn't go great. The girl went silent on him. That was days ago.

Selfish bitch. You sold out a kid for the smallest chance of getting your mate back. Lore played you.

Dawn wasn't giving up on Ehrue. She would never. But she could change how this worked. Warn Talia. Confront Lore. Set new terms. He needed her. Dawn was the only one who knew what they'd face in those ruins. She'd been to Valrotala. He hadn't.

She buckled on her gun belt and stepped out into the afternoon sun, her boots clicking on the rickety staircase. She meant to find a drink. Then she'd talk to Talia.

The fucker was waiting for her.

Lore leaned against a building just across the street. Bastard never left Starfall. What was he doing here? He smiled and walked over.

"Dawn. Perfect timing." He pulled a folded note from his coat. "I need you to handle something for me tonight."

He never delivered assignments himself. She came to him, or he sent someone. She took the note and unfolded it.

Riven Valros

Pentarchy agent. Freight yard, after curfew bell tonight.

What the fuck? She looked up. "This man isn't Pentarchy."

"He is turning over information tonight. That must not happen." Lore said it like a fact.

"I know him." *This has to be wrong. Lore is out of his mind.*

"The garrison will be issuing a warrant for Talent's arrest later today," Lore added. "Riven Valros is reporting to them."

She didn't trust Lore, but when he twisted the truth, it was always subtle. Not like this.

He squinted at her, suspicious now. She might complain, but she never pushed back on assignments. "He is a threat to you and your friends," he said.

"I'll handle it."

"Good." He started to turn away, then paused. "Come by Starfall before midnight. After this is taken care of. We have a lot to discuss."

"Yes, we do. Because I'm gonna warn the girl. Tell her what you really are."

Lore chuckled, then broke into a full-on laugh.

"Are you?" His smile was almost fond. "Well. We'll talk about that tonight. Things are moving faster than I planned."

He turned and walked into the crowd before she could say anything back. Dawn stood in the street. She crushed the note in her fist.

Riven working for the Pentarchy? That didn't add up. He said he'd made one report to Talia's family and that he'd stop. He would never knowingly hurt Talia. There had to be more to the story.

Fuck.

Her pulse spiked. She needed to blow off steam. She found herself walking to Ruby's before she realized where she was going. Ruby answered the door in her undershirt, her wild red hair undone. The room was bright, porcelain figures on every shelf. Boots, spurs, hats. Lived in. Dawn had never stayed anywhere long enough to collect things like that.

"Hey, babe." She read something in Dawn's face and stepped aside.

Dawn pulled Ruby in hard, and she kissed back, hands sliding under Dawn's coat, pushing it off her shoulders. Dawn needed the simplicity of this—skin, breath, teeth, an easy *now* that took her mind off. Ruby worked with wild horses. She got it. Walking backward, she pulled Dawn onto the bed.

Dawn fucked her hard and fast. Ruby took it slower, forcing Dawn's focus down—steady rhythm, teasing, building.

After, Dawn lay staring at the ceiling, Ruby's head on her shoulder. Early lowsun light slanted through the window, dust hanging in the sunbeams.

"You going to tell me what that was about?" Ruby's voice was soft against her collarbone.

She forced out a rough laugh. "Complaining?"

Ruby growled and bit her ear. "Avoiding the question?"

"Lore gave me an assignment." Dawn forced the words out. "It's Riven." *That isn't even his fucking name.*

Ruby was quiet, fingers tracing patterns on Dawn's ribs.

"Lore said he's an informant. That he turned Talia in." Dawn scrubbed both hands over her face.

"Would he do that?"

"I don't fucking know." Dawn's voice cracked.

She pressed the back of her skull into the headboard and closed her eyes. Dawn didn't like intrigue. She liked killing and fucking and drinking.

"I saw him this morning," Ruby said. "Coming out of the garrison."

"Riven was at the garrison?" Dawn sat up straight.

"No, the prophet. Real early. He was chatting with some enforcers. He looked like a normal person."

That was a shock, and she didn't like it. She rolled out of the bed and started tugging on her pants. Threw a flannel shirt over her head, closed the buttons impatiently.

Ruby watched her dress. "Fuck and run?"

"Looks that way." Dawn paused to buckle her gun belt. "We should do this again. It was nice." She leaned back over the bed for a kiss.

Ruby chuckled into her mouth. "Just don't get yourself killed, asshole."

Dawn pulled away, but she paused at the door. She liked this one. A lot. Something told her she wouldn't be back here.

She stepped back into the street, the sun lower now. Hours until nightfall. Until she was supposed to meet her oldest friend at the freight yard.

She drifted back toward the main drag. Hours left to kill. Might as well get that drink.

She was closing out her tab at the Broken Wheel when the

curfew bell rang. It was later than she'd planned. Fuck, she might miss the meeting. One last job. Her terms this time.

21

THE SNARE

TALIA

OFFICIAL WARRANT. Talent 'Talia' Salaren. Scholar. Charges: consorting with rebel sympathizers, western territories. Arrest authorized. Remand to Pentarchy custody upon apprehension. By order of Pentarchy Central Command, Vaelis, 401 AC.

Holloway had been at the garrison all day, some kind of emergency, so Talia spent the day studying Vael's journal. The "gods" described themselves as immortal, but they'd died, one after the other, within fifty years of settling in Sovana. There was a clue there. It had something to do with the mystery of flux channeling.

She was so focused on her work she lost track of time. Three quick raps on the door jolted her from her notes. Her hands shook as she shoved the journal back into its drawer and locked it.

When she opened the door a crack, Webb stood in the hall, coat half buttoned. He was breathing hard, eyes cutting down the corridor.

"Good, you're here," he said quickly. "You need to take a walk."

Webb had never visited her here. How did he even know how to find her room?

Talia frowned. "What? It's almost curfew."

"Exactly." He slipped something from inside his coat, a folded note with a broken seal. "This just came in. I wasn't supposed to see it until morning, but I was working late on field assignments."

She reached for it, but he held on. "Don't read it out here. You need to take a walk. Skip the office tomorrow. Maybe the day after.

Peat and Nadir are being sent on assignment to Haven, leaving tomorrow. Emmer won't be in."

"Wait, *they* get field assignments? What's in that letter?"

He laughed nervously. "It's an arrest warrant. For you."

"No. That's not possible."

"Sure it is." He rubbed a hand over his jaw. "I mean, I read it, so..."

He held it out, and the paper trembled between them. She pinched it between two fingers and drew it to her chest. Now that she had it, she wasn't sure she wanted to read it.

"When did all this happen?" Her mind was racing. Was this about her meeting with Lore? Who told?

"Today. Just now. The enforcers will be by in the morning. Or maybe sooner."

Talia swallowed hard. "Thank you for letting me know."

He nodded, but he was already backing down the hall.

"I can't be seen here," he said, then he turned and ran.

When she shut the door, the room seemed to spin, and her pulse roared in her ears. Holloway said there was an emergency situation at the garrison. What if he was working on this? What if he was coming home now to arrest her? Her mind jumped to the letter she'd burned. She'd thought they were past it, but apparently not.

She packed mechanically. Notebook. Cloak. Riven's revolver. All the contents of her secret drawer. She laced up her sturdiest pair of boots. When she switched off the lamp, the room fell into blue shadow. She hesitated at the window just as the curfew bell started pealing.

"Just a walk," she whispered to no one.

Riven's canvas coat still hung behind the door. She almost left it, but then she tugged it down. Who could say when she'd be back.

She stopped at the end of the hall to knock on Riven's door. She had been avoiding him for the past few days, but he'd know what to do. No one answered. He was either asleep or out past curfew. She told herself she could handle it, but panic burned hotter in her chest.

It was even cooler out than she expected, and she was grateful for the coat. The streets were empty. She kept her head down and walked briskly. The scuff of her boots and the hum of power lines were the only sounds. Every corner felt too exposed. A dog barked, and the echo died too quickly.

Her breath came shallow. She needed a plan. Lore would take her at Starfall, but he was a last resort. Cannon might be an option. The old stablemaster hated enforcers, and there was a hay loft at the corral where she could hide out. But she couldn't shake Webb's agitation, his panicked glances down the hall. She didn't want to put anyone else in danger.

She slowed at the next corner. Someone was there. She heard a scrape of leather, the faint jingle of spurs. She bit her lower lip and reached slowly into her satchel for the revolver.

A voice came out of the dark, soft and amused. "Evening, sweetheart."

Flint Jones stepped out from the mouth of the alley. Birdy loomed behind him, broad enough to fill the space between buildings.

Gods. Anyone but them.

Flint tipped his hat. "Turns out you're more than just a pretty face."

She took a step back. Her hand closed around the handle of the revolver in her satchel.

"Easy now." Flint's smile widened. "We can do this the nice way or the not-nice way. Both work fine for me."

"Whatever you think you're doing—"

"Just delivering some cargo." He nodded toward Birdy. "You know there's a reward for bringing you in?"

She pulled the gun out of the bag, tried to remember what Dawn had taught her. Thumb the hammer.

Flint laughed. "Look at that. Girl's got a gun."

Birdy chuckled, low and thick.

"You know how to use that, darlin'?" Flint took a step closer. "Because I do."

She pointed the gun at his chest, but it was visibly shaking in her hands.

"Go away," she said. Her voice came out thin. "I *will* shoot you."

"Will you?" Another step. "Because you didn't shoot me last time. I'm not sure you really mean it."

She hesitated, and it cost her. Birdy moved faster than a man his size should. His hand—massive, rough—clamped around her wrist and twisted. Pain shot up her arm, and the revolver clattered to the planks. Then his other arm was around her waist, hauling her backward, and she was up against solid muscle. His forearm crushed her ribs, forcing air out of her lungs.

She tried to scream, but his palm covered her mouth, fingers digging into her cheeks. His smell was everywhere, sweat and leather.

"None of that now," Birdy cooed.

His emotions hit her at the same time: anticipation, satisfaction, lust. Simple as an animal. He dragged her deeper into the dirt-packed alley. Buildings pressed close on either side. Flint sauntered after.

She drove the heel of her boot back into Birdy's shin. He grunted but didn't loosen his grip. She twisted, trying to use her weight, but he was heavier.

"Bounty says alive," Flint growled. "Doesn't say untouched. You try and yell again, you'll wish you hadn't."

She thrashed harder. Birdy's grip shifted to her wrists, pinning both her arms behind her back. The angle made her shoulders scream. He forced her forward into a stack of crates. The wood bit into her stomach and knocked the wind out of her lungs.

Flint stepped closer. His hand caught her chin, forced her to look at him, her cheek pressed into the rough wood. A thumb traced her lower lip.

His emotions washed over her, darker than Birdy's. Cruelty edged with pleasure. He enjoyed this. His power. Her panic.

"This won't take long," he murmured. "Then we'll get you where you're going."

Navigator guide me. Thyss protect me. The prayers came automatic, desperate, even when she knew no one was listening.

Flint's hand closed around her throat. "Bet you taste expensive."

She twisted her head and bit down on Flint's wrist. Her mouth flooded with the taste of dirt and blood. He roared and jerked his hand back. She sucked in air, lungs burning, and screamed—

His fist caught her temple. White pain exploded across her vision, and the alley lurched.

She sagged against the crate. Birdy's grip loosened, but she couldn't run. The crates were the only thing keeping her on her feet.

Flint was behind her now. Hands bunched in her skirts, yanking them up.

"There we go," he said roughly. A knee pressed between her thighs, forcing them apart.

She couldn't breathe. Couldn't think past the roaring in her head. A belt buckle clicked open. Leather hissed as it slid through loops.

She was outside her own body, looking down. Flint's anticipation peaked—

A series of metallic clicks was the only warning before a gunshot cracked the air.

Birdy's emotions snuffed out, and her wrists were free. Something heavy hit the ground with a wet thud, and Talia slid down to the dirt too. Her whole body was convulsing. When she looked over, Birdy's lifeless eyes stared back at her.

Flint jerked back, belt hanging loose, scrambling for his gun. He shouted something that got drowned out by another shot. A window shattered overhead, raining glass.

Gun smoke filled the alley, thick and acrid. Her throat burned, and she coughed. She couldn't see, couldn't hear past the ringing in her ears.

Flint backed into the shadows, gun drawn. Someone stepped through the smoke, blue fluxlight catching on a drawn revolver.

And then darkness took her.

22

THE RECKONING

HOLLOWAY

Sennett's early career was distinguished by intense devotion to duty. It is worth noting, then, that when he finally broke, he did not do so for a cause or a principle. He did it for a person.

— *SONS OF THE PENTARCHY: A BIOGRAPHICAL RECORD*, 443 AC

The mist was something he still hadn't gotten used to. Back home, rain fell like it meant it, all in one direction. The sky here couldn't commit; moisture just hung in the air. It turned the freight yard to mud and muffled sound in a way he didn't totally hate, though—good cover for a drop.

Holloway stood with his back to a crate, eyes burning after eighteen straight hours on duty. Thirty paces off, Jack and Rider were passing a flask, shoulders loose, laughing at something.

Good men. A little too green, a little too eager to prove they weren't, but they'd make fine officers. That was his job, to shape them right. He'd made sure to position them far enough out that they couldn't hear tonight's exchange.

As soon as the warrant hit his desk that morning, he knew it was bullshit. It had to be. He knew Talent better than anybody. She folded herself into shapes that other people wanted her to take, and it made her vulnerable. The rebels must have lied to her or tricked her somehow. Just one more example of why she needed someone to make decisions for her. He promised Cordon he'd protect the Salaren girls, and it was his honor to do it.

All day today he'd manufactured red tape and rerouted patrols to buy her time. She'd never know how much he'd done for her. He wouldn't usually run an informant drop himself, but he'd taken that on tonight, too, on the off chance it'd help.

Boots squelched in the mud. Holloway's hand dropped to his sidearm. He turned—

And nearly laughed. Held it to a cough.

"*You're* the informant?"

Riven Valros stopped ten paces away. The hulking sellsword who shadowed Talent to work every day. The man had an edge to him that Holloway had clocked from that first night at the Flux & Fiddle. Talent clearly hadn't.

"Captain Sennett." Riven's voice was flat. "Talia's in danger."

Holloway scrubbed a hand over his face. *Obviously*.

"She's being framed. Someone submitted evidence—"

"It was you." Of course it was this guy. It had to be someone like him. "You made these reports."

Riven's jaw tightened. "I am protecting her."

Holloway did laugh then. "Hell of a job, asshole."

The sellsword didn't flinch, but he seemed ragged around the edges. His beard hadn't been trimmed, and he had a wild look in his eyes. Maybe he did care about Talent. Not that it mattered.

"Captain, everything good?" Jack called.

"Just settling up," Holloway hollered back, waving him off. "Hang tight."

"There's a man called Lore Tavis," Riven kept on. "He's a rebellion leader. He's the one framing her."

Riven shoved a packet toward him. The drop. Had to be. Holloway shoved it back.

"I know who Lore Tavis is. The man's untouchable. Connected at the highest levels of Pentarchy command. And Talent—" Something tightened in his throat. "She's an easy target now, without her family's protection."

Riven narrowed his eyes. "She has a warrant for her arrest. You're defending her. Why?"

Holloway wasn't answering that.

"You limit her choices then show up like a hero," Riven said in that flat, unemotional tone. "Is that it? Think she'll change her mind and wed you after all?"

The fuck? Heat hit the back of Holloway's neck. His hand twitched at his sidearm.

"Here's what's going to happen," Holloway said, fighting to keep his voice level. "You're going to disappear. Tonight. Out of Gateway, out of her life."

Riven's eyes flicked to Holloway's weapon. His own hands stayed loose at his sides. Soldier recognized soldier. Part of him wanted the fight. The excuse. The clarity of pure violence.

Then a gunshot cracked, somewhere close. And another.

Riven's head snapped to the sound. Holloway's did too. His boys stood ready, weapons drawn.

"With me. Now." Then, to Riven, "You're done here. Get out of my city."

He ran toward the gunshots. Behind him, Riven's boots hit mud going the other direction. Holloway's mind was already triangulating a location, likely scenarios, next moves. He could deal with Riven later.

His boots skidded as he rounded the corner.

Oh, gods. Tally.

She was down in the dirt, curled up like a child. Face streaked with flux dust and blood, a man's coat over her shoulders. Someone crouched beside her, talking low and quiet.

There was a body sprawled nearby, face down. Male. Back split open. Gunpowder hung in the air. Blood looked fresh, still wet. Single shooter, probably.

Talent whimpered softly. *She's alive, thank the Navigator.*

"Hold there!" He raised his lantern, pistol ready in his other hand.

The other person's head snapped up.

"Dawn." He lowered the pistol without taking his eyes off her.

"Small world, Captain." Her voice was flat and a little slurred. Was she drunk?

Jack and Rider spread behind him, hands on their sidearms.

His eyes went back to Talent. She wasn't moving. Gods, if she was really hurt he'd never forgive himself.

"What happened? Is she okay?"

"She is now." Dawn shifted, keeping her body between Talent and his men. "Flint and Birdy Jones grabbed her for the bounty."

The Jones brothers. Small-time mercenaries. Violent, dangerous men. Their brother had been sentenced and executed for the murder of Captain Valence, if he recalled correctly.

Damn it all. He'd spent eighteen hours running interference from the inside, trying to keep Talent safe. He'd assumed she was in her room. He'd told himself that was enough. It wasn't at all.

Rider stepped in. "Sir, is that the woman we have a warrant for?"

Holloway waved him off. His focus stayed on Dawn. On Talent. He didn't want to take them in, but he was so tired. He couldn't think right.

Dawn nodded. "If I told you Birdy was a murderer," she said, testing the words, "that he's the one who killed Captain Valence, not his brother. What would you say to that?"

"I'd say it seems convenient," Holloway said. His eyes held hers. *I know you're lying.*

Her grin didn't waver. *I know you know.*

"He bragged about it just now. Said he kept the captain's ring."

Holloway crouched in the mud and checked the man's pockets. Pulled out a sapphire ring. *Way too neat.* He flipped the ring over in his palm. Valence had been a good man. This wouldn't do him justice. But Valence was already dead. Talent was alive, and she was hurting. He stood.

"Good enough for me."

Relief flickered across Dawn's face before she masked it.

For a heartbeat, it almost worked. He'd need to go back and file this report. They could all walk away.

Then Rider stepped forward, eager bastard. Still believed that justice and following orders were the same thing. "Sir, there's still the warrant. That's the Salaren heir, I'm sure of it."

"Stand down," Holloway said, voice low. "The captain's murder takes priority. We'll get the girl tomorrow, on schedule."

"With respect, sir, the warrant came direct from Vaelis." Rider's hand moved to his belt, reaching for restraints. "We have to—"

"I said stand down." Holloway stepped between Rider and Talent. "That is an order."

Rider hesitated. But he always was too godsdamned stubborn. He stepped around Holloway and knelt, wrapping a hand around Talent's arm.

Holloway stepped forward the same instant Dawn's shot cracked the air.

Only took the one shot.

Rider folded without a sound. His fingers slipped off Talent's arm, his body hit the dirt, and the world stopped. Gun smoke hung in the air. Dawn's arm still extended, revolver steady, expression blank. Jack stood frozen, hand halfway to his sidearm.

Talent was awake now, eyes wide with horror, trembling against the wall. Flecks of Rider's blood spattered across her cheek.

Everything narrowed. Five years of service, of following orders. A lifetime of doing the right things, the right ways. It all led him here, somehow.

And Rider—that damn kid—was dead in the mud because Holloway hadn't been fast enough. He'd lost control again, and look what happened.

"What's your move, Captain?" Dawn asked, still armed.

"Shit," he muttered.

He turned to Jack, who still stood frozen, pale in the lamplight. He looked like he might be sick.

"You didn't see this. You'll go back to the garrison and report that Birdy Jones was found dead. The others ran before we could apprehend them."

No mercy in asking Jack to lie, but he couldn't lose another officer tonight, and he wasn't turning Talent in.

Jack's eyes went wide. "Sir, I can't—"

"You can." Holloway stepped closer, lowering his voice. "That's an order. File the report. You understand?"

A long pause. Jack looked at Talent, still trembling, blood on her face. At Dawn, gun ready. At Rider's body.

"Yes, sir," he whispered finally.

"Good man."

Jack backed away, shaking. Turned. Vanished down the side street at a half run.

And just like that, it was done. Holloway's fate was set.

He turned back to Dawn and Talent. His eyes were burning. He'd crossed a line he couldn't uncross. Nothing in his training had prepared him for this.

Talent was in bad shape, her dress torn. Covered in bruises, but the blood didn't look like it was hers. The only person who'd stepped in to protect her, who'd saved her twice, was Dawn.

Violently. Viciously. Without question. But *Dawn* had kept her safe. He hadn't. Not when it mattered.

He should have stopped this, should have come to her hours ago. But he'd followed protocol.

"They'll hang you both if they find you here," he said quietly.

He'd have to arrest them. Or—

"So you're coming with us," Dawn said.

Not an invitation. A statement.

He laughed once. The whole life he'd built would end here, in an alley at the edge of the world. His career as an enforcer. His inheritance. Any chance to honor Cordon's memory. That was all over now if he walked away. If he didn't—he couldn't protect her.

"Yeah," he said finally. "Looks that way."

The mist was thickening to something closer to rain, sporadic drops hitting thick and cold. Holloway scanned the empty streets. They needed to find cover. Make a plan.

"Starfall," Talent said. Her voice was small. "Shelter...with Lore."

That name. *Lore Tavis.* The name Riven had given an hour ago. Apparently, he and Talent were on a first-name basis. Holloway filed that away for later.

"Figures," Dawn said, spitting into the dirt. "That bastard always gets what he wants."

Dawn knew him too. Fantastic. But what choice did they have? Holloway holstered his pistol. "Lead the way."

They walked in silence through back alleys. Fugitives now, all three of them. He'd been on his feet all day, but he kept going for Talent.

Somewhere behind them, Jack would be filing his report. Rider's body cooling in the mud. Lies stacked on lies.

Dawn walked up ahead, checking corners, choosing their path—that one knew what she was doing. Talent fell back next to him. When she leaned on his shoulder, he held her up.

"You came for me," Talent whispered. "You stayed."

At least he'd gotten that part right. That was something. He focused on putting one foot in front of the other as he followed Talent into the unknown.

ACT II

WHAT IT TAKES TO SURVIVE

23

THE TRAP YOU CHOOSE

DAWN

An oath sworn in blood will survive death itself.

— A PROVERB, PRE-CROSSING ORIGIN

Dawn's eyes stayed on the street behind them as she pounded on the gate. Too much open ground. If anyone came around that corner, they were pinned. Talia leaned heavy on Holloway's shoulder. That enforcer boy's blood still painted her face.

Rusty hinges wailed. The door swung open *slowly* and Lore stood in the gap.

"Quickly," he said, but it took him a beat to step aside. "We have a lot to do."

Something about the way he stood—clasped hands, serene smile—didn't sit right. She scuffed the gravel path with her toe while she waited for the gate to close again. So fucking slow. When it finally shut, the metallic clang echoed through her chest. *No going back now.*

Lore led them into his chambers. He pressed a cup of *thavi* into Talia's hands. She shook so hard the drink slopped over the rim.

Dawn couldn't shake the picture of Flint looming over that girl. That tiny sob she'd let out when she thought no one was coming. Sure, Dawn had stopped it, but she was too fucking late. Should've shot Flint weeks ago.

Talia stared at the *thavi*. Lore knelt in front of her. He wrapped his hands around hers to steady the cup.

"I can't go home, can I?" Talia's voice came out a whisper.

"No," Lore said, low and soft. "You cannot go back. But you can go forward. I promised Starfall would protect you, and we will."

Dawn watched Lore as he spoke. He failed to mention that associating with him was what got her in trouble in the first place. Or that they couldn't stay here in Starfall.

"Holloway too." Talia's eyes might be unfocused, but she said the boy's name clear as a bell.

A small line showed between Lore's eyebrows. "Are you sure that's a good idea?"

"I won't go without him."

Lore studied Talia's face. Gave a nod. "Fine. But I need some assurance of his loyalty."

"What kind of assurance?" Dawn cut in. Nothing was ever free with Lore. He might ask for information, or money, or promises. He might get those things and still ask for more.

"An oath," Lore stood and walked to a sideboard, started opening drawers. "His protection in exchange for mine."

That seemed reasonable. She didn't trust it.

"And if he won't swear the oath?" Dawn asked, scanning the room. Holloway's face was pale. Talia was looking into the middle distance, picking at her fingernails.

"If he won't swear this oath, in blood, the captain walks out of my gates." Lore spread his hands. "I won't stop him. I won't help him."

A blood oath? Dawn didn't know how that worked—blood magic was old and messy. Some old families had practiced it, but she'd never had a use for it herself. Lore pulled a knife from the drawer, its blade reflecting the firelight. Holloway's eyes cut to the door.

"This is your choice," Lore purred. "I won't force you."

Some choice. Bind his soul to this asshole or leave Talia alone? This was how Lore operated. He'd put a gun to your head and call it free will.

Holloway rolled up a sleeve. "Do it."

Lore pressed the blade into Holloway's palm. Dark blood welled up, weeping over his wrist and splattering on the table. Then he cut himself. He took Holloway's hand and pressed their palms together.

Sweat beaded on Holloway's forehead. His back jerked straight.

"I accept your service," Lore murmured. "And you accept my protection."

"I accept your protection," Holloway choked out. "And I live to serve."

She knew the moment the oath snapped into place. The air went slack. Flux lamps flickered around the room. She tasted copper and felt a tug on her skin, like metal filings drawn to a magnet. Lore released his grip, and Holloway staggered. Caught the edge of the table. Sucked in a shaky breath.

Lore drew a length of gauze from the sideboard and wrapped it twice around Holloway's hand, tying it off with an expert twist. His own wound bled freely, but he didn't seem to notice. He whispered something to Talia and ushered her out of the room, letting the door click closed behind them. Dawn stared at a smattering of blood on the floorboards.

Just two of them now. Dawn hooked the back of a chair and dragged it to the fire. Holloway dropped into the chair across from hers, eyes on his hand. Heat crawled under her collar. She unbuttoned her jacket and leaned back. *This fucking day.*

"Well, good," she said, kicking an ankle over her knee. "We were short one bleeding fool."

His face stayed neutral as he stared into the fire, but amusement flashed around his eyes as he said, "I do live to serve. Apparently."

She'd expected him to bristle, not joke back. That was a good sign. "Anything you're useful for? Besides ordering people around?"

He gave her a crooked half grin. "Why, you looking for an apprentice in the swearing and shooting department? I *am* looking for a new gig. "

That made her laugh. He held his hands to the fire, and she could see the change settle in. Shock burning off. Training taking over.

"Do we have a route out of town?" he asked.

"The north gate's closest, but it'll be stacked with patrols. South gate might be clear. We'd have to cut across the city and circle back to the Queen's Way."

He shook his head. "All the real roads will be guarded. Need a third way. Rockier the better."

"The old quarry road?" It didn't deserve to be called a road, more like a flat bit of gravel between bigger rocks. Once you took flux out of the soil it didn't come back. The hills near town had been stripped bare for years.

"That sounds like what we need." He nodded once. "My boys never trained on trails. Rough terrain slows them."

She studied his face. *My boys.* He'd lost one of those boys tonight. Shit, Holloway's whole life had pretty much ended tonight. He'd given up his rank, maybe his soul, and he was already putting a decent plan together. Her fingers tapped restlessly against her holsters.

She hadn't planned to respect him, but it was coming on fast.

"Question for you. Ever run into Riven Valros at the garrison?"

Holloway frowned. "Why?"

"Was he...was he really reporting on Talia?"

He tipped his head back and sighed, tired. "Yeah."

Fuuuck. Lore wasn't lying. She didn't know what to do with that. "The warrant. Was that him?"

Holloway rubbed the back of his neck. "I don't know. Someone turned in a full dossier on her this morning. Timelines. Transcripts. That's what did it." He looked down at his hand. "But the informant —Riven—reached out later to schedule a drop. Asked me to arrest Lore."

"Stars above." Dawn shut her eyes. *What was he thinking?*

"Tally can't find out," Holloway said. "She's been through enough."

"Agreed."

The fire snapped as a log collapsed in on itself.

"You better scrounge up some gear," she said finally. "Can't wear black and green on the road. I'll go check on our girl."

She found Talia alone in the library, bent over a map. The girl was tracing a finger up the road that ran north along the coast and then west into those mountains.

Dawn leaned on the table near her. "How are you holding up?"

Talia's eyes were unfocused when she glanced up. "What? Oh." She looked at her own hands, turned them over. "I don't know."

Shock. Dawn had seen it before. The girl's mind had gone somewhere else to survive. She stared at Talia's shaking hands and made herself say it.

"You don't have to do this. If you want out, just say so. I'll get you somewhere safe."

She'd been fighting off the guilt of introducing Talia to Lore. Flipping it into anger, like she did with feelings she didn't need. But it had been building for days now, maybe longer.

It was one thing to run down Lore's hit list or fuck over someone like Lorry. Those pricks deserved what came to them, and she deserved to survive. Talia was different—she didn't ask for any of this.

Talia stared at the map a long time. Then, "I want to see what's out there."

Dawn studied her. Shaky hands, glassy eyes. Still running on momentum instead of brainpower. Dawn wanted to argue. When all your other choices got burned down, picking the last door wasn't really choosing. But the girl looked set.

"If you're in, I'm in," Dawn said.

Talia fidgeted with the corner of the map. "Thank you. For tonight. For—"

"Don't thank me yet." Dawn pushed to her feet. "We're not out of it."

Bells tolled midnight as they gathered in the courtyard, which was filled with Lore's acolytes. A sea of blue cloaks. Lore raised his hands, and the crowd went quiet.

"True gods, bless us on this road," he intoned. "Keep us safe to the end."

His people murmured the words back.

Dawn watched Holloway, standing next to Talia. Felt the magnetic tug of the oath wash over her skin and anchor into Holloway, pulling him forward just a half step. His face went white. Whatever Lore had done, it held.

They were all bound to Lore now, one way or another.

Lore checked his stallion's bridle and tack before swinging onto his back. "Head for the quarry road," he said. "West into the hills, north once we're clear. Dawn leads."

Someone had fetched the horses from Cannon's. Dawn was happy to see Brimstone. She mounted up as the gates groaned open. The street beyond was mostly empty. She drove her heels in and leaped forward. She knew Lore had planned this, every piece of it. She was riding straight into his snare, eyes open, jaw set. She should have resented it.

And yet—

The wind tore at her duster coat as she cantered into the street. They crossed the western perimeter where the wall was still being built, then Gateway shrank to a shadow behind them. She craned her neck back to take in the sky, speckled with stars. She laughed once—short, rough, real. The night stole the sound as they rode out.

24

CROSSING THE THRESHOLD

TALIA

Thyss weeps for his brother, and I stand here. What is there to say? We planned for this, but I never guessed the world could burn that fucking fast. I'll never again smell luriel flowers at midnight, and I didn't know until this moment that I cared for them at all.

— VAEL LAR VARLOHEIM, PERSONAL JOURNAL,
YEAR OF THE CROSSING. TRANS: T. SALAREN

The quarry road was barely that, more like a stretch of loose gravel and shale pointing at the hills. Talia pressed low against Jonquil's neck, just trying to hang on. Every jolt of the mare's hooves felt like it might tear her loose.

Behind them, Gateway screamed awake. Horns cut the night in quick blasts, three at a time. She didn't know what it meant, but it couldn't be a coincidence that the sound was chasing them.

A sharp crack split the air, then another. Stone chips started spraying up from the ground near Jonquil's feet. Bullets. The little mare leaped forward, and Talia's jaw slammed shut, her teeth knocking together painfully. She wrapped the reins around her wrists and held on as tight as she could.

"Let's go!" Dawn's voice cut through the wind somewhere ahead.

A flash of silver light filled Talia's vision, bright enough to hurt. She heard yelling and the clamor of metal striking metal. She tried to twist in the saddle to see, but she was leaning too far forward. The commotion kept getting louder. Between the crashes, a wet thunk and a scream.

Who was fighting back there? She tried to sit up again, but just as she pulled back, Jonquil lost her footing in the loose shale. She felt the mare pitch to the left, felt herself tip to the right. Talia grabbed for the reins and got a handful of mane which slipped between her fingers.

She hit the ground hard and skidded. She'd thrown her arms around her head, palms out, and she felt the little rocks slice her hands open as she slid. Her hip struck something solid, a root or a rock, and her body spun to a stop. Hooves thundered past her head, and hot panic flooded her as she imagined being trampled.

"Talia! Tally!" Several overlapping voices called her name.

Jonquil was bolting ahead down the track, reins whipping in the dark. Talia watched, dazed, as Dawn spun Brimstone, snagged Jonquil's reins one-handed, and hauled the mare in.

"I'm fine," Talia said. She could feel the blood, sticky and slick in her palms, and a deep pulsing drumbeat in her shoulder and hip. That should hurt. Why didn't it hurt? Footsteps crunched through the gravel, and Holloway was there, standing above her. His beautiful gray gelding sidestepped, and he clicked soothingly, then knelt at her side.

"We've got to get moving, Tally," he murmured as he wrapped an arm around her waist. Then, with a dizzying lurch, he lifted her and spun her around onto his horse. He mounted quickly in front of her and reached back to pull her arms around his waist. The heat of his back seeped into her, cutting through the cold deep-night air.

"Hang on to me," he said.

She did, tightly, and his emotions flooded in with the contact. His reactions were clean, like a steady drip of water into a clear fountain. Her fingers relaxed as the hoofbeats below them fell into a rhythm and the sounds of fighting pulled away. Her breathing slowed to match his. She pressed closer, let his calm sink into her until it was all she could feel.

"Half a league to the crossing," Dawn shouted over the wind.

They rode hard. The gorge appeared without warning, stone arches spanning black water that roared below. In faerie stories, crossing water at night could wash away the past. Talia wished that were true.

Torchlight flared on the far side, and Talia could make out a new line of enforcers across the bridge, rifles raised. Then horns sounded again behind them as their pursuers closed in.

"Shit," Dawn cursed. "We're pinned."

Lore's stallion shied, hooves scraping stone. He steadied the horse with one hand. Talia squinted to make out Lore's face in the dark. He didn't seem rattled by the trap springing shut around them, enforcers ahead and behind.

"There's no other way. We have to break through the line." Lore spoke, silky slow, like he had time to spare.

On the other side of the bridge, the enforcers' rifles caught moonlight as they lowered into shooting position. The horns behind them screeched, so close now, Talia flinched. That silver light flashed again—and then she saw him. It was Riven. Her stomach lurched with relief, then confusion. He wasn't riding to meet them. He was standing between them and their pursuers and turning back to engage.

It was dark, but she could see blood running down his face, glinting in the glow of his silver swords. The enforcers' rifles didn't work at close range, so they'd drawn blades too. He parried three attacks at once. Talia looked on in awe and horror as bodies fell in his path, rifles clattering off the stone. The gorge walls threw the sound back in layers—steel clashing, shouting, the crack of gunfire.

"Go ahead!" Riven's voice broke through the clamor.

Ahead of them, the sentries on the bridge were faltering, lowering their guns and shouting in confusion. Dawn spurred forward, rushing the line, with Lore just behind. Holloway held back for a moment, and Talia looked over her shoulder. Riven stood in the mouth of the pass, blades cutting through the dark in silver arcs.

Too many enforcers.

"We can't leave him!" She pulled at Holloway's shoulder.

"He's buying us time. We can't wait."

She held Holloway tighter and turned again just as a blade caught Riven's side. He fell to one knee. His glowing swords dimmed, then flared.

"Riven!" The sound she made was more scream than anything, tearing out of her throat.

But they were galloping through the scattered line of enforcers, across the bridge. Pulling away from the fight. She felt the roughness of Holloway's jacket. The sting of cold night air, laced with gunpowder, in her throat.

She looked back one last time to see a wave break over Riven's head. Green cloaks surged, and he was gone.

"Eyes forward," Holloway said roughly. "Make it worth it."

They turned a corner and lost sight of the battle. Talia couldn't breathe. Her throat prickled and tightened, and she buried her face in Holloway's back.

Dead or captured. Either way, he's gone.

It didn't make any sense. She'd been avoiding him; she hadn't seen him all day. Riven hadn't been with them at Starfall. Why would he be on the quarry road, attacking those enforcers? She couldn't work out the logic, and that made her feel unmoored.

"How did he—" Her voice broke, and she coughed. Tried again. "Holloway, how did he find us?"

Holloway's back went rigid, but he didn't reply.

Dawn's voice carried back on the wind. "We need to keep moving!"

Right. Questions later. Let's just survive.

But the questions didn't stop spinning just because she told them to, and one question above all kept rising to the front of her mind. Had Riven died thinking she was angry at him?

They rode in silence. Time felt strange, stretched thin. It could have been minutes or hours. Talia squeezed Holloway's firm torso with her shredded hands and felt the pain cut through at last, throbbing in time with his breathing.

Eventually the land changed. The ground beside the road got rockier, wilder. The trees grew twisted and strange.

"There." Lore's voice cut through the darkness. He pointed ahead to where a stack of stones rose against the stars.

A cairn stood at the head of a narrow valley, taller than a man on horseback. She could see the carvings even in the dark, spirals and lines cut deep into stone. Not Starscript. Something older.

"A boundary stone," Lore said solemnly. "They won't follow us past here, at least for tonight."

Talia remembered talk of boundary stones in field reports. They marked the transition to fluxborn territory, and patrols had to follow special protocols if they ventured beyond them.

The air shifted the moment they passed the stone. It was thinner, almost brittle.

"What is this place?" she asked, her curiosity spiking.

"Hundreds of years ago, these marked the edges of fae territory." Lore pulled his horse next to the marker and ran his hand over the face of it. "But the stones are older than that."

He kept his eyes on the massive rock, not sparing a glance for the path behind them. Dawn scoffed out loud as she pulled up beside them.

"Can we get the fuck off the road before we start telling faerie stories?" She *did* look back, with a frown that pulled her eyebrows together. If Talia didn't know her better, she'd say Dawn was worried.

Dawn clucked, urging her horse forward. A narrow stream crossed the path ahead, black water sliding over darker rock. The horses splashed through, exhausted from the flight.

On the far bank, Talia turned to face the way they'd come. It felt wrong here, too slow and quiet after the violence they'd just escaped. Gateway's lights weren't directly visible, just a glow in the sky behind the hills. Riven was somewhere in that darkness. Or his body was.

They made a haphazard camp in a clearing between the strange, twisted trees. Talia sat on a fallen log. Around her, the others moved through their tasks in silence, watering horses, checking weapons. They didn't risk a fire. At one point Lore pulled Dawn aside, and based on Dawn's gestures, they seemed to be arguing. Talia couldn't make out any of the words.

She found herself sitting with her elbows on her knees, staring down at her shredded hands. Slowly, she pulled back a piece of loose skin and picked a bit of gravel out of her flesh. Then another. She focused on the sting and took stock. No grief. No rage. She should feel something, but her chest felt empty instead. Scraped bare.

She smelled Holloway approach before he even sat down, clean, like vanilla soap and linen. He took one of her hands and started washing out the wounds with a wet cloth. Each dab of the cloth shot jolts of pain up her arm, but she didn't complain—it would be over soon. When he was done, he took her left hand, turned it over, and brushed his thumb twice across her knuckles. Their signal.

"I was angry," she whispered. "I was acting like a child, and now I'll never be able to tell him I'm sorry." She knew how much an unspoken apology could hurt, how it burrowed in and bit you at the strangest times. An old memory of her sister kept trying to intrude, and Talia pushed it down.

Holloway tensed at her side. "I'm sure he understood," he said finally.

Guilt colored his emotions. There was something he wasn't saying, but she didn't have the energy to probe it. Maybe he was jealous? He'd never had nice things to say about Riven. She let her head fall against his shoulder and closed her eyes.

"You can rest now, Tally. You're safe."

Safe. The word rang empty. This was going to be a long journey, and a dangerous one. Riven had promised to keep her safe, and he was already gone. *Safe* was an illusion, she decided. She couldn't afford to pretend.

25

DAWN ALWAYS TAKES FIRST WATCH

DAWN

Young Clover came to Gateway town,
Said she'd never been astride.
The wrangler perked right up to help—
By morning, gods, that girl could ride.

— DRINKING SONG, VALTA, ORIGIN UNKNOWN

Dawn let the crew sleep in. After the night they'd had, they needed it. The sun was already climbing when they broke camp. They rode till the rocky ground gave way to grassy prairie. Nothing to trip on but a rotting fence post or two under the open sky.

Dawn rode ahead of the others, letting the quiet do what it could for her head. In a group like this, she always rode point. Riven always took flank, kept an eye on her blind spot, watched for trouble coming sideways.

Now her right side felt wrong. She kept glancing back that way and feeling a flash of panic in her chest. She knew he wasn't there, but she couldn't stop looking.

The wind shifted, and voices caught up with her. The kids were arguing again. Dawn didn't mean to, but she smiled.

"—cultural memory," Talia was saying, bright and certain. "Fables and faerie stories carry history we'd have lost without them."

Holloway snorted. "History is history. You just wanted to study bedtime stories at the Lyceum and call it a degree."

"You haven't read an original faerie story, then, if that's what you believe."

"I haven't read one? Don't insult me. You've told me every faerie story that exists, Tally. And a few you made up."

"Were you ever listening? I seem to recall—"

The wind shifted away. Dawn slowed Brimstone, let the distance close until she could hear them again. She breathed easier listening to them argue. It sounded normal. Healthy.

"You talk real serious, professor," Dawn cut in when Holloway's gelding, Ash, pulled even with her. "But tell me, are you reading page by page? Or do you skip to the parts where the fae warrior finally pins the girl down with this—" She made a crude gesture.

Talia sputtered. Holloway bit his fist as he fought to hold in a laugh. Talia punched his shoulder, and Dawn winked at him. The wind carried their laughter on ahead. She rode into it feeling a little less alone.

They made slower time with Talia and Holloway riding double. Ash was blowing hard by lowsun, and the mountains ahead might have been pinned to the sky. Seemed no closer than they'd been that morning. When they stumbled onto a small slip of a creek cutting through the grasslands, Dawn called it.

"We're stopping here," she said, swinging down. Her knees creaked when she hit the ground. "Before the light quits."

Setting up camp was a disaster. Talia tried to dismount and fell instead. When she tugged at a strap, the grain sack thumped open and spilled in wet sand. Dawn crouched and started scooping it up. Her hands moved automatically. Salvage what you can, forget the rest.

Talia made a strangled noise. Tried to help, just made it worse. This wasn't fair to the girl. She'd gone from scholar to rebel-in-exile, just one day to another. Riven should be here to help her.

Holloway led the horses to the creek, voice low and steady. The beasts calmed under his hands, ears flicking forward. Boy knew his way around animals. She hadn't expected that. He was a good addition to the crew, to be honest.

Lore put in the work too. He lay out bedrolls, stacked firewood. Dawn hated how her shoulders eased watching him make order from chaos. For her part, Dawn built a firepit with stones pulled from the creek. She had flint ready when Lore eased down and pulled a flux crystal from his coat.

"Your hands stop working?" Dawn asked, eyeing the crystal. Damn waste of magic, using that for one fire.

Lore didn't look up. Just breathed light through the crystal. The spark jumped too eager, flames catching fast. Kindling snapped and spat.

"There are plenty more crystals waiting in the caravan," he said, unbothered. "This won't give off smoke."

Dawn's jaw tightened. Lore didn't often show his hand, but this was telling. Burning a crystal was a reckless flex, even if it helped them lay low. Whatever. She had her own reserves. *She* wouldn't run out of fuel.

Talia leaned in, eyes bright. "How does it work? The crystal?"

Lore's posture shifted. *Oh good, he's ready to preach.*

"Flux is just energy," he said. "You can store it in crystals like these, then draw from them later. Here, try."

He placed a smaller shard in Talia's palm and covered her fingers with his. The light bloomed and flickered, and Talia's face lit up.

She tied the shard with twine and hung it from one of the trees. Then she did another.

It was a wild risk to burn crystals this early. But Talia was smiling ear to ear. Was that enough for Lore, or did he have another angle? Dawn didn't trust it, and it must have showed on her face.

"It's fine, Dawn," Lore said. "We'll meet up with the caravan tomorrow and resupply. Let her have some magic."

Dinner was campfire rabbit stew. One of three things Dawn could cook. Holloway finished eating first, wiped his hands, and drew a small harp from his pack. He tuned it with the kind of care that had Dawn staring at his hands.

The first notes were slow and sad. Something hooked in her chest that she wasn't ready to feel. Then the melody shifted—same bones but faster—and Holloway rolled the tune into a rowdy drinking song. His voice was clear and shameless. Lore surprised her by joining in with a smooth baritone. Talia tried to follow, stumbled over the bawdy bits, laughed and kept going.

Dawn hesitated, then she gave in. She couldn't sing worth shit, so she hollered. Holloway grinned at her over the harp strings and kicked the tempo faster. They chased it together, voices tangling and splitting. The last verse collapsed into laughter. The silence that followed felt different than before.

Dawn looked around the fire. Holloway's dimples showed, his hands still cradling the harp. Talia's face was flushed, eyes brighter than they had been. Even Lore had eased.

A total mess. Off-key and wounded and held together by spit and blood oaths. But they were alive. The fire crackled. An owl called from the darkness. Laughter still hung in the air.

Later, as the fire burned low, Lore pulled a map from his saddlebag. Dawn leaned in, watching his finger as it traced the road.

"The Queen's Way runs direct from Gateway to Valrotala," he said. "But we are a fair bit west of there. Tomorrow, we hit Pickler's Junction, meet the supply caravan, and cut east with the wagons until we hit the road. Less direct, but we'll travel faster from there out."

Dawn looked over at the half-empty grain sack. At the disaster of a campsite. The exhaustion sitting heavy on Holloway's shoulders. The sooner they met up with that caravan, the better. Safety in numbers, fresh provisions, some extra hands.

"How long to Valrotala after we reach the Queen's Way?" Talia asked.

"Two weeks, at least," Lore said. "Maybe three."

Faster to cut diagonal, but we couldn't take the wagons that way. Dawn kept her thoughts to herself.

"Get some sleep," she said. "We ride at firstlight. No more sleeping in."

After a time, the camp went quiet. Horses shifted on their picket lines. Snores hummed from crooked tents. The creek flashed silver under the waxing moon.

Dawn sat first watch, propping herself under a tree at the edge of camp. In the dark, one of Talia's crystals blinked out. Then another. Then a third dimmed to nothing, light bleeding away into the dark.

"Well, that didn't last long," Dawn muttered.

"Nothing does." Lore's voice cut through the dark. She didn't realize he was still sitting beside the dying fire.

Dawn scoffed. She was over his gloomy prophet act.

"You always this inspiring? Or is it just for me?"

Lore seemed to think about that. The fire crackled. Another crystal died. "You don't trust me," he said finally.

"True." Dawn reached for her knife. The leather grip had worn away many times, but the blade kept doing its job. It felt good in her hand.

"I wouldn't either." She couldn't see his expression. Was he joking?

"That warrant for Talia. That was you." It was an educated guess, but Lore's chuckle confirmed it.

"I recall saying she'd have a choice," he replied, unshaken. "And she did." Stars, he didn't even feel bad.

"And that blood oath you slapped on Holloway is a nasty piece of work."

"He would have turned on us the moment his enforcer friends showed up," Lore said. "This simply prevents that."

"Right, so you're an asshole twice over. Why should I help you drag those kids deeper into danger?"

Lore watched her, gold-flecked eyes flashing in the dark.

"Because you want to reconnect with your mate. And I need all of you to reach Valrotala alive."

Dawn stilled. She hated that he knew more than she did about Ehrue. Every few weeks he'd drop one more detail, just enough to keep her around. She wanted to grab him by the throat and shake the whole story out of him, but she knew he'd just die laughing at her. Then she'd never know.

She forced her voice steady. "And when one of those things stops being true?"

"Then we deal with it." He poked the fading fire, sending up a cloud of sparks. "We can always kill each other later. For now, we're all going the same way."

Dawn wanted to argue, but he was right. Out here, you worked with what you had. Survive first. Settle accounts after. She sat back against the tree, knife at hand.

Tomorrow they'd meet the caravan. Get supplies, reinforcements, maybe even a decent meal. Tonight, she'd make sure they lived to see it. She watched grimly as the last of the crystals guttered out and went dark.

26

SURVIVAL IS A LANGUAGE

TALIA

The fluxlines are structural. STRUCTURAL. I have so many questions. What made the network collapse? Does the grid cross all of Valta? If this is how power moved, where did it come from? How could it work at this scale? The answers have to be in Valrotala, I know it.

— T. SALAREN, FIELD NOTES, 401 AC

Someone was slapping Talia's leg, and she rolled over to see Dawn crouched above her in the shadowy tent.

"Time to move," was all Dawn said before disappearing back through the tent flaps.

The second Talia sat up, pain jolted up her legs, her back, her core. She had never ridden that hard or long before, and she'd definitely never slept on the ground. Everything hurt.

Outside, horses stamped and gear clinked. She slipped on her blouse and skirt as quickly as she could and struggled to pull her boots up over her swollen feet.

The easy mood from last night was gone. The horses were tacked and saddled, the camp packed. By the time she turned around, Holloway was folding her tent.

"Sorry," she said, feeling flustered. "I thought we had more time."

The landscape was eerily quiet. There weren't even birds singing.

"The caravan's moving," Dawn said, wrapping their remaining flux crystals in cloth. "Every hour counts if we're gonna catch them."

After a full day with no sign of a limp, Holloway gave Jonquil the all-clear. Talia swung into the saddle and let out a sigh. It would be nice to get a break from Holloway's emotions.

The sun climbed quickly. Dust lifted from the horses' hooves and hung in the still air. She tried not to think about Riven, but when she closed her eyes, she kept seeing the cluster of enforcers swarming over him.

She focused on the landscape instead. It was hilly country, nearly colorless, all sage and rust-colored rocks. Crumbled foundations peeked from the dry grass like sun-bleached bones. These plains must have been thick with cities. An entire civilization with advanced language, culture, technology. Then hundreds of years ago they'd vanished.

Everyone referred to them as "fae" because Valta was discovered across the Green Sea, exactly like the Lost Continent in the faerie stories. The label was misleading. Talia knew that the people who lived here, who'd died here, were just people.

She'd waited so long to get into the field, and the landscape was flying by too fast to see anything. But she'd already made them late; she couldn't ask to stop. Holloway pulled up alongside her.

"You good?" he asked.

"Yes." She forced a smile. Had he ever noticed she always answered yes to that question? She wasn't good. Nothing made her more uncomfortable than feeling like a burden.

"Your pack's slipping," he said. He reached over and started adjusting the strap.

"I can do it myself," she snapped, pushing his hand away.

"I was just—" His voice went quiet. "Sorry."

His hurt came through when their hands touched, and she pulled back. *Damn it, Talia, he is just trying to help*. She didn't want to need help, but that wasn't his fault.

"Actually, I do have a question."

He pulled up beside her, careful to keep more distance. "Yeah?"

"It's about Riven." Her voice dropped. Saying his name hurt. "Do you know why he did it? Why he stayed and fought those enforcers when he could've run?"

Holloway frowned. "I suppose he saw it as his job to protect you. And you know, it's possible he survived. My boys would want to question him, if they could."

The gentleness in his voice was the worst, like he thought she was too fragile to handle the truth. She knew Riven was most likely gone. She nodded and clenched her teeth. Holloway had been treating her like a breakable object all her life. She didn't know why she expected honest answers from him.

She faced forward and decided not to ask for help again.

The creek was deeper than it looked, pooling and thrashing around a cluster of rocks. Dawn and Holloway rode through, but Lore paused at the bank, glancing back at Talia.

"Follow my line," he said. "Current looks stronger on the right."

She tried to mimic his approach and his posture, but Jonquil was shorter than the other horses. The water rose faster than Talia expected, clear up to her knees. The current grabbed her legs, and she braced, tightened her grip on the reins, looked down at the swirling brown water—

Jonquil spooked sideways, and Talia fell. Cold water shocked the air from her lungs, and her waterlogged boots dragged her to her knees. She flailed for the bank, fingers slipping in mud.

Holloway's hand closed on her elbow and hauled her up.

"You all right?"

She nodded and gasped for air. Everyone was staring at her.

"What did I do wrong?"

"Nothing." He squeezed water from his sleeve. "The ford was too deep for your little mare; we should have stopped. You did tense up, though. Try and stay loose next time."

Nothing she could do, except stop screwing up. She heard him loud and clear. She wanted real feedback, instructions, something she could practice. But he was already moving away.

Her legs were raw where they'd chafed against the saddle, and now the wet fabric was sticking to them. It burned at every point where cloth touched skin, and tugged with every step. She set her jaw and focused on walking up the sludgy bank, slipping half a step back for each step she took. Then her toe hit something solid.

She reached down to brush silt away from a perfectly square stone buried in the muck. It was vibrating faintly.

"Part of an old foundation," she murmured.

Foundation. She recalled the passage from the journal: *Flux channeling was the foundation of civilization.* She'd taken it as a metaphor. It made sense that way. She reached back down and felt the stone hum under her hand. What if it wasn't?

She wasn't sure what she was looking for until she spotted a faint blue line connecting the stone to another one, like some kind of conduit. She followed it. Ahead, Holloway whistled, pulling the group to a stop.

He circled back. "What is it, Tally?"

She traced the conduit through the mud until she reached a cornerstone with a blue crystal embedded in the center. A flux crystal. She pressed her thumb against the crystal, and it clicked free from its casing. As soon as it came away from the cornerstone, the entire conduit line flickered and went dark.

The horses crowded in, their shadows cooling her wet clothes. Talia held the flux crystal up for them to see.

Dawn gave a low whistle. "Nice catch. We need more of those."

Warmth spread through her chest, and she slipped the crystal into Riven's coat. She might be slow and soaking wet, but she was the only person here who'd noticed the fluxline. Maybe she wasn't incompetent after all.

Pickler's Junction finally appeared on the horizon, a cluster of gray buildings. The town seemed empty, no sign of a caravan.

"They must be late," Talia said, fighting to keep her voice level, but her unease only sharpened as they pulled into town.

"Look around," Dawn said. "What do you see?"

She slid off Jonquil carefully, her shredded thighs screaming in protest.

It looked like any other town. A dusty road. A few scraggly buildings. Then she saw a door, smashed, half hanging from its hinges in two separate pieces. It swung a little in the wind, the only movement on the whole empty place.

Holloway stalked the perimeter, rifle in hand. Lore sat motionless on his horse, eyes tracking something in the dust that Talia couldn't see. There was no one else. It was a small way station, but there should have been someone in the saloon. On the street. In a window.

A sign creaked.

"Mount back up," Dawn said sharply.

"What happened here?" Talia asked.

"Don't know." Dawn was already turning Brimstone's head. "And we're not staying to find out."

Talia's heart hammered against her ribs as she climbed back onto Jonquil's back. Where would they go next? If the caravan wasn't here, how would they find it? Dawn pulled off the road and started riding north into the hills.

The sun climbed higher, pressing down as they rode. Talia tried to focus on the ruins they passed. Tried to catalog architectural styles, notice patterns. But every part of her hurt, her skin rubbed raw after just a few days in the saddle. Her thoughts kept scattering.

She was tired of never having answers. She kicked Jonquil into a canter, caught up with Dawn at the front.

"I need to know something," she said.

Brimstone was easily a head taller than Jonquil, and Talia had to look up into the sun. She felt like a child begging for attention, and she hated it.

"Why did Riven do it? He could've run. Or come with us. Why did he stay?"

Dawn's jaw tightened. "I don't know."

Talia reached over and brushed Dawn's knee. Anguish radiated off her, thick enough to choke on. But underneath it, that same twinge of guilt that Holloway had carried. They were both hiding something.

"You do know," Talia said, dropping her hand. "Tell me."

"That warrant had your name on it, Talia. Maybe he wanted to give them a bigger target."

"What does that mean?"

"He's gone." Dawn's voice cracked. "Just leave it."

Dawn pulled ahead to catch up with Holloway, who had dismounted and was looking at something on the ground. Talia reined in, throat burning. Lore's stallion, Vesper, drifted up beside her, and Lore leaned over so she could hear.

"She's broken in her own way," he said quietly. "Grief makes people guard what hurts."

Talia blinked, fighting the sting behind her eyes. "I just want to understand why he did it."

Lore looked straight at her. "He didn't die for the wrong person, Talent."

But what if he had? What if he'd died for her? She was the last person who deserved that kind of sacrifice.

"It feels like I'm the only one here who wasn't built for this." She couldn't meet his eyes. "I'm weak, and I'm holding you back."

"You're not weak," he murmured. "You're new at this."

She swallowed hard and blinked the tears away. Talia had always been *good at things*. She didn't know who she was if that wasn't true.

Lore kept his tone low and steady. "Survival is just another language, and you're already learning it. Fording the creek. Finding that flux. You notice details that carry significance. You have remarkable potential. That's more interesting than perfection."

She wanted that to be true, badly, but she also wondered why Lore was the only one bolstering her as Holloway and Dawn rode ahead. What did he want?

The afternoon dragged. Behind her, Holloway and Dawn spoke in low voices. She caught fragments.

"—tracks back there..."

"—four, maybe five..."

"—since the Junction..."

Something had been shadowing them. That must've been what they were looking at on the ground earlier, some kind of tracks. They all knew, and she'd been oblivious. She twisted in the saddle, scanning the ridges behind them. Saw nothing but scrub and rock.

"Eyes forward," Dawn called.

Talia faced forward, but the skin prickled at the back of her neck. Now that she knew something was circling them, she heard noises everywhere. Footfalls. Twigs cracking. She jumped every time, twisting in her saddle to scan the brushy hills around them, but she saw nothing.

When the sun started to drop and Dawn called for them to stop, Talia thought she might fall off her horse with relief. It took a while to make camp. The others moved through their tasks efficiently. Talia collapsed onto a log, gingerly sticking her legs out in front of her. She almost couldn't move through the pain.

Dawn was tending the horses. As she lifted Jonquil's saddle, she paused.

"Talia. Come over here."

Something about Dawn's tone made Talia's stomach drop. She forced herself to stand and stumbled over.

Dawn angled the saddle. Dried blood streaked the leather.

Heat crawled up Talia's neck. "It's fine. I'm dealing with it."

Dawn's eyes tracked down to Talia's legs. She was wearing skirts over riding pants, so there wasn't much to see, but Dawn sniffed the air and frowned.

"This isn't your monthly blood. You're hurt. Show me."

There was no point arguing. Talia pulled her skirts up around her waist and started to tug her pants down. Every time the cloth moved, it ripped raw flesh. The saddle burn was worse than Talia thought.

Dawn sucked in a breath. "You didn't say anything."

"It wasn't important."

"Bullshit," Dawn said. "You're not out here alone." Then, softer, "I'm getting help. That okay?"

Talia nodded, and Dawn called Lore over quietly. He knelt next to her and carefully lifted her skirts to inspect the wound. She tensed up, but he was careful not to touch her.

"Hold still," he murmured. A flux crystal glowed in his hand. "This will only heal the surface, but that should do."

She stared up at the sky, trying to pretend this wasn't happening. Prickling heat washed over her raw skin, and she was extremely aware of how exposed she was. When the sensation faded, her thighs were still pink, but the bleeding had stopped.

Lore stood, the crystal now dim and cloudy in his hand. He tossed it aside.

"Nine left," Dawn said quietly.

Nine. Because of her. She felt her shoulders curl inward. She just wanted to disappear, but Lore made a soft *tsk* sound and shook his head.

"Not wasted," he said quietly. "And not negotiable. We'll all need to ride hard tomorrow to catch that caravan."

She forced herself to meet his eyes. "Thank you, but I'm fine."

She pulled her pants back into place, straightened her skirts, and walked back to the fire. She wasn't fine, but she was capable. She could learn this survival language. She had to.

27

ONLY A STORY

DAWN

The happier ending resolves cleanly: the princess and bodyguard fall in love. The darker variant is likely a later addition, a cautionary revision reflective of more cynical modern times. The original almost certainly ended in joy.

— *THE LOST FAE PRINCESS: A FAERIE STORY WITH TWO ENDINGS*, T. SALAREN, 398 AC

The fire had burned down to good old-fashioned coals with no flux crystals to sustain them. They pulsed like a heartbeat, red fading to black, red again with the wind.

Dawn stretched her boots into the heat; flask balanced on her knee. *Liethi.* The good stuff. She took a slow sip. Felt it burn down her throat, settle heavy in her stomach. Not enough to dull shit.

After the hard ride and tending Talia's wounds, no one had energy to hunt or cook or pitch tents. They lay the bedrolls in a tight circle around the fire. Dinner was hardtack and jerky. Talia had crawled into her blankets, but she wasn't asleep. Holloway stared at nothing. Lore sat still, like he was waiting.

No wagon train. No supplies. No solid plan except to follow the wheel tracks, and only nine crystals left. Someone needed to say something. Fill up the quiet.

She took another swig. "Ever hear the real story of the lost fae princess?"

Dawn didn't look at anyone. Easier to lie about the past when you weren't watching them believe it.

Holloway nodded. Lore didn't move. Just watched her with that snarky smile, like he knew what she was about to say.

She poked the coals with her stick. A log shifted, sending embers drifting.

“You’ve all heard the faerie story,” she started. “Gowns spun from starlight, palace in the clouds, a princess who fell in love with her sworn protector, and when darkness fell, their love saved the world.”

The fire snapped.

“That’s the kids’ version. The truth’s meaner.”

She leaned forward. Firelight caught the fluxborn teeth strung around her throat and cast jagged shadows.

“Her name was Elanwei. Beautiful, powerful, spoiled to the core. She held power over light and illusion. Could bend sunlight or starlight into any shape, make any fake thing look real. She played princess while her servants worked themselves bloody.”

No one spoke. The wind sighed, and Dawn went on.

“One of those servants had a son who thought duty was the same thing as love. They made him her bodyguard. Poor Althen never stood a chance. All honor and no sense. You know the type. Loyal as a dog. Clueless as one too.”

Talia shifted. “You say that like you knew him.”

Dawn took a long pull from the flask. Didn’t meet Talia’s eyes. “It’s a faerie story. They all sound that way.”

After a pause, she picked up again. “He’d have followed her into the void. So when she asked him to follow her to bed, he went. The night they escaped the city to explore their love under the open sky was the night the servants struck. When they got back that morning, the city was on fire. Her family had been twisted into starlings and flown away.”

Dawn stared into the coals.

“If the bitch had cared about her people, she could’ve rebuilt. Stepped up to lead. Instead, she went into the flames chasing vengeance and didn’t come out again. Some say she still lingers in Valrotala—a figment with ink-black hair and empty eyes—cutting down anything that reminds her of what she lost.”

A log collapsed inward. The night pressed closer. Stars bright overhead, cold and distant.

Dawn shrugged. "That's the story anyway."

"What's the lesson?" Talia asked quietly. "If the darker version is true, it must mean something."

Dawn rolled the flask between her hands. Thought of Riven's laugh. The way he'd stepped between her and danger, always, even when she didn't want it.

"*Love conquers all*," Dawn said sarcastically. "Or maybe *hate conquers love*. I always get those mixed up."

Heavy silence followed until Holloway said, "It's only a story."

Dawn looked hard at the boy who'd sworn a blood oath two days ago. Like Althen, he'd given up duty and honor for the woman he loved. And Dawn would bet good money that Talia, like the princess, did not share his devotion.

"Sure," she said. "Just a story."

Across the fire, Lore's smile deepened. "Stories have their own kind of power," he said softly. "We will see the truth of Valrotala with our own eyes soon enough."

He was looking at Talia when he said it. Dawn saw the way the girl leaned forward, hungry for meaning in a dark place. Lore knew exactly what he was doing. Turning trauma into prophecy. Making chaos feel like destiny. Stories were weapons, and he knew how to wield them.

Dawn stood abruptly. "Get some sleep. We ride again tomorrow."

Someone added a log to the fire, but Dawn had turned away. Heat pressed at her back as she walked, and the wind cut through her coat, sharp enough to hurt. Good. She needed something that felt real.

The night smelled like iron and flux charge. Some kind of storm was coming. She shivered. That caravan should've been at Pickler's Junction. They should all be approaching the Queen's Way by now.

Out here, when things weren't where they should be, it meant blood.

28

THE CULL

TALIA

The first decade produced three schools of thought on the fluxborn. The Pentarchy funded eradication. The Lyceum funded research. The prospectors buried their dead quietly and kept digging.

— *FLORA & FAUNA OF THE VALTA INTERIOR,*
VERACITY NIN, 409 AC

Talia was up before anyone came for her. She was dressed and ready in time to help break camp, and Dawn noted it with a nod and a smile. That was her version of praise.

"We're being followed, right?" Talia asked. She met Dawn's eyes.

"Since Pickler's Junction. Five riders, maybe six."

Talia bit back the rest of her questions. Now that Dawn knew she was paying attention, maybe she would include Talia next time. Lore had called survival a language, which implied there were rules. Patterns. She could learn a language. She was determined to be a better student today.

The landscape grew drier as they rode. The dusty ground was peppered with rubble where homes and roadways once stood: collapsed arches, broken pavers. She saw flashes of Starscript etched into stone, faded, nearly lost to time. When she paused to check foundations, all the fluxlines had gone dark. The crystals she did find had all been shattered, just like a flux lamp after a power surge.

Her research seemed frivolous now compared with the pressure of staying alive. Soon they'd run out of flux crystals and food, and then what? So they rode on, and the relics she might have studied were ground to powder under Jonquil's hooves.

It was near midday when they topped a low rise and Dawn slowed, hand raised to stop the others. When Talia saw the circle of wagons in the valley, she let out a sigh of relief. But nothing was moving down below, just a thin curl of smoke off an old campfire. No people. No horses.

Something glinted from one of the wagons, blue flux light. It fluttered quick and erratic, like a dying heart.

A strange smell met them halfway down the incline—the tang of copper and wet fur with something sour behind it, like vinegar. A wall of flies rose off the nearest wagon in a black cloud.

Closer up, the wreckage came into focus. A wagon lay on its side, axles broken. Another wagon had its canvas slashed and hanging like a fallen flag.

The first body she saw lay face down near the wagon wheel. A man. Older. His hand reached for something. Blood pooled black beneath him. Her stomach lurched, and she looked away.

This was the language she needed to learn. She made herself keep going.

A second body. Then a third. Talia's breath came shorter. She counted because she didn't know what else to do. Four bodies. Then five.

Holloway swung down from his saddle and walked in. Dawn followed on foot, a revolver in each hand.

Six, seven. Some in sleeping shirts. Some half dressed, caught unaware. Eight, nine, ten. She made herself keep looking, keep counting, until she couldn't anymore. It was a horrific scene, but there was something strange about it. Something missing.

"Where are the horses?" Talia asked, looking around.

Holloway stepped up beside her and grimaced. "No horses, no way to escape. Whoever did this must've driven them off first."

Her stomach clenched. Bile surged up her throat, and she spat into the dust.

"No looting either," Dawn noted. "All the coin is still on them."

Dawn checked another body. The man's chest had been opened,

ribs cracked down the middle, but not like an animal mauling. It was neat, almost surgical.

She frowned, then shook her head once, sharply, as if ruling out a thought she didn't want.

"This wasn't a raid," Dawn said. "This was a cull."

The word lodged under Talia's skin.

Cull. Like thinning a herd. Choosing who lived and who didn't.

Something scraped under the nearest overturned wagon. A whisper of movement, then a low groan.

Dawn's guns came up. "Show yourself."

A man crawled into view, dragging himself with his hands. His left leg was bound in bloody cloth.

"Don't shoot," he gasped. "Name's Sorrel. I'm the cook."

Holloway was already there, crouching to take the man under the arms. "Easy. You're all right."

"'All right' is generous," Sorrel rasped. "You got water?"

Dawn passed her canteen, her eyes scanning the ridges around them.

"What happened here?" Holloway asked.

Sorrel swallowed hard. "Wolves," he said. "But not like any I ever saw. Bigger, with blue eyes."

"Fluxborn direwolves," Dawn muttered under her breath. "A pack of 'em, I'd wager."

Talia edged closer. Her empathy twisted awake, humming behind her ribs.

"Enforcers were checking papers at the Junction, so we aimed to cut around." Sorrel's hands shook. "The wolves followed. Thought they were just scavengers, waiting for scraps. Then I saw they were...counting us."

Talia swallowed. "How could you tell?"

"They shifted when we did," he said. "Every time we moved a wagon, two of them traded places. We had five guards, there'd be five wolves. Six, then six."

Talia knelt beside him. "I can help," she said, reaching instinctively with her empathy.

Dawn caught her wrist. "Don't. You don't know this man."

She did know he was suffering. After days of feeling like a burden, she wanted to help more than she needed to stay safe. She reached into Sorrel's mind, projecting calm.

His trauma hit her in a series of sharp bursts.

Terror.

Horror.

Searing pain.

The emotions slammed into her chest, too vivid, too fast. A barrage of feelings, each hitting sharp and separate. Her vision flashed red, starbursts of silver, then black. She tried to pull back, but her gift didn't listen.

"Talent," someone said from far away. "Let go."

She couldn't. Sorrel's fear wrapped around her like barbed wire.

Then she was falling, and hands were catching her. A cool touch brushed her temple; someone braced the back of her neck.

"Breathe." Lore's voice. "You're here, Talent. This is not your fear. It belongs to someone else. Let it pass."

His calm reassurance cut through her panic. The emotions pressed on her eyelids like an impending headache, but she breathed slowly, in and out, and the pressure eased. Lore held her until the world stopped spinning.

When her vision came back, she was on the ground with her back against a wagon wheel. Lore knelt beside her, hands gently cradling her face.

"That," Dawn said tightly from somewhere behind him, "is what I said not to do."

Talia's cheeks burned. "I'm fine."

Lore lowered his hands to her knees but didn't break contact. His emotions came across as a pool of confidence, and she was grateful to draw from it.

"You keep saying that." He looked straight into her eyes. "You're not fine now. But you will be."

That's when a new sound cut across the wreckage. A dragging, scraping sound. Everyone froze, then Dawn was on her feet. Holloway pulled his rifle off his back.

"Tally, stay here," Holloway said as a huge wolf dragged itself from behind a wagon.

Gray fur matted dark around its hindquarters. One back leg hung uselessly, bone glinting white. Its head lifted. Blue eyes scanned the scene. Not wild and rolling but focused. Assessing. Her empathy hooked on the wolf before she processed what she was doing.

Pain. Deep and constant. Fatigue. A thin, taut thread of fear, not animal panic but cold flat certainty. The wolf knew it was dying. Talia wasn't touching it, wasn't touching anyone. The connection shouldn't work like this, untethered from anything physical. It was just like before, with the gryphon.

The wolf's gaze found Talia. The wreckage and bodies seemed to fade around her. Just two crystal blue eyes. Curiosity flickered through the pain. Recognition.

Talia took a step forward.

"Tally." Holloway's voice was tight with warning. "Stop."

"I can ease its pain," she whispered. "We don't have to—"

A gunshot cracked, and the wolf's body jerked. The connection snapped. The shock of the severing hit like a physical blow. One second the wolf's mind had been merged with hers, curious and aware. The next, a hollow space.

Her knees buckled and hit the ground. The air left her lungs with a small involuntary sound.

She looked up, dazed, to see Dawn with one revolver raised, smoke curling from the barrel.

"You didn't have to kill it." Tears blurred her vision. The horror of the wolf, the bodies, Riven, all of it tangled together until she couldn't separate which loss hurt the most.

"It killed these people," Dawn said.

"I know." She did know. But the wolf's pain had felt so familiar. "It couldn't even stand up—"

"Even worse. Wounded animals are unpredictable. The smart ones hold grudges. You want that thing crawling back to its pack?"

Talia stared at the wolf's corpse. Blood pooled around its body, soaking into the dust.

"There had to be another way."

Dawn shook her head once. "Not out here."

Was that the secret to survival, then? Dawn just drew a line and killed everything on the other side of it. Yes, the wolf had been dangerous, but it was intelligent too.

Talia held her questions in, but they burned in her fingertips. She wanted to write all this down, to unspool the threads that were tangling and reforming in her mind.

But there was too much work to do. Dawn and Holloway dragged the bodies under the cover of an intact wagon. Lore and Talia gathered what they could find—waterskins, dried food, flux shards pulled from broken lanterns. It wasn't enough, but it was more than they'd had.

Talia had stopped seeing the bodies by the end of it. She pressed a cloth to her nose to keep out the worst of the smell and focused on working methodically, one wagon at a time, so she didn't miss anything. She was sifting through a pile of mostly ruptured waterskins when Lore approached her.

"You touched the fluxborn's mind," he said.

"I didn't mean to. It just kind of pulled me in." She focused on the task in front of her, trying not to spill the water.

She could feel him drawing closer. "It's the flux in the air here. It makes your affinity stronger, less predictable. It will destroy you if you don't learn to shape it."

"I don't know how." Her voice came out small.

"I do." He took her hands and squeezed them, tugging her attention to his face. "Control is a skill. It comes with practice."

Control. She hated how much she wanted that.

"Can you teach me?"

"Yes. I can." His smile barely touched his mouth. She was struck again by his beauty. The grime of the road didn't touch him the way it clung to everyone else.

A howl broke the air. It carried, sad and long and low, from a ridge to the north.

Every muscle in Talia's body went rigid. Sorrel whimpered. Dawn's head snapped up, eyes locking onto the ridgeline. Another howl answered the first, from the east. Then a third, between the two. Calling and responding, like a conversation.

"They're still out there," Sorrel said hoarsely. "They never left."

"We've gotta move," Dawn said. "Now."

"It'll be dark in a few hours," Holloway warned.

"Then we use those hours," she snapped. "I am not sleeping in this valley."

No one argued. They mounted quickly, taking what they could carry. A fourth howl rose, closer, and Talia's empathy brushed something vast and angry before she yanked herself back.

Dawn set their course into a cluster of low mountains to the northwest, and the wolves paced them from the ridges, one wolf per person, just like Sorrel had described.

"They're herding us," Dawn said quietly.

Talia looked ahead at the mountain pass narrowing ahead. No way through but forward.

29

BECOMING IMPOSSIBLE TO KILL

DAWN

The drought was dire, the kitchen garden near gone. At highsun, the prophet stood in the courtyard and called the storm. By lastlight, rain had reached Starfall. He's never once let us go hungry.

— PRIVATE JOURNAL, STARFALL ACOLYTE,
IDENTITY UNKNOWN, 398 AC

They rode hard into the night with wolves on both flanks. The mountain path was steep and slick. By deepnight the horses were blown. Ice-studded rain bit their faces. They needed shelter.

The mining camp appeared out of nowhere like a stripped carcass in the moonlight. Tailings in gray heaps, an old fence slumped and rotting. Seemed abandoned until Dawn spotted movement, a woman picking through slag. Then a kid burst from a shed, a hearth fire throwing light across the yard. Laughter echoed, too happy for a place like this.

Dawn hated bringing trouble to strangers, but dropping dead on the road wasn't an option. She gave a short whistle to catch Lore's attention.

More figures stepped out of cabins and lean-to shelters. Dawn's hand went to her revolvers. Fifteen, maybe twenty souls. Enough to be trouble if they didn't care for company.

Lore swung down from his horse like this place belonged to him.

"We're just passing through," he called out. "We need rest and a roof till morning."

An older man came forward to speak for the rest. He spat on the ground. "You bring trouble, it lands on us."

"The night's half over," Lore said. "We have food we can share. I'll mend your fence myself before we go."

The man studied him, then gave a single nod. "One night," he said. "Then on your way."

He jerked his chin toward a low cluster of sheds. "My name's Ridge. Take those. Not watertight, but warmer than nothing."

They led the horses to the largest of the sheds. Dawn stripped Brimstone's tack, checked her hooves, made sure the mare had water. Simple habits. Keep your horse sound, she'll keep you alive.

Behind her, Talia wrestled with Jonquil's straps until Holloway stepped in to help. The girl flinched like he'd hit her before apologizing. She'd been doing better, but today broke her all over again.

"Hey, it's okay," he murmured. "We'll be safe here tonight."

Dawn turned away. *Safe*. Sure. Enforcers, wolves, no hope of resupply. Still, the girl needed to believe in safety. And Holloway needed to believe he could give it. Let them have their stories. Dawn would keep watch.

She walked the perimeter. The rain thickened to full sleet, and she felt the icy water slip down the back of her neck. She'd kill for the fur felt hat she'd left back in town.

She came upon Lore at the east side of camp. "You're expecting trouble," he said by way of greeting.

"Just what always comes." She didn't look at him. "The question is when it shows."

"I have faith." The man was sitting there in the full sleet. Didn't even wear a coat. "If violence finds us, we'll pay what is due."

"This place doesn't care about your sermons," Dawn spat. "It only respects who survives."

"Then we'll survive."

"Not the way we're going. You're putting soft people in a bad spot. We're way off road here, and we need supplies. Keep this up and you'll get people killed."

"Some missions are worth dying for."

Bastard. He really believed it. He walked away and left her watching the empty road. She thought she saw a flash in the distance, but then it was gone.

They came just after firstlight. Five riders. Just like she thought. They rode in a straight line, the gray morning light catching on silver stirrups. Too clean for bandits. Enforcers, for sure.

"We got company," she hollered, and the camp jolted awake. Women shoved children inside, men reached for picks. Mining tools against military-grade rifles. *Great.*

Lore was already striding out to meet them. "I'll talk to them."

"Talk?" she said. "Let's shoot them."

"There's no need for violence." His voice was calm.

"Those enforcers are hunting us," Dawn pressed. "We hide, they chase. We're all dead if they catch us by surprise. We can see them coming now."

He ignored her and started down the muddy track on foot, unarmed. His arms were spread wide.

Fuck that. She slipped behind a slag pile, revolvers out. Holloway crouched beside her. He squinted through the sleet.

"I know him," he said under his breath. "Front of the line. That's Jack."

Dawn followed his line of sight. The lead rider was younger than the others. She recognized him too. The kid Holloway sent back with a false report.

Lore was already out front. The patrol reined up, confused. Good. At least he'd draw their eyes. She moved, boots quiet in the mud. If she could get a clean shot, this could be over quick. She was almost past the open stretch when a hand clamped her arm.

Talia. The girl looked half wild.

"No," Talia whispered. "Wait. Don't—"

"You're fucking kidding," Dawn hissed. "Get out of here."

"Please," Talia whispered. "No more killing."

She wasn't loud, but the sleet had stopped suddenly. The air carried every word.

The closest enforcer turned his head.

Dawn felt it the second they were seen, like a gun cocked beside her ear. She shoved Talia behind her, but they were out in the open.

"Hold there!" the lead officer, Jack, barked. "Identify yourselves!"

Two of them dismounted, fanning out. Jack leveled his rifle at Lore's face. Point blank.

"We're here for one fugitive," Jack said. "Turn over Talent Salaren and the rest of you can go."

Dawn saw a flash of movement at the edge of her vision. Holloway stumbled out, off balance, his body jerking like he wasn't in control. There was pain carved across his face.

Jack's gaze snapped to him. "Captain?"

Holloway tried to answer, but what came out wasn't words. *The oath*. She could feel its power crawling under her skin from here.

"Don't," Holloway rasped. "Jack, don't."

Jack froze, rifle still pointed at Lore. "Sir, please stand down."

Holloway's hands shook. "Jack—listen to me."

Lore hadn't moved. He watched the exchange with a smile playing at his lips.

Holloway's whole body locked. Every muscle seized at once, like he'd been hit with a live wire.

Dawn saw the oath take hold—blood blooming in his eyes, a thin red line from his nose, hands jerking up like a puppet. *So this is what Lore put in him*. No wonder the twisted bastard was smiling.

"Captain Sennett?" Jack's voice went sharp. "What are you—"

Holloway's mouth opened. Closed without a word. His hand was moving for his rifle.

"Go." The word tore loose from between his teeth. "Run."

But his body wasn't his anymore. The gun slid off his back smooth and fast, leveled at the enforcer boy's head.

Jack's eyes went wide. "Sir, stand down!"

"I can't—" Holloway's voice broke. Blood streamed from his nose, down his chin. "Jack, I can't—"

He was fighting it. Dawn saw it in every line of him. Tendons straining, shoulders tensed. His hand shook, but the rifle stayed level.

Jack saw it, too, just then.

"Captain," he said softly. "It's okay."

He really wasn't going to fight back. *Damn.* Holloway's pupils were blown wide. Tears and blood streaked his face. He stared at the boy like he was trying to remember this moment.

"I'm sorry," he whispered.

Then the rifle went off.

The shot cracked across camp. Half of Jack's face was gone. His horse screamed, reared, and dumped the body in the mud with a wet crash.

Holloway stayed standing, arms outstretched. Then his knees gave. He hit the ground hard, body convulsing.

"I'm sorry," he gasped into the mud. "I'm sorry, I'm sorry, I'm sorry—"

Like if he said it enough, it might change what he'd done.

The other four enforcers split up, found cover, took position. Holloway had trained them well.

Dawn dragged Talia behind the slag heap and dropped to one knee, both revolvers out. The first enforcer went down fast. Took two shots—shoulder, then chest. The second died behind a wagon. Three shots through the boards.

Two targets left.

Return fire cracked. She rolled right, emptied both cylinders, reloaded. Someone was shouting orders. Dawn tracked the voice, a female enforcer on horseback, turning toward the main building. Toward the settlers.

Dawn fired. Missed. The horse reared, broke her angle.

Fuck. Motion in her periphery. The other was circling around, trying to flank her.

She spun, fired without pausing to aim. Heard him hit the dirt, but he was still moving.

A settler bolted from the main building, pickax raised.

"Get down!" Dawn shouted.

The mounted enforcer's rifle cracked. The man's chest burst open in a blast of red spray. He dropped face-first in the mud.

The enforcer swung her rifle toward Dawn.

Dawn landed all three shots: throat, chest, face. The woman toppled backward off the saddle.

The last enforcer tried to run for it. Dawn tracked him. Forty yards. Fifty. She fired.

The man stumbled, dropped. Then silence. Just ringing ears and the taste of gunpowder.

A woman's wail cut through the silence. She was on the ground, pulling the mangled settler's body close. Blood soaked her dress. A child ran out, too, and started screaming.

A small crowd stared at the bodies. Five enforcers. One of their own.

Talia stared at the dead settler, then at her hands. Her shoulders curled forward. Good. Intentions didn't matter out here. Just consequences. The sooner the girl learned that lesson, the better.

Dawn wanted to leave. She'd warned Lore he'd get someone killed, and look what happened. He shut her down again.

"We stay," Lore said. "These people deserve a proper burial."

Ridge looked like he wanted to argue, but he eyed the bodies. Big enough mess, few enough hands. He gave a tight nod.

Holloway sat slumped against a wagon wheel, face gray, eyes vacant. Blood crusted across half his face. He stared at his hands. Talia knelt near him, but she avoided touching him.

The day crawled by. Lore dug the graves himself. Cleaned the bodies and set them to rest. By lastlight, all five enforcers and the settler were in the ground.

Folks gathered in a half circle around the graves, hats in hand. Some stared at the dirt. Others stared at Lore. He held the silence for longer than comfort allowed. When he spoke, his voice was deep and musical. It rolled over the crowd like a spell.

"These people didn't die because they were weak," Lore started off. "This world burns its brightest souls for fuel. That's hard to hear, but I respect your intelligence too much not to be honest with you."

Dawn hadn't watched him preach before, and she was surprised at how quick his words set in. The widow still wept, but softer now. A few people were nodding.

"I know you want to build walls against the pain of loss," Lore continued. "I've wanted that too." His voice dropped so folks had to lean in. "But pain is not your enemy. Pain is the gateway through which we access the divine."

Someone in the crowd whispered, "He's the prophet from Gateway."

The words jumped and caught on like fire in dry grass. Heads bowed. The mood in the air changed. Anger drained from their faces. Dawn's hands found her revolvers. She didn't draw, just felt their weight.

"Today we bury six bodies. Their pain is ended, but ours must not. Think about what I just said: Pain is not your enemy. When you avoid pain, when you mistake numbness for peace, you let survival make you smaller. Isn't that a kind of death?"

He was looking at Talia, and Dawn saw the moment the hook went in. Exactly what she needed to hear. No reassurance or gentle lies. The kind of truth that hurt. That's how he got them. Dogma just sharp enough to make folks feel brave.

"The true gods passed through agony," Lore said. "They endured loss, embraced sacrifice, and ascended to power. The false gods ran from pain and were consumed by it."

Holloway had been staring at the mud all afternoon. Now his head was up, eyes on Lore. Like a drowning man who sees a ship in the dark. *Fuck. He has them both.*

"May the true gods stand with us now." Lore stepped forward, stopping before the widow. "May we honor the dead by choosing to live. Feel it all. Carry what you can. That is how we outlive death itself. That is how we become impossible to kill."

The settlers had fallen silent. Then the widow nodded and squeezed her child's hand. More than one person was crying. Cold ran up Dawn's spine. She'd seen swindlers work a crowd. Lore was worse. He believed he spoke the truth.

When the crowd broke up, Holloway went straight to Jack's grave. Stood for a while with his hat in his hands. When he moved on, he picked up a fence post and drove it into the ground.

Lore grabbed an ax and went to work beside him. Two men who'd gotten people killed today, building something in the last of the light. She couldn't say if Lore was mad or brilliant. She knew for certain he was dangerous.

"Should've shot the bastards when I had the chance," she muttered under her breath.

Dawn was done asking permission to survive. Next time she saw a threat, she didn't plan to hold back.

They shared their food with the settlers. Let them keep the enforcers' horses too—all but Jack's, a white mare called Larkspur. Holloway didn't want to leave her, and Sorrel needed a mount.

Dawn avoided small talk as she packed her gear. She wanted this place behind her—the graves, the sermon, all of it. She watched Talia chatting with a few of the settlers as they tidied after dinner. Her eyes looked brighter. She even smiled once. Lore's words had done that.

They set out at firstlight. Mist rolled low over the slag heaps, and the camp quickly faded to gray nothing behind them. Lore led the column. Talia rode just behind him. Then Holloway, pale and silent. His hands shook on the reins. Sorrel rode behind him, just as broken. Poor man had nowhere to go but along with them. Dawn brought up the rear, revolver resting easy on her thigh, eyes on the road behind them.

Lore doesn't need chains. These people forge their own.

FIRST ONE'S FREE

VAELIS • 7 YEARS AGO

When she turned nineteen, Talent Salaren started signing *Talia* on her papers. The characters in the stories she studied had names like Elanwei and Althen. Never noun names like Talent. She was still Talent at home, but she savored the small act of rebellion. It made her feel more like a person and less like an object.

She wore black these days. Structured collars, dark lipstick, thick kohl her grandmother hated. When she dressed that way, people didn't look too closely at what was underneath. She attracted enough attention as the youngest graduate in the school's history. She taught Starscript seminars that students much older than her fought to attend. Her essays circulated through the Lyceum with little stars scribbled in the margins.

Praise made her uneasy, but she kept working harder, trying to deserve it.

The problem was her source material. Every approved text led back to the same narrow corridor of history. The hidden archive had ruined her. She'd tasted real mystery, real magic. Now the university's relics felt like toys. She told herself she needed more because her research demanded it. That sounded better than admitting she was restless.

That was the year Wren entered her life. He appeared in her office doorway on a rain-dark afternoon, dripping on her polished floors.

Talia didn't look up. "Office hours are posted outside."

"You're the one who reads dead languages, yeah?"

Her pen stilled. The dockside accent was out of place in the Upper City, let alone this deep into Lyceum grounds.

The boy was maybe ten, maybe even younger. He was skinny enough she doubted he'd seen three square meals a day in his life. There was mud on his boots, and the fishy smell of the docks clung to his coat. *Very much* out of place.

The rebellion was growing bolder and security was tighter than ever. She had no idea how he'd made it this far, and she should have called security on him.

"Starscript," she corrected. "That *dead language* is called Starscript. And you shouldn't be in here."

"Sure, sure." He slouched against her doorframe, eyeing the clay bowl on her desk. "Pretty. Shame it's fake."

"Excuse me?"

"The real ones hum," he said. "Yours doesn't."

She pushed her chair out as she stood up. "Who are you?"

"Wren." His smile had a gap in it. "I work the docks. Lots of crates come in. Sometimes stuff falls out, and I pick it up."

"That's illegal," she said automatically.

"You say illegal." He shrugged. "I say nobody misses it."

He stepped into her office, flicked the clay bowl with one dirty fingernail. "You want to see something older than this?" He pulled a scrap of paper from his pocket and held it out. An address in the Lower City. "Come tonight before sundown. First one's free."

He was gone before she could refuse.

For hours, she kept glancing at the address. She shouldn't go, obviously. But what if legitimate relics were rotting in some warehouse? She'd just look. It was just research.

The Lower City stank. Piss, rot, old smoke. Bodies pressed too close in narrow streets. Dim flux lamps threw shadows that made everything look haunted. Graffiti bled across brick walls:

THE GODS ARE DEAD. WAKE UP.
PENTARCHY LIES.

Talia's gaze jumped between the paper and the house numbers, trying to look less lost. Finally she found the address, a timber-sided townhouse with boarded-up windows. Wren sat on the porch.

Instead of going inside, he hopped to his feet and gestured for her to follow. He threaded through the crowd without looking back, and she followed. Turning around now would make her feel foolish. Plus, she was curious. Where was he leading her?

He finally paused in front of a heavy door. "Don't break anything expensive," he said over his shoulder. Then he yanked it open.

The whole room glowed blue.

There were tables heaped with relics—a mess of cracked ceramics, bone flutes, glass jars etched with Starscript so dense and delicate she wanted to run her fingers over it. Everything hummed faintly, a vibration she felt deep in her chest.

On a table in the middle of the room lay a round blue crystal the size of her fist with Starscript etched in parallel bands around it.

"Where did you get this?" she whispered, approaching the stone to get a closer look at the etchings.

"I thought you might like that one." Wren seemed pleased. "That's from Valta. They find those inside the ruins. The fae built houses on top of them."

She couldn't help it; she had to touch it. The moment she did, energy surged through the grooves—not just light but power, thrumming up her arm and into her chest. She gasped and pulled her hand back, but some of the power lingered. It felt like there were moths trapped behind her sternum.

"That's not possible. Flux is just fuel."

Wren was grinning. Heat curled under her skin. It felt like waking up. She wanted to touch it again. To take it apart and understand how it worked.

"This is dangerous," she finally said. "You shouldn't have it. I shouldn't—" Then: "How much?" The words just slipped out.

"Told you, first one's free." He pushed off the doorframe and stalked over to the table, wrapping the relic in a cloth and handing it to her. "You'll be back anyway."

Her heart fluttered the entire way home, and her satchel tugged at her shoulder. She locked the door and drew the curtains. She gathered all the books and papers cluttering her desk and piled them on the floor. Then she set the stone under her desk lamp.

She copied the script carefully—first in pencil for accuracy, then in ink. When she spoke the words in Starscript, a glow broke over her like firstlight. Silver and blue and gold, pouring through her fingers, flooding her veins. She felt it in her teeth, her blood, her bones. Every nerve lit up.

Then it cut out, and the room went dark.

She sat breathing hard, palms flat on the desk, staring at it.

Flux wasn't just fuel. It was some kind of magic. And she had touched it.

She didn't care if this was dangerous. Didn't care if it was illegal. She needed more.

Wren came back the next week, and the next. He learned what she wanted: the pieces that still hummed, the fragments that glowed in the dark. She paid whatever he asked.

That was around when the empathy started.

She had been holding the door open for a student when a flutter of the girl's worry brushed her thoughts. Later, her shoulder clipped someone else in the hall, and the man's shame hit her like cold water. More and more often, when she touched someone else, her skin would prickle with feelings that weren't hers.

She told herself she was working too hard. She was just overtired. There was no one she could tell, and even if she did, it was too ridiculous to say out loud. So she withdrew into herself, taking on a lighter teaching load, working on relics at night when the campus was empty.

"Knew you'd be a good customer," Wren said once, sifting coins with his clever dirty fingers.

"Bring me something rarer next time," she said, lifting her chin with all the false confidence in the world.

He always did. And she always needed it.

30

THE FLUX STORM

TALIA

Flux is neither divine nor magical, no matter what Pentarchy propaganda claims. It was produced by the elein *and absorbed into rocks and weather systems over millennia. Those gentle beasts are gone. Notice that the land around a spent flux mine is stripped of life. It does not replenish.*

— LORE TAVIS, *ON THE NATURE OF FLUX*,
UNPUBLISHED

They rode hard for three days. Once they'd cleared the foothills, they made decent time over the open prairie. They didn't see the wolves again, but howls threaded the nights, near enough that no one slept well.

The hills had been laced with small streams, but the Central Plains were dry. Sorrel had decided to ride with them as far as Heller's Ridge, and between five people and their horses, water quickly ran low.

The wolves' howls clung to Talia's nerves even in daylight. When Lore asked her to look for water with him, it was a relief to step away from camp. The prairie shimmered with flux-dusted blades of grass, bright and endless.

By midday the heat rippled the perfect horizon line. They'd found the faint edge of an ancient road but no sign of water.

Talia pulled the flux stone she'd found from her pocket and sketched its inscriptions as she rode, half to study, half to stay ahead of the intrusive thoughts: Riven under a pile of green cloaks, the ravaged caravan, the look on Holloway's face when he shot his friend. Starscript was easier than parsing emotions. Each translation gave her something clean to focus on.

"You're enjoying yourself," Lore said.

"This is all I ever wanted," she answered, tipping her chin up to feel the sun on her face.

His gaze slid over her—assessing, amused. "A dry prairie? If this is your dream, Talent, you've been starving yourself."

She tried to ignore him, scanning the horizon, but she saw nothing but brown grass and crumbling ruins. When she let herself glance in his direction, Lore was still looking at her.

They were out in the open when the wind died. The whole world went still. Then the sky darkened like a light had switched off. Lore was off his horse and moving toward her when the bolt of flux lightning hit.

It happened so fast, she didn't have time to scream. There was a blinding blue flash, and she felt bits of loose hair float around her face. A metallic taste flooded her mouth. Jonquil was rearing up, shrieking, but Lore already had her reins. He calmed the horse first and then tugged Talia out of the saddle.

"There was a stone structure back that way," he yelled over the wind. "If the horse spooks again, let her go. We're safer on foot."

They ran, the dry prairie churning to mud under their feet. When Talia tripped, Lore was there at her elbow, pulling her back up. Her pulse jumped. *Just from the flux storm. Just the lightning.*

The sky filled with blue fire behind them, chased immediately by a peal of thunder. Another strike. Fifty paces to their right the earth fountained up, blue flames licking grass.

Then the cluster of ruins was right in front of them, a few broken walls and a partially collapsed roof. It wasn't much, but it was stone. The walls weren't conductive, and the foundation stones should ground the flux in the air. They stumbled through an archway as a wall of rain slammed down behind them. Inside, stone muffled the roar. A few rivulets of water poured in through the broken spots in the ceiling, but it was mostly dry.

Talia braced her back against the wall. She wasn't used to

running, and her lungs were on fire. Water had soaked through every layer of her blouse and skirt and riding pants, and her braid had come undone. She was shaking so hard her back kept hitting the wall. Lore turned to check on the horses, who were shivering just inside the entrance.

"Are we safe now?" she asked.

"From the storm." He rubbed the horses' noses, making soothing sounds. Rain poured in silver curtains behind him.

Her brain finally caught up. They needed water. She blinked at the streams running down the stone. *Water*. She crossed to Jonquil and unhooked three waterskins from her saddle, propping them under the gaps in the roof. When she turned back around, Lore was watching her.

"Good thinking," he said with that smirk, just half a smile, that made her think he was holding something back.

"What?" she asked, but he shook his head.

They huddled in the back corner of the shelter, shoulder to shoulder, watching the rain fall in sheets outside. Over time, the roar of the rain dimmed to a drumbeat, then staccato tapping, and finally to a soft crush.

When a stretch of time had gone by without a flash of lightning, Lore stood and started gathering bits of wood and grass. Talia frowned when he took one of their precious flux stones out of his saddlebag.

"There's no point in hoarding flux and freezing to death," he said. "I do wonder what it will take for you to see yourself as worthy of comfort."

He stacked his ragged kindling with practiced, efficient movements. She watched his long fingers coax flames from the flux stone, and she didn't look away fast enough when he caught her staring. The half smile flashed again.

"How did you learn all this?" she asked, desperate to fill the quiet.

The fire flickered to life. "I grew up in the Lower City. On the streets. You figure out how to survive, or you don't."

She'd been to the Lower City a few times with Wren, and it was a wretched place. She tried to imagine being a child in that place.

"What was that like?" The words spilled out, and she immediately regretted the question.

He didn't hesitate. "It was like being small in a world built for bigger people."

Her throat felt tight. She'd grown up blissfully unaware of the class disparities in Vaelis, but the more she learned, the more uneasy she had felt about what her family's comforts cost. She was sure that if she reached over to take Lore's hand right now, she'd feel a surge of bitterness. At least that's what she would feel in his place. He must hate her.

He went on in a quieter voice. "I knew of you, of course. Talent Salaren, the Starscript prodigy. They put your essays in the newspapers. I read them whenever I could."

The fire popped.

"What you wrote about the parallels between fae mythology and orthodox religious rituals led me to Valta, in fact."

"Ironic, isn't it? The Starscript prodigy who wasn't allowed to advance her own research. You had more freedom than I did, then." She looked up, startled by how her own words came out. "I know it sounds petty compared to—"

He cut her off. "A cage is a cage." Then he looked up, meeting her eyes. "Even if the bars sparkle."

She searched his face for mockery, but it wasn't there. This, right here, was dangerous. He shouldn't know her so well. This same man had hurt Holloway with blood magic, but she didn't feel repelled. She felt deeply curious. He was a puzzle she wanted to solve.

She hadn't noticed when it happened, but they were sitting closer now, leaning into the fire. She was acutely aware of the space between their knees. Her skin prickled as if he was looking at her, but she focused on the fire.

"The other day, you asked why Riven stayed behind," he said suddenly. "Do you still want to know?"

The question surprised her. "Yes, of course. No one will tell me."

"He felt guilty for his part in the warrant. It wasn't random, Talent. Someone was reporting on your work, our meetings."

The fire crackled between them, and Talia found it hard to breathe. The space felt too small, the ceiling felt too low. Riven had died saving her. Was Riven the reason she needed saving? The contradiction sent her mind spinning, searching for the logic it couldn't find.

"Dawn and Holloway both knew," Lore said quietly. "I'm surprised they didn't tell you."

Talia's hands were shaking. She pressed them flat on her thighs. If Holloway had kept this from her, he had a reason. He always tried to protect her, even if he did it wrong sometimes. Lore didn't say anything on accident, himself. He had a reason too.

"Why are you telling me this?" She concentrated on keeping her voice steady. "I think you want to make me angry. To isolate me from my friends, again."

She reached over and took his hand, on impulse. She told herself she wanted to read his reaction, but her whole arm tingled when she made contact. His emotions shocked her—he was thrilled. She'd expected defensiveness, maybe anger, but he was genuinely delighted that she'd accused him.

He didn't pull back. Instead, he slowly threaded his fingers through hers. He was watching her face with a funny expression, like he'd forgotten his script.

"This is what you do," she said, looking down at their interlaced fingers. "You break people down until they lean on you."

The noise of pattering rain and crackling fire filled the space, and instead of denying it, he grinned.

"Yes." He said it with force, like she'd cracked a puzzle. "I do isolate. I provoke. It's how I test what people are made of. Some crumble. Some sharpen."

He leaned forward, bringing his other hand over hers. The firelight carved shadows across his face, catching the gold in his eyes.

"You." His voice dropped low. "You sharpen."

He said it like he was pleased she'd challenged him. Like he wanted her to do it again. She couldn't look away from his mouth when he smiled like that. He was looking at her like she was capable. Like he couldn't wait to see what else she could do.

"That doesn't make it untrue." He leaned back from the fire, releasing her hand. "Riven did betray you. Repeatedly. Dawn and Holloway are keeping secrets. And I want you to rely on me. What you do with that information is up to you."

He wasn't lying to spare her. He was trusting her with the unfiltered truth, and it almost felt like respect. Some part of her—the part that was tired of being handled gently, tired of being shielded—woke up.

He's very good at this. She met his eyes, determined not to give in so easily.

"If you want me to rely on you, then stop playing games," she said firmly. "It's insulting."

Her heart raced, and she didn't know why. She wasn't sure it mattered whether it was anger or attraction. They felt equally dangerous.

She stood, forcing her legs steady. She had to put distance between them because she was dying to know what he was thinking now, and if she stayed within reach—if she touched him again—

"I need air." The words came out strangled.

She pushed past him, nearly stumbling in her rush.

The rain had slowed to a fine mist, leaving the whole world clean and sharp. She stopped and leaned her forehead against Jonquil's neck. The mare's earthy scent steadied her.

Riven had reported on her, gotten her exiled, then sacrificed himself to buy her escape. He'd cared about her and betrayed her and saved her, all three at once. The contradictions sat there, jagged and hurtful, refusing to add up.

And Holloway had known. He knew how she spiraled when she didn't have all the information, and he'd let her wonder and grieve without giving her the truth. That almost hurt more.

She heard footsteps, but she didn't look back.

"I underestimated you," Lore said. "That's a first for me."

She didn't answer, she couldn't. She was finding it hard to breathe. She heard him take another step. With Jonquil there, she had nowhere to go. She turned around just as he moved into her space. Their eyes were level.

"You don't have to like me. But understand, I don't waste honesty on people who can't take it."

She should have pulled away. Instead, she stood there, back pressed against Jonquil's flank, watching a raindrop trail along his temple.

"I'd like us to be allies, Talent. Maybe even friends. The kind that make each other stronger." He smelled like amber and smoke, and his chest was nearly touching hers. They were the same height, and if she tipped forward just a little—

She did pull away then, pushing past him and putting the horse between them. "I think we should go back."

He frowned, just for a second. Then he smiled, like he knew a secret.

"Maybe we should," he said. "If that's the thing you want." Then he moved to clean up the fire.

She could tell he was trying to use her. He probably had been since she met him. At the same time, he was the only person who treated her questions like the main event instead of a distraction. Who trusted her to be strong enough to hear the truth instead of some watered-down version of it. And some part of her responded to his confidence in her like a flame to fresh air.

That was the problem.

Not the fact that he would use her. She could see the pattern of manipulation, and she wasn't falling for it, exactly. The problem was that even when she saw what he was doing, even when she knew better, she wanted to see how far it would go.

She should have been more afraid of that. Of him. Of herself. But she was curious what would happen if she let herself be sharp.

They didn't speak on the ride back. Dawn met them at the edge of camp, her eyes flicking over the mud, the bruises, the strange new energy between them.

"He didn't hurt you, did he?" she asked.

"No." Talia answered too fast.

Dawn narrowed her eyes. "Be careful, Talia. That one is good at making his choices feel like yours."

"I can handle myself," Talia said, swinging off Jonquil and unhooking the waterskins. She'd been able to fill twenty before the storm ended. The water would buy them a couple days, at least.

"That's what he wants you to think," Dawn called to her back. "And he likes a challenge."

Talia tried to focus, but her pulse was still racing, and her hands were shaking again. She told herself it was exhaustion from the storm. The shock of the flux strike. Riven's betrayal. Anything but the truth.

The truth was, she'd been alone with Lore for hours, soaking in his attention. And gods, if she didn't want it to happen again.

31

STEALING BREAD

DAWN

Any lesser person can be grateful for good fortune. Be grateful instead for the heartache, for the pain, for the mistakes you loathe to face. These things sharpen you.

— *COLLECTED SAYINGS OF LORE TAVIS*, COMPILED BY THE ACOLYTES OF STARFALL SANCTUARY

Three days after the storm, Dawn watched Holloway portion out the last rations. A handful of dried corn was nothing. She chewed the kernels one at a time to distract from the noises coming from her stomach. The horses were worse off. If they didn't find food soon, they'd be walking.

The sun burned overhead, a flat white coin in the empty sky. Shimmering heat blurred the horizon line. Lore rode ahead. His cloak was drawn close despite the heat. Talia's hands shook on the reins. Holloway's jaw was clenched so tight she heard his teeth grind.

Riven would have said something sharp to break the silence. Made her laugh against her will. When the wind shifted, she swore she heard his voice. He'd taken more than one bullet for her. It killed her to think that he'd fallen and she'd just watched.

He couldn't be gone. He was too tough to die, too stubborn to stay down. She wouldn't believe it until she saw a body.

A twist of smoke curled into the sky. She sat up in her saddle and whistled to Lore.

He shaded his eyes to see. "A camp?"

"Think it's a homestead," Dawn said. She caught the scent of woodsmoke and warm bread drifting on the breeze.

The cabin was set in a ragged field, children picking rows of late-season corn. A hard life, but they had food. Lore rode down alone. The man who came to the door closed it behind him. Wind brought the rhythm of voices, not the words. When Lore came back, his jaw had gone hard. He shook his head.

Talia straightened. "Did you offer to pay?"

"They have no need for coin. Winter is coming on, and they've got seven mouths."

Holloway exhaled slow. "Okay then, we move on."

"On what horses?" Dawn asked. "Jonquil is already faltering."

He turned on her, his voice raw. "So we steal from children? Is that how we operate now?"

"Children can survive a lot." Did she like it? No. But staying alive was the priority here. She wasn't going to have this conversation with Holloway, of all people. He'd never gone hungry a day in his life.

Lore spoke slow and even. "Nobody wants this, but we cannot go on without provisions, and we cannot go back. The gods set us on this path, and we must see it through. By whatever means."

Dawn agreed with the sentiment, but the calm in his voice made her skin crawl. Same tone he'd used over those graves, marking grief as sacred. Men with his kind of conviction were the most dangerous. They could make the worst atrocities feel holy.

Holloway's gaze darted to each of their faces. "This is your faith?"

"This is reality." To Lore's credit, he did not look away.

Lore went down again. When the man lifted his rifle, Lore raised a hand. The air shimmered. There was a crack as the gun shattered, wood and metal dissolving to splinters. The woman started screaming, and the children were hauled inside.

Dawn's hands went to her revolvers. She knew Lore had power, but this was something else. If he could do that to a rifle, what else could he unmake? Maybe it wasn't so bad the flux crystals were running low.

Lore's voice echoed from the doorway. "Take what we need. Nothing more."

Holloway grimaced and rubbed his palm. Dawn wondered if the blood oath was hurting him or if he obeyed on his own. She watched him pull out his coin purse, hefting it once before setting it on a fence post. The farmer might not be able to use it, but Holloway needed to try.

Dawn moved toward the smokehouse when Talia's voice stopped her.

"We're really doing this?"

Dawn turned. Talia sat rigid on Jonquil, staring at the little house.

"You want to starve?" Dawn asked.

"I want—" Talia's voice cracked. "I want people to stop treating me like I can't handle the truth. If we're robbing these people, just say so."

Dawn went still. She clearly had something bigger on her mind. Lore must have told her about Riven. *Shit.* Talia looked up at the sky, avoiding her eyes.

"We're getting food," Dawn said. "Don't overthink it."

Talia stayed mounted as Dawn stepped on into the smokehouse. The scent of smoking meat turned her stomach and made her hungrier at the same time. She found a burlap sack in one corner and started filling it up. Behind her, Lore stood at the gate and watched Talia, his shadow stretching long across the yard.

Holloway worked in silence, hands shaking worse now as he tied sacks of cornmeal, bread, potatoes. Kept dropping knots, retying them. Sorrel stepped in wordlessly, set a hand on Holloway's, and took over. Dawn watched him gather some herbs and a cut of fresh meat. It was nice to have a real cook with them.

They loaded the last sack onto the horses. Dawn pulled the final cinch tight. The family huddled in the open doorway. The father's rifle lay in splinters at his feet. The smallest girl clutched a wooden toy, staring at them with shock as they rode away. Something about the scene got under Dawn's skin, and as Brimstone fell into a steady rhythm, she was transported to a memory she hadn't visited in a very long time.

The waif ran on the balls of her feet, cobblestones pressing hard and round against her toes. Not even the glass in the gutter was sharp enough to pierce her bare soles.

When footsteps sounded, she ducked into an alley and crouched low, breath shallow. A boy came into view, maybe her age but taller, with the look of someone who'd eaten yesterday and the day before. He carried a heel of bread, still steaming where he'd torn it from the loaf.

She sprang on him. Her teeth sank into his wrist. Instead of dropping the bread, he caught her arm in a steady grip. His eyes were gray, and they didn't blink.

"Are you some kind of dog?" he asked, cocking his head to the side.

"I'm a dragon," she hissed. "And I'm going to eat you."

He laughed, soft and startled, then broke his bread in half and pressed the bigger piece into her hand. "This'll taste better. And stop biting people, it's not nice."

She tore into the bread so fast she choked. He didn't move, just watched her swallow and cough. Then he handed her his half too.

She'd thought hunger only made people meaner. He proved her wrong. Something sharp caught in her throat when he showed up the next day. She wiped at her eyes, furious with herself for feeling anything at all.

The gray-eyed boy came back again and again with bread, salt pork, whatever scraps he could scrounge together. He never stayed long, but he always shared. She still growled at him, but she'd follow that boy anywhere.

Dawn jolted from her reverie as they pulled off the road. First the faerie story about Elanwei, now some sappy childhood memory. She was going sentimental, and she didn't like it.

They passed through five broken pillars that Dawn recognized. Ashenfell. Fuck, they were too far west. She made a note to turn them north in the morning. The boundary of the Whisperwood was always shifting, and they wouldn't want to cut too close.

Sorrel built the fire and cooked the fresh meat over it. Lore passed out the portions. Before he ate, he held his plate loose in both hands and bent his head.

"For this food, we give thanks," he murmured. "Not because it was freely given, but because it keeps us alive. May the hard choices fall on those strong enough to bear them."

Holloway ate without hesitation, shoulders tight, eyes fixed on the fire. Talia took her portion and moved off. Sat with her back to them.

The first bite filled Dawn's mouth with salt and smoke. It hit every empty place in her body. She'd gone longer than a few days without food. She'd done worse things than steal from children. Every feast had a cost. She'd add this one to her tab.

She took first watch, let the others settle. Tomorrow they'd eat stolen food again. And the next day. And they'd survive. Out here, guilt hurt less than hunger.

The moon rose, nearly full. Dawn walked the perimeter, hands on her holsters. Movement on the ridgeline caught her eye, and both guns came up.

"It's not nice to shoot people."

The voice stopped her cold.

Riven stepped into the moonlight. He looked like shit—face tight, shirt torn and crusted with blood. He was favoring his left leg.

Relief hit her so hard she had to catch her breath.

"You bastard," she coughed out. "I thought you died."

How *had* he survived, let alone made it this far? Over those mountains, across the dry grassland. They were well off the Queen's Way.

"Not yet." He swayed, caught himself. "Is she okay—"

"Talia? She's alive. For now. Lore's got his hooks in her."

He looked past her toward the camp, where Talia slept. "This is my nightmare," he said, barely above a whisper. "I failed before to save our friends, and it's happening again. I don't know how to stop it."

"Well, you're not invited over." Dawn's grip tightened on her guns. "Lore will kill you. Or have Holloway do it. He made the kid take a fucking blood oath."

Riven grimaced.

"What were you thinking?" she asked, punching him on the arm. He felt solid. "Giving Lore's name to the enforcers? He put a hit out on you. Asked me to handle it."

Riven sighed. "Want to take a shot? Best chance you're gonna get."

When Dawn glared, the bastard just opened his arms wide and grinned. She looked him over again, then she reached into her pack. "You'd better take this," she said, pulling out the bread they'd stolen. Shoved it at his chest, hard, so he had to grab it.

He looked down at the bread in his hands. Then up at her.

"Take it. Just"—she paused—"stay close. This whole thing's going bad. I can smell it."

They didn't need to trade more words, the gesture said plenty. Her gray-eyed friend nodded, took the bread, and stepped away. She waited until she lost sight of him in the dark before turning back for camp.

Made sense, she supposed. Why he'd stayed. Why he'd made the calls he did, maddening as they were. Riven had been lost a long time, and now he'd found someone worth protecting again. He deserved it.

She'd kept his betrayal from Talia once. Tomorrow, she'd have to lie about his loyalty. Add that to her tab too.

32

WOLVES

TALIA

I will say plainly what my colleagues will not: the fluxborn are not animals. Whether they are sentient, I cannot say. But they count. They coordinate. They seek revenge.

— *FLORA & FAUNA OF THE VALTA INTERIOR,*
VERACITY NIN, 409 AC

Talia woke choking on someone else's terror.

She couldn't tell where it was coming from, maybe the edge of camp? Her blankets tangled around her legs, and she struggled to get free, to get air in her lungs. Had she imagined it? Then a scream tore the night open.

Outside, Holloway swore as he fought to calm the shrieking horses. A tent was ripped open, streaks of blood on the ground outside. Dawn was already moving—hair wild, revolver in hand.

Another scream sounded, farther away now. Emotions latched onto her out of the dark—terror, confusion, helplessness. Talia stumbled, grabbing Holloway's shoulder on her way down.

"It's Sorrel," Holloway panted, helping her up. "This way."

Talia reached back to grab her boots and ran without lacing them. They turned a corner and skidded to a stop on a ledge where the ancient city simply—stopped.

Beyond the last row of foundation walls, the ground fell away into a jagged black gash. Blood trailed down into darkness.

Something was moving down there. *Many* somethings. Shapes shifted among the rocks, and the scrape of claws echoed.

Sorrel's terror spiked again in Talia's chest. He was still alive.

"We have to go now," she said. Her voice was shaking. "I can feel him down there."

Holloway didn't ask how that was possible. She didn't explain.

A narrow gravel path cut down the steep slope. Talia's unlaced boots wobbled on her ankles. The air from below smelled musty, of wet fur, old blood, and something sour that made her throat close. She half slid, half climbed down the broken slope.

Sorrel's fear guttered and flared like a dying candle. Every time it dipped, Talia's stomach dropped with it.

A growl rumbled from her left. Very close. She froze.

Rocks skittered off the side of the path, bouncing into darkness. A pale shape moved at the edge of her vision. There and gone.

Another growl answered from her right. Then one from below. The tones repeated, almost like a conversation.

The path narrowed as they approached the bottom of the ravine. Walls pressed close on both sides, slick with moss. Above, Ashenfell's broken skyline shrank to a thin strip of stars.

Lore was just behind her, and his hand found her shoulder. "Keep moving, Talent. I'm with you."

Sorrel's mind flared again with pain so bright it whited out her own vision. It felt like her own bones were cracking. Then his terror dropped. Flickered. Held on by a thread.

"Faster," Talia gasped.

Just before they reached the bottom, a sound echoed around them. Not a scream this time. Bone cracking. Wet. Messy. Sucking and tearing. Then a gurgling breath that didn't resolve. Her tether to Sorrel's mind snapped and went quiet.

The absence hit her in the chest. She bent forward, hands on her knees, trying to breathe around the hollow where she'd felt him.

They found the body just around the corner. What was left of it. He lay at the mouth of a tunnel, propped against the wall, throat torn, chest opened, organs spilling out in a pool of red. His right leg was gone below the knee. A thin trail of steam rose in the chill air. He'd been alive moments ago.

Dawn stepped over the ravaged body and stalked into the darkness. "I'm getting his fucking foot."

Talia hesitated. Dawn was already gone. Holloway and Lore exchanged a look, then Holloway's hand found her shoulder.

"You okay?" he asked softly.

"Yeah," she said, swallowing back the lump in her throat. "Let's just get Dawn."

The dark tunnel opened into a vast cavern, and Talia gasped. It was beautiful in a way, tiers of rock cascading down the far wall, green moss glowing with eerie light. The floor was scattered with bones. Old ones picked clean. Fresh ones still speckled with blood and bits of flesh. Movement flickered at the edge of the light. A shadow detached from deeper shadow. Then another.

Wolves materialized from the darkness, shapes shifting in the rock formations above. Talia's empathy brushed against their minds. She didn't find the frenzied hunger she expected. Instead, a feeling of calm settled behind her ribs, a sense of *waiting*. Then a growl rolled from behind them. Another from the right. A third from overhead.

Without warning, a single wolf lurched toward them.

Dawn's revolver cracked. The wolf twisted mid-leap, hit the ground, whimpered, scrambled back.

Two more shapes darted in. Holloway's rifle boomed, and they scattered.

"They're testing us," Holloway said. "Back up. Slowly."

Talia turned toward the entrance they'd come through, but the path was blocked. Another wolf appeared at the side tunnel to their left. Talia's skin prickled. The wolves' minds pressed closer. They were focused and patient. Clearly working together.

"This isn't an accident," she whispered. "They want us here."

Then she saw why. At the back of the cavern, tucked under an overhang, a hollow was filled with small shapes all huddled together. Pups. Five of them, with round bellies and oversized paws. Watching with bright, curious eyes.

One had a human leg between its front feet, gnawing with

clumsy puppy enthusiasm. Another tugged at the boot, tail wagging when the laces came free.

The pups' minds were simple: hunger, satisfaction, curiosity. Her stomach churned. Sorrel was just meat to them. One stumbled forward on unsteady paws. Made a soft chuffing sound.

"We need to—" Talia began.

Another wolf lunged, jaws snapping. Dawn fired. It dropped, but the others surged forward.

The world narrowed to teeth and claws. Wolves surged from every shadow. Holloway fired, reloaded, fired again. Each shot bought them less and less time. Dawn's revolvers cracked in the distance, deeper in the cavern.

Lore's hand found Talia's shoulder, a steady weight. He stayed there, his other hand throwing fire. A wolf veered away, yelping, fur smoking, and Lore dropped a spent flux crystal.

"Stay by me," he commanded.

Another wolf lunged. Holloway took a shot and it dropped.

But more came. So many more.

A furry body slammed into Holloway from the side. He went down hard. Razor-sharp jaws snapped for his throat. He drove the rifle stock into its skull once, twice. It yelped but kept coming. Lore threw fire with his free hand. The wolf recoiled, snarling, and Holloway scrambled back.

Then one broke through the line. Flux-blue eyes locked on Talia. Intelligent. Determined. It lunged.

Talia didn't think. Her mind reached out—clumsy, desperate—and grabbed hold of the wolf's mind. Either panic or proximity, or both, reversed the flow of emotions, and she shoved with every awful feeling she had. Sorrel's terror. The caravan bodies. The feral certainty she would die here.

The wolf flinched mid-leap. Its body stuttered, claws raking air inches from her face. Holloway's rifle stock came down. Bone crunched. The wolf dropped, and pain lanced through Talia's skull. She gasped, hitting the wall behind her. Lore's head snapped toward her, pupils blown wide.

"That," he said through his teeth. "Do that again."

She felt the praise sink into her chest, warm and thrilling, but she couldn't do it again. She didn't know what she'd done, and she could barely think through the pain behind her eyes.

Holloway's rifle clicked empty. He swung it like a club, driving one wolf back as another circled around. Lore threw fire again, but it flared weaker this time. His hand on Talia's shoulder shook, and she watched in horror as black seeped up from his fingernails, up the back of his hand. *Burnout.*

Through the chaos, Talia saw Dawn fighting toward the back of the cavern, farther and farther away from them.

"Dawn, fall back!" Holloway roared, but she ignored him.

A wolf lunged at Lore. He turned to meet it, his grip leaving Talia's shoulder for just a moment. Fire burst from both hands. The wolf twisted away, singed. When Lore turned back, his face was gray. Sweat tracked down his temples.

"We can't hold this," Lore gritted out.

Talia pressed her back against the wall, weaponless. Useless.

A wolf circled to their right, cutting off any retreat. Another moved in from the left. Their eyes gleamed in the dark, their fur glowing green in the strange moss-light. They could be patient. They knew they had won.

Holloway's shoulder was bleeding heavily. Lore's power was spent. They were going to die here. A massive wolf stepped forward, shoulders low. Her blue eyes fixed on Talia. She watched the wolf's haunches clench, gathering herself to spring.

Then silver light exploded from the side tunnel, and Talia saw a ghost.

Riven.

He launched into the cavern, twin blades shining, his shirt already dark with blood. His movements were unsteady, but his blades found their marks. He hit the big wolf mid-leap, drove one blade into her ribs, then twisted, using its momentum to swing around and open her throat with the other. They went down together in a spray of blood.

Two more wolves turned on him, and he came up fighting. He slashed, spun, drove them back with sheer physical power.

"Move!" he shouted, jerking his head toward the tunnel behind him. "Get her out of here!"

Holloway wrapped his good arm around Talia's waist and hauled her toward the open path that Riven had cleared of wolves. Lore stumbled after them. Riven held the tunnel mouth. Somewhere behind them, Dawn's revolvers cracked once, then twice. She was still fighting, beyond their reach.

They scrambled up the slope, gravel sliding away under their feet. Riven staggered behind them. Each step was slower than the last. His silver light dimmed. When they reached the top, he fell to his knees, blades clattering onto the stone. Blood soaked the entire left side of his body.

"Where's Dawn?" Talia asked, looking around. Panic twisted in her stomach.

Then a gunshot cracked up from the dark.

Sharp. Final. Echoing off ruins. Talia held her breath.

A second shot.

A third.

Fourth.

Fifth.

Somehow, her empathy registered each little death. Confusion flared, then nothing. Fear spiked, then nothing. Five times, almost too fast to process. When Dawn emerged from the ravine, she walked steady. Holstered her revolvers as she reached them, then brushed grit from her palms.

"The pups? Really?" Talia asked, but Dawn just stalked past her and rounded on Riven.

"You just couldn't stay away, could you?" she snarled. "I told you to hang back."

"Wait," Talia said. "You knew he was alive?" Dawn kept ignoring her.

"Seemed like you could use a hand." Riven coughed, blood

tracking a line down his chin. Then his eyes rolled back, and he slumped to the ground. Talia screamed.

"No—" Dawn dropped to her knees, but Lore shoved her over and took her place at Riven's side.

"You still have that flux crystal you found, Talent?" Lore's voice was unrecognizable, so hoarse it took Talia a moment to understand him.

She nodded frantically, pulled it out of her pocket—Riven's coat pocket—and placed it in Lore's outstretched hand.

"Last one. I can only fix the surface wounds. It'll have to be enough."

He pressed both palms flat on Riven's chest with the flux stone between them and murmured. Light poured into the wound just as dark veins spiderwebbed farther up Lore's arm. He swayed on his knees, cutting the spell short.

"That's all we get," he gasped.

Riven's breathing came steadier. Blood had stopped streaming down his side, and there were spots of pink on his cheeks.

"Why did you save him?" Talia whispered. Lore had done everything he could to undermine Riven. It made no sense.

"We're a week from Valrotala. We need every sword. And there are no"—he coughed—"degrees of burnout."

No degrees of burnout. Once burnout set in, it progressed. Lore might as well keep casting at this point. But she couldn't imagine Lore giving up. It felt like there was something he wasn't saying. It seemed to Talia, true or not, like he'd saved Riven for her.

They returned to camp, plenty of night left to go. Dawn kept watch. Lore tended to Holloway's shoulder the old fashioned way—with bandages—then wrapped his own wounds. He worked one-handed, tearing strips of cloth with his teeth. Riven lay by the fire, chest barely moving. Even after Lore's healing, blood seeped through the bandages. Talia sat apart, arms around her knees.

The fire crackled between them all, throwing sparks. Dawn sauntered up behind her, and Talia didn't look back.

"You're angry," Dawn said. "About the wolves?"

"The pups were innocent." Talia's throat felt raw.

"They were small predators. Give them a year or two, they'd hunt every road from here to the coast."

"You don't know that!"

"I know what smart hunters do." Dawn's voice was hard. "They learn. Adapt. Kill more efficiently. That pack was smart enough to lay a trap for us. Imagine each of those pups leading its own pack."

"So we just kill them? Because they might be dangerous someday?"

"Yes." No hesitation. "Before they kill us. That's how survival works."

"Then what makes us better than they are?"

"Nothing." Talia smelled Dawn light a twist of *savuthe*, heard her take a deep breath. "You're mixing up 'good' and 'not dead.'"

"You're right," Talia said quietly. "I would have spared the pups. And maybe that'd be naive of me." She looked at Riven bleeding by the fire. At Lore's ravaged arm. "Or maybe we'd be fine. And they would be too. They were intelligent, Dawn."

"So are humans. And they do plenty of damage." Dawn inhaled, and smoke curled around her face. "Hate me all you like, but you're alive to do it."

Talia pressed the heel of her hand to her chest. She'd done something new with her power tonight when she pushed into that wolf's mind. She would have kept going if she'd known how—it had been life or death. But there was a difference between fighting for your life and killing the way Dawn did.

"What's the point of surviving if you have to be a monster to do it?" Talia asked.

Dawn didn't argue. She just tossed away her smoke and stalked into the darkness with a scoff. Talia hugged her knees to her chest and smiled. It had been a horrific night, but she was getting sharper. That part felt good.

33

TRUTH OR BLOOD

DAWN

It's said of the Whisperwood: 'Those that enter find what they've lost and join it.' The boundaries are rumored to shift around unwary travelers. Most folklore has a grain of truth at its core—the wilds of Valta are treacherous.

— *THE DEFINITIVE GUIDE TO PRE-CROSSING FOLKLORE*, FEN ALDAINE, 399 AC

The Whisperwood was fucking with them, and it wasn't Dawn's fault.

Lore had been in bad shape at breakfast that morning. Riven was worse. Talia refused to speak to Dawn and the others followed her lead, so Holloway stepped up to play captain. His voice went clipped and arrogant in a way she did not appreciate. They had two choices, he said—turn due north, hit the Queen's Way, and proceed west on the road to Heller's Ridge. Or cut the corner and head straight for town.

"North is the only choice," Dawn insisted. She tried to explain about the nightmare forest with fuzzy edges, but the soldier boy fucking interrupted her.

"Tally is worried for our injured," he'd said. "We should take the shortest path."

His precious *Tally* was being a stubborn prick, so Dawn's warning went ignored. Now they were trapped. Even the horses knew it—ears flicking, eyes rolling white. Smart beasts. At least someone was paying attention.

"Still with us, old man?" Dawn asked. She caught Riven's shoulder just as he pitched forward in his saddle. He was riding

Larkspur now that Sorrel had no use for her. Poor girl's riders didn't stay alive long.

He cracked one eye open. "Oh, takes more than this." His hand squeezed her wrist. Dawn tied him on, just in case.

Lore wasn't much better. Black veins branched from his wrist to above his elbow. Sick-sweat hung in a cloud around him. Dawn told herself she didn't care, but she caught herself checking his pulse. Burnout was a nasty way to go, even for him.

The forest was wrong. No other word for it. The sunlight came through weak and gray. The horses' hooves made no sound, like the ground wasn't solid. When she spat, a coppery taste stuck to her tongue. The fog thickened, curled, licked at her calves.

"Cut that out," she growled at whatever. The fog. The trees.

When the road split, Dawn's temper was up. Twelve paths ahead. Twelve identical dead ends. She'd seen this before, illusions that ate feelings like fuel. Not great with a crew this emotional.

"It's you," Riven whispered, staring into the forest.

Dawn looked where he was looking. Nothing there. Poor bastard was seeing figments. Then Dawn saw her own.

Sunlight. Real sunlight, not this gray shit. Ehrue sat in the grass, hair loose around her shoulders. Two boys wrestled by her feet. A little girl laughed—white hair like Ehrue's, dimpled chin like—

No.

Dawn's breath caught. Everything she'd lost. The forest had found the only thing she wanted and ripped it from her chest. She slid off Brimstone's back. Took a step toward the clearing and felt her foot slip forward like it was soft sand, tugging her in.

"Don't move!" Holloway's voice cracked across the clearing. "Nobody take another step!"

The vision shattered. Her family vanished. The forest pressed in again, darker and hungrier. It sucked at her ankle as she pulled back. Branches pressed closer, and thorns caught at her coat.

"Fuck!" Dawn yelled, yanking her sleeve back. The branches *pulsed* when she said it.

"There's a pattern," Talia said, staring at Dawn. "Every time you get mad, the forest feels it. We all need to stay calm."

"Yeah? Good luck with that." Dawn laughed under her breath as she climbed back onto Brimstone.

Of course no one listened, or else they had no fucking self-control. They rode on best they could, and the forest went right on thrashing. Jasmine bloomed in Riven's wake, reaching for Talia. Flux sparked whenever Talia's gaze slid to Lore.

"What happened to staying calm?" Dawn asked as blue sparks crackled around Talia's head. Whatever that said about Talia's thoughts, it wasn't something pure.

"Will you shut up?" Talia snapped.

Dawn raised her eyebrows. Everyone here wanted to protect that girl, and she wanted to throw herself at Lore. That was fucking funny. Then Riven slouched in his saddle, deadweight on the ties.

Dawn turned back and shook him. "Damn it. Not now."

His eyes opened. "You know"—he coughed—"how it works."

"Are you seriously lecturing me right now?"

His mouth twitched. "Thought you might listen...if I was dying." His breath hitched. "You have to...let go."

She snorted. "I'm fine. You're the one bleeding all over your horse."

"Forgive yourself." His eyes closed. "She would." Then his body went slack again.

Dawn felt a spike of cold, then prickling heat. *Don't panic. He's alive. We'll get out of here, then get help.*

The path opened into a clearing that was even stranger. Birches ringed the space, roots knotted to create a sort of arena. The air felt off. Cold and still as a crypt. Bones jutted from the moss.

Holloway's horse balked. "We're not the first to get lost here."

No shit. Dawn felt that quicksand pull again, tugging her forward. The forest wanted her here.

The fog pulled together at the center. It thickened into a column, then a shape. Bark and shadow, seven feet tall, eyes like burning coals. The stink of rot and old blood rolled off it. Dawn's hand found her revolvers, one on each side. Her fingers traced their etchings like a little prayer. She might not believe in gods—old, true, or otherwise—but her sidearms had always come through.

"Truth or blood," the thing creaked. *A dryad*, she realized. Same category as blood magic, weird and fucked.

Holloway slipped off his horse and stepped forward, all soldierly calm. "We mean no harm. We only ask for passage."

The dryad tilted her head. Runes flared down her arm. "Lies."

Roots erupted under Holloway's boots, spiraling up his legs. He hit the ground hard. The vines burrowed and bit through fabric. He cried out in pain, and Dawn smelled fresh blood.

"Let him go!" Talia shouted, but the air around her shimmered, locking her in place.

Dawn raised her gun. The dryad turned those ember eyes on her. The weight of its stare squeezed her heart.

"Ancient one," the thing said. "Speak. Truth or blood."

Dawn's gut clenched. She glanced around at her companions, but they seemed more alarmed by the talking tree than by what it had called her.

"Dawn, it's you," Talia gasped. "The forest is reacting to you."

Dawn flashed her teeth. "Sure, blame me. I told you to avoid this fucking place."

Roots started twisting around the horses' legs, and they screamed with panic. Branches bent low. The fog surged higher, so cold it burned. Sound went muffled.

"Truth or blood," the dryad repeated. Waiting.

Fine. They wanted truth? They could have it.

"You think I chose to be like this?" The words ripped out of her. "I do the hard shit that needs doing, and you hate me for it. So hate me. But when the next monster comes crawling out of the dark, you'll beg for my help."

Light burned up from the ground. Roots wrapped around her boots, climbing her legs.

"I wasn't there, all right?" Her voice cracked. "My love died screaming while I was off with my friends. That's the truth. I failed her. That's why she's dead. That's why he broke his oath."

Her eyes cut to Riven. No saying how much time he had left. She'd say whatever she needed to. Spit out whatever guilt she pretended not to carry and swallow it all over again. She wouldn't lose him too.

The forest shuddered. Vines loosened on Holloway's legs. Fog pulled back. The dryad came apart like smoke in sunlight, scattering into nothing.

Silence. Then the canopy above cracked open. Real light broke through. The ground went solid under their feet. Dawn let out a shaky breath. The only thing missing was birdsong—but birds never sang in Valta these days.

Holloway stared at her like she'd grown a second head. "What the hell was that?"

"It was a toll," Lore said quietly. "She paid it for us."

Closest thing to thanks she'd get from this crew.

They rode on, and the mist started to thin. Talia laughed a little hysterically. By late afternoon, trees gave way to meadow. They came on an old stone temple, and the air smelled like clean water. The forest could've spit them out anywhere, so Dawn checked the temple gates for clues.

"Oh shit." She turned back to Riven. "You picked the right place to die dramatically, old man." A grin slipped out before she could stop it. "This is Elanvesi."

"Water of life," Talia murmured.

Dawn nodded. "You two"—she pointed at Holloway and Lore—"make camp. Watch the horses. Keep the fire going. We'll be back."

No one argued. Apparently, they were listening to her again. Dawn spat the last taste of the Whisperwood from her mouth. Then Talia gasped. "He's not breathing. Dawn, he's not—"

Riven lay slumped over Larkspur's neck. *Fuck.* She had no idea if the springs could catch a man this far gone, but she'd drag him there anyway.

"He'll be fine. It's a hike. Let's go."

34

THE HEALING SPRING

TALIA

I was wrong. Flux channeling isn't a lost technology.

— T. SALAREN, FIELD NOTES, 401 AC

The hot springs cut the white limestone cliffside into dozens of cascading pools, each one darker blue than the last. Thick steam glowed gold in the dying light. The beauty felt wrong. Dawn was wrestling Riven down off the horse, and she didn't know how to help. He was breathing in fits and gasps, but at least he was breathing.

"Give me a hand, will you?" Dawn said. She'd backed into the bright blue water, tugging Riven's shoulders back with her, but his hips caught on the stone lip. "Get him in."

Talia was still upset, but Riven was more important than Dawn being a murdering liar. His legs were deadweight in her arms, and she stumbled forward on the loose pebbles, nearly crashing face-first into the pool after him. The water soaked through Talia's boots and skirts, hot and shocking, dragging at the loose sleeves of her blouse.

It wasn't too deep, just to Talia's armpits, and it had a salty, chalky quality that made her feel buoyant. Riven was floating between them, his breathing a little stronger, maybe.

She traced a line of looping Starscript carved into the white stone rim with her finger: *Healing requires touch from the source.*

"What's the source?" she asked. Riven's ragged breathing seemed to echo in the steam. Talia's glasses had fogged up completely, and she set them aside. The world slipped into a fuzzy blend of shapes and colors, like a pattern cast by stained glass.

Dawn didn't answer, and now Talia couldn't see her face. The water lapped and tapped at the limestone. Steam curled between them. Somewhere in the distance, a squirrel chittered.

Talia took one of Riven's hands in hers, pressing fingers to his wrist. Blood seeped from the wound in his side, ribboning into the bright blue water. She could see the colors: red to purple, then pink dissolving into blue water. His pulse fluttered, then dropped so sharply Talia gasped. The water didn't do anything. It didn't glow or shift or change.

"What did the inscription say? Something about touch?" Dawn was reaching down to peel off her shirt.

Talia's hands froze around Riven's wrist. Every inch of her body sparkled with awareness as Dawn's wet shirt hit the rim with a slap. Every governess she'd ever had screamed in the back of her skull: *Not proper!*

Riven's breathing hitched. Stopped. Started again. She stopped caring about the rules. Her fingers worked the ties on her bodice, then her blouse and skirts. They stripped him down together, Talia's fingers slipping on the buttons. She tried to keep her focus on the wound at his side, cataloging damage instead of exposed skin.

Dawn positioned herself on one side of Riven, Talia on the other. They held him upright between them, hands clasped under his arms.

Skin to skin. Three bodies in the water, stripped to the waist. Was that what it had meant?

"Come on," Dawn muttered. "Fucking heal."

But the water around them was clouded with blood, and it stayed that way. Riven's life force unfurled faster into the water.

"I think the springs need a power source." Dawn's hands stilled on Riven's chest. "They amplify flux, but they need something to draw from." She met Talia's eyes. "We used our last crystal yesterday."

It took Talia a second to process what she was saying. No flux. No healing. No way to save him.

"There has to be another source," Talia said desperately. "Something we can use. I'll find a foundation stone—"

Riven's chest went still, and his pulse vanished under Talia's fingers.

"No." Talia pressed her fingers to Riven's wrist, his neck. Nothing.

"There is a way." Dawn's voice was subdued, but it cut through Talia's panic. "It's called a channel bond. You have an affinity, right?"

None of those words made sense in that moment.

Dawn tried again. "You connected with Sorrel, and with those fluxborn direwolves. Some kind of mindweaving." Talia could only nod. "Okay, then this can work. I'll be the power source."

"You have flux? Without crystals?"

"Something like that." Dawn's face was a smudge in the steam. "I can generate extra power with your affinity. But the bond is permanent. Once it's done, we're connected. You and me."

Permanent.

She looked at Dawn through the whorls of steam. Her, of all people.

"Will it save him?"

"Yes? I've never done this before." Dawn sounded scared. That was a bad sign.

Talia squinted at Riven. His lips were bluish. His skin looked gray. She knew what he'd say if their roles were reversed. He'd stayed behind in Gateway. Thrown the enforcers off their trail to make sure she escaped. Saved them from the wolves. This was the least she could do.

Talia nodded. "What do I need to do?"

"Take his hands. When you hear the question, you say yes. Out loud."

Talia's fingers found Riven's in the water. Dawn moved behind him, bracing his shoulders.

"Close your eyes. And Talia—" She paused, then let out a breath. "You're choosing this. Not me. Not him. Got that? You can say no."

She got that this was a commitment she wouldn't understand until after she'd made it. Trust without clarity. A step taken on faith alone. But Riven was dying, and she didn't know what else to do.

She closed her eyes.

The water lapped against her ribs. The steam was warm and wet as she breathed in. Then something brushed her mind. The impression of Dawn, her presence. Like standing in a dark room knowing someone else was there. Talia held her breath, and the presence pressed closer. A wordless question.

May I?

This was it. The moment. No turning back. No way out but through. Her fingers tightened around Riven's stiff hand.

"Yes," she whispered.

Heat exploded up through Talia's palms, racing through her veins like liquid fire. The world went white. Then it cracked open. She couldn't explain what happened next. It felt like her empathy, except with pictures.

She was drenched in Dawn's memories. Sun on her shoulders, a woman's laugh, wide open skies, the feeling of flying, a baby's fist curled around her thumb. ***This must be her family***, Talia realized, remembering Dawn's confession in the Whisperwood. Warmth stretching—

—and tearing.

Smoke thick enough to choke. A doorway on fire. Roofs collapsing in sparks. Running barefoot, screaming a name Talia couldn't catch.

Then years slipping past in flashes. New faces. New towns. New graves. Grief settling like sediment, layer on layer, hardening to stone. The sheer number of scenes, decades stacked on decades, it made her dizzy.

Then the whole scene shifted like a page flip, and Dawn moved through Talia's mind, sifting through memories she'd never shared.

Her grandmother's study—light on polished floors, the smell of ink.

"You were right to tell me," her grandmother had said.

The night I ruined everything.

Merit's empty room. Lanterns on the water. A mother's anguished cries.

The mirrors showed her own face three times over, none quite right. Running from truth. Searching for love she'd never deserve.

She tried to pull back, to hide the worst angles of herself, but it was too late.

Dawn's presence settled beside the shame, steady and scarred. Quiet recognition. Understanding. Support.

They were back in Elanvesi, but it had changed. The entire cascade of pools glowed electric blue, and power was pouring into Talia's chest, hot and endless. Her veins lit up like Gateway's power lines. The water around her went from blue to white, the glare mirrored in the steam.

Dawn was translucent, a bright glow pouring out of her into the water and through Talia, coursing into Riven. His body arched, his head snapping back as his hands gripped hers. Silver lines reached up from between their clasped fingers, flaring up his arms and around his muscled shoulders. Glyphs curled down his chest and torso. The wound in his side knit shut, muscle weaving back together. Skin sealing over it pale and new.

Talia had never seen this much power. Had never heard of a person wielding magic like this, even in the stories. What had she just done?

Riven gasped. His eyes flew open, shining silver and wild, and the power cut off, and everything went dark.

The world came back in pieces. Steam. Stone. Her glasses were somewhere on the rim of the pool. Everything was blurry.

The three of them stood in the water. She was aware, suddenly, of her own body. His knee pressing against hers.

She looked down. She hadn't imagined it. Silver script covered his chest, his arms, wrapped around his ribs and torso. Presumably under the water too. Fading now from bright glow to dull swirls, but still visible, like tattoos. She knew those glyphs. She'd copied them from artifacts, translated them one at a time. Liturgical Starscript. Reserved for fae nobles and those in their service.

"You're one of them," she whispered. Riven squeezed her hands. He didn't argue. She turned to Dawn. "And you knew."

Dawn's mouth twitched. Then she was grinning. "We grew up together, remember?"

Grew up together.

Talia thought back on what she'd just seen in Dawn's mind: cities burning, years and years of graves. The two of them must have lived entire lifetimes before she was even born. And now she was bound to one of them.

A *channel* bond. She had so many questions. She'd need to read the journal again with this new context. This whole time she'd been looking for answers, and Dawn had them. It was infuriating, and still—gods. What she'd been through. Talia didn't fully forgive her, but she was starting to understand the weight that Dawn carried.

Suddenly Talia felt dizzy, like she was standing on the edge of a cliff. The bond hummed in her chest, and Dawn's ancient heartbeat folded next to her own.

"What does it do?" she asked, sharper than intended. "The bond. What do you know about me?"

"I can feel you, physically." Dawn met her eyes. "Your location. Your heartbeat. Things like that. I can't read your mind. Or your emotions, unless you share them. That's your ability, not mine."

"What's your ability? Can you control me?"

"It's a fire thing, don't worry about it. No. I'm just the source. The bond amplifies my power, and we share it." She sounded tired.

Talia pulled her hands back from Riven's. The knotted feeling held tight inside her chest, but at least she could pretend she had some space. She moved to the edge of the pool and struggled to pull on her sticky wet blouse.

They hiked back to camp as the last light died. Water squished in her boots.

Holloway looked up from the fire, eyes widening at Riven. "You're—"

"Alive again," Riven agreed. He sat down heavily.

Lore hadn't moved from where they'd left him. The black veins had spread to his neck. It seemed like he was struggling to breathe.

Dawn started pulling supplies from the packs. "I'll get dinner going. You can help him now." She nodded at Lore. "Burnout shouldn't be a problem from here on. Plenty of flux to go around."

Lore let Talia help him up. He leaned heavy on her shoulder as they pulled away from camp, far enough for privacy.

"You're soaking wet," he said with a low chuckle that turned into a cough. "And not the way I'd like."

"You're delirious." Talia glared at him. "Be quiet, let me try something."

She closed her eyes and reached for the bond, feeling the coil of power somewhere in her chest. She wasn't quite sure what to do, but she tugged, like she'd done with the flux stone, and energy prickled in her fingertips.

When she opened her hands, blue light bloomed in her palms. She pressed both hands to Lore's chest. He went still, then his eyes opened wide.

"Oh, Talent. What did you do?"

The black veins in his neck pulsed, then she watched them pull back. Lore held his arms out, rolling one sleeve up to inspect where the burnout had spread. The skin was clear. His hand trembled slightly as he tugged his shirt back in place.

"Thank you," he said quietly. "I wasn't sure I would see Valrotala." He flexed his fingers, testing. "The power you just channeled. You didn't have a crystal."

"Dawn did something," she admitted, not sure how much she could say.

His eyes raked over her, then a smile broke over his face. It wasn't the slow deliberate one she knew. It was wider. Unguarded. He pushed a hand through his hair.

"She bonded with you?" He was still staring, and she found herself looking away. "Truly? How fascinating."

Warmth crept up her neck as she nodded. Gods, she wished she wouldn't blush. Not in front of him.

"Do it again. I want to see how it works."

She pressed a palm to his chest and tugged on the bond. When she opened her eyes, her fingers were glowing blue. She felt a little tug on her fingertips, as if Lore was drinking it in.

"By the gods, Talent." His voice dropped. "You are dangerous."

It was a strange compliment, but his praise sparked something warm in her gut. She caught herself smiling.

"We should get back," she said, pulling her hands away.

Dawn was stirring a rabbit stew over the fire when they returned to camp. Was that the only thing she knew how to cook?

They ate in silence; everyone was so tired. Talia curled into her bedroll and stared up at the stars, trying to breathe normally, to calm her mind and sleep. In her chest, two heartbeats rattled instead of one.

THE TRANSACTION

VAELIS • 6 YEARS AGO

Axel checked all the boxes. He was a friend of Holloway's, wealthy and well connected. Attractive enough. And he was interested—he'd made that clear when he first approached her weeks ago. The act itself had been built up for so long. Maybe actually doing it would make her feel more like everyone else, less like an outlier.

Talia took her contraceptive teas. Put it on the calendar weeks in advance. Now it was time. Everyone else had done it, and it was her turn.

She kissed Axel at the door, cataloging sensations. His mouth was warm. Eager. His cologne smelled like figs.

"I've wanted this for so long," he murmured. Desire radiated off him in waves. *Good.* She'd read that right.

"Oh, me too."

He pulled her to the bed. Fumbled the buttons of her blouse. She reached down to help. What she'd felt at the door was just a prelude. When he palmed her breast, his full passion crashed over her like a wave, crushing all other sensation.

Her empathy was soaking him in at every point of contact. These weren't her feelings, they were his. She could taste what he wanted, the shape of it flooding her senses. Her body arched, and her mouth made sounds she hadn't decided to make. It felt like the one time she'd tried to ride a horse and it'd spooked beneath her.

He groaned. "Gods, Talia. Tell me you want this as much as I do."

She *did* want the experience. She was just surprised *this* was the thing everyone had been talking about. His hands were everywhere, slipping her shirt over her head, sliding into her pants.

"Can we go slowly?" she asked. "I want to feel you."

He grunted an affirmation, and his hands were gentle. But he wanted her to touch him, she could feel it. She slipped his pants down his hips and ran her hands over him. His manhood felt warm and rubbery. What a strange thing.

She let it slip against the palm of her hand, chasing his flares of pleasure. She enjoyed how directly he responded.

"You're incredible," he said, and she soaked up the praise.

He rolled her onto her back and perched over her, propped on his elbows, all muscles and freckles. He brushed a curl away from her face and kissed her sweetly. Smiled. Asked permission. When he pressed into her, she felt sharp pain, then pressure, and then his pleasure crashed through her, sparking across every nerve.

It wasn't bad. It was just that none of the best parts felt like hers. The way he moved inside her felt good in a frustrating way, like a massage that just missed the spot. She borrowed his pleasure instead and observed it like an experiment.

When it was over he pulled out and collapsed beside her, breathing hard and grinning. "That was amazing."

She lay still. Carefully peeled herself away from his skin. She wished she felt *amazing*.

"You okay?" He was propped on one elbow, head in his hand. He was an attractive man, muscles flexing up his arm, sandy red hair falling loose in his eyes.

"Of course," she said, smiling. "You were great. Thank you."

She closed her eyes, and he stroked her hair. Nearly an hour passed before he stood up and kissed her, pulling on his trousers. Once he was gone, she sat on the edge of the bed to assess.

That had been interesting. She could see herself doing it again. But it had clearly done more for him than it had for her. She decided that her grandmother was right; sex was a tool. Potentially a useful one, so long as no one used it against her.

A few days later, she ran into Axel at lunch. He was sitting with

Holloway and their usual group. When she approached with her tray, their laughter stopped. Axel smiled at her, bright and unbothered. She waved and smiled back. Holloway stared hard at his plate. His jaw was tight, his shoulders set.

"Morning, Talent." He didn't look up.

Her stomach dropped. He'd always called her Tally. Never Talent.

"Morning," she answered, hurrying to find a different table.

She didn't understand. They were friends. Why would this—any of this—matter to him? Sex was normal, practically a milestone assignment. She'd done everything right. But the way Holloway avoided looking at her, that was new.

Later, she caught him between classes. "Hey. Are you mad—"

"I'm fine." Still not meeting her eyes. "Just busy."

"Holloway—"

He stopped. Exhaled. "Did he treat you well?"

The question surprised her. "Yes, of course. He's your friend."

He nodded once, jaw still tight. "Good." Then he walked away.

She stood in the hallway after he was gone, confused, heat creeping up her neck. Somehow, he seemed more affected by the entire thing than she was.

That night, she sat on the edge of her bed again. Same sheets. Same room. The echo of someone else's pleasure still ghosting beneath her skin like a bruise. She pressed her hands flat to her thighs. Breathed slow. Her body felt like a traitor. Too porous. Too easy to drown in someone else. Too easy for the consequences to spread.

She hadn't meant to hurt Holloway. She hadn't meant to absorb Axel's pleasure, to let it override her own. She'd just wanted to try something new. Better to keep some distance. Just until she figured out how to maintain boundaries.

At the time, she thought it was temporary. Avoid touch, learn control, then go back to normal. She didn't realize how quickly the distance would start to feel safe—no expectations to fail, no one close enough for her to hurt.

35

TOO MUCH INFORMATION

TALIA

One detail I've observed over the past year, and I'm not sure what to make of it. There is no birdsong in Valta. If there are birds here, they do not sing.

— *FLORA & FAUNA OF THE VALTA INTERIOR,*
VERACITY NIN, 409 AC

It was a familiar dream, a recurring fantasy since she was young, and it always ended the same way. An embrace. A promise. A bright, inhuman gaze fixed only on her. Except this time, the dream was alarmingly specific.

Gray eyes burned into hers. Starscript glyphs glowed across a bare muscular chest, wrapping around his ribs. Careful calloused hands slid along her jaw, tilting her face up. A mouth dropped to her throat, teeth grazing tender skin, and she heard herself whisper his name—

She woke with a start and realized two terrible things. First, this dream was not some random fae prince—it was very specifically Riven's mouth she'd imagined on her throat. And second, she'd been broadcasting the scene to everyone. Not just the emotions behind it, actual images.

She'd projected her emotions once, in that wolf cave, but that was nothing like this. The bond had warped her gift.

Oh gods. No, no, no.

She tried to yank the mental images back wherever they came from. They only pulsed brighter—*his mouth swept down her neck, his hands slid lower, her dream-self arched into his touch—*

"Could you not?" Dawn's voice cut through the morning quiet. "It's too early for whatever this is."

Across camp, Riven was staring hard at the horizon, his jaw clenched tight. Holloway was saddling Ash with aggressive tugs on each buckle. Lore watched it all with barely contained glee. Elbow propped on his knee, chin in hand, mouth curved in a cruel smile. *Of course he would think this was funny.*

"Fascinating," he said. "That bond really amplifies your range."

"Please don't," Talia muttered.

"I'm only saying, the detail in some of those images—"

"Lore." Riven's voice snapped flat and dangerous. "She asked you to stop."

Talia squeezed her eyes shut. Yesterday's ritual had broken something in her. She could feel every emotion in the camp—Dawn's irritation, Riven's strained neutrality, Holloway's horror. Her own mortification weaving between them like a panicked bird.

Everyone else had the decency to avoid looking her in the eye, but Lore was staring. He seemed fascinated, like he was cataloging every detail to study later.

Finally, he stood and crossed to her. "It's time to learn control. Come. Let me help you."

Letting Lore into her head seemed like a terrible idea, but when Talia glanced over at Dawn, she scoffed.

"Absolutely not," Dawn snapped. "I don't want any part of this."

Great. Whatever this horrible bond did, it didn't make Dawn a decent person.

So Talia followed Lore until the camp was out of earshot.

"Flux amplifies your empathic abilities," Lore explained. "We practiced with crystals, remember? Now you're drawing from the bond. You need to be able to disconnect from that power source." He motioned for her to sit. "Close your eyes and feel for the bond. Where is it?"

She concentrated. It wasn't solid, exactly, but she could feel the pressure of it in her chest. "Right here." She touched her sternum.

"Good. You're going to put a filter in right there. Imagine a lens of dark glass, and slide it between the bond and the flow of your emotions."

He wasn't making sense. How was she supposed to slide something that didn't exist into a space she was imagining? This was too abstract. Her frustration flared so hard that Lore flinched.

"This is never going to work," she muttered.

She pulled away and tried to calm down, plucking anxiously at a patch of grass. A halo of worries circled her head, fading out and swapping in for new ones. What if this was her life now? What if she never learned how to control it?

Her fears felt more solid now that she knew the others could see them. Irritation flashed like lightning, and she sighed.

Riven's voice cut in. "May I try something?" She startled, not realizing he'd joined them.

When she nodded, his hand settled on her shoulder. "Breathe with me."

She matched her breath to his, and the static in her head quieted to a low buzz. *Oh, thank the gods.*

"Flux always wants a path." He knelt, guiding her hand to the damp grass. "You're projecting it out, but you can give it a different path. Send it down."

She focused. Felt the thread of power inside her, imagined it flowing through her palms. For one perfect moment, the noise stopped.

"That's it," Riven murmured. "You're grounding it."

But her mind kicked in—how did this work, why did it feel this way, where did the power go?—and she lost it. Emotion surged back.

"You're overthinking," Riven said. His voice was gentle, but it sent shards of irritation under her fingernails.

"That's kind of what I do," she snapped.

She knew how her own mind worked. It needed a system, a set of rules. She thought back to the other time something like this happened, in the wolf fight. She'd shoved her emotions into the wolf's mind. It hadn't been a filter, exactly, but she *had* directed her empathic power. Kind of. Could she do that again?

She felt for the bond and concentrated on her anger. It had the most surface area of all her emotions, hot and prickly. She tried grounding her rage, except instead of pushing it down, she pushed it toward Lore. The bond pulsed once, like it was giving her a boost, and the heat in her chest eased. It had worked.

Lore tipped his head to the side, and she could feel him staring.

"You're both wrong." She stood up abruptly and walked a few steps away, fighting to ignore Lore's eyes on her.

She reached for the bond and tried again, peeling off a thread of gratitude. She focused on Riven, concentrated on what she appreciated about him. His steady patience. His dry humor. Then she aimed those feelings right at him.

His eyes widened. She was actually doing it. She held the projection steady. Three seconds. Five. Ten. Then gently pulled it back.

A smile played at Riven's mouth. "You figured that out yourself."

Heat flooded her face. This time when her attraction flared, she caught it mid-broadcast. Focused it. Pulled it back. It wasn't perfect, but it was better.

"Nicely done, Talent." Lore's eyes flicked back and forth between her and Riven, clearly wondering what had passed between them.

"I combined your methods. The grounding and filtering together." She couldn't hold back her smile.

"I noticed." Lore stepped closer, studying her face with intense focus. "You're going to be dangerous when we figure out what you're capable of."

There it was again, that word. *Dangerous*. It didn't sound like a warning. When Lore said it, it sounded like a promise.

The day fell into a rhythm. Riding northwest, stopping when her emotions flared, practicing grounding.

Holloway rode up ahead. He hadn't said ten words to her all morning. He always did this, drew into himself when she made him feel—what? Jealous? She never knew what she was supposed to do to get him back.

On the other hand, she caught Lore staring at her more than once. The second time it happened, she held his gaze, a silent challenge. His small nod made her pulse kick, and she bit back a smile. Whatever game *that* was, she was pretty sure it was a bad idea to crack first.

By midday, when they stopped to water the horses, she could maintain control of her emotions for at least twenty minutes at a time. She was making real progress, but not everything was fixed. She found Holloway at the far edge of the clearing, checking straps that didn't need checking.

"Holloway—"

"I need some space, Tally." He didn't look up. "Please."

She swallowed. "I didn't mean to broadcast that. The bond, it's new, and I—"

"I know what the bond is." His voice was level, but the muscle in his jaw kept twitching. "Dawn explained. It's not your fault."

"I don't want you to hate me."

His hand stilled on the harness. "I could never hate you," he said quietly. "And you don't have to apologize for what you feel."

She stepped closer. "I didn't even know I felt that way." Her cheeks were burning. "I mean, I'm not sure I do. I wasn't trying to—"

"I know." He cut her off again, softer this time. "That's the problem."

She blinked. "I don't understand."

He finally looked at her. And gods, she almost wished he hadn't. The grief in his eyes wasn't sharp. It was old. Settled. Like he'd carried it a long time and it was just slipping out now.

"You never mean to hurt me, Tally." His voice frayed at the edges. "But you don't have to try. It happens. Every time."

An ache opened in her chest. "Holloway, you're my oldest friend. You're important—"

"Don't." A whisper now. "Please don't do that."

The silence between them was so thick she could hear wind whispering through the dry grass.

"I don't want to lose you," she said in a small voice.

He closed his eyes, just long enough to pull something fragile back into place.

"You're not going to lose me." He gathered the reins. "I just need to let go of what I thought we were."

The words knocked the breath from her. He turned away before she could answer.

She would fix this, figure out how to make the two of them okay again. Holloway was the only other person left who'd loved Merit and Cordon the way she had. He knew her better than anyone. She wasn't sure who she'd be if he *let go* of his feelings for her.

That night they made camp at a ridge sheltered from the prairie wind. Riven sat alone by the fire, polishing his blades. He'd stripped down to a sleeveless vest, and the silver tattoos on his arms caught the light. She wanted to turn and run and pretend none of this ever happened, but she forced herself to approach.

"Can we talk?" she asked.

Riven's hands stilled. He set his sword down carefully. "About this morning?"

Heat flooded her face. "Not sure I'll ever be ready for that conversation."

His mouth twitched, smile lines showing at the corners. "For what it's worth, there are worse ways to find out someone's thinking of you."

Her breath caught, and he looked away, giving her space to recover.

"Start wherever you need to."

Straight to it. She drew a breath.

"The reports," she said. "I need to know what you did, what you told them. I want to hear it from you."

He nodded. "Your grandmother hired me in Vaelis. I told you this. But she gave me a contact at the Pentarchy garrison, and they offered to extend my contract."

The honesty landed hard, even when she'd expected it. "So you reported on me?"

"Twice." A muscle jumped in his jaw, and he shook his head. "It was after I heard where Lore planned to go, what he asked you to do."

"That wasn't your decision to make."

"Agreed." He turned his body toward her, giving her his full attention. "It seemed the lesser evil. Valrotala is a dark place, and I have—history there. I hoped to shield you."

"So you protected me by betraying me."

"Yes." No hedge, no apology, but regret lived under the words. She could hear it in his voice.

"And then you stayed behind. I thought you died."

"I came after you to explain myself, but I found enforcers on your tail. Distracting them was the best I could do."

She was finding it hard to breathe. Did he think one heroic act would clear the board? She thought back on the voyage, their morning walks to the office, that conversation on the roof. How much of that had he shared with her grandmother, of all people?

"You should have told me." It felt good to say out loud.

"You're right." His voice rumbled. "But I wasn't sure you'd listen to me. Keeping you alive mattered more than honesty for its own sake."

That answer was so *him*. Practical, direct, infuriating. She laughed, then she groaned. "I'm still mad."

His mouth twitched. "You have every right to be."

He shifted just slightly, his knee brushing hers, a subtle point of contact she could have pulled away from, but she didn't.

"That can't happen again. I need you to be honest with me."

He nodded slowly, thinking. "I was raised to be an oathsworn protector. It was my whole purpose. This"—he gestured between them—"is less familiar. I can do my best."

Her throat tightened. What did he think *this* was? "What if it goes both ways? I get to watch out for you too? I saved your life back there, you know."

He chuckled. It was a nice sound, deep and rumbly. "Like partners? I suppose I couldn't call you boss."

"Exactly." They were going to be okay. Something in her chest unknotted, just for a new kind of panic to set in.

"It's a deal, then." His knee pressed into hers, and he gave her a smile, a real one.

Talia turned away before the wave of emotions could hit her full force. She dropped to a crouch, pressed her palms hard into the cold earth, and grounded every emotion clawing up her ribs—pushed it down, through, away—before it could spill over.

Whatever she was feeling for Riven, she didn't want it. She certainly didn't want him to want her. She'd crushed Holloway without even trying. If that was love, if that's what it cost, it wasn't worth it.

36

THE WANTED POSTER

DAWN

WANTED. Lore Tavis, preacher of Gateway. And associates. Charges: theft and assault, Mallory homestead. Reward offered. By order of Sheriff C. Mallory, Heller's Ridge.

Two days of hard riding brought them to the Queen's Way. They couldn't be far from Heller's Ridge. Dawn would kill for a real bed and a hot bath. Maybe a warm body that didn't have a dick or a death wish.

But clouds were piling up, dark ones. That storm would hit tonight; she'd bet money on it.

"We should find shelter," Riven said. "This storm'll break soon."

"We push on," Lore countered.

Talia's emotional control slipped while the two men argued. Dawn picked up a flash of panic over the bond, like the girl didn't know whose side to take.

By midday, Heller's Ridge shimmered in the distance. Rows of crooked buildings crowded a wide empty street. A little *too* empty. Townsfolk stepped back into doorways as their group rode into town. Shutters slammed shut.

Riven reined in. "Something is off here. We should go around."

Lore didn't slow. "We need to resupply. We'll get what we need and carry on."

Riven rarely spoke up unless it mattered. He was making a lot of sense, and Lore was a fool to dismiss his concerns.

"Can you feel it with your affinity, Talia?" Riven asked. "There's tension in the air."

The girl froze. Not at the danger. At the men. Her gaze jumped from Riven to Lore. Her shoulders rose, like she could make herself thinner. She was trying to disappear.

Lore frowned and shook his head. "Just follow me."

What the hell was going on? Talia's nerves were rattling their bond every time those men tugged her different ways. Holloway clenched his reins. His eyes shot between Talia and Lore. He was tracking it too.

Riven slid off Larkspur and sauntered up to the feedstore wall. Tugged down a bit of paper that was flapping there.

"Shit," he said under his breath. Then louder, "Hey, there's a wanted poster here. Names Lore Tavis of Gateway and associates. Theft and assault."

Talia leaned in. "The Mallory homestead. That must be the family back on the prairie."

Thunder rumbled in the distance. That storm was coming in, right on schedule. The first drops hit the dust. What was it Lore had said after they robbed that family? *May the hard choices fall on those strong enough to bear them*. Well, he'd been making all kinds of choices today. Guess they'd see what he was made of.

Riven's jaw flexed. "We need to get off the Queen's Way. Now."

The same road they'd started on. It would have taken them the whole way, if they could have stayed on it for one damn minute.

"Running draws attention," Lore countered. "We act normal, resupply, leave at firstlight."

"Agreed," Holloway said, reining up alongside Lore.

Dawn would love to agree. She wanted that damn bed. But Riven was right. "We passed a gorge back there that'd make a decent windbreak. We should head back, camp there."

Lore smiled at Talia. "You're the deciding vote."

The girl chewed her lip. Rain started coming down harder. They needed to take shelter or go, now.

"Talia," Riven pressed. "We need to move."

She opened her mouth, closed it again. She seemed frozen.

"We stay," Lore said. And just like that, the choice was made.

Dawn watched Holloway's face go tight. Damn, he was pissed. Couldn't say she blamed him.

Every head in that saloon turned when they walked in. Conversation didn't stop, exactly, it just got quiet. The way it does when folks want to hear better. Dawn clocked the exits. Kept her hands loose. Smiled at no one.

Lore leaned on the bar, murmuring to the barkeep. Talia sat next to him, close enough their sleeves brushed. Dawn saw the moment Holloway snapped. Talia's fingers grazed Lore's arm, and the soldier boy just lost it.

"Unbelievable," Holloway muttered.

Talia turned in her seat. "What's wrong?"

"You." His voice cut through the room. "Burning time while you figure out how to commit to exactly nothing."

The saloon went even quieter. Dawn loosened her revolvers. This was a hell of a time to pick this fight.

"That was a wanted poster out there, Tally. And you froze. Again." He had stepped closer and dropped his voice to a whisper, but Dawn had excellent hearing. She caught every word. "You let Lore choose for you. Again."

"I was trying to understand—"

"No. You were waiting for someone else to make the call so you wouldn't have to carry it." His voice cracked. "You're so scared someone will notice you're not perfect; you erase yourself. You mirror whoever makes you feel wanted. Lore. Riven."

Dang. That was harsh, but it was a little true.

His throat worked, like the words scraped coming out. "It used to be me."

Talia flinched. Then her jaw set. Her eyes went hard. Dawn felt heat through the bond as anger flickered to life in the girl's chest.

"That's not fair—"

"Then say it," Holloway said. "Right now. Tell me what *you* think we should do next. Not what *he* wants to hear."

She opened her mouth. Nothing. Holloway let out a long, tired breath.

"Yeah," he said softly. "That's what I thought."

Before she could defend herself, the saloon doors slammed open. A man stepped in real slow, spurs clattering. The sheriff, with two deputies at his back. The man's eyes shot straight from the wanted poster in his hand to Lore's face.

"That's them," he said flatly.

Lore raised both hands. "Sheriff, there's been a misunder—"

The gunshot cracked before he finished. A glass bottle behind the bar exploded, sending shards flying. No warning. No negotiation. These boys wanted blood.

The barkeep screamed and dove behind his counter. Three more guns fired. Four. Dawn tracked the flashes. Two from the door, two from upstairs. *Fuck.* They had boys on the balcony.

Her revolvers were out, safeties off, cocked and loaded in four quick clicks. Dawn aimed and fired, and a deputy on the stairs flipped over the rail. Riven drove the men at the door back with two quick slashes.

"Way's clear!" Holloway shouted, already on the move. "Let's go!"

Dawn fired twice more, covering shots, just keeping heads down. The five of them burst into the street. The storm was out in full force now. Rain slammed into them. Thunder rattled the shitty buildings. Shots flashed from porches and windows. This whole damn town was in on it.

"We have to split up!" Talia's voice cut through the chaos. Clear. Commanding. Dawn sent a pulse of support down the bond. "Lore and I will draw them south through town. Riven, you cut north. Dawn, Holloway, get the horses out of here. Regroup at the gorge at firstlight!"

Dawn barked a feral laugh. *Fuck yes.* Angry looked good on the girl. Maybe Holloway's little speech had done the right kind of damage.

"You heard her! Move!" Dawn cried.

Riven was so fucking fast. He went left and just melted into the rain. Holloway swung onto Ash's back, spurring hard. Dawn caught

Talia's eye. The girl's jaw was clenched, her hackles up. Mad enough to make a point. Dawn knew that feeling well. Then bullets kicked up between them. Dawn wheeled Brimstone and rode hard for the gorge.

Thunder. Rain. Gunfire. Shouts. Hard to tell who was where. Dawn rode north, hard and fast. Riven appeared from the darkness ahead, and she dropped Larkspur's reins. Didn't look back, but he caught up with her a few minutes later, mounted now.

They pushed toward the meetup point. This storm was a doozy; everything was mud and water. When the sounds of pursuit faded, they dropped to a trot, then a walk, steam rising from the horses' flanks.

Holloway beat them to the gorge with the other three horses. He'd wedged himself under a shelf of rock for a bit of shelter.

"Where's Talia?" Riven shouted.

"She and Lore ran the other way." Holloway's face was pale. "Thought they'd circle back."

They waited. And waited longer. The rain never stopped. Dawn just felt static across the bond. Either the storm was scrambling it or Talia was too far away.

"We need to go find her," Riven said, voice tight.

"In this?" Dawn gestured at the sky. "We'd ride past her in the dark and never know."

"She said firstlight," Holloway reminded them. "We should wait."

So they waited there. Huddled under the overhang. Watched the storm rage. Riven paced. Holloway sat with his head in his hands. Both useless with worry. Dawn tested the bond again. Still nothing.

The girl was out there, alone with Lore. In the dark. In enemy territory. Angry. Reckless. Trying to prove she was bolder than she looked.

Well, shit.

NO GOING BACK

VAELIS • 2 YEARS AGO

Holloway was exactly on time, like always.

Talia's heart fluttered. Three years since they'd done one of these—careful meetings in neutral places where they could pretend they were still the people they'd been.

The café off Scholar's Row was buzzing with fluxlight and conversation, its brass service rails polished to a mirror shine. Talia had claimed the back corner, a pot of *thavi* steaming between empty cups.

He looked her over and smiled faintly. "That's a different look for you."

She shrugged. "Easier to paint my nails black than scrub out the ink."

His enforcer's uniform—black wool, brass buttons, green cloak—suited him. He'd shaved the sides of his head, trimmed his curls. Sat straight, looked her in the eye. But when he grinned, his dimples hadn't changed. For a moment, she almost believed they could go back.

They spoke about safe things. The weather. Her teaching. His work at the docks.

"Still on smuggler duty?" she asked, keeping her voice light. As if it were a game. As if the people he arrested didn't hang.

"It's relentless." He poured *thavi* for her first, then himself. "We caught a merchant last month trading in illegal relics." His hand stilled on the pot. "They executed him three days later."

He sighed and shook his head, as if he could shake off the memory.

"I'm sorry that happened," she said quietly.

"He kept saying he didn't know they were illegal." He set the pot down carefully and paused. The silence between them felt off. "But that's grim. I'd rather talk about you."

The way he said *you* made her chest ache.

"I've been working on something incredible," she said, grateful for the change in subject. "Liturgical Starscript. I'm calling it that because it looks just like the script in early religious texts. But these were tattoos. Used to seal an oath between fae rulers and their guards."

His expression shifted, and something closed behind his eyes.

"I've been reading your essays," he said carefully. "Don't you think it's a bit risky to draw comparisons between faerie stories and the gods?"

"I have dated artifacts showing very strong parallels across the locations and timelines. The evidence is solid."

"Strange. The relics trade is highly regulated. I haven't seen many pieces that old come through academic channels."

His tone shifted, like a pressure change before bad weather rolled in. All the warmth had gone out of it.

"Well, the Lyceum has..." She trailed off at the look he gave her.

He leaned forward. "Tally. Where are you getting these artifacts?" The question came out clipped, professional.

She should have deflected or changed the subject or laughed it off. But this was *Holloway*. They didn't lie to each other.

"Does it matter?" She didn't break eye contact. "The research is legitimate."

"Does it matter? Tally, it's the law."

"It's not like I'm running off and joining the rebellion." Her pulse thrummed. This conversation wasn't dangerous, was it? This was her friend. "I'm a scholar, a successful one. I want the truth, not some sanitized version of history."

He reached across the table and covered her hand with his. His thumb brushed her knuckles once, twice. Their old signal.

I'm here. You're not alone.

But his next words shattered it.

"If you keep this up, you'll be arrested. And if that happens, I don't know if I can protect you."

"I'm not asking for your permission or your protection." She heard how cold she sounded, how much like her grandmother. "This is my life's work. I'm not doing anything wrong."

Something closed down behind his eyes.

"The people I arrest, they aren't bad people," he said. "It's not enough to save them."

They sat in silence, *thavi* cooling between them.

"When did this happen?" he asked finally.

She wanted to ask him the same thing. When had he chosen to side with the people who burned books? When had duty replaced wonder? It was tragic.

"Maybe we've both changed," she said.

He stood, dropped coins on the table, too many, like he was paying for more than *thavi*.

At the door, he turned back. "If I find out you're involved in something illegal, I'll have to call it in. You understand that?"

"Of course."

"And you're going to do it anyway."

He was looking at her like she was already gone. Like he was memorizing her face.

"Goodbye, Talent."

Not *Tally*. Not *see you next time*. The door closed. The bell chimed.

She sat alone in the bright café. Conversation swirled around her. A couple near the door eyed her table, but she ignored them and sipped her cold *thavi*.

In the stories, this would be the moment the girl changed her mind. Ran into the street. Chose love over ambition. But Talia had never been one to chase the happy ending. She'd wait until it came to her.

It was raining on the walk back, but Talia didn't bother with a coat. She liked the feel of cold rain on her skin, found it grounding.

Wren was waiting outside her office. She'd grown so used to his visits; she'd stopped wondering how he got into the Lyceum. This time she panicked, pulled him inside, and checked the hall.

"You shouldn't be here. They're cracking down—"

"I know. Been dodging patrols all week." He shrugged out of his coat. "But this was worth it."

He pulled a small parcel wrapped in oilcloth from out of his coat.

"Oldest book I've ever seen," he said. "Found it in a vault, right here in Vaelis. Been sealed up for centuries."

Her hands trembled as she untied the string. Inside lay a narrow journal bound in leather. Simple and unmarked but cracked with age.

Warmth flooded through her fingertips as soon as she touched it. She opened the first page. The script was familiar—she'd read religious texts in this hand. But seeing it here, in a personal journal, made her breath catch.

"What is it?" Wren asked.

She couldn't speak. Couldn't stop flipping pages.

This was written in liturgical Starscript, but it wasn't a liturgical text. Not a ceremony or a sermon. This was a personal diary. Written by Vael lar Varloheim. The Divine Navigator. The god. She closed the journal carefully.

Holloway thought she was studying smuggled vases and trinkets. If he had any idea she had this journal, he'd arrest her on the spot. She should burn it. Hide it. Give it back.

Instead, she asked, "How much?"

Wren grinned. She paid him extra, for the risk. After he left, she sat at her desk with the journal open under her lamp. Heresy scrawled across every page.

She pictured Holloway's face when he'd walked out. The clipped way he said goodbye. He walked away from her that day, but she crossed the line. She picked up a pen and started translating a dead god's journal, and there was no going back after that.

37

TOTAL DESECRATION

TALIA

The heroine doesn't trip and fall into someone else's story. She jumps into her own. She takes what she wants.

— T. SALAREN, PRIVATE NOTES, UNDATED

Who made this awful plan? She hated running. She and Lore had drawn the lawmen away from their friends, but now they were at the edge of town. Beyond this last row of crumbling buildings, they'd be completely exposed. Lore grabbed her wrist and pulled her through a split in a rotting wooden doorframe.

Inside, a cavernous space echoed with their ragged breathing. The air smelled like damp stone and old incense, something her body recognized before her mind caught up. Her hands clasped together purely on instinct.

A white stone altar stood at the far end of the room, carved with ships and stars. Broken pews ran down each wall, and stained glass gods stared down through fractured windows. How many afternoons had she knelt in places like this? She wondered what the Divine Navigator would have to say about how far his name had spread and how little it mattered here.

"We can't stay—" she whispered.

Lore's hand clamped over her mouth.

Footsteps sounded outside. Voices called out. He held her mouth closed long after the sounds had faded.

"I think they're gone," he murmured, finally releasing her.

She nodded, her breath coming shallow. He stepped back only

far enough to strike a match. A candle stub flared in a wall sconce, throwing violent, shifting shadows across the broken gods.

He scanned her face. "You're bleeding."

He reached up, tilting her face into the candlelight. A thumb traced her cheekbone. The touch was deliberate, experimental, like he was daring her to pull away. She held her ground and watched him. What game was he playing?

"It's not serious," he murmured, but his thumb stayed on her cheek, tracing the same line again, slower.

Warmth rushed up her neck, and she knew she must be blushing. She couldn't hide it and she wouldn't look away, so she met his eyes instead. He nodded, like that told him something.

"Holloway was right, you know," Lore said. He slid a finger along her temple and tucked a runaway curl behind her ear. "You never let yourself have what you want. But when you do, you will be more capable than any of them."

Holloway's words still stung, and Lore must know that. He was obviously trying to provoke her, but there was enough truth in everything he said for his praise to feel good. She'd play along.

"And if I let myself have what I wanted," she said, aiming for confident and landing closer to breathless, "you think I'd want you?"

That got him to smile.

"I think"—his lips just brushed the shell of her ear—"if you did, you'd be surprised by how much you could take."

Was it a challenge or a threat? She shivered. She didn't like to be touched, but his fingers felt so soft. It made her wonder. She curled a fist into his shirt, and that spicy amber scent wrapped around her.

"But you hate me," she said, breathing him in.

"You want that, don't you." His voice rumbled through the church, deep and ominous, but he was smirking. "You broken, hungry thing. You don't want to be loved at all. You *want* to be used."

Her shoulders relaxed, and she let out a shaky breath. She *did* want him to use her, she realized, with a shock. She wouldn't have to worry about hurting or impressing him. She could just let go and let him—she pulled her imagination back, but not before a warm feeling spread through her, liquid and aching. He had *way* too much control. If they were doing this, she couldn't make the first move.

His mouth hovered over hers, daring her to give in. His hunger flooded every point of contact. She could hardly breathe through it, but she held on.

It was worth it when those gold-flecked eyes blinked first. With a burst of irritation and a surprised chuckle, he tipped forward and claimed her mouth. *Finally.*

"You'll pay for that," he said in a muffled voice before his tongue swept back in.

She should have pulled back, but the sheer force of his desire was intoxicating. He wanted her, and she wanted more of that. They stumbled backward through broken pews, tongues and teeth clashing. She didn't think. Didn't care. Didn't stop until her back hit the altar.

The stone was shockingly cold on her spine. His hips ground into hers. Lightning flashed through the broken glass, throwing red and gold across his face. He broke the kiss to speak against her lips.

"Is this what you want?"

"Yes."

"The bond—Dawn will feel—"

She didn't want to think about Dawn. For once, she wanted to make a choice without worrying about everyone else's feelings.

"I don't"—she pulled him in harder, biting his lower lip—"I don't care."

The black in his pupils expanded, swallowing the color.

She watched it happen, his physical reaction to her words, and she shivered. What else could she make him do?

"You're done pretending to be perfect, then," he murmured, pressing back her curls on both sides of her head, looking her straight in the eye.

He'd been working toward this for weeks. He was using her, and she knew it. She reached for him anyway, slipping a hand beneath the hem of his shirt. Two could play that game.

She traced a slow path from the coarse hair below his navel, over each ridge of his stomach. His skin was velvet-smooth, just like she'd imagined, and he flexed under her hand.

"I want you to take this off."

His smile sharpened and he pulled the shirt up and over his head. His bronze chest was lean, nearly hairless, and taut with muscle.

Lore kissed her harder, fingers moving under her blouse, over her ribs. His mouth slid down her throat, teeth dragging on the spot where her pulse thrummed out of control.

"We're desecrating this place," she breathed.

Lightning cracked overhead, chased by a peal of thunder.

"We will," he murmured. "Unless you want to stop."

She didn't.

"No," she breathed.

He dragged each button open down her blouse, and she let it slide off her shoulders. She shivered, half from chill, half from the way he looked at her, like he was taking inventory.

"Talent," he said, quiet and absolute. "Get on your knees."

Her breath caught. The demand in his voice shocked her, but her body thrummed: *Yes.* Wet stone bit her shins as she sank in front of him. The altar loomed at her back.

"Good. Now look up. At me." He pinched her chin and pulled her face toward him. When their eyes met, he inhaled sharply. "Oh, Talent. You do want this."

He reached down, palming himself through his trousers. The bulge of his desire strained against the fabric, taut and undeniable.

"Let me show you how much." Her voice echoed back like it belonged to someone else.

He hummed his approval as she reached up to unlace his pants. Her hands shook, and the knots slipped under her fingers. He watched her fumble for a moment, then let out a low, dark laugh and undid the ties himself with three quick, practiced pulls.

When his cock sprang free she took him in her hand, pulled his silken length gently to her lips. He hissed, his hips jerking, as she took him in.

Her palms braced on his thighs as his shaft pressed deeper, and his pleasure flooded in—ecstasy, and beneath it, the tense edge of control. She felt powerful, and she pushed that feeling back into him.

"You see it," he said, threading his fingers into her hair as he fell into a smooth rhythm. "That's how you take power back."

Power. Something unlocked in her. If he was going to wreck her, she'd wreck him harder. Her knees were soaked through and raw on the wet stone, but she drew him deep, past the point of comfort. He pressed into her throat with each thrust, and she took it all.

"Fuck," he gasped. "You won't yield."

She swirled her tongue as she pulled back, and his whole body shuddered.

"No, but I think you might." She smiled sweetly up at him.

His jaw flexed. Oh, he didn't like that. She would have laughed, but his fingers tightened in her hair and his hips jerked forward, rougher than before. When he hit the back of her throat, she felt his control snag like a loose thread, then start to unravel. He pulled out with a sharp gasp and glared down at her. His chest was heaving as he gathered her hair in his fist and tipped her head back until she was looking up at him.

"No." His eyes dropped to her mouth. "It's not that easy."

Isn't it, though? I almost had you.

He slipped his fingers between hers and pulled her up. Then he reached behind her and used one arm to sweep the altar clear. Relics smashed to the floor. Musty books slapped stone, pages flying. The clatter echoed obscenely through the empty church. He slid both hands beneath her thighs and lifted her to the altar's edge.

He looked into her eyes, thumbing her waistband. "You asked for this. Tell me you're ready."

She knew she'd pushed him, and she was about to find out what that cost. But she wasn't backing down now.

"Go ahead and use me."

He exhaled sharply through his nose, almost a laugh, and reached for her. He deftly unbuttoned her skirts and peeled them down her legs, taking everything with them until she was bare on the wet, cold stone.

One finger traced the goose bumps rising along her thighs before he pressed her legs apart. He slid his middle finger inside her, drew it out, and watched her intently as he pushed back in.

"You don't have to be quiet." His lips brushed her temple. "Don't overthink it. You know exactly what you want."

She couldn't think if she wanted to. The analytical part of her brain was drowning in sensation.

"Say it." His voice was calm, but his emotions were cycling too fast to pin down. Desire and anticipation and need, frantic and unbalanced.

"Please—Lore—I want—" She struggled to find words as a second finger pressed into her. "I need you inside me. I want—I want you to—" She broke off, heat flooding her face. "Gods, I can't say it."

"Try," he commanded, fingers curling. She gasped.

"I want you to fuck me." The word felt foreign in her mouth, embarrassing and filthy. She looked up at the ceiling as his satisfaction washed over her.

He pulled his hand away, gripped behind her knees, and tugged her to the very edge of the slab. One hand braced on the altar beside her hip as he stepped between her legs and positioned himself.

"Talent Salaren," he said in a rough voice. "Gods. Look at you. I've waited so long."

He watched her face as he pressed in, paused, and pushed a little deeper before drawing out again. She let out a frustrated whimper. The slowness was maddening.

"Oh, now she's in a hurry," Lore said, that half-smile drawing the dimple out as he took his time. "You really shouldn't rush me, Talent."

"You can't make me beg," she said between shallow breaths. Her hips bucked, chasing more friction, and he laughed.

"But you already are." He pulled out and his thumb traced a slow circle on her hip as she writhed. Then—without warning—he thrust all the way in, filling her completely.

He groaned, pulled back, and drove in again. The altar shifted beneath them with each thrust, the church echoing with the shriek of old stone and the slap of skin.

"I knew you were brilliant," he growled, hips driving forward. "They tried to make you small—but look at you—more powerful—than any of them." His rhythm stuttered. "You're perfect. So stubborn. So broken. Fuck—you deserve to be worshipped. I'll crown you myself."

The praise and insults mixed together made her brain short-circuit. Pleasure scattered through her, low in her stomach, down to her toes.

"Oh gods," Talia said, fighting for breath. Then, softer, "Oh, fuck."

Everything shattered. She heard herself cry his name, wordless sounds, prayers to gods she didn't believe in anymore. The Divine Navigator stared down at her from the rafters, watching her unravel on his altar.

Lore wasn't far behind. She felt his cock pulse, the liquid warmth of his release. His forehead dropped to hers, both shaking, locked together. Through the bond—distant, muffled by weather—she felt a flicker of Dawn's concern. She concentrated on the warm feeling in her chest and hoped it sent the right message: *I'm okay.*

For a moment they just breathed. Bodies locked together on a cracked altar. Then Lore pulled out and stepped away with his head bowed. Her body hummed, hollowed clean, as she watched him gather their things. She slid down and stood barefoot on soaked stone.

They dressed in silence. A pleasant ache settled between her thighs as she stepped into her skirts. He helped button her shirt with surprisingly gentle fingers. Adjusted her jacket. Brushed hair from her face.

"Tell me you wanted that," he said softly.

She nodded and smiled. "Trust me, it wouldn't have happened if I didn't want it. You're not as irresistible as you think."

"No?" He kissed her forehead. "That sounds like a challenge."

He led her to the back of the sanctuary, farthest from the broken windows, and made up a bed with his cloak and some musty curtains.

After he tucked her into the makeshift nest, he left to stand watch by the door. His face took on that boyish look it sometimes did as he gazed into the distance. She wondered, just before she drifted off, if she should have asked whether he'd wanted it too.

The mix of emotions she'd picked up from him was confusing. Desire, yes, and dominance, but none of the bitterness that laced his words. And at the tail end, a twist of something that almost felt like regret.

38

THE MIRROR BRIDE

TALIA

Scripture and faerie stories share the same characters and moral stakes, but they approach belief differently. A good faerie story doesn't tell you what to believe. It makes you feel. You discover your own truth in it. That kind of emotional connection is very hard to uproot.

— T. SALAREN, "FAITH AND FOLKLORE," *THE VAELIS COURIER*, 399 AC

The first hints of rosy firstlight just touched the horizon when they made their way out of the church, and the streets were eerily quiet. Talia felt Lore just behind her and to the left as she picked her way through the mud. It was a tense trek. Every second she expected their pursuers to reappear, but they made it to the rendezvous without incident.

The soft nicker of horses echoed through the gorge, and she followed the noise to their friends. She scanned the group, and everyone was accounted for. No new wounds that she could see.

The bond flickered to life, and she felt Dawn scanning her. She did her best to shield her emotions, but she couldn't know how much slipped through. Dawn smirked, which told her something. No privacy between bond-mates, apparently.

"You're okay, then?" Holloway asked, oblivious to the flurry of context passing across the bond.

"Just fine," Lore said easily. "Storm broke their trail. We waited it out, and no one followed us."

Riven glanced from Lore to Talia. She couldn't meet his eyes.

They rode north through the morning, further from the Queen's

Way with each step. Holloway tried to make conversation, but no one answered. Dawn kept scanning the horizon line behind them, watching for pursuit.

They made camp a little after highsun, when it seemed clear no one was behind them. Everyone was exhausted, but that didn't fully explain the tension.

Dawn seemed more prickly than normal. Riven stalked off to set a perimeter. Holloway kept shooting confused glances between them, trying to figure out what was going unsaid.

When Riven returned, he watched Talia with a concerned crease between his eyebrows. It was worse than anger would have been. If he was being territorial, she could have dismissed it, but this? His stoic concern irritated her, and she couldn't explain why.

When evening fell they built a fire. Still, no one talked.

"What about a story?" Holloway asked hopefully.

Riven stirred the coals, and sparks drifted up like fireflies. His voice, slow and ceremonial, snapped Talia out of her head.

"There was once a fae prince who took a mortal bride. He loved her beauty so fiercely he feared losing her. So he gave her a mirror, polished silver, that would show her everything she desired.

"She gazed into the mirror each day. First to see herself as she was, then to imagine herself as she wished to be. The mirror gave her what she longed for. Each time she looked, her reflection grew more vivid, while she herself grew dim.

"When the prince saw what was happening, he tried to pull her away, but she no longer heeded him. She belonged to the mirror more than the living world.

"One day he came to look for her, and she was gone. Only her perfect reflection in the mirror remained, smiling back at him from the silver glass. And there her beauty has continued to sparkle, the mirror bride, long after her body turned to dust."

Talia wanted to laugh. Leave it to Riven to break the silence with the most depressing faerie story possible. She glanced at Lore and he smirked back, shaking his head a little. He thought so too.

"They were doomed from the start," Holloway muttered,

tugging his blanket up to his chin. "Mortals and fae magic don't mix."

Dawn snorted. "Lesson's simple. Get off your ass and take what you want before wishing carves you hollow." She grinned at Talia.

Lore's smile caught the firelight. "You're all so convinced that it's a sad story. The prince gave her exactly what she wished for. Most people call that love."

That brought the silence right back down. The fire popped, and stillness settled over them. There was clearly a warning in the story, but they'd each heard a different one.

Talia wasn't sure what to take from it, herself, but she couldn't get the image out of her head. The bride staring into silver glass until there was nothing left but the reflection. Until she *was* the reflection.

She looked around the campfire.

Holloway was watching her sheepishly. Lore's eyes flashed gold in the firelight. Riven's face was unreadable. Three men. Three different versions of who she could be with each of them.

The fire burned lower. One by one, folks drifted to their bedrolls. Lore's hand brushed her shoulder as he passed, but he didn't ask her to follow, and she didn't offer.

Riven caught her eye. "Everything okay?"

"I'm fine," she said quickly. "Just tired."

He looked like he wanted to say more, but he nodded and gave her space.

She lay awake, her mind spinning. The story clung to her thoughts like cobwebs, uncomfortable and sticky. Finally she gave up and slipped from her bedroll. The night air stung her lungs, and she tugged on Riven's old canvas coat. She found Dawn at the edge of camp, perched on a boulder overlooking the dark river.

"Figured you'd come by at some point," Dawn said. "Could tell you weren't sleeping."

Talia leaned on the boulder. The water churned noisily down below.

"You're going to torture yourself over this, aren't you?" Dawn said. "I can feel you spiraling." She tapped her temple. "Bond goes both ways."

"I'm not spiraling—"

"You fucked Lore. Good for you." Dawn kicked a pebble off the edge. "You wanted to do it, right? Don't second-guess it."

"But you told me not to." If Dawn was going to judge her, she'd rather hear it head on.

"You ever do that before?" Dawn asked, glancing over. "Make a bad call on purpose?" Talia didn't have to answer, Dawn just grinned and shook her head. "Shit, it was probably past time."

Talia's throat tightened. "What about Riven?"

"What about him?"

"I hurt him."

Dawn just laughed and slapped Talia's leg. "No. You definitely didn't. He's worried, not hurt."

Talia wanted to argue, but her shoulders relaxed. Dawn didn't sugarcoat things, and she knew Riven better than anyone. If she said he was okay, he must be.

"Look, Lore uses people," Dawn said. "Riven sees that. He wants what's best for you, and he'll fight for it. Maybe let him."

Talia nodded slowly. She felt almost...disappointed? Had she wanted Riven to be jealous? That made no sense.

"Just do what you want," Dawn said, looking her over. "It's not your job to make these men happy." She stood and brushed off her pants. "Get some sleep. You look like shit."

She sounded dismissive, but Talia got a different message over the bond. There was concern there, a protective hum that gave Dawn away. She cared. It was sweet, in its own way.

Dawn stalked off to prowl the perimeter while Talia lingered at the riverbank. The cool breeze felt good on her warm cheeks. Her body hadn't stopped humming.

You mirror whoever makes you feel wanted.

Holloway's words still stung. She sighed. She didn't regret what had happened with Lore. Last night was the closest she'd ever gotten to putting her own desires first, and she didn't want to apologize for it, not even to herself.

She didn't want to care what Dawn thought, either, but her support felt surprisingly good.

When Talia got back to camp, Riven was awake, studying the fire. He didn't look up, but he shifted to the side, making room.

She hesitated before settling next to him. "I've never heard that faerie story before. I thought I'd heard them all."

"It's an old one."

She was getting more used to the cadence of his silences, the non-answers and the quiet that seeped between them. He wasn't being evasive, she realized. He just didn't make things about himself.

"Where did you hear it?"

He was quiet long enough that she thought he wouldn't answer.

"My mother loved the old stories. That one reminds me of a good friend. Someone I let down."

"Can I ask what happened to him?" It was a personal question, but she was suddenly desperately curious about Riven's past.

"She wanted the wrong things," was all he said.

The fire popped. She pulled his coat tighter around her shoulders and stared at the coals.

"Do you think I made a mistake?" she asked.

He didn't answer right away. When he did, he didn't answer the question.

"Are you happy, Talia?"

She opened her mouth to say she was fine, like she always did, but she paused. That wasn't the question.

"I think so," she said finally. "I'm trying to be."

He nodded and dropped a hand to her knee, rubbing it before he stood. "Then no," he said quietly. "I'm glad you kept the coat, by the way. I like that one."

39

SOMETHING OFF ABOUT HAVEN

DAWN

~~Cordon Sennett. House Sennett. Fae bloodline: lar Vuorlar, direct lineage. Affinity potential: moderate.~~ Status: terminated.

— PENTARCHY BUREAU OF BLOODLINE RESEARCH, INTERNAL RECORD, 391 AC

The road was nice while it lasted. They were cutting their own path again. Making decent time until a patrol burst from the tree line. Fucking green cloaks. Six enforcers spread across the narrow trail and swung their rifles around.

Dawn was ready for a fight. She counted three rifles, two carbines, one scattergun. She could drop the scatter first, pivot left, maybe get one more before they tore her to pieces. The math was ugly.

Talia nudged Jonquil up before Dawn could fire, blocking her sightline. Raised both hands. "Stand down. I'm the one you want. Talent Salaren of Vaelis."

Wild move. She must have trusted that whatever the Pentarchy wanted from her wasn't a roadside execution. Got them to lower their guns, at least. The leader circled back to the patrol and said something under his breath. Dawn caught *Salaren heir* and *early*. Then the man dismounted and dropped to one knee.

"Forgive us, Lady Salaren. Haven is honored by your presence. We were not expecting you so soon."

They ended up riding through Haven's streets as honored guests instead of in chains. Made no fucking sense.

Crowds surged forward as they rode past. Men swept off their hats, children pressed hands to hearts. A whole city kneeling to a bunch of strangers. Dawn's hand stayed near her guns. It all gave her the creeps.

Her chamber had a feather bed piled with pillows, and a huge copper bathtub. The wardrobe held a charcoal jacket lined with pink satin, trousers reinforced at the knees, and a wide-brim felt hat. If this was a trap, whoever was setting them up had impeccable taste.

She checked the windows. Three stories up, clear sight lines to the courtyard. Two exits, one into the hall, one to a servant's passage. The bath was too hot, and the soap had been carved into little flower shapes. She sank into it anyway. Four hundred years of dust and blood taught you to take pleasure where you could get it. She didn't trust any of it, but damn, it felt good.

The jacket fit like it was made for her. Must have been. Was this what that enforcer had meant when he said they weren't expected so soon? Why were they expected at all? Satin whispered when she moved. In the mirror, she looked dangerous and civilized. When an orderly summoned her to dinner, she went armed.

The banquet hall was packed. The table sagged under buttered fish and perfect fruit. Servants moved in sync like clockwork. Talia sat in the middle of it all. The girl was glowing in a red corset dress that showed off all her curves. Those soft Consortium men were here, and she was putting on a show. Correcting their Starscript. Laughing at their jokes. After everything they'd been through, here she was again. The girl Dawn had met in the flux shop, polished back down to nothing.

Fuck. Everything about this felt wrong. Dawn couldn't put her finger on it, exactly. The enforcers shouldn't have welcomed them. They shouldn't have fancy clothes and sweet-smelling soap. The whole place was too polished for a military post this far from the coast.

Dawn caught Riven's eye across the table and tilted her head toward the door. He nodded. After the twelve millionth toast, she excused herself. He followed. It seemed they got out clean.

They were a few blocks outside of the complex when she picked up a familiar vinegar smell. She followed it down an alley to a warehouse. The door had an ironbound frame, new hinges, and a shiny new lock. Riven had it open in ten seconds.

The wash of smells hit her as soon as the door creaked open. Blood and vinegar. Burned fur. Old piss and shit underneath.

Rows of cages stood empty. Straw darkened where bodies had been. A drainage trench cut through the floor, sloping toward a grate. Dawn's hands tightened on her revolvers. She moved down the row. Some cages were small enough for cats or lapdogs. Others big enough for worse things. Water dripped from somewhere, otherwise it was dead quiet.

"How many can they hold here, you think?" she asked.

Riven studied the cages. "At least forty. Maybe more if they double up."

Forty fluxborn. So where are they?

Just then, footsteps echoed in the alley outside. Dawn killed her lamp and spun, guns ready. Riven tensed beside her, hand on his blades. The footsteps paused. Then moved closer.

Dawn set up next to the door. When a figure stepped through, she almost shot Holloway in the face.

"What the fuck." She lowered her guns. "What are you thinking sneaking in here?"

"I wasn't sneaking," he said, all defensive. "I was following you."

"Same damn thing."

"I saw you come in here, and I thought—" He stopped, color rising in his cheeks. "I was just walking down the street, and you both ducked in here. I thought I'd have your back while you—" He gestured at the air.

Dawn stared at him. "While we what?"

His face went from pink to red.

Riven's rare laugh rolled through the warehouse. Dawn snorted.

"You thought I was fucking him?" Dawn jerked a thumb at Riven. "Soldier, he is *not* my type."

Holloway's gaze darted between them. He looked like he wanted the floor to swallow him up. "Right. Obviously. I just—you both stepped out, and I thought—"

Dawn cut him off. "We're looking into this." She holstered her guns and gestured at the empty cages. "Forty-some cages, all empty. Fresh enough the blood's still wet."

"What did they have in the cages?"

"Why don't you tell us, Captain? These are your people."

He stood up straight. "Have you checked the offices yet? Pentarchy loves paperwork. I bet they wrote it all down."

The office upstairs smelled like dust and old paper. Filing cabinets lined the walls, unlocked and unguarded. The officials here must be absurdly confident. This was all too boring to be a trap. Riven started sifting through piles of papers.

"These have to be fluxborn," Riven said, showing her a table with what looked like numbers and dates.

"What about fluxborn?" Holloway asked, pulling out another drawer and leafing through some files.

Dawn and Riven exchanged a look. He shrugged. She rolled her eyes. *Fine.*

"Pentarchy's been caging monsters," Riven said. "They're transporting them here, and we think"—he glanced at Dawn—"it resembles a kind of fae technology."

Holloway went still. "I knew they were building something out here. Research facilities, fortifications. But I didn't know that, exactly. Not in those terms."

"You knew they had a *secret research facility*?" Dawn snapped. "When the fuck were you going to say something?"

Riven cut in. "Stop. You both need to see this."

He held up a thick folder, flipped through it. Pages and pages of branching lines, what looked like names connected by ink strokes. Family records, Dawn realized. Going back a long time.

He leafed through the drawer and pulled out a file, which he handed to Holloway. Dawn tapped her foot, watching them read. Fidgeted with her guns. Useless fucking symbols. She hated needing other people to parse the world for her every damn time things turned to text.

"Find anything good?" she asked finally.

"Genealogy," Riven said softly. "Family trees for all the ruling families of Sovana. Detailed notes on bloodline strength, magical potential." He glanced at Holloway. "I gave him his family's file."

Holloway's finger traced down the sheet, then it stopped. His face went three shades lighter.

"What is it?" Dawn asked.

"Cordon." His voice broke. "My brother. They crossed out his name. There's a note—" He looked up, eyes wet. "Terminated."

The folder slipped from his hands. Papers scattered.

Dawn went to say something. Stopped. What the fuck was there to say? His brother's name was crossed out like a canceled order. She dropped a hand on his shoulder and squeezed.

Something creaked below them.

Riven's head snapped up. "Company."

Dawn killed the lamp. "Grab what you can. Let's move."

Holloway dropped to his knees, scrabbling for papers in the dark. Riven snatched a handful of folders.

Boots echoed through the warehouse. Four, maybe five men. Voices drifted up: "Records audit's tomorrow... chancellor's orders..."

The steps paused directly below them. Dawn grabbed Holloway's sleeve and hauled him under a table. The footsteps moved again, slower now, like the guards were checking the cage doors. Then they faded without coming up the stairs.

Dawn counted to sixty. "Out. Now."

She put both hands on the railings and slid down. Her feet hardly touched the stairs. Riven and Holloway followed just behind her, bolting into the night air without a word. The fluxlight was a strange golden color. Everything seemed too bright, too clean. They paused three blocks away, just long enough for Riven to hand

Holloway the files. He shoved them in his harp case one at a time, then let out a low groan.

"I need to go back. It's not all here."

"Not tonight," Dawn said. "That's suicide."

"They know what happened to Cordon—"

"And they'll still know tomorrow." Dawn met his eyes. "I'll go back there with you first thing in the morning. Just not tonight."

Riven looked down at his hands. "I found something in Talia's file."

"What'd it say?" Dawn asked.

He hesitated, looking at Holloway.

"A little late for secrets," Dawn said. "Just spit it out."

He huffed out a breath and took his time. Something big, then. "It's her affinity. She was already channeling flux in Vaelis, as far back as seven years ago."

"Channeling flux? What's that mean?" Holloway sounded a little frantic.

"You didn't know she had an affinity for mind weaving?" Dawn tried to sound gentle. Wasn't sure she got it right.

"I don't know what that means," Holloway snapped.

Riven cut in. "There's more. They've been grooming her for Pentarchy leadership. Since she was a kid."

"Well yeah," Holloway said. "The Salarens are one of the Five Families. But what do you mean—"

"Did you know they always planned for her to come here? To Haven?" Riven asked, turning to Holloway. To the boy's credit, he didn't shrink.

"No, that's not right. I was told to make sure she didn't leave Gateway. She was never supposed to come here."

"Never, or not yet?" Dawn asked.

It would make sense. Talia had asked about channeling the very first time Dawn met her. Could she really study something like that without the Pentarchy knowing? Maybe even helping? Made Dawn wonder what Lore knew. He had agents planted all up the Pentarchy command chain. Hard to imagine he hadn't come across this information.

They walked the rest of the way in silence, sticking to shadows, avoiding the main streets. Back in her room, Dawn should have felt safe. Soft bed. Locked doors. Weapons within reach. But she didn't even try to sleep. She stood by the window and counted patrols as they passed below.

They hadn't stumbled into Haven. They'd been expected here. All of them, but especially Talia. The question was, for what?

The bond spiked. Talia was struggling. Dawn was on her feet before she realized what was happening.

The girl wasn't in pain. She was with Lore.

Fucking hell. Good for her, I guess.

Dawn sent a pulse of strength down the bond. She didn't have to like her friend's taste in men to support her. Then she built a wall and stayed on her side of it.

40

THE LESSON

TALIA

Sometimes I see light under his door at deepnight and again at firstlight, and I wonder if he sleeps. Has anyone ever taken care of him the way he cares for us?

— PRIVATE JOURNAL, STARFALL ACOLYTE, IDENTITY UNKNOWN, 400 AC

The banquet had stretched late into the evening. It had been a pleasant surprise to reconnect with Peat and Nadir, to talk about research and laugh and drink. She had to wonder if the warrant for her arrest had traveled this far. They didn't bring it up, and she wasn't about to ask.

Nadir leaned forward and refilled her wine. "I want to hear more about your work with flux, Salaren. Didn't you have a fieldwork proposal on that topic?"

The question surprised her. Had Nadir ever expressed interest in her work? But she had new data and no one to share it with, and the wine made it easy. She told them about the fluxlines, the foundation stones, the way Starscript interacted with flux. She worried briefly that she was boring them, but they both leaned in for more.

Peat and Nadir asked detailed questions. When she mentioned how the wolves' eyes glowed blue, exactly like flux, they exchanged a look before asking about her companions. They were especially curious about Dawn for some reason.

As the meal wound down, she made plans to join Peat in the archives in the morning. He promised to show her what they'd been working on, and he seemed genuinely eager for her input.

The wine still burned warm in her chest when she left the dining hall. She wasn't ready for the night to be over, but her companions had slipped away early. She took slower and slower steps as she approached her room—this dress deserved an after-party. The corset did extraordinary things for her bust.

She was startled, then thrilled, when Lore caught her elbow.

"How would you feel about a lesson?" he asked. "There's supposed to be a fabulous library here."

"A lesson," she echoed. "On what?"

His one dimple came out. "Whatever you're ready to learn."

Not innocent, then. Not even remotely. Amber and smoke curled around her as he moved into her space, and her pulse tripped. Lore hadn't said anything since the church, but they'd been circling each other. Teasing comments. Little touches when the others weren't looking. She'd been waiting for him to make a move, and here he was. It'd taken him long enough.

The bond with Dawn felt distant, like a thread drawn tight. Maybe Dawn was distracted. *Good.* Talia had gotten to be a Starscript scholar again tonight, and she wanted the feeling to last—to pretend that her mind was wholly her own.

"Let's see the library." She looped her elbow through Lore's.

The library doors whispered shut behind them, sealing out the rest of the world. Globes burned a steady white along the walls. She'd never seen flux glow that color before. Shelves packed with volumes bound in silk and leather stretched toward a vaulted ceiling. A lock clicked.

She turned and found Lore standing closer than she expected.

"You promised a lesson." She reached over and straightened his collar. "Or did you have something else in mind?"

He caught her hand, removed it, and set it at her side. "Always." A table in the center of the room was carved with glyphs, and he approached it, gesturing for her to follow. "Come here. Tell me what you know about burnout."

She blinked. "It's what happens when you channel too much flux. It almost killed you."

"Close." He was arranging a set of crystals on the table. "Burnout happens when you draw from a source that's too weak for the task. You run out of flux; it drains you instead." He fit one last crystal into place and stepped back. "There's an inverse condition. Did you know that?"

She shook her head.

"What do you know about how gods are made, Talent?"

"The gods aren't real," she answered quickly. "They're metaphors for virtues and vices, based on old faerie stories."

He chuckled and shook his head. "No, Talent. I read your essays. It's a clever theory, but godhood is very real." He gestured at the table. "When you channel an excess of power, it primes you instead of burning you out. With enough power, anyone can become a god."

"I thought you brought me here for something else," she admitted, looking down at her dress.

"We'll get to that." He smiled thinly. "I would like to try something new, but I don't know if you're ready. It's very advanced."

"I think I can handle it."

He hummed, skeptical or approving, she couldn't tell. Then he stepped behind her and took her wrists, drawing her forward over the table. His chest pushed against her back and held her there as he pressed her hands into a glyph at the center of the crystals.

Power surged from the glyph the moment her palms touched it, racing up her arms in waves. She gasped as his lips brushed her ear. "Do you trust me?"

She didn't even think. "Yes."

"Good."

One hand slid down each notch of her spine, coming to rest on her hip. His other hand pressed on the small of her back. She tried to turn and look at him, but he didn't let her.

"You're going to let go and let me take over," he said, voice dropping. "We'll draw from this together. You'll feel everything I feel."

Her stomach twisted. This was all moving too fast. "How does that—"

"Don't overthink it." A hand slipped between her knees, up her skirts. "Focus for me."

His hand slid higher, between her thighs. He was about to find out exactly how her body reacted to his attention, as soon as...

"Good girl," he murmured, tracing his fingers over her wet center. "You've been thinking about me, haven't you."

Something about that phrase—*good girl*—landed wrong. Like something you'd say to a child, or a pet.

But then his fingers dragged her underwear aside and plunged into her, and the thought dissolved.

"Imagine," he whispered. "Every day like this. Learning. Growing stronger." His breath brushed her ear while his fingers pumped slowly. "And every night, I will take you apart."

She closed her eyes. She could imagine that. Gods help her, it didn't sound so bad.

"You don't have to pretend with me. You can't hurt anyone when I make all the decisions. You just let go."

A wave of relief hit her before the wrongness did. No choices, no consequences, no one else paying for her mistakes. But—he'd make all the decisions? That didn't sound right. It was getting harder to focus.

"What if I say no?" she gasped.

"Then we stop. But you won't." Certain. "You've been starving yourself your whole life, Talent. I know exactly what that feels like."

A single small twist of loneliness slipped across the connection before he locked it down. Talia tried to look back, but he was still holding her.

"I'm going to fuck you now." His voice vibrated down her back. "Hold still."

Cool air washed up her legs as he pushed her skirts up around her waist. He ran his hands down the back of her legs, and she shivered. There was a rustle of fabric, but she couldn't see. What was happening back there?

"Breathe for me," he murmured. "This might feel a little strange."

She waited there, pitched forward, exposed. Then—

Her empathy crashed open, a door blown wide.

She was still in the library, but everything had shifted. She was standing, looking down at a woman on a table. She was strikingly beautiful and coming apart—red dress hiked up around her waist, breasts spilling over her corset with every ragged breath. Talia had the strongest urge to hold her down and keep her there. The woman's braid was unraveling, and...

"Oh gods," she breathed. "I'm in your head."

His gaze. She was seeing through his eyes—and feeling what he felt—but she wasn't in control. She rode along, fascinated, as they approached her prone body from behind. Took their time, shifted layers of silk skirts and slid her underwear down, drew out their aching cock and stroked themselves to fullness.

The throbbing tip slipped just inside her silken folds. Then—pushed up and inside her tight, wet heat. At the same time, she felt the intrusion, the stretch and pressure of being filled.

She gasped, and the woman on the table gasped too.

Lore chuckled darkly and rolled his hips in slow, deliberate thrusts. The velvet drag on his cock as he pressed deeper into her body—she felt that. She felt everything.

It was strange, looking at herself from this angle. Her skin glowed in the low fluxlight, and her hair spilled over her back. Beautiful and broken. Each thrust drew a small squeak from her lips—too stubborn to give him the sound he wanted, but too undone to stay silent. An emotion stirred that Talia couldn't place. Almost possessive, but more primal. A sense of coming home.

The body on the table shifted, started to turn, and panic spiked. They didn't want to meet her eyes. A hand pressed flat between her shoulder blades. *Not yet. Don't turn around.*

"Look at her," Lore said. "She takes it so well."

"Gods—it's so hot," she moaned, fighting to catch her breath.

"That's you. That's how you feel." His voice came out rough. "Stubborn and desperate and so fucking—"

He nearly pulled out and she felt the drag on both sides. Loss.

Anticipation. Then he drove back in hard and fast, all pressure and tight heat.

"Mine," he growled, driving home.

Talia was slipping. She tried to separate what she was feeling. Her mind, his body. Her body, his pleasure. But every time she found the edge of herself it slipped away. She'd been trying to—what had she—

He tugged one of her hands off the glyph, guiding it between her legs. Light flared, but the energy was inside her now, lighting up every nerve.

"Touch yourself. Feel what a perfect mess you're making."

Their fingers laced together, pressing in where their bodies met, and she felt the jolt from both sides—her pleasure spiking, his satisfaction echoing back. She felt something brush the base of his cock—her own fingers—and she shuddered. For one dizzy moment she was Talia again—and then she slipped back under.

"That's right, let go," he murmured. "I have you."

The channel bond flickered with Dawn's distant concern. Talia didn't have the energy to block it, but she didn't want Dawn here. Didn't want her to see how far she'd slid. But Dawn's presence didn't intrude or try to stop her. It *steadied* her. Dawn's heartbeat next to hers gave her a rhythm, and Talia followed it. Suddenly, the room came into focus.

Her emotions separated from Lore's like oil and water, and her thoughts were her own. She watched along with him as his cock slid into her body. Witnessed, each time, the flare of his satisfaction. He *needed* this—the power, the domination. He felt close to something very big, something that he wanted, and *she* was the threat. If he let her look, she might see how much he needed her.

He doesn't know I'm here, Talia realized. He thought she was gone, dissolved into his spell, but she was wide awake now. She felt powerful standing there. In control. She could do anything, try anything, and no one would know.

Harder. Talia pressed the thought into Lore's mind. *Fuck her harder, Lore. She can take it.*

That shocked him. She felt it ripple through him—a surge of surprise, then approval, then crackling desire that nearly swamped his self-control. He took a breath to steady himself. It was almost funny, how easy that was.

Talia felt stronger with each stroke, watching her body rock forward, feeling Lore coming undone. The pinching need to push deeper, take her harder, seemed to overwhelm him. He was frantic with it.

He tugged one of her knees up onto the table to hit a better angle. His muscled back hunched over her like a rutting animal. Savage. Rhythmic. He thought he controlled her. Possessed her completely. She let him think he had.

Enough.

She closed her eyes and slipped back into her body. She felt him behind her, hammering home almost to the point of pain. Knowing how feral he was for her made her giddy, and she let herself sink into the other side of it—the excruciating pleasure of being destroyed.

"I hate how good this feels," she gritted out, each word wavering in time with his thrusts.

"I know," he hissed. "Fuck."

She felt him pulse and erupt, and she cried out as her own pleasure crashed down behind it. He groaned and pumped into the grip of her body, fast and off-beat, and then it was over. He pulled out and took a step back.

When she turned to face him, his eyes were mostly black with just the faintest halo of gold. He searched her face, frowning in concern.

"Still with me?" he asked.

"That was—"

"Too much?"

"Absolutely not the lesson I expected."

Relief washed over his face. Her hair was loose and wild, and he brushed it back behind her shoulders. "You continue to surprise me, Talent. Next time, I'll let you stay longer."

He had no idea.

"Tomorrow?" She surprised herself with the question.

He hesitated, just for a second. Then he smiled. "Of course. Same time?"

She nodded, still catching her breath.

He adjusted his pants and shirt and paused to look at her. "You're so fucking broken, Talent," he said with a crooked smile. "I wish I'd known sooner. I have so many plans for you."

He shook his head and turned on his heel. The door clicked shut. *If I'm the broken one, you're beyond repair.* Too late with the comeback, as always.

The bond pulsed at the edge of her awareness. Had Dawn felt all that? The library's thick walls, the flux humming in the air, maybe it had muffled the connection. Talia felt a flash of annoyance and gratitude mixed together. She was sure it was Dawn that had pulled her out and given her solid ground. She'd wanted to keep Dawn out of her head, but she was glad she hadn't been alone tonight.

Her body still buzzed with power, and her palms tingled where they'd touched the glyph. She'd never channeled that much before. Even with the bond, she'd never felt that strong. *And yet.* She wrapped her arms around herself, suddenly cold despite the flush heating her skin.

Lore had *told* her what would happen. He hadn't asked or made a suggestion. Told her. As if she'd already made the choice and just didn't know it. She'd actually enjoyed the sex, but the way Lore had taken possession of her affinity was alarming. What else could he do, if he could tap into her power? His need and isolation went deeper than she could have guessed. Even his desire for her was laced with fear.

And what was all of that about becoming a god?

Talia's legs shook, and she sank into an armchair. She pressed her hands to her face. They smelled like sex and amber and smoke.

Do you trust me?

She'd said yes. Hadn't even hesitated. She wondered when she'd stopped asking herself that question.

41

MORE BAD CHOICES

TALIA

Flux is depleted when used, and we cannot create more. Once, the fae kept magical beasts as pets—now effectively extinct—that were able to produce new flux. Not only that, they could amplify a person's affinity in proportion to their own capacity. Imagine the potential.

— LORE TAVIS, *ON THE NATURE OF FLUX*, UNPUBLISHED

Talia barely slept. Every time she closed her eyes, she was back in that library, pressed into that table. She kept hearing Lore's voice rasp against her ear.

Good girl.

Her stomach twisted the same way it had then, and she gave up on sleep. It was technically morning now, but the sun hadn't yet risen. She sat by the window, watching Haven's lights reflected on the rain-slick streets. Her body still felt like it was glowing. That part felt good. So why wasn't she satisfied?

I make all the decisions. You just let go.

That part had sounded wrong too. But her alarm had faded in the moment. Like he'd turned off the part of her brain that questioned things. That wasn't normal. She always asked questions, it was fundamental to who she was. Except with Lore.

The first time she had sex with Lore it had felt like freedom, like choosing something wrong and delicious for herself. This time, she had the nagging feeling she was letting someone else define her again. She'd just traded society's approval for his.

Except she *liked it.* Just thinking back on what they'd done in that library made her toes curl. If he was here now, she'd let him do it again. Maybe she *was* broken.

You know in the old stories, when someone offers you everything you want? There's always a price. That's how it is with Lore...

Dawn's warning from weeks ago surfaced, like a splinter she couldn't dig out. She scrubbed her hands over her face. She was overanalyzing. She always did this. Picking apart every moment of joy until nothing good survived.

A knock on the door broke her spiral. It shook hard enough to rattle the latch.

Dawn's voice called through the wood, too loud. "You up? We've got a problem."

Talia scrambled to open the door, grateful for the interruption even as dread pinched in her stomach. Dawn stood in the hall in a full gray suit and matching hat, but her usual swagger was gone. Her fingers tapped at the doorframe.

"Holloway's gone."

Talia froze. "What?"

"He was supposed to meet me." Dawn grimaced. "Haven't seen him since last night. I'm worried he did something stupid."

Dawn woke the rest of their party, and they gathered outside the dining hall, clothes half fastened, weapons belted in haste.

"We split up," Riven said, voice clipped. "Lore, take the archives. I'll check the stables and alleys. Dawn, lower levels. Talia, guest wing. Meet back at the central fountain."

Talia noted that Riven gave her the most boring possible assignment. The guest wing was where they all slept. Obviously if Holloway was there, they would've found him already.

She searched the guest wing, the common rooms, the garden. Nothing.

By the time she reached the fountain, her chest was tight with worry. Riven was already there, shaking his head. Lore joined them, empty-handed. They waited. Five minutes. Ten. Fifteen. Dawn didn't come back.

Talia reached for the bond, and it was muffled, like it had

been in the library. They waited another ten minutes. Then the connection went quiet between one breath and the next. Just gone. Talia pressed a hand to her sternum. One heartbeat instead of two.

"Something's wrong. I can't feel her."

Riven's expression went deadly. "We search everywhere. Every room, every passage."

Two hours later, they'd found nothing. Nearly four hours since they'd last seen Dawn. The broken bond ached in Talia's chest. She couldn't stop reaching for it, hoping each time that Dawn's presence would bloom back, but it never did.

"I'll check the council hall," Riven said when they reconvened. "If Haven took her, they'll have records of some kind." His jaw tightened. "Go back to your room, Talia. Lock the door."

Talia nodded. Then, the moment he turned the corner, she did the exact opposite and headed for the archives. Lore fell into step beside her, the gold flecks gleaming in his hazel eyes. Had he been waiting there for her to disobey?

His hand brushed her arm, and he grinned. "Smart girl."

Peat's face went pale the moment he saw them. He tried to back away, but Lore caught him by the shoulders.

"Peat," Talia said calmly, laying a hand on his arm. "We're looking for Holloway and Dawn. Where are they?"

"I—I don't know. I haven't seen anyone."

Fear spiked sharp, but underneath she felt a thread of guilt.

"You're lying."

"I shouldn't be talking about this," Peat stammered, trying to pull away.

Talia stepped closer. Her heart was racing, but she fought to keep her expression blank. She slid her empathy forward, hooking into his devotion, weighting it with urgency. She didn't just suggest, she *steered* his emotions. His eyes snapped back to hers, pupils blowing wide, breath catching.

"You will tell me where my friends are," she said evenly. "Because I'm asking nicely."

"Push harder, Talent," Lore murmured beside her. "We'll be here all day if you're gentle."

The approval in his tone spread through her chest like sunlight. He wanted her to do this. Wanted her to break Peat's mind. And she wanted...to impress him? The realization was horrifying, but she shoved that down. Later. She couldn't worry about it now. She pushed harder.

Peat shook his head frantically. "I can't. They'll know I told."

Talia layered calm over his fear, urgency over his hesitation. The same gift that let her hear Dawn's heartbeat now bent Peat's will like soft clay. *Help me find them*. She shaped her desperation, turning the plea into a command.

She hadn't known her gift could do this. This was manipulation. Control. And it was terrifyingly easy. Peat whimpered. Tears blurred behind his glasses. She smelled urine.

Talia felt sick, and tears pricked in her eyes. Her hand shook on Peat's arm. She should stop. This was wrong, and gross. But she couldn't feel Dawn anymore, and all the gentle options were gone.

"Just tell me where they are, Peat," she said, her voice wavering. "This can all be over, just tell me."

"They said—" He scrubbed at his eyes, voice hitching. "They said Holloway was reading restricted material. They're holding him for questioning. For his own safety."

"And Dawn?"

He shook so hard his teeth clicked. "A live donor. The first real channel bond anyone's seen. They want to study it. See if they can replicate—"

The words washed over her, refusing to sink in. *Donor*. *Study*. *Replicate*. Clinical terms for a specimen, not a person.

"Where is she?" she gritted out.

Peat sagged in Lore's grip. "Under the council hall. Service stairs by the northern cloister. It's marked as storage, but it's not—" His voice cracked. "Please don't make me go there."

She leaned close enough to see her reflection in his tear-filled eyes. No time for pity. No room for mercy. "Show us."

He nodded frantically. Lore let go, and he stumbled forward. He led them through the corridors to a narrow service door. Talia tugged it open revealing a wide staircase heading straight down.

Riven emerged from a doorway farther down the hall, chest heaving. He looked between the three of them, his brows pressed together.

"Figured you wouldn't listen," he said. He took in Peat's flushed face, the piss soaking his pant leg. "What happened to him?"

A strangled cry escaped Peat's throat. He took a step back, then another, then fled down the hallway. Talia let him go.

Lore's voice brushed her ear as they watched him run away. "Power suits you."

Pride bloomed hot in her chest before she could stop it. But he wasn't praising her strength. He was praising her cruelty. The way she'd wielded power to take what she needed. Hurting a friend of hers to do it. When she glanced at Riven, he was taking in the whole scene, a dark expression on his face.

She let out a deep slow breath. This was bad. It was irrecoverable. She knew in her gut that she would have to peel herself away from Lore. But she pressed the feeling down. Later. She'd deal with this mess after Dawn was safe.

The stairwell reeked of vinegar. The air was too cold, flux lamps too white, each footstep echoed weird and hollow. As they neared the final landing, she heard machinery hum somewhere behind the walls. Liquid gurgled through unseen tubes.

An archway loomed ahead, sealed by double doors etched with flux glyphs. Blue light shimmered across the surface, pulsing faintly. Not to keep people out, she realized. To keep something in.

Then a scream ripped through the layered soundscape. A raw, hoarse cry filled with fury and pain.

Dawn's voice.

It tore through Talia, shattering her last shred of restraint. She pressed her palm against the cold metal door, feeling the flux wards hum against her skin. Her friends were in there, and she would get them out, no matter what she had to do.

42

PRISON BREAK

DAWN

The only people worth dying for are the ones who won't let you.

— FRONTIER VERNACULAR, ORIGIN UNKNOWN

Dawn cracked one eye open, but all she could see was a white glare. A band across her midsection held her flat on a table. She clawed for Talia's brightness over the bond, but there was nothing there. Panic tightened in her chest. She was cut off. Alone.

Tubes ran from her veins to bags overhead that filled with that blue light. Replaced. Filled again. She tried to make a fist. Her fingers barely twitched. *Well, fuck.*

White coats drifted in and out of her field of vision. Someone laughed under their breath. Someone else scribbled notes, avoiding her eyes.

Dawn started counting. Three exits—two normal-size doors, one wider service entrance on metal hinges. Four guards, standing at attention. Based on the uneven pattern of the footfalls, one of them walked with a limp. Some kind of wards hummed at a pitch that hurt in her sinuses. The far wall was lined with tanks and cages. She couldn't see much flat on her back.

They wheeled a table past her. Some kind of fluxborn lay strapped to it. Barely breathing. The researchers cut into it, no sedative that she could see. The creature's body seized against its restraints. They pulled out wet organs that dripped into steel bowls. Everything else—meat, bone, fur—got slapped into a bucket.

They rolled the mangled body away, and Dawn's stomach twisted. Not at the blood—she'd gutted hundreds of fluxborn—but at the attitude. Indifference. Like the fluxborn were ore to be mined. She wondered what would happen when it was her turn.

"—told you that bath was too good to be true."

A voice snapped her out of her daze. She twisted and saw Holloway smirking like a jester behind some bars. Relief hit so hard she almost passed out again.

"Ah, Dawn," he said, all casual. "How's the service? I'm giving it two stars."

"Only two?" Her voice rasped.

"Well, the beds are small, and they never brought breakfast. But"—he gestured around—"this room is spectacular. Nothing says luxury like a wall of torture equipment."

One of the white coats glared at him. "Shut up."

Holloway shrugged and winked at her. He looked like shit, and his hands had a tremor. He was doing a terrible job of pretending he wasn't terrified, but Dawn respected the act.

"How long have you been here?" she asked.

"Few hours before you. I went back for the files." His tight smile warned her not to say she'd told him so. "They're holding me here for my own safety, of course."

For your own safety. Sure. Not likely either of them would walk out of here alive.

The white coats came back with surgical trays and clamps. A crown of needles shaped like a halo from hell. They cut her nice new jacket away. Cold air licked her skin, gooseflesh rising. Pants next. What a waste. She wondered idly if one of them would enjoy wearing her hat when this was all over.

Across the room Holloway looked away. "Could use some music. Any requests?"

"Just something loud."

He started singing. Boy had a lovely voice. Even the white coats paused, glancing up before they forced their eyes back to their instruments.

Dawn swallowed a lump in her throat. The damned music cut through all her emotional shields. "You think that'll help?" she croaked.

He paused and grinned at her. "Better than screaming. Anyway, we're not going to die in here. Lore will come."

Lore. Not Talia. Not Riven. Not the gods he'd grown up praying to. The certainty in his voice caught her off guard. She wanted to believe him so bad, she almost did.

Holloway kept singing until they dragged him out of that cage. He fought, or tried to, but there were too many of them. They sliced his clothes away and heaved him onto another table. They pinned him down too. Naked, shackled. Another way to make them less than human.

When the white coats stepped out, Holloway twisted his head toward her. "Don't look at them," he whispered. "Look at me."

He didn't shut up. He told her about growing up in Vaelis. About his dead older brother. About sneaking into taverns and charming all manner of girls and boys with his music. The jokes got darker as the time crawled. Gallows humor dressed up as levity. Dawn hung on every word.

Her vision blurred at the edges. Just breathing felt like work. When she tried to talk, her throat closed. Four hundred years she'd been alone. Her choice. Now, strapped down and dying, that felt like a mistake. When the scholars came back with the needle crown, she was grateful for Holloway. At least she wouldn't die alone too.

"Neural bridging requires direct interface," one of them was saying, not to them but to the others. Explaining. Teaching. "We'll establish connection through the device, directly on the brain stem."

Dawn didn't follow all the words, but she understood enough.

They wanted to carve a bond into her skull. Her blood wasn't enough. They wanted inside her head. The scream ripped out of her, shredding her throat. *Fuck them. Fuck all of them.*

The doors didn't open. It sounded like they exploded. Silver light split the air, and there was a confusion of noises. She heard the guards and scholars shout and scream and fall silent. Talia yelled her name, and she recognized Lore's laugh.

Then Riven was at her side. His blades cut through the restraints like nothing. The bands fell away.

The bond slammed back. It hit her straight in the chest. Not gentle. Not gradual. After hours of nothing, Talia's stubborn sparkling energy hit so hard Dawn gasped.

"Took you long enough." The words cracked in her throat.

She tried to stand and just sagged into Riven's arms. A laugh and a snarl bubbled up together. She was alive. She wasn't alone. Talia cut Holloway loose. He tugged on his pants, but his shirt and jacket were shredded.

"Well, this is happening," he said, holding up the shreds of fabric. "Naked prison break. Totally normal."

His ridiculous chatter didn't annoy her so much anymore.

Then a wave of enforcers marched through the broken doors and spilled into a line. Dawn counted twelve. Lore tossed her one of her revolvers. She almost dropped it; her hands were shaking so bad. But she braced herself on Riven's shoulder and got it up. The shot went wide but close enough to scatter the line.

Talia stood in the middle of the room, Lore at her side. No weapon Dawn could see. She was about to shout for the girl to get down when Talia lifted a hand. The first few enforcers charged, then stopped, eyes going glassy. Their arms jerked like puppets with fucked-up strings. The girl's face was blank. Lore just stepped back to let her work, a smirk on his face.

That's when the fight broke open for real. They fought like a pack. Talia pushed confusion. Lore broke their weapons, a fresh flux stone in both hands. Holloway propped himself behind the metal table with a rifle he'd picked up: aim, fire, reload. Riven sliced through anything that got close.

And Dawn—weak, shuddering—leaned on them. Let them fight for her. Hated it. Needed it. Loved it.

The room was a smoky hellscape when the last enforcer hit the floor. Bodies piled in the stairwell. Gunsmoke and flux dust choked the air. Dawn had swiped a lab coat from the rack, and the white front of it was splattered with—well, better not to think about it. She cackled. The ragged fluxborn packed into that wall of cages growled and shrieked and slammed into the bars. She almost felt bad for them.

The sound of boots hit the stairs, and twelve more enforcers marched in. They had to break formation to get around the broken doors and bodies. They looked confused. Probably wondered how five random prisoners had done this much damage. A figure elbowed to the front of the group with his hands up. He looked vaguely familiar.

"Talent! Stop this!" the man shouted.

The girl stepped forward. "Nadir, get out of here. I don't want to hurt you."

"What are you doing?" he demanded, looking around with wild eyes. "I don't understand. This was your work, and we were so close."

Their group was moving, pulling together behind her in the middle of the room. They cut quite the picture. Lore's dark curls floated in a halo of flux static. Holloway shirtless, splattered with blood and flux juice. Riven looked like a statue, huge and square, and—was he growling? Dawn hefted her revolver and aimed it at Nadir's face.

"Can I take him?" she asked, pulling the hammer back. Talia raised a hand.

"We need to move, Talent," Lore said, and his hand brushed her waist. *Eww*.

Talia waved them both off. "What do you mean, this was my work?"

Whatever Nadir was going to say was broken by a growl and a crash. Dawn spun around to see fluxborn pouring out of the cages. Looked like eight or nine of them had enough energy left to do some damage. The cages must have lost power in the attack.

She shot one, and Riven sliced another through the midsection, but the rest of the fluxborn flowed past and set on the guards. They were small, ragged things, hard to tell what they'd started out as. But they had teeth and claws. She watched Talia's friend catch a raking claw swipe across his face. Then Riven grabbed her elbow and pulled her back.

"Time to go," he growled.

They fell back to a door that opened to a set of stairs, going up. More guards were pouring into the room behind them. Lore was the last one up. He waved a hand and exploded every light in the room. Glass and flux and fire swirled at their backs. But they were running up and out through a service door.

Cold winter air hit Dawn in the face. She gulped it in and collapsed against a wall. Blood and sweat slicked her skin under the tattered lab coat. The rush was fading. She could barely feel her legs.

Riven wiped blood from his blades. "Everyone alive?"

"Close enough," she rasped.

Talia draped a big bulky jacket around Dawn's shoulders, and she realized it was Riven's old one. A little worse for wear, but it'd do.

They staggered through alleys, keeping to shadows. The stables were a mess of enforcers and stable boys. They slipped three horses before shouts rang out, then ran hard for the gates. Alarms rang behind them, but no one seemed to be in charge.

By the time they cleared Haven's walls, highsun had peaked. They didn't stop until the city was a white smudge behind them. Talia swayed. Riven caught her elbow.

"I'm fine," she said, but her voice sounded thin, and a track of blood seeped from her nose. Her face was pale, with deep purple bruises under her eyes. She'd torn through dozens of minds that morning. Would have been a burned-out husk without the bond.

They'd escaped with the clothes on their back, except her and Holloway, who had less than that. Three horses and whatever was in the saddlebags. Lore looked to have stocked up on flux stones, and he'd grabbed Holloway's harp case and both of Dawn's revolvers.

"Well, this is a mess," Dawn rasped. "Where to next?"

Talia stepped forward. Didn't look to Lore. Didn't wait for a vote. "Valrotala," she said. "That's our destination, and we're close now."

Lore's smile curved, like he owned her. "I agree—"

But she was already walking away. Chin high, shoulders squared. Not waiting for praise or approval. Dawn blinked. The girl who'd been paralyzed by the simplest choices was gone. This one had shattered minds and fought through hell tonight. This one had teeth. When had that happened?

"Good plan," Dawn said. "Love it. Let's go."

And for the first time in a long, long time, she felt the ground shift in the right direction.

ACT III

TRUE GODS & NEW GODS

43

I'VE NEVER

DAWN

Sennett's first love was music. This surprises many who know only his military record and ultimate fate. He set his harp aside at age fifteen when he took on the mantle of Sennett heir, but he never gave it up entirely.

— *SONS OF THE PENTARCHY: A BIOGRAPHICAL RECORD*, 443 AC

Dawn had been looking over her shoulder every ten minutes for the past four days. She kept expecting to see a squad of enforcers. A pack of fluxborn. Something. It turned out, the scrubland west of Haven was fucking empty. No deer soft-stepping through the woods. No squirrels in the trees.

They were in red rock country, and the horses needed water. Their steps had shortened. Their ears drooped. Back in Haven, they'd barely made it out of the stables with Brimstone, Jonquil, and Larkspur. Three mounts for five riders meant a slow shuffle—ride, walk, swap, repeat. It wore on everyone, the animals most of all.

She and Talia had been testing the bond to pass the time. Working out signals. A sharp pinch to the left shoulder meant danger. Two hands to the chest meant all clear. Basic, but it worked. Next time one of them got in trouble, they had a plan.

"Let's stop up here," Riven called out.

A few scraggly trees leaned over a shallow creek. About as good as they were going to get. Valrotala was close now. A day or two at most. She wasn't too eager to see that fucked-up city again.

They all dismounted and brought the horses to water.

Holloway stretched his arms and leaned back until his spine popped. "Ugh, I'm getting old."

"You're not old," Dawn said. "You're a baby. And you're soft."

"You call this soft?" He flexed his arms and playfully muscled into her space with a shit-eating grin on his face. "I'm an enforcer, ma'am. Very intimidating."

The bruises from Haven had faded to yellow. The oath scar was a thin red line across his palm. He cracked those jokes to stay sane, and she got it. She really did.

"And you're what? Going to arm wrestle me to death? Get out of here." She shoved him back with both hands, and he cackled.

Talia laughed at them, and her delight glowed warm and fuzzy through the bond. It settled in Dawn's chest, tugged her lips into a smile too. She'd never imagined taking on a channel bond. Ehrue was the one who used her power to help others. Dawn was the loner. The survivor.

But she liked this just fine.

Holloway looked over at a fallen log near the water. He grinned. "Not arm wrestling. Rock throwing."

"You serious?"

"Afraid you'll lose?"

She snorted and picked up a smooth river stone, weighed it in her hand. Her arm was weaker than it should be. She compensated, adjusted her stance, and threw. It smacked the perfect center of the log with a satisfying crack.

Holloway's shot sailed wide.

"Best two out of three," he said, already picking up another rock.

The contest escalated. Rules, wagers, heckling. Holloway was better than he let on. Dawn relied on instinct, the kind honed by hunting things that hunted back.

Lore picked up a stone and turned it over like he was feeling out some invisible current. His throw cracked a branch clean off. She frowned. They were all a little outgunned by Lore, she thought, until Riven stepped up. He didn't even pause to aim. His shot took out three brittle leaves in a row with a little *thunk, thunk, thunk*.

Dawn threw a pebble at his head. He caught it without looking.

"Arrogant bastard," she muttered, but Talia's affection rippled through the bond. *Well that was new*.

Lore raised his hands. "Fine. We have a new champion." He plucked a handful of grass and braided a crooked crown. He dropped it onto Riven's head. Riven endured the ceremony with dead-eyed dignity while Holloway and Talia cheered.

They traveled another few hours before making camp. Red dust stuck to everything. The sun was nearly down, and the sky was bruised purple. She'd say it was bad luck, except by some miracle she caught two rabbits. Talia dug up some wild onions and garlic.

Riven cooked. They fell into an easy rhythm. She split the meat, cut the onions. He built the fire, added the herbs. Shook the pan like he'd been doing it for centuries. When he passed her the first piece, the meat was charred outside, tender inside, dripping fat. The onions had burned down to candy.

She eyed the darkening horizon. They couldn't see the spires of the city yet, but she could imagine them out there. Then she turned back to dinner. No sense in worrying. They ate with grease on their fingers, smoke in their hair. Lore pulled out a flask and passed it around. The *liethi* burned like fire and cinnamon.

Talia sniffed it suspiciously. "Where did you get this?"

Lore just smiled. "I found a few useful things in Haven."

On top of the slow travel day and good food, the liquor loosened them up.

"One more game!" Holloway announced. "For the crown." Everyone groaned. "This game is called 'I've never.'"

The rules seemed simple. Each person had to say something they'd never done. Everybody who had done that thing had to drink.

"I'll start," Holloway said. "I've never broken off an engagement." Then he shoved the flask at Talia.

"Damn, boy," Dawn said, letting out a low whistle. "Guns blazing."

Talia groaned and rolled her eyes, and Holloway giggled. She drank.

"Well I've never read a book." Dawn stood and pointed at Talia, making the girl drink again.

"Rude!" Talia said, but she drank like a good sport. "Fine. I've never killed anyone. Not with my own hands."

Everyone else had to drink. The laughter thinned to silence until Dawn broke it. "Well. Good. Keep it that way if you can."

Lore leaned forward toward the fire. "I've never told a lie."

"You're full of shit." Holloway punched his shoulder.

Lore only raised an eyebrow. "Name one time."

Dawn tried to come up with an example. Couldn't. "Huh, maybe he's telling the truth."

"That's—gods, that's worse somehow," Holloway muttered, taking a sip and leaning forward, elbows propped on his knees.

"Old man," Dawn said, pointing the flask at Riven. "Your turn."

Riven shifted, clearly uncomfortable. "I've never died."

The circle fell into stunned silence. Then Dawn started laughing. "What?"

Riven's brow furrowed. "I mean, I've almost died, but I haven't, so—"

"That's not the game!" Holloway was laughing, too, leaning against Lore's shoulder. "You say something the other people *have* done that you *haven't* done."

"You're terrible at this," Dawn said, wiping her eyes. "This is why I never invite you to do fun shit."

"I've never begged," Riven said, stubborn, like he didn't see the problem.

The mood shifted again. Lore slipped the flask from Holloway's hands and tipped it back slow, his eyes on the fire. Dawn raised an eyebrow.

"Is there a story there?" she asked, reaching for the flask and drinking herself. She'd judge Lore for plenty, but not that.

He brushed a hand through his loose hair. Kept his eyes fixed on the fire. "Just my childhood. It won't happen again."

Talia's hand made to reach for him, then stopped. She looked away. Holloway touched Lore's shoulder, whispered something only he could hear.

The fire burned lower. Someone added more wood. The game kept going until they were all loose limbed and the flask was empty.

"I've never been to Sovana," Dawn said sleepily.

"You should come home with us." Talia leaned on Riven's shoulder. Her eyes were almost closed. "You all should. I'll show you Vaelis. The harbor. The market at sunrise."

"Maybe," Dawn said. She didn't plan that far ahead.

Holloway wore the grass crown now, crooked on his curls. He played a soft tune on his harp. Firelight lit up each of their faces—Talia sitting close to Riven, Riven relaxed for once in his life, Holloway lost in his music, Lore softening around the edges.

Dawn leaned back and watched them, this pack she hadn't asked for. This thing they'd built? Annoying, loud, messy. She liked it despite herself.

She took first watch, like she always did. Sat with her back to a big old rock, grass crown perched on her head, listening to her pack snore lightly in the dark. They didn't have many of these nights left before they got to Valrotala.

And that's where it would end.

She didn't see a way both her and Lore walked out of there alive.

44

THE THREE SUITORS

TALIA

I don't know what I expected the end of the world to look like, but it wasn't that. It wasn't blue flames and orange skies. What even are we now?

—VAEL LAR VARLOHEIM, PERSONAL JOURNAL,
YEAR OF THE CROSSING. TRANS: T. SALAREN

Lore and Holloway rode ahead together, an unlikely pair, dark prophet and golden knight. Riven rode slightly behind, ever the guardian. They'd passed out of the red dirt desert and entered a thin forest, the Thol Amras mountains a jagged line just over the treetops. That's where Valrotala was supposed to be.

She touched the bond in her chest. Dawn was scanning for danger, as always, and that sharp awareness felt like an anchor.

"We should stop soon," Dawn called back. "Rest up before heading in."

As the group spread out along the creek, Talia noticed Holloway watching her. He approached as the others unpacked. He looked serious, but his hands tugged nervously at his jacket.

"I need to apologize," he said immediately.

Her heart skipped, and she tilted her head, leading him away from the others. "For what?"

"Back in Heller's Ridge. The things I said." His eyes fell. "You didn't deserve that."

She studied his face. When had he gotten those lines around his eyes? "You were upset. I get why."

"Do you?" He stepped closer, voice dropping. "Tally, you're the one good thing in my life. You're solid ground. Remember when we were children and we made that promise, to explore the world together? I thought that was real."

Talia squeezed his hand and felt the pain leaking between them, sweet and salty.

"I know you don't feel the same," he said softly. "I need to let it go; I just don't know how. After we lost Cordon, I thought if I could keep you safe, it'd make sense. There'd be a reason I survived when he didn't."

His other hand closed over hers, and she felt the full weight of his love and loyalty and grief. Guilt twisted in her stomach. His pain was her fault, and he had no idea. It's why she'd always offered him comfort; it was the least she could do.

"He's been gone ten years, Holloway," she said quietly. "Nothing we do is going to make it make sense." She squeezed his hand before pulling back. "You were right to call me out back in Heller's Ridge, but if you're asking me to be honest about what I want? It's not us."

He nodded slowly, but a line had formed between his eyebrows. "But would it be so bad," Holloway asked, "a life together in Vaelis? We'd both sit on the Council of Five. We could make things better. Write songs together. We wouldn't have to—we'd need an heir, but after that we could keep separate rooms."

He smelled like that vanilla soap he always used. Familiar and steady, clean and safe. If she'd never found the journal or come to Valta, if she was still Talent and not Talia, she could imagine a life where they cordially coexisted like that.

But she *had* changed. She had the channel bond with Dawn now and more power than she knew how to use. She wanted to explore that, and she couldn't fold herself back down into the tidy shape Holloway wanted for her.

His thumb brushed across her knuckles twice. For one dizzy heartbeat she wanted to stay there, wrapped in the comfort of his unwavering love. But that wouldn't be fair to anyone.

"No not bad, exactly," she admitted. "I just want more."

"I know." He radiated sadness, but he still smiled. "I've known for a while."

He pulled her into a hug that was tight, and warm, and then over. He was letting her go, and it felt real this time.

She was checking Jonquil's hooves when Lore materialized, humming under his breath.

"We'll be in Valrotala tomorrow." He paused, a little dramatically. "You should be ready to meet the gods."

"You know I don't believe in your gods." She shook her head, but she couldn't keep from smiling.

"Belief isn't required."

He leaned against a tree, watching her. "Back in Haven, you handled more power than most of us see in a lifetime. You and I push each other to be stronger. That's rare."

She stepped back. "What happened in the library. I don't want to repeat it."

"Don't want to?" He kicked off the tree and walked slowly around her. "Or won't allow yourself?"

"Both." She forced herself to meet his eyes. "You controlled my affinity, and you told me you'd make choices for me. After what happened with Peat..." She swallowed. "He was a friend, and I hurt him. I haven't stopped thinking about it, but you don't feel bad at all, do you? You'd tell me to do it again."

"Of course I would." He frowned. "We needed the information. We barely made it in time as it was."

"You always do that," she said. "It doesn't matter who gets hurt, you're always justified in the end. You *have* made me stronger, Lore. I just hate the person I become when we're together."

As soon as the words were out of her mouth, she knew they were true, and she wished she could take them back. His hands curled into fists at his sides, and she wanted to reach for them. She held herself back.

"If you say so." He let out a weary sigh. "I'd be surprised if you need my help to hate yourself. That's why you enjoyed what I did to you in the library. You want to be punished."

She bristled at his arrogance, but heat flooded her body at the mention of the library. Oh gods, was she turned on? He watched her struggle, a mean little smile tugging at his lips.

"Maybe I'm exactly what you deserve." He turned to leave, pausing only long enough to add, "Be ready for tomorrow, Talent."

She curled her fingers in Jonquil's mane, breathing through the urge to run after Lore and ask what he meant and how to prepare. She'd turned him down, but he hadn't accepted it. Apparently, her body hadn't either.

She clearly couldn't trust her own judgment around him, and she had no idea what would happen if she found herself alone with him again. She'd just need to keep her distance.

The sun bled orange across the horizon by the time they made camp. Talia sat close to the fire, hands nearly touching the flames, but she couldn't get warm.

Riven grinned down over a stack of firewood and dropped it with a crack, then took a seat next to her. He leaned forward, elbows on knees, but the tension in his shoulders didn't ease. He always carried more than he let on.

"Heading for bed?" she asked, glancing over at him.

"Not yet. Don't want to waste what time's left." His eyes stayed on the fire.

She surveyed the others. Holloway sat across from them, shaping chords on his harp. Dawn and Lore murmured in low voices at the perimeter.

Riven leaned closer. "Walk with me?"

He led her through the trees and up a short hill that opened into a clearing. They were at the edge of a bluff, a rocky shelf that dropped off steeply into a tree-filled valley. Across that valley, set into a row of jagged mountains, the silhouette of a city stood out against the stars. Valrotala. Riven walked to the edge and sat, very slowly, with his legs hanging over.

Talia joined him, feeling a dizzy rush as her feet swung in the open air. They sat looking at the ancient city, Holloway's music fading in and out with the wind.

"When I was here last," he said finally in a low voice, "the sky was orange." He paused. "When an entire city burns, the smoke gets into everything. You carry the smell for years."

His face was impassive, but he was breathing quick and shallow, like he couldn't shake the panic he'd felt that day. She had to imagine the city's fall had cut him deeply. Who had he lost? She squinted at the shadowy towers, trying to picture what it had been like.

"I wasn't here when it happened," he said. "I should've been."

"When Valrotala burned? You would have died."

"Very likely."

Oh. Her chest felt tight. She couldn't feel his emotions with her affinity, but she traced the edges of her own guilt and grief and tried to imagine if she'd lost *everyone*. How long had he hated himself for surviving?

"You can't really want that," she murmured.

His hand flexed once, knuckles going white. "Not anymore, no."

Relief washed over her. The devastation of Valrotala was tragic enough, but for Riven to blame himself after so many years seemed worse. The souls lost when the city was destroyed could rest, at least, but he had to go on living.

"What changed?" she asked.

"You would've loved the library," he said instead of answering, his voice growing steadier. "Glass ceilings. Reading rooms that changed with the light. More books than you could count."

"That sounds beautiful."

"Yes, it was. Not sure what's left." He squinted at the shadow of the city as if the library might come into focus. "I assumed it was lost. Every book. Every work of art. Then I found the journal in your cabin, and you spoke Starscript." He paused and exhaled slowly. This was a lot of words for him. "Your accent was not so bad."

She hadn't considered how it made him feel that everything she studied, he had lived. It made more sense now, why he stuck around. She must have reminded him of home. She wished she'd known—she might have made different choices.

Nighttime forest sounds filled the space between them. She didn't mind the quiet. With Riven, she didn't feel like she needed to fill the silence or prove anything. His cedar scent grounded her.

"Do you remember our first night in Gateway?" she asked.

That made him chuckle. It vibrated through his chest and rolled through the valley.

"How could I forget?" he asked. "You made such a generous offer that night."

She groaned. "I thought I was so brave and clever, but I really was a child."

He shook his head. "I never should have said that. You *were* brave and clever. But you thought I was a beast. I couldn't prove you right."

She settled her head on his shoulder. He froze, then let out a small sigh and relaxed. Their hands were pressed to the rock beneath them, and when his pinkie finger brushed hers, it sent a jolt up her arm.

"I'm not with Lore," she said suddenly. Her throat felt scratchy, and she swallowed to clear it. "In case you thought—I don't know. I told him it's over."

"That's good." She liked the way his voice rumbled under her head as she leaned against him. "It's up to you, of course, but you deserve better. He doesn't even call you by your name."

She was sharply aware of her legs dangling over a free-fall drop and of every point where her head and shoulder and hand touched his. Her whole body felt alive, like she could do anything.

"Well, I refuse to proposition you again," she said, doing her best to sound casual. "It was embarrassing enough the first time."

"I can appreciate that." He wrapped one hand lightly around her braid and stroked the length of it, tugging a little at the end. It was weirdly intimate. "I promise that I won't make you ask the next time, if that's what you'd like. Just not tonight. You should have a choice, when it happens. A real choice, not one you're backed into when the world feels like it's ending."

This man was so different from Lore. He wasn't challenging her; he was guarding her choices like they mattered. Like she mattered.

"*When* it happens?" she asked.

"Mm-hmm. If you want." His whole chest vibrated with the affirmation, and the nervous energy she always felt rattling around in her brain just—calmed. She let out a small sigh.

He wrapped one strong arm around her and pulled her closer. She folded against his solid chest, his heartbeat thrumming steadily beneath her ear. They stayed like that, tucked against each other, as the valley wind got colder.

"We should go back," he murmured. "Before Dawn sends a search party."

"One more minute." Talia burrowed into his warmth.

His chin was resting on her head, and she felt him smile. "Sure."

When they finally stood, he kept her hand in his. They walked back toward the glow of campfire. Riven laid out their bedrolls, close but not touching.

Talia lay down and fought to slow her breathing. Tomorrow they would venture into the ancient ruins they'd glimpsed from the cliff. They'd find out what Lore's gods amounted to and what was left of the library Riven described. But tonight...

Tonight, she reflected on what it would take to forgive herself. She'd made a devastating mistake that she couldn't take back, but still—it'd been ten years. Maybe it was time.

If Riven was willing to face his ghosts, she could too.

45

SEALED GATES & FAKE FLOWERS

DAWN

Met the twins in the orchard again. Sweet as sin and eager as anything. They rode me like they were racing each other. I lost. Or won. Hard to say.

— VAEL LAR VARLOHEIM, PERSONAL JOURNAL,
TEN YEARS PRE-CROSSING. TRANS: T. SALAREN

Well there it was. Valrotala sparkled ahead of them in the late-autumn light. Its white towers echoed the jagged peaks of Thol Amras behind it. The city spilled into the valley, districts and neighborhoods she used to wander through. All surrounded by a massive white wall with copper gates.

The weird thing was, nothing looked ruined from here. Riven went stiff at her side.

"The city burned," he said. "When we left, it was ash."

Dawn studied the perfect walls. Four hundred years and not a crack showing. She called bullshit.

They rode down toward the gates. The same gates she remembered. Same stone faces glowering down at her from the walls, every Valtaren king going back however long. They could all rot.

Talia gasped at the Starscript curling over the archway. Dawn was getting used to the flavor of her curiosity. Sweet on her tongue, like spun sugar.

"It's a riddle," Talia said, reading the translation out loud for Dawn's benefit. "*I am born from mouths, fed by hearts, and bind the living to the lost. Name me, and the gate remembers its part.*"

Dawn hated riddles. Lore motioned for the others to stay back.

"*Avatei leipi*!" He pressed his palm to the stone. *Open for passage.*

Nothing happened.

He tried a different pronunciation, getting louder.

Dawn folded her arms. "The door doesn't like that."

Lore ignored her. "Talent. You try."

He didn't have the courtesy to ask, just summoned the girl up like a tool. Talia pressed a hand against the metal gate. Her mind snapped awake, sparkling across the bond.

"*Born from mouths...fed by hearts...*" She traced the letters in the air as she thought through it. "Something said aloud. Or read."

She paced while she thought. "Not prophecy, that's too literal. Not an oath, wrong structure." Then she stopped and smiled. "Bind the living to the lost. Stories do that."

She turned back to the gate. "Story. That's the answer."

The gate flared to life. Starlight raced across the archway. Crystal veins lit up bright enough to throw shadows.

Lore stepped forward like it had responded to him.

"Of course," he murmured. "A story. A tale. A prophecy."

Dawn didn't bother rolling her eyes.

The light reached the center seam—

—and died with a soft little fizzle.

Silence slammed down around them. Lore froze, hand still hanging in front of the unmoving gate.

"No," he said. Quiet. "No, that's—try it again."

Talia lowered her voice. "I don't think—"

"Try it again!" he snapped.

She didn't flinch. She just knelt and brushed away dust to reveal cracked crystal veins set into the ground, blackened and dead.

"The answer was right," she said patiently. "But the gate can't open. The whole mechanism is blown out."

Well, damn. This wasn't a trial they could win. It was a system, and the system was cracked. As dead as the foundation stones they'd been kicking over all the way here. As dead as the bastards that built this place.

Lore's expression changed—fear, fury, humiliation—cycling so fast Dawn almost missed it. Then his mask slammed back in place. "It's a divine trial. If the answer is correct—"

He slapped the stone arch. "Open."

Nothing.

"*Avatei!* Open!" He hit harder this time.

The door absorbed his outburst. The sound didn't even echo back.

Lore turned to face the group. His control shook loose. Raw need flashed across his features before he smoothed it away.

Dawn couldn't help herself. "Four hundred years is a long time, *prophet*. Shit breaks."

She'd thrown the title like a slap. His neck flushed red. *Good, it landed.*

Talia approached a gnarled old apple tree near the base of the wall and pulled a piece of fruit down. She'd been keeping the bond open ever since Haven, letting Dawn in on her emotions. The girl's curiosity spiked.

"An orchard," Talia breathed. "Vael wrote about an orchard." She fished a battered old journal out of her satchel, flipping pages fast.

"The Moon Garden." She looked between Dawn and Riven. "Do you know where it was?"

"Inside the walls," Riven answered. "Southwest corner. We can't get there. though. It's beyond the gate."

"Oh gods," Talia breathed. "Except we can. There has to be another way in."

She led them through the overgrown apple orchard toward the southwest corner. Just outside where the Moon Garden was. She stopped, took a deep breath, and opened the journal.

"So, this was Vael's journal," she said quickly, cheeks flushed. Holloway swore under his breath.

She flipped pages until she found what she was looking for.

"I'll just read it," she said, her face flushing pink. "*Met the twins in the orchard again. Sweet as sin and eager as anything. They rode me like*"—

she choked—"sorry, that part's not important. Use your imagination."

She flipped another page. "Here, *Nearly dropped onto a patrol cutting back through the Moon Garden. They stared like I'd come down from the heavens and not the damned wall.*"

Talia closed the journal softly. Holding it closed like the words might jump out and bite her.

"He snuck out, and he didn't go through the front gate. He did —some stuff—here in the orchard, then he climbed over the wall and dropped into the Moon Garden." She pointed at the ivy-choked wall. "Somewhere around there."

The pride in Riven's smile hit Dawn square in the chest. Hadn't seen that look from him in a long time.

Didn't take long to find the spot once she knew to look. There was an ornamental carving of a massive dragon hewn into the wall. The notches along its spine almost looked like a ladder. The facade was crumbling in places, but it was worth a shot.

Dawn tested the first foothold. Solid. Then she paused. She glanced back at their dusty, restless horses. They weren't taking animals into a place like Valrotala. Certainly not over a wall.

"We need to cut the horses loose," she said.

Holloway blinked. "What do you mean? We're just letting them go?"

"Better they run free than break a leg in that place," Dawn said, untying Jonquil's lead and rubbing her nose, then moving on to Brimstone. She felt her throat go tight. Brimstone was a good girl.

They'd have to figure out how to get home without horses, but that only mattered if they survived.

They stripped the saddles, gathered the packs, and stepped back. The horses didn't need urging. They bolted into the orchard at a gallop, tails snapping. No going back now.

"All right," she said. "Let's break into this fucking place."

Dawn took point. The second handhold crumbled under her grip. She cursed, found another. Riven followed, and Talia came next. She climbed pretty well for a scholar. Holloway grunted behind her. Lore came last, sour as ever.

The incline got steeper. Roots dangled overhead and Dawn grabbed one, pulled herself to a narrow ledge. Riven was just behind her.

Talia climbed careful and quick, until her boot slipped.

She yelped, weight dropping—

Riven caught her around the waist with one arm, but the force of it yanked them both sideways. For one breathless second, Dawn thought they'd both go down. Then Riven's other hand locked onto a root and held.

Dawn felt dizzy from the ripple of feedback from Talia's shock, then the clean drop of relief. She cursed under her breath. The fucking city was already working against them.

The ledge opened into a cramped tunnel, some kind of garbage chute, from the smell of it. The walls scraped Dawn's shoulders. Roots snagging in her hair. But she could see light at the end.

Dawn dragged herself out onto another narrow ledge. She brushed bits of crap out of Riven's old jacket, which was hers now. That was when she looked down.

The Moon Garden had been a jewel among Valrotala's many treasures. Even Dawn hadn't hated it. The *luriel* blossoms only opened in starlight. Their vines had been woven into arches and benches and mazy paths. To come here on a clear summer night, when the air was warm and the sky was full of stars—it was something to see.

The place was a dusty tangle now. Heaps of dead vines. Dry pools. Crystal chimes that made no sound. She dropped off the ledge. When she hit the ground, a thin cloud of dust rose around her.

Riven stood frozen at the edge. Whatever she felt, this was worse for him. After a beat, he dropped down next to her. Talia came down next. She crouched to touch a shriveled *luriel* flower, the petals dissolving in her fingers.

Riven knelt next to her. "These flowers stored up moonlight. They glowed brightest on the darkest nights."

"It's still beautiful," she said, rubbing the dust between her fingers.

Lore crushed dead petals under his heel as he stalked past them all. "Welcome to Valrotala."

Dawn adjusted her grip on her revolvers and led the way. They slipped under a low arch, and she felt an itch between her shoulders. Something was off. She turned a corner and stopped hard enough that Lore ran into her. She expected bones and dust. She expected more decay. She didn't expect this.

It was a market, but it was *perfect*. One wooden stall held pyramids of apples, peaches, oranges. The fruits were all perfectly round. Their skins glistened. There was a bakery stand with bread set out half sliced. The air smelled like honey.

She didn't see a fleck of dust. No footprints. Everything looked cozy and lived-in, but she was shivering. Talia pressed her palm to the loaf of bread. Over the bond Dawn felt her heart flutter with surprise.

"It's warm," Talia whispered.

Lore came up beside her. "The true gods keep this place. They welcome us."

"Gods don't bake bread," Talia said back.

She moved on to a flower stall and tugged a round pink bloom out of its bouquet. She spun it in front of her nose and frowned.

"It's a good copy, but it doesn't smell like anything." She looked up at all of them. "It's an illusion. It's all an illusion."

Dawn scanned the pristine street. The impossible food. Whatever was doing this must have known they were here. Was probably watching. And now they were trapped inside with it.

46

THE GHOST CITY

TALIA

The figment differs from the ghost in one essential way: it still carries part of a soul. A ghost is an echo. A figment is a prisoner.

— *THE DEFINITIVE GUIDE TO PRE-CROSSING FOLKLORE*, FEN ALDAINE, 399 AC

"But why?" Talia asked, twirling the peony between her fingers. It looked so real. "Who made the illusion? And where is the power coming from?"

Lore was smiling like he knew a secret. "Don't worry about it." His hand settled on Holloway's shoulder. "The gods preserve what they choose."

Lore usually encouraged her curiosity when it came to magic. Shutting her down now was odd.

"We'll go to the citadel," Lore continued. "If answers survived the fall, we'll find them in the library."

The library. Talia couldn't wait to see it.

She tried to take in everything as they moved deeper into the city, scanning columns, the seams of doors, the bases of lampposts. No signs of decay.

Riven was quiet. She wished she could take away his heartache, but the best she could do was let her knuckles brush his every few steps. Then they turned a corner, and the road looped back on itself—the same fountain, the same fruit stalls, the same overturned cart. Not just similar, identical.

"We've been here already," Dawn said, kicking an apple that had rolled into the street.

Lore walked up beside her. "The true gods test our faith."

Talia didn't believe in Lore's gods, but if they did exist, they had a cruel sense of humor. Dawn bent down to swipe a bit of stone from the path and scratched an arrow into the wall pointing the direction they were walking.

Ten minutes later they stepped into a square with a fountain in the middle and a big white arrow on the wall. The back of her neck prickled, and she looked over her shoulder.

A child stood beneath a red-striped awning. She looked translucent. Her dress fluttered in the still air.

"Hello?" Talia asked.

The child pressed her palms into the air. Beneath her fingers, cracks spread in the illusion like breaking glass. She lifted one hand and pointed through the widening fissure, down a narrow side street.

A wash of emotion struck Talia then, grief, old and heavy, threaded with a warning. What kind of being could crack open an illusion with her fingers and hum with human feelings? Was she seeing a figment?

"Tally!" Holloway called. "What are you doing?"

When she turned back, the child was gone, but the grief lingered in the air. "Let's try this way," she said, guiding them to the side street.

Dawn made a face, but they followed her, and the fountain finally fell behind them.

A sharp pain grew in Talia's side as they climbed a narrow street so steep the pavers were almost stairs. She pressed her hands into her waist. The city spread out below them, a sparkling maze of twisted alleys and wider avenues.

Halfway up the slope, a door stood open, and the figment was waiting. Talia could make her out more clearly now, a girl of eight or nine, dark hair, eyes wide set and too old for her face. The girl turned and stepped inside, and Talia moved to follow.

Riven started to follow her inside, but she held up a hand. She didn't want him to see the girl—or, worse, say she didn't exist. She was overcome with the strongest urge to go in alone.

"Wait for me?" Talia asked with a pleading smile. "I'll only be a minute."

Riven scowled, but he called to the others to stop and took a position outside the door.

The air was stale and dry, and Talia's nose burned with an almost-sneeze. She moved deeper, drawn into a hallway with a door at the end.

It was a child's bedroom. She took in a small bed in the corner, the blankets folded neatly. Then her vision stuttered. Claw marks scored deep into the bed frame, feathers scattered everywhere. The room flickered between states—whole, ruined, whole again—until her eyes hurt. It settled on destruction.

Something violent had happened here, but there was no sign of blood. No bones or bodies. As if whatever had attacked hadn't found anything to kill. The girl stood in the corner. Emotion rolled off her in waves: grief, fury, fear.

Talia followed her gaze to a charcoal sketch pinned to the wall. Stick figures, some tall, some short. The smaller ones wore circles at their necks. Beneath them, a single word in Starscript: *elein*.

She knew the word. In the oldest lexicons, *elein* referred to pets or companion animals, ranging from lapdogs to oxen. But these figures stood on two legs. She looked again at the crude necklaces. Or—collars. She couldn't recall an example of people being called *elein*, but it was possible the word had been sanitized in translation.

"They enslaved them," she whispered to herself.

The scene distorted and rippled again. The child strained against it, her outline breaking apart. Talia reached out, but the air snapped and everything stilled. The bed stood neatly made. The gashes in the wall were gone.

There was nothing else to see, and Talia squinted against the daylight as she stepped back into the street. From outside, the house looked like every narrow townhouse in the row.

They kept climbing the narrow street, pausing every few blocks to let Talia catch her breath. Eventually the street widened into a boulevard lined with statues, pairs of people and animals. Each of the animals wore a marble collar.

Talia's stomach dropped. Collars. Like the picture in the room.

"The *elein*," she said slowly. "What was their relationship to the fae?"

Lore walked a step ahead. "Dawn, why don't you tell her?"

It sounded like a jab. Talia was missing the punchline, but it clearly got under Dawn's skin.

"Asshole." Dawn stared at the ground as she spoke. "The fae didn't have magic of their own, Talia. They drew power from their pets."

"Through the collars?" Talia asked.

Dawn grunted. "Those were more about restraint, but sure."

"Did they—" Talia hesitated. "Did they ever put people in those collars?"

Lore clicked his tongue, spinning on his heel and walking backward. "Very interesting question! Rumor has it that the *elein* were people, in a manner of speaking. They could shapeshift."

"Not *in a manner of speaking*," Dawn snapped. "They *were* people, shifted or not." Anger sizzled through the bond. Talia noted that Dawn spoke in past tense.

"What happened to them?" Talia asked, running her hand over a marble lion. She might have been imagining it, but his eyes looked sad.

The sun was sinking lower in the sky, and shadows pooled beneath the statues. Dawn had walked ahead of the group, her silhouette framed by the citadel ahead.

"The night that Valrotala fell, the *elein* went wild," Riven volunteered. "We don't know why, but they destroyed the city. Slaughtered the fae. They even killed each other, Dawn's family..."

He trailed off. Riven and Dawn had been away when the city fell, and if the *elein* had ravaged the city, what they'd come home to—the scene must have been horrific.

"Where are the *elein* now?" Talia asked. She didn't want to press, but she was too curious. It seemed improbable that so many deadly creatures could just— "Oh."

"Yes," Riven said quietly. "You know them as fluxborn. Those monsters are feral. There's nothing left of the people they were."

Talia had more questions, but she held them in as they caught up with Dawn at the entrance to the citadel. The doors were massive and shut tight, but they made their way through a service entrance into a wide, empty hall. The air was colder inside, and their footsteps rang sharp on the polished marble. At the far end of the room, a portrait took up most of the wall.

Talia walked down to look at it. Five figures—a king, a queen, three girls. Her gaze snagged on the woman in the center. She was beautiful in an otherworldly way, the kind of beauty that felt sharp around the edges. Beneath her image, a plaque read *Elanwei lar Valtaren, Voice of the Voiceless.* Riven made a low broken sound in his throat.

She squeezed his hand. "You knew her."

He didn't answer, maybe he couldn't. He squeezed so tight, it crushed her fingers. She thought back to the faerie story she'd studied, the one Dawn had told around a campfire once. Was this the same Elanwei? Was that even possible?

Lore walked up and gazed at the portrait. "Voice of the Voiceless." A slow smile tugged at his mouth. "How appropriate."

Talia only had to tip a little to bump against his shoulder. He was at ease, relaxed, his emotional signature laced with amusement. There was something sticky to his emotions, too, but she couldn't quite place it.

He nodded at her, like he knew she was reading him and he didn't mind. Then he hooked Holloway's elbow through his and steered him toward a doorway at the end of the hall. Talia had started to follow him when the child flickered in at her side. The girl's gaze moved between the portrait and Talia.

"What happened to you?" Talia asked the girl before she could stop herself.

No answer, just emotions: fear layered with urgency. But Talia felt her feet shuffling toward Lore before she'd decided to. Then suddenly the scent of roasted meat rolled through the hall, then fresh bread, then spiced wine. Her exhaustion doubled, vision blurring at the edges.

Lore's voice carried from the doorway. "The banquet is ready. We'll eat before we descend."

Talia tried to hold on to the child's warning, but her thoughts slipped. Her hunger surged, and her eyelids went heavy. She was moving through the arched doorway after Lore, into a hall lined with tables heaping with food. Platters of fruit glistened. Bread steamed, fresh from the oven. Cups brimmed with wine.

"We shouldn't—" Talia started. Her thoughts kept sticking, like slow-dripping honey.

Holloway reached for a fig. "This looks delicious."

"No—" She tried to step back, but her legs wouldn't listen.

Panic spiked as her body moved on its own. Riven's hand tightened on hers, but the sensation felt muffled and distant, like they were touching through water.

The air shimmered.

She blinked.

When she opened her eyes, she was seated at the table. A cup pressed into her palm. Wine on her tongue—tart, sweet, wrong. She hadn't poured it. Hadn't lifted the cup. Couldn't remember moving at all. Her mind tried to trace back what had happened, the sequence from standing at the door to sitting here, but the memories weren't there. Not fuzzy, just gone.

Holloway was smiling, juice running down his chin. "See? Delicious."

The child's terror pulsed at the edge of her awareness, but she couldn't remember why it mattered. And underneath that, a deep hum kept time with her heartbeat, steady and patient, waiting somewhere below the floor.

47

POWER IN THE WALLS

DAWN

Of all the pets in the fae menageries, dragons were the rarest and most powerful. A dragon-bonded channeler's access to flux would have been effectively limitless.

— LORE TAVIS, *ON THE NATURE OF FLUX*, UNPUBLISHED

It made no damn sense. This food shouldn't be here. The fire shouldn't be dancing over fresh logs. The wine shouldn't taste this sweet. Flux crystals in the chandelier threw blue light, warping all of it with a creepy glow.

Dawn's stomach growled. Her body ached from the steep climb. The smell of roast meat and honey made her knees go loose. She carved off a slice of pork, shrugged, and took a bite. Salt. Smoke. Fat. A hint of something her tongue remembered but couldn't name. Fuck. It was good.

"Think it's poison?" she yelled down the table, chasing the bite with a long pull of wine.

Holloway grinned around a mouthful of fruit. "Don't ask questions you don't want the answers to."

Talia laughed. Even Riven's shoulders had eased. Lore moved down the table, pouring wine that never seemed to run out. His hand brushed Talia's wrist as he refilled her cup, and Dawn felt the girl's heart skip. Damn bond. She didn't want to be in the middle when this mess between Talia and Riven and Lore came to a head.

The chandelier hummed overhead, crystals flashing. You didn't need that many flux crystals to power a damn light. Dawn clocked it. Then she took another bite. Her head felt stuffed with cotton.

Today had sucked. This damned city. The *elein* conversation. Elanwei's portrait. She wanted to forget. Let her guard down for once. Drink this fancy wine and worry about it tomorrow.

Holloway was telling a story about a drunk captain and a runaway wagon. Dawn smirked. She'd heard the story before—years ago in a bar in Gateway. He hit the punch line. Everyone laughed.

Ten heartbeats later, he told the same story. Same rhythm. Same grin. Same hand gesture. The laugh came again—on cue. Like the room was playing them a recording.

The fire popped. A shower of sparks leaped up—

—and hung frozen in the air for two heartbeats before they remembered how to fall.

Dawn frowned and shoved her chair back. The legs scraped the floor, the sound echoing too slow. So much for letting her guard down. She knew what this was, and she hoped she was wrong.

"Riven," she said, kicking his chair. "With me." He was already pushing back.

The heat of the dining hall dropped off quick. It just kept getting colder as they walked down a corridor. Behind them, muffled laughter echoed, rewound, played again.

"Feel here," Riven said quietly, pressing his palm into the marble wall. Dawn did the same. The stone thrummed beneath her fingers, an undercurrent of energy buried in the walls.

"This is more than an illusion." His jaw flexed. "It's warping time. There's only one person strong enough for this."

He looked at her. Really looked, right in the eye. She blinked and looked away.

"You said Ehrue was dead," he said quietly.

Dawn swallowed. "When I found her, she was drained. I tried to get her out, but those fucking monsters were everywhere—"

"I know." His voice was soft. "We had to go."

"But this—" Dawn pressed her forehead briefly against the marble, feeling the hum in her skull. "It's her. Lore wasn't lying."

Riven's voice rumbled on, deep and unrelenting. "She wouldn't have chosen this. If it's her, then Elanwei is using her. Channeling her dry."

The implication hung in the air between them.

"Could you do it?" Dawn asked, turning to lean against the wall. "If that's true. Could you kill Ellie?"

He looked away. "I don't know."

She was about to tell him she'd do it for him, when the bond flashed in her chest. Talia's heartbeat was racing. Then a pinch on her left shoulder. Hard and desperate.

The signal they'd agreed on. *Danger.*

"Talia. She's in trouble." She barely got the words out, and Riven was already running.

The hall warped around them—doorways stretching, torchlight bending, floor gleaming too bright. They hadn't gone far, but the illusion was trying to steer them off. Dawn shoulder-checked a door that shimmered into existence.

The banquet hall flared ahead, and they burst in together. Wet heat hit her like a wall, gluing her shirt to her skin. The room stank of wine and something sour—arousal and flux and rot.

Talia was on the couch, dress rucked up to the thigh, between the two men. Lore leaned back behind her, his shirt open and askew. Holloway sat on her other side, cheeks pink, hand half up her skirts. Lore was leaning forward, saying something in Holloway's ear.

"Lore." Riven's growl rippled through the air. "Stop."

Lore looked up with the widest smile. Like this amused him. Like Riven's reaction was *funny*. Dawn didn't bother arguing with the fucker. She lifted her revolver and shot the chandelier. Flux crystals exploded in a cascade of blue and silver. Shards of crystals fell like rain. Pinging off silver platters. Skittering across stone.

The illusion tore apart like tissue paper, and Dawn knew for certain it wasn't just Lore. Illusion magic was Elanwei's domain.

She and Riven locked eyes. He saw it too. A grim understanding passed between them. In the morning, they would free Dawn's lost love—and kill Riven's.

48

A FALSE FEAST

TALIA

I felt trapped for so long, but I could have said 'no' so much sooner. What if the cage door was never even locked?

— T. SALAREN, PRIVATE NOTES, 401 AC

The world had softened at the edges somewhere between the first bite and the second cup of wine. The flavors startled her. Sweet as honeycomb, then salt, then something like her favorite pastry from home. How could it taste exactly right this far from Vaelis? The warmth uncurling in her chest felt too good to question.

Her head buzzed, warm and fuzzy. Her shoulders relaxed for the first time in weeks. Her laughter felt too loud, but it didn't embarrass her. Even the fact that they all might die tomorrow seemed less scary. She could worry about that later.

She heard chairs scrape back, Dawn's and then Riven's. They moved toward the door, shadows stretching in front of them across the floor. She could still feel Dawn in the bond. They'd come back if anything bad happened. She leaned back and sucked sweetness off her fingers. She closed her eyes, just for a moment.

When she opened them, she wasn't at the table anymore. She was standing at the far end of the hall near the fire. Lore and Holloway sat on a low couch in front of her.

Holloway was rigid, hands braced on his knees, breath uneven. Lore lounged beside him, shirt unbuttoned, one knee bent at an angle. His arm rested along the back of the couch behind Holloway's shoulders.

She watched as Lore's fingers brushed Holloway's jaw, turning his face. Holloway's breath hitched. His eyes fluttered closed. Then Lore leaned over and kissed him.

It was a real kiss, deep and claiming. Holloway's hands fisted in the cushions. He let out a low moan, then a tiny inhale, as if he could take the noise back. Lore's eyes opened mid-kiss and found hers, watching her watch them. His mouth curved against Holloway's.

You want this too, that look said. Lore pulled back slowly, leaving Holloway flushed and gasping. Then he lifted two fingers in a quiet summons.

She'd been terrified of what they'd face tomorrow, but when Holloway saw her, a smile broke across his face, pure and reflexive, and her fears relaxed. All she had to do was exist, and he loved her. She didn't deserve it, but gods it felt good.

And Lore—the cut of his bare chest, the curve of his smile. She had wanted to put distance between them, but she couldn't quite remember why. His hands were on Holloway, but she knew exactly how they'd feel on her. If this was going to be her last night, there were worse ways to spend it.

Lore shifted to make room between them, but as she sat, he tugged her back into his lap. The cushions dipped, and Holloway's thigh pressed warm against hers. Lore's hand settled at her waist, and his free arm reached behind her along the back of the couch. Through the haze, she caught a flash of his emotion—satisfaction and relief. Like pieces of a puzzle clicking into place.

"You've been holding everyone else up for so long." Lore spoke softly to Holloway, sliding a hand through his golden curls. "Following rules you had no say in, that asked everything of you. You're allowed to want this."

Holloway's throat worked. He tilted into Lore's touch like he'd been starved for it. "Tally," he whispered. "Will you really join us?"

Lore turned his gaze to Talia. "It will all be worth it," he said quietly. "It will all be worth it."

Lore's hand slid higher on her waist, his thumb stroking up her ribs. Her pulse fluttered in her throat, and she swallowed hard.

She was seated fully on Lore's lap, and he dropped both hands to her hips, twisting her to face Holloway. "Go ahead. If you want her, she's right here."

Holloway's eyes went wide. "Tally—are you sure?"

"It's okay," she whispered.

She felt like she was in a dream, half-lucid, watching herself from a distance. She might wake up at any time, and she didn't want to. She wanted to see what happened next.

The kiss was soft at first, tentative. Then Holloway made a low, broken sound and deepened it, his hand coming up to cradle her jaw. When he pulled back, Holloway was breathing fast and shallow, and Lore was watching them with dark, hungry eyes.

She couldn't feel the bond anymore.

Lore's grip tightened at Talia's waist, pulling her tight against his chest. His arousal pressed into her back, hard and insistent.

"We could have this forever," Lore murmured into her hair. "The true gods can make new gods. Imagine the three of us. Ascended. Infinitely powerful."

It sounded absurd. And yet. Some part of her whispered, *if* this was true, *if* this power existed, what could she do with it?

Lore's lips brushed her ear as he whispered, "Let me show you."

She felt his teeth graze her pulse point, his hand sliding to her breasts. Every place he'd touched before, he touched again, reminding her body what he could do.

The bond was dead quiet now. The fire snapped and flared.

Holloway leaned into them both and kissed her again. A trail of sweat tickled down her spine. Between three bodies and the raging fire, the heat was oppressive.

Holloway pulled back, gasping. "Tally, I—gods—I shouldn't—"

"Keep going." Lore's voice was a silken rumble. "She wants you to give her an excuse."

Lore guided all three of their hands to rest on her thigh, fingers laced, dragging them slowly higher.

Holloway let out a choked sound as her skirts peeled back. "Can I—please—can I touch you?"

Lore chuckled darkly and bit her ear. "I didn't realize you'd never let him fuck you, all this time. You must have been curious."

What if she let this happen? Even if they died tomorrow, she would have made this one indulgent choice. Lore might be dangerous, but Holloway was here, and he would never hurt her. The two men's desire and desperation pulsed and crackled like the fire, a heady sensation that made her twist in Lore's lap.

She closed her eyes and tipped her head back until she felt the sharp edge of the couch. She bit her lower lip and tasted honey. How had they gotten here again?

"Tally?" Holloway was still waiting for permission. He wanted it so badly his hands were shaking.

She glanced back to the table, but it was empty. Right, Dawn and Riven had left. How long had they been gone?

She was alone here, and if she kept going, she knew she wouldn't stop. She tried to stand up, and Lore's hand tightened on her waist. Holloway's fingers tickled her leg, gentle but eager.

"Wait—I need a minute—" She reached across to pinch her left shoulder, hard enough to bruise.

Lore's hand slid to her jaw, angling her face back toward him. Away from the door.

"Stay with me," he murmured. "Stop thinking so much, just feel this with me. Please."

That one word, *please,* broke the spell. Lore never begged. He needed her, Talia realized, but it didn't go both ways. She was stronger without him.

"No," she said. The word came out thin but steady. "Stop."

He might have let her go on his own, but she'd never know. As soon as Dawn burst into the room, her revolvers cracked. Bits of chandelier rained down, clattering off the table, skittering across stone. The food sagged, green-black mold blooming across the bread, fruit collapsing in on itself.

Talia yanked her dress down, tearing herself out of the tangle of cushions and hands. Holloway jerked back, too, face going two shades lighter, then flushing so hard he looked fevered. He stared at his hand like it belonged to someone else.

Dawn stood in the doorway, gun smoking, a terrifying scowl on her face. Riven was moving, then he was at Talia's side.

He crouched in front of her, one hand hovering near her shoulder. "Are you hurt?" he asked. His voice wavered, the control in it razor thin.

She clutched her dress closed, hands shaking. "I don't think so."

Holloway sat on the edge of the couch, staring at his hands. "I didn't—" His voice cracked. "Gods, Tally, I wouldn't have—not if you didn't want it—"

The vacant look in his eyes made *her* feel guilty. He'd been so purely happy, and she shattered him again. Why had she waited so long to stop it?

Her mind was starting to spiral when Riven's hand fell to her shoulder. Solid. Real. He radiated calm assurance, but when she looked up, his jaw was clenched tight, his eyes cold and flat. He looked furious.

"You're safe now," he said. "You're in control."

She leaned forward, pressing her forehead against his shoulder, sucking in air that tasted like cedar instead of rot. He wrapped one arm around her, and it was just enough pressure to prove she wasn't floating away.

He looked at Lore over her head. She felt his voice vibrate in her chest. "If you touch her again, you are dead."

Lore's tone was unrepentant. "Illusions don't invent desire. They just remove the excuses." There was a pause. "I didn't force anyone," he added quietly.

Talia's cheeks burned. She should have stopped it sooner. But then again, would it have gone so far without the glamour, without the wine, without Lore steering their hands? No. It wasn't her fault. He did this.

She borrowed a flicker of Riven's anger and let it kindle in her own chest.

THE OTHER SISTER

VAELIS • 10 YEARS AGO

Everyone loved Merit best. She gave thoughtful gifts and remembered every servant's name. Once she nursed a wounded kestrel back to flight. Her laughter made you feel special, like sharing a secret. When Merit danced, people forgot to breathe.

Talent planned the mischief and spun the stories that bound their little group, but Merit was the soul. She made the stars sparkle brighter.

That night, Vaelis glittered. After yet another social ball, the adults had retired to the smoking parlor, and the house had gone still except for the faint hum of flux chandeliers.

Talent sat cross-legged at her desk, bent over a gift she'd worked on for weeks: a star map for Cordon Sennett's name day. Every constellation drawn by hand, silver ink for the brighter stars, deep blue wash for the sky. They'd talked about mapping the heavens the way explorers charted new lands, once they were married.

When the last line was dry, she smiled and wrapped it in silk and ribbon. A perfect gift.

The eastern hall lay half dark, moonlight pooling over marble. A thin line of candlelight glowed beneath Cordon's guest suite. The Sennett boys stayed here when the Council of Five was in session.

She hesitated, then knocked once. No answer. Her hand brushed the latch. The door gave a quiet click and opened just enough.

Candlelight spilled across rugs and tangled sheets. Her sister's dark hair fell loose over Cordon's bare shoulder. They were tangled together, whispering and laughing.

For a heartbeat, Talent couldn't move. She forgot to breathe. *Wrong*. This was all wrong. Cordon was engaged to her. What would society say? She'd be humiliated. Merit had everything—why did she need this too?

The box slipped from her fingers. It hit the floor and burst open, the star map unrolling and spreading, a spill of silver across the carpet.

Merit gasped. Cordon sat up. She caught a flash of their faces—beautiful, shocked, guilty.

Talent ran. Her feet slapped the marble, the echo chasing her down the hall. Her reflection blurred—round face, wide eyes, a ribbon still clutched in her hand.

She didn't stop running until she reached her grandmother's study. The air smelled of ink, paper, old perfume. The window stood open to the harbor, tide whispering as it ebbed below.

Her grandmother looked up from her desk, silver hair perfectly pinned back. She frowned. "What is it, Talent?"

"I saw something," Talent said, pausing to catch her breath. "Merit. In Cordon's guest suite."

"Was she—" Her grandmother's pause was delicate. "Compromised?"

The word hung in the air. Talent hadn't fully thought this through. She nodded. Her grandmother's pen didn't waver. She didn't even set it down. The clock on her desk ticked.

"You were right to tell me," her grandmother said at last. "Leave it. I'll see to it."

That was all. No questions. No comfort. Unease flickered in Talent's chest. She'd expected her grandmother to send a servant to break them up. Marionette Salaren rarely saw to domestic matters personally, and never gently. But Talent knew better than to talk back. She hovered in the doorway for a moment.

"Go to bed, Talent."

She nodded, backing out the door. Her grandmother had said she would fix it. Cordon might not be allowed to stay here anymore, but that would be temporary. Everything would go back to normal soon, she was sure of it.

In the morning, Merit's room was empty. Her dresses gone,

combs and ribbons vanished, the bed stripped of sheets. At breakfast, her grandmother read her correspondence as the *thavi* steamed.

"Where is Merit?" Talent asked.

"It was best handled quietly."

Her grandmother refused questions and would not post her letters. Talent gathered Merit had been sent to school in the south, but the staff were forbidden to speak Merit's name. It was as if she'd been erased.

A week later, Cordon's body was found in the river.

They held the memorial at sunset. Lanterns drifted on the water where he'd gone under, golden light flashing over dark waves. People said he died of heartbreak, but Talent blamed herself. Her choices had sent Merit away. If that's why Cordon had taken his life, it was her fault. All of it.

Talent stood on the balcony above the harbor, watching the lights float away. She wanted to scream, to confess, to take back the words that had created his disaster. But the house stayed silent. The city glittered on.

When she turned back, the flux chandeliers were already lit for dinner, humming with steady light. The house looked the same, but something in it had gone dark.

49

THE MORNING AFTER

TALIA

Holloway Sennett never got over his brother's death. It was as simple as that.

— *SONS OF THE PENTARCHY: A BIOGRAPHICAL RECORD*, 443 AC

The night fell apart quickly after Dawn and Riven showed up. Lore had excused himself and hadn't returned, which was smart because Riven seemed ready to throttle him. No one was hungry after watching all that food rot in front of their eyes, so they each claimed a dusty bedroom and did their best to sleep.

Talia had risen early to get some fresh air, walking through the empty, eerily perfect streets. She couldn't help but wonder where all the bodies ended up after the city was destroyed. Had they been buried? Or were the bones still here, just below the surface of the illusion?

At least the air outside tasted clean. She walked for an hour and watched the sun rise over the eastern wall.

She was on her way back to her rooms when she paused in a courtyard just outside the citadel. Morning dew clung to the pale vines that crept up through the cracked patio. The illusion couldn't stop weeds from reaching for the sun.

She hadn't been looking for Holloway, but she wasn't surprised to find him here. He sat on the rim of a fountain, harp in his lap, plucking a few tentative notes. The melody faltered, then drifted away. His curls were damp, and there were dark circles under his eyes.

"You sound terrible," she said.

He looked up. The corner of his mouth twitched. "Good morning to you too."

She sat beside him. "You're up early."

"Couldn't sleep. Weird dreams."

The fountain's gurgle filled the space between them as Talia tried to organize her thoughts. They kept slipping sideways as she reflected on last night and what they'd almost done.

"I'm so sorry, Holloway," she said at last. She twisted the fabric of her skirt between her fingers. "I knew how you felt, and I shouldn't have let things—"

He cut her off. "You always blame yourself. Don't do that. You don't owe me an apology for last night."

Her chest felt tight. She kept her focus on her feet, noting how scuffed her boots were. "That wasn't real, Holloway. It was cruel to lead you on—"

"It was an illusion," he supplied. "You didn't choose to get enchanted, so don't take that on."

"I don't know what I was thinking," she said, shaking her head. "No offense."

"Oh, I'm sure Lore promised you something irresistible." Holloway's voice was knowing and just a little wistful.

You don't have to pretend with me, Lore had said back in the library. *You can't hurt anyone...*

She felt Holloway's eyes on her, measuring her reaction, and she finally looked back up. The firstlight caught in his lashes, turning them gold. He'd always been beautiful in an easy, obvious way. Like the sun reflected on water.

"Do you still think about Merit and Cordon?" he asked.

Something squeezed in her chest. "Most of the time."

He hesitated, then said quietly, "I didn't tell you. I found out what happened."

Talia's heart stopped. He couldn't know what she'd done. How would he know that?

He took a long breath. "In Haven, before I got arrested, I found some records."

Goose bumps ran up her arms, and her fingers curled around the lip of the fountain, gripping the cold stone.

"He didn't kill himself. It was an execution. He was working with the rebels, and the Pentarchy found out."

The world tilted around her. Her *grandmother* was on the Council of Five, which ran the Pentarchy. So was Holloway's father. That was—well, that was horrific. But if Cordon hadn't taken his own life, then it had nothing to do with Merit.

"I always thought it was my fault."

He blinked. "What are you talking about?"

She swallowed the tears burning in her throat. "I told Marionette that Merit and Cordon were...together. I didn't know what she'd do. I thought—" The words stuck in her throat. "I thought she'd just scold them. But she sent Merit away. And then Cordon was gone too."

Holloway moved to kneel in front of her, hands braced on the fountain's rim on either side of her knees. "Tally. You were sixteen. Your grandmother, my father, they did something that monsters do. You did nothing wrong."

She pressed her fingers to her eyes, the shame old and fresh all at once. "I wasn't thinking properly. I never should have told on them."

Holloway's voice softened. "He'd forgive you if he could. So would Merit."

"How can you say that?"

"Because I do."

Her breath hitched. "You're a good person, Holloway."

He made a small skeptical noise in his throat. Then he let out a long sigh.

"How do we go back?" he asked in a broken voice. "Once you see what the world really is. What it's built on."

His hands were touching her knees, and the grief coursing through him felt so intense, it was hard for her to breathe. She didn't know what she could say.

"The people we're supposed to go home to—" He stopped and

shook his head. "They gave the order. And we're supposed to just, what? Accept that's the price of peace?"

He'd lost everything since he came to Valta, she realized: his career as an enforcer, his gods. Now, faith in his family. Holloway had always been her safe space, but who was that for him? He was adrift, and she didn't know how to pull him back.

An uneasy feeling twisted in her stomach. "What did Lore promise you, Holloway?"

"Everything." His smile was sad. "A new world. Your family's power and mine. Justice for Cordon. No more lies." He stood, brushing dust from his hands, something raw in his expression. "He said we could build something better together."

It sounded almost like a confession.

"That tempts you," she said quietly.

His beautiful blue eyes were full of tears. "Wouldn't it tempt anyone?"

Of course, she wanted to say. She *obviously* knew how tempting Lore could be, how brilliantly he latched onto people's desires and fears. She'd assumed—vainly—that she was the sole object of his attentions. How long had he been working on Holloway?

"I used to dream about saving you, you know," he said. "From the world, from your grandmother. But you don't need saving."

"I do need you, Holloway. Please." This was sounding too much like a goodbye.

He smiled faintly, and she knew it was too late. "Just promise you'll stop blaming yourself for something that happened when you were sixteen. You're allowed to live, Tally."

He stood then and walked away, toward the citadel. He didn't even look back.

She sat alone for a while watching the light change on the water. Sorting her thoughts. Cordon's execution. Holloway's despair. Her own choices. The fountain's steady rhythm was comforting. Her legs had gone stiff when she finally stood up. She noticed Riven leaning on the colonnade, hands tucked behind his back. He must have been waiting, giving her space.

She crossed to him. “If you’ve come to tell me how naive I am—”

“I haven’t. I came with my own apology, actually.”

She blinked. “For what?”

“You were alone last night, in that room. I should never have left you.”

“You came when I called—”

“I shouldn’t have left.” He stepped closer. “I’m sorry.”

“You’re angry,” she said. She was getting better at reading his face, the set of his shoulders. Was this how normal people tracked emotions? It felt so messy and primed for misunderstanding.

“Only at him.” His jaw locked. “He made you believe you were safe. If I had been in that room—” He cut himself off. Exhaled slowly. “You would have been safe. Whatever else you wanted to do.”

It wasn’t the physical act he was angry about; it was her autonomy. Every time, that was his line.

“Never let anyone take your choices from you, Talia.”

“It won’t happen again,” she said. “I know what he wants now, and it’s off the table.” She reached for his hand. He took it immediately, threading their fingers together. “How can I convince you to trust me again?”

He made a small noise that she realized was a laugh. He was amused. “I trust you completely. My place is to guard your life, not your decisions.”

“Even if my decisions don’t lead to you? You’d still protect me?” He didn’t look like he was lying. A soft, affectionate smile broke over his face.

“Especially then.” He didn’t hesitate.

She brushed her fingers along his wrist. “Okay, so what if they do? Lead to you.”

He was staring at her. “I’ll be here whenever you’re ready.”

Talia looked toward the citadel’s glowing white spires and drew herself up. “In that case, let’s get this over with.”

Riven inclined his head. “Lead the way.”

50

THE SURVIVOR IN THE LIBRARY

TALIA

My power lasted just long enough to reach these fluxless shores. Now I'm going gray at the temples like a fucking mortal merchant. The irony! I survived the fall of my homeland, just to die somewhere worse. On the bright side, everyone wants to fuck a god.

—VAEL LAR VARLOHEIM, PERSONAL JOURNAL,
APPROX. 48 AC. TRANS: T. SALAREN

Riven hadn't exaggerated. Behind the wide bronze doors, the Grand Library rose up like a temple inside the citadel. Columns carved with spiraling script held up galleries stacked three floors high. Flux ran between marble tiles in faint blue lines, humming softly. The air was cool and dry with the scent of paper, dust, minerals, old magic.

There was no fake food here, no scenes of violence phasing in and out, no figments that Talia could see. For the first time since she entered Valrotala, the world felt solid under her feet. She pressed her palm to the nearest pillar, and something relaxed in her chest.

The library was real. And it really did contain a lot of books. The mosaic floor brightened under her boots, sigils waking briefly at each step.

She pulled a tome from the shelf, and the wood binding creaked softly. Inside, ancient Starscript filled the page in tight lines: lists of spices and teas, furniture and lighting fixtures. For a moment, everything inside her steadied.

Then she turned the page, and a single line snared her attention:

— Transfer of 20 thuolev units to Chamber Three —

She blinked. Read the line over again. The word *thuolev* translated to "mortal," as in fae with no magical abilities. She rubbed the back of her thumb over the ink, thinking about the implications. Referring to people as "units" was strange. She could have the translation wrong.

A rustle sounded between the shelves behind her. Talia closed the book gently.

"Hello?" she asked.

A chittering sound. Then a tiny head poked out around the stack. It had wide black eyes and silver-white fur, and its whiskers were trembling. The creature was no bigger than a squirrel, tail tipped with a faint flux blue shimmer. They crept out on cautious paws.

"You read the old script?" they asked in a breezy whistle.

Talia knelt down. "Starscript? Yes, I can read Starscript."

They edged closer, clutching a curled scrap of parchment.

"Good," they said. "The books need reading. Pip keeps the lights awake, but Pip cannot read them."

A curl of loneliness filled Talia's nose and prickled in her throat like unshed tears. "How long have you been here, Pip?"

Pip's silk tail twitched once. "One hundred and forty-six thousand nights," they squeaked. They looked up at the high shelves as if counting. "Maybe more. Pip loses count sometimes."

Four hundred years alone here.

Talia kept her voice gentle. "Pip, can you help me find records about what happened here when the city fell?"

Their whiskers twitched, eyes jumping to the exits, the shadows, her hands.

"You are not like the others," they said finally. "What are you?"

"I'm a scholar."

Their tail twitched. "Scholars read. Pip shows the reading place."

They led her deeper into the stacks, staying close to the shelves, tail brushing each aisle marker as they went.

Pip stopped beside a narrow reading table. "These," they said softly. "The youngest ones."

Talia set down her satchel, pulled out a heavy wooden chair from a reading desk, and unrolled the first scroll: *Extraction Protocols, Lower Chambers*.

She pulled a few books off the table and weighed the scroll down. It was dense with diagrams and sigil-grids designed to draw energy from living bodies. Notes comparing "yield efficiency" across different varieties of *elein*. One of the illustrations made her pause. It was a wall of smaller cages, interwoven with tubes, almost exactly like what they'd seen at Haven.

The next stack of documents appeared to be a census. Pip had pushed it toward her while she was reading. It opened with columns of names, then categories:

ELEIN

Flux generating: dragons, lesser beasts

Labor: oxen, horses, thuolev

Talia's throat tightened. There was that word again, *thuolev*, listed alongside livestock. On the right, a column denoting ownership. It appeared to list family names, which would make sense if *elein* were considered household property.

She pressed her palms flat to the table until her hands stopped shaking. If she was understanding correctly, *thuolev* were mortal people born without magic and *elein* were sentient shifters with an abundance of magic. The fae had enslaved them both.

The next document was different. It was written in hurried, imperfect Starscript:

We are not collateral. We are not tools. When the collar breaks, we choose freedom or death. There is no third path.

The pile of documents was getting thin. This must have been one of the last records captured.

"Pip," she said quietly, "who wrote this?"

"Peoples," they said. "In the lower halls. Pip hid under the shelves so they would not think we listened."

She turned the page to a table with short, time-stamped entries.

We are grossly outmatched. The white dragon says she can reverse the core arrays to ignite the flux channels. Break the collars. Free the elein. A desperate plan, but we have no choice.

Talia's pulse quickened. This wasn't what she'd imagined when Riven had described the *elein* as killers and aggressors. These people were desperate, but whatever happened in the end, she found it hard to imagine they'd been on the wrong side of history.

The next entry, written just a few hours later, hinted at an answer.

Dragon's light—blinding. When sight returned, fae positions empty. Beasts in a killing frenzy—bloodlust? We are overrun, must quit the city.

Whatever they had done to free the *elein* seemed to have gone horribly wrong. The *elein* must have been turned to fluxborn, but that wasn't anyone's intent. It was a tragedy more than anything.

"Pip. Do you know what happened to the white dragon?"

Pip's ears flattened. "Everything fell. Shelves. Lights." They shivered. "But Pip heard her after. Crying. Quiet crying. Down below."

Talia went back through the documents one at a time, looking for patterns. Time slipped. She didn't know how long she'd been reading when the door creaked open.

"Talia?"

Riven stepped inside, carrying bread wrapped in cloth in one hand and a carafe in the other. He took in the table—scrolls spread out, books holding down the edges. Then he saw her face.

"Talia." He said it with an edge of concern.

She didn't trust herself to talk, so she slid the extraction protocol documents across the table to him. He set the food down and read without sitting. His face was as impassive as ever, but his jaw twitched. He picked up the census. Then the manifesto. Then the rough notes. When he reached the entry about the dragon, he inhaled sharply.

"What is it?" she whispered.

Riven's throat worked once. "The white dragon. Her name was Ehrue," he said finally. "She was Dawn's mate."

Dawn's mate had helped lead the uprising. Talia tried to imagine explaining this to Dawn, to picture how she would react. Then she remembered what Pip had just said.

"I think she's still alive." Talia was almost afraid to say the words. "Pip said he heard her crying."

Riven closed the logbook with one careful hand. She had his full attention.

"Dawn thinks the fluxborn killed her mate," Talia said. "That's not what happened."

"No," he agreed.

"Ehrue *created* the fluxborn somehow. And the fae..." She gestured to the spread of documents. "They didn't fall to the fluxborn either. The blast—whatever it was—"

"Ended them," he said, finishing her thought. "Except for the thirteen who made it out."

"What thirteen?" She sifted back through the papers on the table, but she was sure she hadn't read that.

"The ones you call gods." He tapped his fingers on the table as he said it.

"That wasn't in these records." She stared at him, shocked, but it made sense, didn't it? If thirteen magic-wielding fae had escaped from Valrotala, they would appear godlike to people without magic.

It would explain why the religious texts and faerie stories echoed one another. They were two sides of the same history.

She thought about the churches built over the years. All the children raised in the faith. The people who'd been executed for heresy.

"We need to tell the others," she said finally. "We have to tell Dawn that Ehrue is alive and the *elein* didn't kill everyone."

Riven didn't answer at first. "It doesn't have to be you," he said finally.

"Yes," she said. "It does."

She'd uncovered these truths, and she was done avoiding hard conversations.

She gathered the documents and slid them into her satchel. Pip watched from their shelf with wide eyes.

"You've done something important," she told them. "Keeping this place awake."

They dipped their head. "Pip remembers," they whispered. "Even when it hurts."

Talia reached toward them but was careful not to touch. They quivered a little, and she could have sworn they smiled.

"Thank you, Pip," she said.

Riven stepped beside her, and she reached for his hand. He squeezed lightly.

"Ready?" he asked.

"I guess I'll have to be."

Pip padded after them until the doorway. They stopped there. "Will you come back?" Pip squeaked.

"If I can," Talia said.

They gave a small nod. "Pip will keep the lights awake."

She pushed open the bronze doors, and together, they stepped into the corridor. Dawn was waiting right there in the hall. She looked up, her face flashing from annoyance to relief, then concern. Talia took a deep breath and got ready to break her friend's world open.

51

DESCENDING

DAWN

It appears the fluxborn mate for life.

— *FLORA & FAUNA OF THE VALTA INTERIOR,*
VERACITY NIN, 409 AC

Dawn had been pacing the corridor for hours with nothing productive to do. Holloway wasn't talking. She hadn't seen Lore since the night before. Riven had gone into the library with food for Talia and hadn't come back. She kept tapping her foot, drumming the wall. She hated fucking waiting.

She could tell Talia was worked up about something. The girl's heartbeat picked up as the hours passed, but Dawn couldn't do much in a room full of books. By the time the library doors cracked open, the girl's heart sounded like a hummingbird. Something was wrong.

Shit. Talia had been digging around in those books for hours, looking for an edge against Elanwei. What had she found? What if all that reading just told her they were fucked?

Didn't matter if it was impossible. Dawn was going to find Ehrue anyway.

A noise down the hall drew her attention, and look who decided to show up. Lore leaned against the wall like he hadn't been missing in action all night. Jacket immaculate. Hands folded, cocky smile on his face. She'd love to break his nose.

Not just her, apparently. Riven growled and drew one of his blades. He closed the distance in no time. Dawn followed for damage control, and Lore stayed put, still smirking.

"Apologize," Riven snarled. He had Lore by the throat with one hand, his sword in the other. His voice was low and lethal.

Lore sighed, rubbing his temple. "You're angry I removed her shame? Fascinating."

Riven took a swing. Lucky Dawn was there—she grabbed him by the arm and hauled him back. Lore didn't even flinch.

His gaze slid to Talia. "Tell him, Talent. Did I force you?"

Talia's mouth tightened. "Lore, please. This isn't necessary."

"You came to me." Lore spread his hands. "You asked for lessons. You asked for power. I only gave you what you wanted, and you fucking loved it."

"You didn't ask what I wanted," Talia said, pushing back for once. "You just think you know everything."

He smirked, and Riven lunged for him again. Dawn only just pulled him back. She drew a revolver, and stars above, she didn't know who she wanted to shoot.

Lore must know that willing partners didn't need wine or illusions as a warm-up, right? And Riven was snarling like something rabid. *Fucking men.*

"Enough," she snapped. "Why are you here, Lore?"

His smile sharpened. "Because it's time. Ehrue is asking for you."

Dawn's vision tunneled to Lore's face. The smirk that touched the edge of his lips. She heard Riven swear under his breath, but sound was doing funny things.

"Say that again."

"I said," Lore spoke slowly, "your mate is alive. I've spoken with her. She'd like to see you."

Talia spoke up. "Stop it, Lore. Honestly, why are you being like this?"

Lore raised an eyebrow. "What, you wanted to share the news? Go ahead. Tell her the rest."

What did he mean, *the rest?* What could Talia know about Ehrue? And why were they still fucking standing here? If Ehrue was alive, if she was being held, they had to get her.

Dawn swung the revolver over to Lore's face. "No more talking. I can find her myself."

He made a scolding click with his tongue. "You can try, but I know exactly where she is. I know how to reach her, which passages are real and which are illusions." His smile widened. "Kill me, you may wander these halls for months. Who knows what state she'll be in when you find her."

Dawn's thumb hovered. One shot could end him. But if he was telling the truth—

"Fuck," Dawn said. "Fine."

Talia pulled a stack of documents from her satchel, but Dawn waved them off. She couldn't read them. "Just tell me."

They sat on the floor, and Talia did her best to share what they'd found in the library.

"The mortals and some of the *elein* rose up, rebelled," Talia explained. Her voice warbled with nerves. "They were losing, then a dragon had this idea to overload the flux conduits—"

"Ehrue," Dawn whispered.

"Yeah," Talia agreed. "Ehrue. There was some kind of explosion, and she was hurt. But we think she survived."

Dawn looked to Riven. He nodded.

"The fluxborn didn't kill her," Riven added quietly.

The hum in the citadel's walls. Illusions for miles. Power that hadn't faltered when the rest of the continent went dark. It had to come from somewhere. It had to come from someone. Dawn had thought so before, but this was proof.

"And now she's Elanwei's power source," Dawn said.

The words felt numb on her tongue. Rage and grief had fueled her for so long, but her chest was hollow now. Hope? No. Too many things could go wrong. She felt nothing.

Talia reached for her arm. Dawn pulled away and made for a door at the end of the hall. She couldn't let Talia read her emotions before she figured them out herself. She didn't want comfort. She needed space.

Out on the balcony, Dawn took a deep breath of icy air and

leaned on the stone parapet. Familiar boots sounded behind her. Riven stopped a few paces away.

"May I join you?" he asked in his baritone rumble.

Dawn didn't look up. "You're already here."

He chuckled and leaned forward on his elbows, propped against the ledge. The silence between them felt familiar. They didn't need words to understand each other. She'd lost count of the battles they'd prepared for quietly like this. This one tomorrow could be the last.

Finally, he let out a tired sigh. "I should have gone back. After I got you out."

She still didn't look at him. "It wouldn't have mattered." She wondered if the tears would ever come, or if they'd choke her to death someday. "The city was gone. Ehrue was—" Her fists clenched. "We thought she was gone."

Riven's voice stayed low. "Thauni, we didn't leave her on purpose."

Dawn let out a rough breath at hearing her true name, half laugh, half cough. "Don't soften it, *Althen*. We ran."

"Yeah, we ran," he said, turning to look at her. "You'd been back for two days alone by the time I got here. You were bleeding everywhere, killing everything. You couldn't shift. The city was on fire. Ehrue was *gone*. Ellie was *raving*. She would have collared you. We had to run."

"You broke your oath for me," Dawn admitted. She'd never thanked him. She hadn't wanted to live, let alone for that price.

"Then you threatened to kill me in a few creative ways." Riven was smiling.

"I probably should have. Wouldn't be fucking *bonded* now. You know I swore I'd never do that."

"Oh. I know."

Then, quieter, she asked, "So what now? How do we fix it?"

Riven watched the horizon. "Well, if Ehrue is alive, she's hurting. If she's hurting, we will get her out."

Of course, Dawn agreed, but it was good to hear him say it.

"What will you do," he asked so gently, "if there's nothing left of her to save?"

That was the question. She pictured Ehrue's smile. Her laugh. Then cages. Flux channels. Four hundred years of pain.

"If the Ehrue I knew is gone," Dawn said steady, "then I'll take her out. We'll go out together."

It felt honest when she said it. That was her only goal—to live or die with Ehrue. The whole point of putting up with Lore all these years, of coming back to this fucking place. But it felt wrong in a way that surprised her. She would miss Holloway's bawdy jokes and Talia's endless questions. She'd miss Riven. It felt strange, having people to lose.

Riven's jaw flexed, once, but he didn't argue.

"I'll stand with you" was all he said. "Whatever you choose."

She was done waiting. When they rejoined the group, she told Lore it was time.

He led the way. Moved like he'd walked these halls before. Strange, since he'd been trying to get in for a decade at least. Holloway followed close behind him. Too close. Dawn marked it, but she had more important things to worry about.

Each level down, the temperature dropped. The flux in the walls shifted from warm blue to harsh steel to something darker, a purple-black that made her teeth ache. Both hands stayed on both revolvers.

A memory surfaced—Ehrue laughing in sunlight. *Come on, little one. You're not scared, are you? There are no collars here.*

Dawn had never been scared. Not of heights or speed or falling. She was scared now.

When the stairs ended, they were at the top of a long hall. The black stone floor had channels of flux pulsing down each side of it. There were cages in the walls. The extraction chambers, empty now.

The only sound was the shuffle of their own feet. It smelled musty. When Dawn closed her eyes, she could hear the scratch and rattle of the cages in Haven. The door at the end of the hall got closer with each step. Before Dawn knew it, Lore's hand rested on the handle.

"She's through here," he said. "Though I should warn you, she's not what you might expect."

Her heart was racing. Hot pins prickled all over her body. Would they find a dragon waiting? A person? Would she be in one piece? In a cage? Dawn flipped all her anxiety into anger. She was happy to point it at Lore.

"Open the fucking door," she hissed.

He smiled, all teeth, and shoved the door open. Light poured into the dark hallway—blinding white, shot with gold.

They stepped into basically a giant cave. There was a dais at the far end with two thrones. Dawn didn't notice any of the details. Her vision tunneled to the figure standing on the dais, and her knees slammed down hard on stone.

She tried to laugh, tried to scream. She just choked on air. When her voice finally tore loose, it cracked in her throat.

"Ehrue. You're alive."

Her mate was in her human form. As she sat there, gazing blankly at the floor, unease prickled up Dawn's spine. There was something wrong. Ehrue was still beautiful, but she seemed smaller. Her shoulders curled in like a child being scolded. Her skin was translucent, and light bled from it to pool below the throne. She wasn't wearing chains.

When her winter-gray eyes lifted, they were strangely flat. They slid past Dawn and didn't catch. That blank gaze hurt worse than any gut punch. Dawn's chest burned. Her vision blurred, she felt hot tears on her cheeks. Dawn hadn't cried in four hundred years. Grief had its claws in her now.

52

THE BETRAYAL

TALIA

There is no 'fae' race. These were people who could absorb flux power, which extended their lifespans and amplified their abilities. The thuolev *had no power to speak of. The* elein *had an excess of it—enough to shift form—but that only made them a target. The distinction the fae drew between themselves and everyone else was never biological. Fitting, then, that 'fae' ultimately became synonymous with fantasy.*

— T. SALAREN, FIELD NOTES, 401 AC

Talia didn't know where to look first as she stepped into the cavernous space. Every surface seemed to be etched with Starscript.

The room was oriented around ten pillars, arranged in a circle. There were shallow channels cut into the floor, branching from the base of each pillar to meet in a basin of liquid light at the center. Her fingers twitched. She wanted to touch everything and figure out how it worked.

But an uneasy sense of déjà vu tightened in her chest. Something about the layout, the geometry of it, caught on a memory. Glass globes between each of the pillars swirled with flux, and tubes and coils connected these to the basin at the center. The design wasn't ceremonial, it was functional. The sigils, the conduits, the reservoir of light—it wasn't just *like* the lab equipment at Haven, it was nearly identical.

Talia tore her eyes away from the flux system to look up at the thrones. Elanwei was unmistakable from the portrait in the hall. Four hundred years hadn't softened or faded her. Talia felt goose bumps prickle up her arms. This was the lost fae princess, in the flesh.

Another figure sat on the second throne. A woman, pale, luminous, with white-blond hair spilling over her shoulders. Light escaped from her skin, pooling into a network of thin streams under the thrones. Her hand pressed to her temple as if she was fighting a headache.

Shock rippled through the bond like a drop in air pressure, sudden enough to make Talia's ears ring. She saw Dawn stumble forward and fall to her knees.

"Ehrue," Dawn whispered. "You're alive."

The woman didn't answer. Her head tilted, gray eyes curious, like she was studying a stranger. Talia saw nothing behind those eyes. No recognition. No emotion. Tears streaked down Dawn's face. Talia had never seen her cry before.

Elanwei's eyes flicked over to Dawn before they settled on Riven. She rose from her throne and descended, step by deliberate step.

"Althen." The name cracked across the chamber. "My shield. My sword. My coward. It has been some years."

Riven said nothing. His face could have been made of stone.

Elanwei's eyes cut to Talia. "And what is *this*?"

Lore stepped around the group and knelt before the princess with effortless grace, his head bowed low. She had never seen Lore bow either.

"May I present Talent Salaren, Your Majesty," he said smoothly. "She has an exceptionally strong affinity for mindweaving."

Elanwei's lips curved faintly. "That *is* interesting. We will need to build back the bloodlines once we eliminate the mortals."

"Eliminate?" Talia heard herself say.

The princess cast a sharp look at her. "Vermin. Burning our relics, building nests among our ruins."

"You enslaved them," Talia hissed. "You called people *units* and transferred them like property."

"*I* did nothing like that," Elanwei said. "Did you know they called me Voice of the Voiceless? I advocated for kindness toward the mortals and beasts, even quarreled with my father. But he was right, in the end. They repaid me with his ashes."

"They were desperate," Talia pressed on. "That's what rebellion is. The last act of the powerless."

She thought back to the notes in the library scrawled in the city's final hours. She looked at Lore for support. She knew he must agree, but he had a strange expression on his face. It didn't look like he was going to step in.

"Enough." Elanwei flicked a hand.

The whole world suddenly locked in place.

Talia's breath froze in her chest. She couldn't turn her head. She felt Dawn's fury through the bond. Heard Holloway's muttered curse cut short. Elanwei and Ehrue seemed unaffected—as did Lore, who stood with his hands loose at his sides. Why had she spared him? Talia tried to blink, to send him some signal, but her eyes just watered.

Elanwei approached with unhurried grace. She gestured at Riven, and he moved back against a pillar, his arms reaching above and behind his head like a puppet, before shackles clicked into place around his wrists. Her fingers brushed his cheek, and he flinched. Then she turned to Dawn. Fire guttered and died in Dawn's palms as Elanwei snuffed her power out.

"My little dragon," the princess murmured. "You refused to bond with me, but I found a decent alternative, don't you think?"

Dawn was trying to fight it, veins standing out on her neck, but she was pressed into a pillar near the door, facing Ehrue, forced to watch her lover drain herself away.

Holloway went next. He was trembling, eyes wide with disbelief. When Elanwei turned away, he appealed to Lore. "How could you—"

"Quiet," Elanwei commanded. His voice died in his throat.

Then she came for Talia. The paralysis eased just enough for her to stumble to the pillar. The stone was cold against her spine. The cuffs clicked shut, then kept tightening until the metal bit her skin. Four prisoners lashed to four pillars.

Elanwei stepped back to admire her work. Then she turned to Lore. "Well done. You brought me everything I asked for."

"I came as you called," Lore said simply.

The truth hit her all at once. *The true gods.* All those nights he'd whispered philosophy, all those sermons about power and pain. She thought he'd made it all up, but it was real enough, if you fashioned Elanwei a goddess. She wondered if Lore truly did, or if this was another one of his games.

"Are you sure you want to keep this one?" Elanwei gestured lazily at Talia as she spoke to Lore.

Lore looked over at Talia. Let his eyes rake down her body and back up again in a way that made her shiver.

"She's worth hearing out." He approached her slowly, and she could smell the amber and smoke on his clothes, sickly sweet as he leaned in. "You're meant for more than this, Talent."

The look on his face was intent and unreadable.

"You lied to us," she hissed.

"No. You just didn't listen." His smile stayed fixed. "I told you exactly what I wanted. I'm done living at anyone else's mercy." He tilted his head. "I know you want that too."

He stepped even closer, his fingers ghosting over her ribs, his voice low enough for only her to hear. "You know, you could stand beside me. Imagine it. No doors closed to you ever again."

She could imagine it. Her grandmother couldn't control her. Her colleagues wouldn't consign her to busywork. She would be the one granting access to knowledge or withholding it. It felt so close, the possibility ached in her chest.

"You're terrified to lose them," he murmured. "I can feel it, what they mean to you. The bond will show you everything, you know. Every second of Dawn's pain. Up to the end." He tucked a curl behind her ear. "I can spare you that."

Talia's heart hammered against her ribs. The bond surged with Dawn's feral defiance. Whatever she chose, Dawn would stand behind her. She could take Lore's offer. Knowledge. Power. Safety for herself. Or she could stand with Dawn and Riven and Holloway. Knowing it meant pain. Knowing she'd probably watch them die.

But Lore had overplayed his hand. He'd tried to manipulate her, intoxicate her, trick her with pleasure and promises. He didn't know how to love without controlling her, and she still had that spark of anger burning in her chest.

"I already told you no." It felt right. "You need to respect that."

His expression flickered—something like disappointment, then nothing at all. "Pity. You would have been extraordinary."

He turned away. "She made her choice. Now make yours."

Holloway's gaze met Talia's, grief and resolve warring behind his eyes. "I have nowhere else to go," he said, barely getting the words out. "I can't go back. Not after what they—" He choked. "They killed my brother."

Horror washed over Talia as she realized what he was saying. "Holloway, don't. This isn't who you are."

"I wanted to stay with you, Tally, but this is the only way." He drew in a slow, shaking breath. "I'll go." His eyes never left Talia's. "I'm sorry, Tally."

Elanwei flicked her hand, and Holloway collapsed forward off the pillar. Lore caught his hands, light coiling around their joined fingers.

"Then we ascend," Lore said, tugging Holloway toward the apex of the flux pool.

Ascend to what? Talia thought, but the pillars ignited before she could ask.

Pain slammed through her. Flux burned in her veins. She tried to scream, but only light came out. The world narrowed to heat and crackling static and the bond. Riven convulsed, silver flashing beneath his skin. Dawn cursed in languages Talia didn't recognize. Dawn's pain crashed through her, braided with her own, until that was all there was.

The smell of iron and burning flesh filled her nose, and she choked on it. Her heart hurt, each beat weaker than the last. The last thing she saw was Lore's gold-tinted stare, his fingers laced tight with Holloway's. The two men stood together, bathed in energy, and she was kindling.

Her vision collapsed to a pinprick of light.

Just before it went black, a pulse flickered through the bond—hot pink, fierce, unbroken. Dawn was still fighting.

53

THE SACRIFICE

DAWN

If we are the gods, what happens to our souls?

—VAEL LAR VARLOHEIM, PERSONAL JOURNAL,
APPROX. 50 AC. TRANS: T. SALAREN

Everything faded but Ehrue. No collar. No cage. Hands folded in her lap. She wasn't restrained, or fighting, or running away. There was something wrong about her face, a faint tremor in her left cheek, there and gone. When Elanwei's hand settled on Ehrue's shoulder, she tilted into it like a tamed cat.

How long had she been this way?

Elanwei's voice buzzed like an insect in the background, then her hand moved and the floor tilted. Air turned to syrup, and Dawn's muscles refused to cooperate. She reached for fire and hit a wall. Something was blocking her.

Ehrue's power, Dawn knew with sick certainty. *Elanwei and Ehrue have a fucking channel bond.* Elanwei's affinity for illusion was exceptionally powerful. Drawing from a dragon's magic reserves would make her nearly untouchable. Ehrue was ten times older and more powerful than Dawn was.

Elanwei shackled them one by one. Cold metal closed around Dawn's wrists. She shut her eyes, and time seemed to ripple. She was trapped in two places at once. The pillar in Valrotala. The metal table in Haven. Dawn growled, fighting to keep it together. If she survived this, she would crush every flux conduit on this continent.

Her vision kept short-circuiting, cutting to black before coming back into focus. Lore was up and walking around. *That fucker.* He came for Talia, and she refused him.

"That's my girl," Dawn muttered through gritted teeth.

Then Holloway—fucking Holloway—took Lore's hand. Dawn wanted to scream at him. *Your brother is ash and memory, and your perfectly alive friends are right here.*

"I'm not dying for this shit," she growled to herself. No idea if she was making any sense.

Then the pillars ignited.

She screamed.

Agony. Pure and uncut. Flux tore out of her flesh like barbed hooks. She watched Riven's magic burn out, silver tattoos going dark one by one. The bond made it worse. She felt Talia's heart falter. Dawn was dying twice over.

She saw Ehrue through the haze. Still and shining, trapped in whatever fog had claimed her. Power flowing out of her.

Dawn couldn't lose her again.

She reached out with her mind. Their mating oath had withered to a thread, but it was still there. She tugged on that silver thread gently, like a lifeline.

My love, she sent.

The connection caught. Held. She felt a flicker of presence on the other end, faint as starlight.

Thauni? Ehrue used her old name. The only one she knew.

Relief crashed through Dawn so hard she nearly passed out. *I'm here. I'm right here.*

Physically, Dawn was shackled and fading. Within the mating oath, her mind was all there. She pushed forward.

Ehrue's mind was *not* all there. Deep cracks scored through it. Dawn went carefully, following the thread through Ehrue's ruined consciousness.

The first layer was Elanwei's voice. *The mortals killed us. They killed your friends. They must pay.*

Dawn bared her teeth. *Bullshit. That's poison she fed you. That's not the truth, and you know it.*

She pushed deeper. Past the lies. Toward the truth beneath.

The second layer was mired in guilt, crushing and absolute. Images hammered her: blood in the streets, Ehrue racing through the citadel, white light breaking everything. Screams. Bodies breaking.

I killed them all. I deserve to be punished.

No, Dawn snarled. Outside, her body was failing. She was aware, numbly, as her vision blackened. Her heart skipped beats. *You broke their chains. It was never going to be clean, but you did your best.*

Dawn pressed forward, toward what remained of the woman she loved. Her own heart.

The deepest layer was theirs alone. Mountain air under unclipped wings. The frost caves where they'd made love in every possible form while snow swirled outside. Promises whispered: *Always, no matter what...*

The fog shattered, and Ehrue's presence surged into focus, frayed at the edges but whole. Dawn felt her mate's soul wrap around hers like a pair of wings.

You came back, Ehrue thought, wonder threaded with grief.

"I never stopped looking for you," Dawn said aloud, voice raw.

You're dying, Ehrue observed. *Your friends are dying.*

"I'm right here."

Oh, Thauni. Warmth spread over her, scattered and steady at once. *This body is an echo of a dead star. My true light burned out when I broke the chains. We can't keep this.*

Dawn wanted to argue. Wanted to rage. But she could feel the truth across the connection. Ehrue's awareness was flickering. Those cracks in her psyche ran too deep. That's what this was about all along. Lore brought Dawn here to be Elanwei's new power source. *Over my dead body.*

"Take me with you," Dawn whispered.

That was when Ehrue shared an image of her lingering starlit power channeled through Dawn's fire. They could shatter every conduit in the chamber. Free her friends. But it would burn Ehrue out to do it.

"No." Dawn's chest cracked open. "I just found you."

You never lost me. Warmth again. *I waited, and we're here.*

Talia's pulse was slipping. Riven's body arched toward her. Even in agony, he tried to shield Talia from what came next. Dawn's own vision was going black. They were all out of time. Dawn had come here with every intention of living or dying with Ehrue. But it was either that or save her friends.

"Do it," Dawn said. "Burn through me."

I love you.

"I love you too. Always—"

Power flared and filled the room. It didn't hurt. Ehrue's power was silent and white, and it poured into Dawn. Dawn's own magic surged to life behind it, wild and clean, and for the first time since she'd flown with Ehrue, all those years ago, she let her fire run free.

The shackles on her wrist detonated, throwing off shards of metal. Dawn's bones lengthened and cracked into new alignment. Scales erupted over her shoulders and down her back before locking into place with a cascade of small clicks. Wings tore free between her shoulder blades—*that fucking hurt*—and she beat them furiously, sending wind swirling through the chamber.

Somewhere in the background, Talia's voice echoed. "Oh, shit—"

Dawn threw her head back and roared.

She didn't go for Elanwei. She ignored Lore and Holloway standing at the apex of the channel network. She went to Ehrue. One gliding leap took her across the floor. She curled herself around Ehrue's small human-shifted body, wings creating a sheltering cave.

Ehrue stood, shaking, light leaking from her eyes and mouth. She smiled and pressed her forehead to Dawn's nose.

I'm glad you're the last thing I'll see, she sent, tender as ever.

Dawn made a sound low in her throat, between purr and whimper. *I'm sorry I left. I'm sorry I wasn't here.*

I'm not, Ehrue thought. *You lived. That's all I wanted.*

We're doing this together? Dawn asked.

Together.

Power slammed out, down those little paths in the throne and straight into the pool of flux at the center of the room. Runes flared white and died. The channels blew out like glass under a hammer. The reservoir erupted in a fountain of liquid light that rained down and hissed on the stone floor.

The pillars split and fell one at a time. Fractures spiderwebbed across the floor. Stone screamed as millennium-old enchantments shattered. She felt Elanwei's control falter as Ehrue ripped the power out from under her.

At the confluence of the channels, a surge of fire overtook Lore and Holloway. The look on Holloway's face was frozen somewhere between bliss and horror as white and blue fire crawled up his legs. Dawn saw the two figures wreathed in flame, hands clasped together, arms lifted, before it became too bright to look. When her vision cleared, there was nothing left.

The power pulsed once and then surged through the channels, reaching beyond the room and away. Who knew how far.

She should probably be more affected by watching their companions get incinerated, but she found it hard to care. All her attention was on Ehrue.

Her mate was burning out from the inside. Her skin went translucent, black lines shearing across the surface. Light poured from her eyes. From her mouth. Dawn could see the magic tearing through her, unmaking her. She still smiled. Kept her forehead pressed to Dawn's scales.

And in those waning moments, Ehrue's mind touched hers and placed something there. An image of a cold cavern with a cache of pale shells. A secret location with a treasure. A future. Dawn's breath caught as she understood what she was seeing.

Then Ehrue thinned like smoke, and the shape of her came apart between Dawn's claws. Dawn howled until the sound ran out, and she could only stand there, wings trembling, cradling ash that had been the center of her world. Quiet settled in. Smoke. Scorched stone. Slowly, she became aware of the damage around her.

Talia and Riven stood, free from the broken pillars. Talia was staring with her mouth open. Riven gave a single nod. *We're with you.*

Movement flickered from a collapsed area of wall. Elanwei rose from the wreckage, silks torn, face streaked gray. Her hands fisted at her sides as power swirled around her—dimmer than before, but still deadly.

"You bitch," Elanwei said in a low shaky voice. "She was all I had left."

Dawn set the ash down gently. She spread her wings and moved her body between the princess and her friends.

Flux coalesced into a blade of pure light in Elanwei's hands.

Dawn bared her teeth as Elanwei stepped forward and lifted her sword.

54

THE FINAL BATTLE

TALIA

Every faerie story ends the same. The villain faces justice. The hero is rewarded. We repeat these stories because we need a world that makes sense, even if it's fiction. Especially then.

— T. SALAREN, "FAITH AND FOLKLORE," *THE VAELIS COURIER*, 399 AC

Talia was living out a faerie story. That was all she could think about as she scanned the ruined chamber and watched Elanwei emerge from the rubble. It was time for the final battle. At the end of the epic quest, the small band of heroes faced off against the monster.

All ten pillars had cracked, jutting from the floor like jagged teeth. Smoke curled. Bits of plaster crashed from the ceiling. The stage was perfectly set.

At her right stood Riven, her fae protector, blades drawn. To her left, Dawn had transformed into a real-life dragon. And here Talia was, the scholar caught in the middle of the fantasy she'd spent her life studying.

The thrill was tempered by the void at her shoulder. Lore had stood just behind her in every fight that mattered. He might have been dangerous and manipulative, but his support had steadied her, lending her more strength than she realized.

And Holloway—*gods, Holloway*. She didn't want to think about him, but she couldn't stop. The look in his eyes as white flame overtook him had shattered her heart.

Why did they betray her? And what was she supposed to do without them?

The rustle of silk pulled her focus. Elanwei stepped forward, a magic blade cradled in her hands. Her steps were slow and deliberate. The hum of her weapon filled the chamber.

"I bet you hate that," Elanwei said, her gaze cutting to Dawn. "Being the kind of monster you spent centuries hunting. A little hypocritical, don't you think, monster slayer?"

Dawn hissed, and Talia couldn't get over the fact that *she was a dragon*.

Elanwei smiled faintly. "You could have stayed," she went on. "She could have gone free if you had joined me instead. But you ran. Now you come back just to end her life? Some mate you are."

She swished her sword idly in broad arcs as she closed the distance. Her smirk widened.

"And you." She turned to Riven, her tone going soft and poisonous. "You know what I realized, *oathbreaker*? Centuries too late, but I got there. Betraying me was the most interesting thing you've ever done. You're *boring*."

Her gaze slid to Talia, gleaming with malice. "Are you not bored yet, darling? The broody protector act gets old. Trust me."

Heat flared across Talia's cheeks. This wasn't how she'd pictured this moment. She glanced at Riven. He grimaced but said nothing.

Elanwei raised her blade. Light bled down its edge, painting the cracked marble with jagged shadows. "That annoying little priest did his job well. The three of you have all the power I need, I just need to get you into your collars."

Talia's pulse surged in her ears. Riven shifted his weight, coiled to move. Dawn crouched low, wings mantling wide. The tableau felt timeless, like a tapestry in her grandmother's hall. The hero, the dragon, the villain. Ready for the final clash.

Elanwei lunged, blade raised—

—and the dragon moved first.

Dawn was breathtaking. Scales shimmered pink and violet,

every plate refracting the light. Her fangs curved past her lips as she tipped her head to the side, waiting, almost playful.

Every story Talia had studied culminated in a balanced confrontation. Good versus evil, the past versus the future. This fight didn't go quite that way.

Dawn's jaws snapped shut on Elanwei's shoulder with a sickening crunch, shredding silk and flesh. The sound echoed wetly. Elanwei screamed, eyes wide, arms flailing as blood sprayed across marble. She was still alive when Dawn wrenched sideways and bit down again, cracking her spine in her jaws. Talia flinched back, too shocked to scream.

The dragon lifted her head with a violent jerk, the princess's body dangling like a rag doll. Then, with predator's ease, she snapped her neck back. The corpse slid down her throat in one smooth motion. Muscles rippled along her neck as she swallowed, and she spat a ragged scrap of fabric onto the floor.

It was so suddenly quiet, Talia could hear her own breathing.

Blood dripped. A piece of silk floated to the ground. Elanwei's silver circlet rolled and came to rest with a hollow clink, her abandoned sword guttering out beside it. Talia stared. Her mind couldn't reconcile what she'd just seen.

Riven exhaled slowly, pinching the bridge of his nose. "What the fuck, Dawn. You can't just eat people."

Dawn's tongue flicked across her teeth, catching a smear of red. "It shut her up, though." The reptilian voice echoed through the chamber, deep and rasping, but with Dawn's familiar lilt.

The absurdity and horror cracked something in Talia. A laugh burst out before she could stop it, ringing off blood-spattered marble. The faerie-story illusion was shattered—no speeches, no duel, no epic victory. Just the crunch of bone and a self-satisfied dragon licking her teeth.

Maybe that was the point. Dawn had never cared about prophecies or patterns. She'd always made her own way. She didn't even read; of course, she improvised the endings. What would that feel like?

Talia had spent her entire life twisting herself to fit expectations. To play a role. She suddenly, desperately, wanted what Dawn had. To write her own story.

The chamber was quiet. No army of fluxborn rushed in. No more walls collapsed. When they cracked the door open, the halls beyond were coated in a thick layer of dust and ash. Elanwei's illusion had shattered.

Dawn's scales shimmered, her bones folded inward, and in a rush of light she looked human again, wiping her mouth with the back of her hand. She was maddeningly pleased with herself, bouncing on the balls of her bare feet.

"Well." She grinned, manic and bright. "We won. The bad guys are gone. Who wants to raid the castle?"

"Baths," Riven muttered. "Food. Beds. In that order."

Talia's gaze drifted to the place where Lore and Holloway had been standing when the flames consumed them. There was nothing there. Not ash, not scorch marks. Just empty stone. She'd seen Holloway's despair in the courtyard earlier. She should have done more for him, but it was too late now.

Were they dead? Transformed? Ascended to godhood like Lore had craved? She didn't know, and maybe she never would.

55

BABY UNICORNS

DAWN

Nearly every folklore tradition from before the crossing describes the peaceful mythic beasts of the Lost Continent, but they've never been seen. There are reports of ghosts and figments, dryads and sea serpents, but never a unicorn.

— *THE DEFINITIVE GUIDE TO PRE-CROSSING FOLKLORE*, FEN ALDAINE, 399 AC

Water came out black at first. The tap spat, shuddered, and clicked. The spray turned gray before it finally ran clear. Dawn hissed when it bit her skin. Ice cold. No hum from the pipes, no hint of heat. The citadel's plumbing ran on gravity and meltwater now.

"Fuck," she muttered, rubbing her cold-stung fingers together. "We had to blow up the power grid."

She stepped into the shower, and the icy water burned clean and honest. Not unwelcome after days of blood and illusions. They'd chosen rooms at random after the ordeal in the throne room, but the beds were moldering and she'd slept on the floor.

She wandered naked through the halls until she found Ehrue's rooms. She didn't take much. An old locket. A knife. A pair of dragonscale pants and matching vest, close enough to her size. What had happened to that fancy hat back in Haven? Damn shame she couldn't keep it.

The halls were dark, just whatever light filtered through the arched windows. Every footstep echoed too loud. Her shadow jumped between pools of moonlight on the inner wall.

She didn't pay attention to where she was going, but when she reached the cage-filled hall, she stopped. The space was vast and silent. A single feather lay on the floor, as long as her arm. This is where the *elein* had been kept, but they were long since gone.

A side door hung open. She was surprised when she stepped through and found herself in an outdoor garden. A slope fell away, and mist rose from a grassy field below. Her breath fogged in the air. Then, down among the broken statues and wild hedges, something moved. A bulky shape. Many of them.

Dawn dropped to a crouch. Her mind cycled through possible threats. Fluxborn? Elanwei's missing followers? She felt for her revolvers and cursed. She hadn't strapped on her holsters. She'd have to fight this out by hand.

The shapes were pale in the mist. Moving slowly. Not prowling. Not hunting. *What the hell?* Then one lifted its head, and moonlight caught on a spiral horn.

Unicorns. A whole herd of them. No hint of flux corruption. They were perfectly peaceful. Free. She went still, heart hammering. One of the creatures approached. When it got to her, it lowered its head and pressed its muzzle to her palm. The velvet softness undid her.

Her legs buckled, dropping her in the grass. Sobs tore through her body for the second time in two days, and she rocked forward on her knees. She didn't hear Talia until she spoke.

"Hey." Talia placed a hand on Dawn's shoulder. "How can I help?"

Dawn felt a surge of support and love; emotions pushed straight into her chest. She knew Talia had been practicing projection, but she'd never felt her affinity so directly. It felt...nice.

She focused on breathing, in and out, until her hands stopped shaking.

"I don't know." Dawn's voice cracked, and she paused, collecting herself. "I don't know what the fuck I'm for now. I've been killing for so long. Every fluxborn I found. Told myself I was doing it for her."

She waved her hand at the herd of glittering creatures. One of them skittered away and snorted, but the rest ignored her.

"But what if I was wrong? They didn't kill her. What if they weren't all—"

She couldn't finish.

"You couldn't know," Talia said quietly.

"Doesn't matter." Dawn's throat burned. "I didn't ask. I just killed them."

She tugged at the necklace. Hundreds of teeth. Some of them, she knew now, weren't fluxborn at all. For the first time it felt heavy. Her fist clenched and the sharp edges bit into her hand, but she wasn't going to take it off. She didn't deserve to. The unicorn pressed closer, warm breath on her hands. Trusting her. After everything.

"I just assumed they were all monsters." She looked up at Talia, eyes raw. "What if I'm the monster?"

Talia didn't answer right away.

"You might be," she said finally. "But aren't we all a little bit monstrous?"

"You used to be more optimistic."

"I've had some bad influences." Talia squeezed her shoulder. "Plus, you'd just say something mean if I tried to comfort you."

Dawn let out a broken laugh and dragged a sleeve across her face. "Gods, this is pathetic. Ignore me."

"Dawn. I can literally feel your heartbeat in my chest."

"It's kind of gross, when you think about it," Dawn said.

"I think you love it," Talia answered with a laugh. Dawn didn't look at her face.

She chuckled and wiped her nose. "So, no secrets?"

"Not possible," Talia agreed.

Dawn laughed weakly and smiled in spite of herself. They sat and watched the mythic creatures in silence. Talia was a steady comfort at her shoulder.

The herd shifted, ghostly in the fog. Two young ones pushed through, gangly and fearless. One came right up and shoved its nose against Dawn's knee. Its warm breath made her eyes sting all over again.

She pressed her face into its velvety mane. "I'm sorry," she whispered—to the *elein*, to the city, to herself.

The foal nuzzled her cheek. When she finally stood, the ache in her chest was smaller. Still there, but less so. The mist was thinning. Firstlight was glinting over the eastern wall.

It hurt like hell. Ehrue was gone. Dawn had grieved her once, but this hit worse—the comedown from hoping, only to lose her again for good. But she'd seen her mate one last time. That was a gift.

Dawn had one thing left to do for Ehrue. Then she could figure out the rest.

56

HERS

TALIA

This warrior is sworn to the lar Valtaren line. If by blade or breath or death he may deliver them, it is already given.

— OATHSWORN INSCRIPTION, UNNAMED FAE,
TRANSLATION: T. SALAREN, 401 AC

Talia couldn't shut any of it off.

Dawn's grief. Elanwei's fury. The ghost of Lore's fingers on her skin, and the quicksand pull of Holloway's loss. Every emotion in the citadel scraped raw against her nerves, until she couldn't tell what was hers.

She'd scrubbed herself clean in cold water and pulled on silk pajamas from Elanwei's wardrobe. They were the only clothes that hadn't disintegrated.

Now she sat on a balcony over the gardens, buried in cushions and blankets she'd dragged here herself. The morning air bit her bare ankles, and it helped. The sting felt real.

She flinched when she heard footsteps.

Riven filled the doorway, shirtless, pants loose around his hips. The silver glyphs across his chest glowed faintly in the firstlight.

"You look like you want to be alone," he said quietly.

"I wouldn't mind company."

He hesitated before stepping outside. "It would be understandable after yesterday. Taking time for yourself."

"It doesn't matter," Talia sighed. "I can hear every heartbeat in this cursed city. There's no alone."

He lowered himself cross-legged beside her but stayed at arm's length. "There are only three heartbeats in this city," he said softly. "One of them's mine."

It held a question, an offer to leave.

She wanted him to wrap his arms around her, and she wanted him to go away. She reached for his hand before she could think too hard about it. She traced his knuckles, each tendon and raised scar.

"I feel everything," she whispered. "Dawn's heart is breaking, and it's right here, in my own chest. I tried to help her, but—I'm not sure I'm capable."

She was shaking. He was going to think she was broken. Too much. Too strange. But he didn't pull away. He just drew a slow breath and went still.

She felt it right away. The noise around them folded in like a tide drawing back. The static in her body eased. For the first time in days, she could breathe. She'd been so afraid he would be another person to drown in. This was the opposite.

"How—"

"It's my affinity. I'm a shield." A crooked, apologetic smile.

She laughed. "I could have used this a while ago."

"I wish I'd known. How do you feel?"

She didn't know. She drew in a slow breath, feeling the air in her lungs. Listening to her own ragged exhale.

"I feel like a swarm of bees just flew away, and I didn't realize how loud they were buzzing," she said, then immediately regretted it. "I'm sorry, that doesn't make sense."

"You make perfect sense," he said in a low rumble. "And you apologize too much. Get some rest, Talia. It'll stay quiet for as long as you need." He started to pull away, but she reached for his arm.

"Stay," she said. Then, after a pause, "You promised you wouldn't make me ask."

He shook his head. "I don't think that's a good idea," he said, but he settled back into the cushions.

Talia's body felt like it was sparkling. Sunlight was just breaking through the clouds in wide diagonal lines, so beautiful it looked made-up. Like a painting. When she met Riven's gray eyes, it felt a little hard to breathe.

Was it just a few minutes ago she'd wanted to be alone?

She reached forward, hesitated, then pressed a hand to his chest. Testing the silence. Waiting for the noise to come roaring back. He tipped his chin down, watching her fingers slip through the wiry hair.

He went still for a moment, just looking at her. His jaw tightened. Then he traced one hand up her stomach, mirroring the speed and pressure of her touch.

Each sensation was hers alone: the scrape of his calloused hands through the fabric, the catch of her breath.

She ran a finger up over his shoulder, watching the sigils light up under her fingertips, fading from blue to silver as she traced them.

This warrior is sworn to the lar Valtaren line...

Riven cleared his throat. "Are you reading my shoulder?"

"Shit, sorry," she said, feeling her face flush.

"Stop. Apologizing." His voice was a growl, but he was chuckling softly under each word. She'd give anything to know what he was thinking.

She glanced down and was surprised by the thick outline straining against his pants. Her empathy usually alerted her to that level of desire, but the air was clear. He followed her gaze.

"Ignore that," he said, shifting his weight and tugging the fabric loose. His fingers traced the thin straps of her silk camisole. "What would make you feel better?"

She fought to keep from glancing back down. He'd looked—big. "I don't know. I can't tell what you want, so I'm not sure where to start."

He stilled. His expression softened.

"Talia." He slipped a finger under her chin and tilted her head up to meet his eyes. "Has it always been loud for you? When you're with someone?"

She bit her lip and nodded. The only time she hadn't been

distracted by her partner's emotions was that time with Lore, when he'd nearly erased her.

Riven swore under his breath, then he looked her over. "But it's quiet now?"

She nodded.

"Okay. Fuck. Come here."

She pressed her fingers into his outstretched hands and he tugged her closer. He slid her glasses off, folded them carefully, and set them aside before asking, "May I kiss you?"

As an answer, she sat up on her knees and kissed him first. His mouth was wide and soft, and his beard tickled her face. His hands fell to her hips, tugging her against his chest.

The kiss was slow and long and searching. His hands roamed around her ass and up her back, gentle and curious.

His body pressed through her silk pajamas—ridges of muscle, a very thick erection—and she pushed into him, chasing more contact. She'd spent so long managing everyone else's need, she hadn't known she had this much of her own.

He pulled back. "Hey, I've got you." He ran his fingers through her hair and searched her face. "If this is too much, or not right, just say something."

Too much? She glanced down, but instead of baring himself, he tugged her forward until she was straddling his hips. They were both wearing pants, but the fabric was thin enough to feel everything between them.

"Oh gods," she gasped, pressing her lips together and looking up at the sky.

"Hey," he said. "It's okay. Just take what you need."

Her hips were already rocking, and a whimper slipped out. She should feel embarrassed by her raw need, how frantically she moved on him, but the burning pleasure racing down her legs was too good. She pressed forward, dragging herself over the whole hard length of him.

"You're doing so good," Riven said, kissing the end of her nose. "How does that feel?"

She twisted her hips and felt the tip of him slip up just inside her, fabric and all. A jolt shot through her, there and gone. *Not enough.* She needed to give him more. She placed one of his hands on her breast and guided him to pinch it. Her nipple hardened between his rough fingers and he groaned.

"You can have it. Whatever you want," she gasped. Her whole body felt warm inside, a deep, loose sensation. She wanted him to feel that good too.

He squeezed her breast, then dropped both hands to her hips and lifted her back to where she'd been. "Let's start here," he said. "We've got time."

It did feel good, the press and pulse of him, the gentle rock of his hips, his calloused hands scraping down her back. She closed her eyes and tried to concentrate on the way each ridge of his cock made her body shudder as she raked over him. She kept waiting for the next thing to do, and worry ate away at the edge of her joy.

"Isn't this frustrating for you?" she finally asked, bracing both hands on his solid chest and watching the sigils flare.

"Absolutely fucking not." He laughed, and the vibration rumbled through both their bodies. "Do you know how sexy it is, watching you take what you need? Knowing I can do this for you?"

His mouth found her jaw, the curve of her throat, unhurried. Like he knew where he wanted to be and wasn't in any rush to get there.

It felt like the world was telescoping down to this, the pressure between her legs, the rhythm of their bodies, the rasp of his beard against her cheek. She was almost entirely present.

"What can I do"—she gasped—"for you?"

"You're doing it," he said, a little breathless. "Ride me, just like this. Tell me what you like."

He wrapped his hands around her hipbones, and they were so large they nearly circled her waist. Then he pressed his thumbs into the sensitive area at top of her mound.

"That," she breathed, surprising herself. She'd never known what she enjoyed clearly enough to ask. "Do more of that. Please."

He hummed, and she moaned and rocked harder. She was close now. His thumbs kept pressing in slow circles as his thick shaft throbbed between them.

"Can I take this off?" He slipped a finger beneath the strap of her camisole. She nodded, and he drew it over her head before tossing it aside. They were both bare now, and she found herself just —looking at him. He was looking back. It felt more intimate than anything she could remember.

"I'll tell you what I want," he said, as if he knew she'd just keep trying to guess. His eyes slid over her, and a smile drew deep lines around his mouth and eyes. "There are so many things."

He ran one hand, slowly, down her neck. Along the sensitive edge of her breast. His thumb tweaked her nipple, drawing a squeak, before falling back to that place between her legs.

"I'm dying to hear every sound you make. To know how you taste. But what I really want"—he paused to kiss her again, drawing her into his chest—"is to take my time with you."

She didn't need to read his emotions after all. He was telling her everything she needed to know. He saw her—she could feel it in every careful, deliberate touch—and he wanted her. All of her.

It all hit, all at once, and she stopped trying to be quiet. The sound that came out of her was guttural and indecent, and she didn't care at all. She grabbed Riven's shoulders, pulled him closer, and writhed gracelessly. His solid arms just wrapped around her and held her close, tipping back just a little to help her ride it out.

She felt weightless and electric, like a cloud just past the verge of storming. There were tears on her face.

No one else's pleasure crested next to hers. She had nothing to prove or perform. Just wave after wave of pure sensation that belonged to her alone, and Riven's broad hands steady at her back, holding her up as she came apart.

She felt giddy. Her pleasure. Her desire. Her body. It was all hers.

"Thank you," she whispered when she could talk again. "That was—I've never felt anything like that."

He was grinning. "Good. That was the idea."

He helped her shift down so she was lying against his chest. She pressed her face into his shoulder, and he kissed the top of her head. His hand moved in slow circles on her bare back, absentminded, like he couldn't help it. She didn't want him to stop.

The silence felt like a gift. Just the morning air, the warmth of his skin against hers. For the first time in her life, pleasure hadn't felt like surrender.

"Feel better?" he asked, handing her back her glasses.

She smiled faintly. "Almost."

"Oh no." His fingers were in her hair now, gentle and reverent. "What else can I do?"

"No, not that. It just won't stay like this. Nothing like this ever lasts."

He pulled her closer. "Then we'll make the most of it while we have it. And if we lose it, we'll get it back."

She closed her eyes, letting his words settle in her chest.

A soft sound drifted up from the gardens below, first one birdsong, then another. Talia relaxed and listened as the new morning found its voice, clean and bright against the silence in her head.

57

ONE DAY AT A TIME

DAWN

In the aftermath of the flux surge, things changed. Birdsong returned to Valta for the first time in living memory. Peaceful creatures reappeared. And shifters who had been locked into fixed forms for four centuries found, without warning, that they could change shape again. We didn't understand the full implications at first.

— T. SALAREN, FIELD NOTES, 401 AC

Dawn walked back to the lower halls, the stone stairs cold on her bare feet. The citadel was quiet now. No hum of illusions. No heartbeat in the walls. Just shadows and echoes.

She eventually reached the place where Ehrue had burned out.

Nothing remained but a patch of silky ash. Dawn sank into a crouch. For a second she thought something flashed as the ash caught the light, but it was just ash.

Dawn scooped a handful in her palm. It clung to her skin, gray against her fingers. Too insubstantial for all the years of love and grief.

"Sorry," she said. This wasn't how it was supposed to go.

She found a scrap of cloth and folded the ash into it. Wrapped it tight. Held it close to her chest. Then she left the extraction chamber for the last time. She had planned to die here, but she had to live to find that clutch of eggs, to safeguard their children. Ehrue had given her that one last task, and she wasn't going to fail.

Outside, the air was cool and clean. Mist curled around broken statues as Dawn crossed the sloping garden. The unicorns moved among the overgrown brambles. The herd parted for her when she got to the field.

Dawn knelt in the wet grass. "This is better," she said quietly. "You shouldn't be alone in the dark. Now you can see the sky and the sparkly horses."

She dug a shallow hole with her hands. Put the bundle in and covered it with soil. Pressed her palm to the mound. That was all she could do. One of the elegant creatures bent its head, touching his muzzle to the disturbed dirt. She let herself take it as a good sign.

"Yeah," she murmured. "You'll like this."

The tightness in her chest didn't crack open again. It eased. Just a notch. Enough to breathe around. She stood, wiping mud on her new pants. The sun was trying to break through the clouds.

Movement caught her eye. Talia and Riven walked across a balcony, standing close. Riven had his fingers in Talia's hair. The girl leaned into his touch.

Dawn snorted. "Took them long enough."

She watched Talia smile just a moment longer than she needed to. Then she turned toward the citadel—still broken, still standing—and made her way back up the path.

She met her two friends upstairs. They were pretending things were normal, but Talia's heartbeat was thrumming with joy.

"Hey," Talia said. "Everything okay?"

"Nope," Dawn answered. They'd promised no secrets.

Talia nodded.

"We should get moving," Dawn added. "I'd like to sleep somewhere that smells less like death."

Riven looked over. "We can be ready in an hour."

"If you two drag your feet, I'm flying away without you," Dawn said, brushing past him.

He huffed a breath. "Half an hour, then."

She kept walking. Thinking.

She'd spent her whole life pretending to be mortal, choosing life on the streets over wearing a collar. When Valrotala fell and the channels exploded, pretending became the only option. Four hundred years locked in one skin.

She rolled her shoulders. Her dragon was right there, coiled and ready, like a muscle she'd forgotten how to flex.

She could fly them home in an afternoon if she wanted. Ironic, after all they'd been through, that it could end this quickly. They'd be back in Gateway tomorrow.

58

MYTHMAKING

TALIA

History is not faithful to events. It is faithful to those in power. Even the false gods understood this. It's why they claimed to be gods.

— *COLLECTED SAYINGS OF LORE TAVIS*, COMPILED BY THE ACOLYTES OF STARFALL SANCTUARY

Flying on dragonback was everything Talia dreamed it would be. Dawn's iridescent pink scales shimmered beneath her palms. Riven's arms wrapped around her waist. The wind tore her braid loose as Valta unfurled below them. Forests blurred, rivers flashed silver. For one weightless afternoon, she was purely happy.

The bond thrummed with Dawn's fierce joy as their excruciating weekslong journey wound backward in hours. Talia's mind raced ahead as they flew. Lore was gone, so Starfall should be leaderless. She could claim the archives, build something real there. She closed her eyes, felt the wind on her face, imagined what might come next.

When she opened her eyes, the horizon was black with smoke.

The haze thickened. Ash stung her throat. Riven's hand locked tight at her hip. A city below them was burning. She recognized the thick walls, the tidy grid of streets. Haven. Dawn banked low, and they landed just outside the city.

Char crunched under their boots as they approached. The pristine order of the military outpost was gone. Whole blocks had collapsed inward, coals breathing red. The eastern districts still roared with flame, which leaped roof to roof. The air was so hot it blistered Talia's lips.

Could Lore have done this? Movement flashed in the streets.

There were people down there. They were huge and mostly naked. Some had faint sigils glimmering across their skin.

"Who are they?" she whispered.

Riven's arms tightened around her waist. "My people."

The words stopped her breath. Dawn's hand lifted to the necklace of teeth she always wore. Horror flooded the bond.

"Stars and fucking moons." Dawn's voice was small. Stricken.

The records in the library said the fae had vanished after Ehrue's blast. The fluxborn appeared at the same time. Then when Ehrue overloaded the channels yesterday...

"They weren't *elein*," Talia's voice cracked. "The fluxborn were always fae."

She caught flashes of violence through the smoke—a body dragged, a scream cut short. She looked away, but she couldn't unsee it.

Her mind flashed to the fluxborn wolf den, Dawn killing those pups in cold blood. They had been fae too. Transformed and trapped. Now those people were slaughtering citizens in Haven. Where did justice begin? Where did it end?

Haven was ash. There were already figures peeling out of town and moving east toward Gateway. Violence marching across the continent, unstoppable as a flood. The future she'd imagined—that was gone. No archives. No joyful life beside Riven and Dawn.

She'd spent her life studying myths—heroes and monsters, good and evil—but she'd missed the point. She'd been so focused on the characters, on stories and symbolism. She should have asked who was writing those stories, and why.

The gods weren't just real. They'd had agendas. The Divine Navigator and Elanwei and Lore were all gone, but someone would fill the void they'd left behind. Someone would write the next myth, become the new divine authority, reshape the world.

She'd turned down Lore's offer, but she hadn't understood what he was truly seeking. Not just power. Agency. The ability to decide whose story would be recorded as history.

She got it now. And she wanted that for herself.

59

THE NECKLACE

DAWN

Some of our number chose sleep over death. I wish them well, but that fate isn't for me. When my time comes, I plan to stay down.

— VAEL LAR VARLOHEIM, PERSONAL JOURNAL, APPROX. 51 AC. TRANS: T. SALAREN

The fluxborn were always fae. Talia's words rang through Dawn's whole body. Every tooth on her necklace. Every kill. Not mindless monsters. There'd been people in there.

Smoke hung thick in the air above Haven. The streets were just carnage. Streets she'd walked, buildings that caged her. All smoke and coals. She didn't give a fuck about Haven. She'd have burned that hellhole herself. But she doubted the violence would stop here. She'd be damned if she let them reach Gateway. There were people there worth protecting.

Fire surged under her skin. She wanted to rage and kill. Reduce the cursed continent to ash. But Talia stood beside her with tears streaking her face. Riven was steady at her back, blades in hand. She wasn't alone. And her story didn't end here.

Her mate's last gift, a location pressed into her mind in those final moments. Deep in the frost caves of Thol Amras, a clutch of pale moonshell eggs waited in the dark. Their children. Violence burned in Dawn's blood, but protecting that fragile future mattered more.

She lifted her gaze to the smoke, the ruined city, the fae ripping through it. She bared her teeth. Not in grief but in resolve. Dawn had always been a little feral. But now? She was something worse.

Something stronger. A mother. A bond-mate. And gods help anyone who tried to touch what was hers.

Talia must have felt the surge of resolve through the bond, because her friend's hand found Dawn's shoulder. "We can be dangerous too," Talia said.

Damn right. They fucking would be.

EPILOGUE

GODHOOD

HOLLOWAY

They stood on a ridge above a mortal city and watched the wave of death emerge. Just a few at first, stumbling from the ruins. Then dozens from the plains. Hundreds from the mountains. The transformation spread outward. In every corner of the continent, fluxborn became fae, and fae became death.

The city in the valley below was on fire. He tasted the smoke. A man in a green cloak fell with a blade in his back. A woman sobbed over a small body.

He felt the balance tilt away from humanity. Still nowhere near an equilibrium.

He lifted his hands, and light pooled in his palms. When he flexed his fingers, the air straightened itself, light bent at new angles. The grass at his feet turned brown and crumbled to dust. A halo of corrosive power spread from wherever he stood. He could stop the bloodshed down below. He had that power. Maybe he should care, but he didn't.

He didn't remember arriving here.

One minute he was looking at his friends. Fingers laced with the prophet's. Then the channel system overloaded and white fire licked up their legs, and then—nothing.

Someone else—was it the prophet?—was inside his head, sifting through his memories like fingers through sand. Taking what it wanted. Discarding the rest.

A mother's laugh. Rain on summer evenings. A thumb brushing his knuckles.

Gone.

The reasons those things mattered.

Gone too.

The man he'd been before had wanted something. A name lingered on his tongue—*Cordon*—like the memory of a bitter taste. But it wouldn't quite stick. The memory kept slipping away.

"Holloway."

The prophet's voice pulled him back into his body.

Holloway. That was his name. When had he forgotten?

"The bloodshed here will play out within the week," the prophet was saying. The fae were quitting Haven and turning east. "They will seize the shipyards in Gateway and move on to Vaelis. When we arrive, the city will be ready to receive us."

"How do you know?" Holloway asked.

The prophet's smile sharpened. "I see further than I used to."

"Are we going to Vaelis now?" Holloway asked.

"We have someone to collect first."

The prophet's hand found Holloway's face, a thumb tracing his jaw. The touch was cold, numbing everything that was wrong beneath his skin. Glimmers of feelings froze and withered.

The numb was pleasant. He wanted more numb.

"Do you remember our companions?" the prophet asked. "From before?"

Faces flashed through Holloway's mind, but he couldn't hold their names. They slid away like water.

The prophet's smile sharpened. "Forget them. They were a disappointment, in the end."

The shadows around Holloway's wrist tightened. He leaned into the prophet's touch. *I live to serve*. The echo of an old oath hummed between them—tugging, soothing, erasing choice.

Maybe it was okay that he couldn't remember. He let the fragments of memories fade.

"Where are we going, then?" he asked.

The answer didn't matter. He would follow the prophet anywhere. He had nowhere else to go.

The prophet's hand slid to the back of Holloway's neck, pulling him close. His voice dropped to something almost tender.

"There's another in the bloodline." A pause. "I know where to find Merit Salaren."

"Merit," Holloway echoed.

The name came out flat, hollowed of everything it should mean. Some distant part of him remembered a girl. He'd cared about her. The feeling lingered like an echo, orphaned from its source.

Something in him tried to resist, hadn't he promised to protect...but the oath in his palm burned, and the feeling died. The prophet's fingers traced down Holloway's throat.

"Merit Salaren is alone. Estranged from her family. We can use that."

Holloway followed the prophet away from the burning valley. Behind them, thousands of fae marched toward the coast. Ahead of them, a woman in exile that his prophet wanted to collect. And somewhere out there, the friends he left behind, with names he couldn't remember.

The grass died where he stepped. Reality skittered and smoothed in his wake. The prophet moved ahead, and he followed.

The man he'd been had wanted something. Justice, maybe. The god he was becoming had the power to take it, if he could remember why it mattered.

ACKNOWLEDGMENTS

I always said I'd write a fantasy novel someday, as if it would just happen on its own.

Creating this book cost more than I expected. I stepped away from my career, typed in my car through kids' soccer practices, and chose late nights at the keyboard over sleep.

Absolutely none of it would have been possible without my best friend and husband, Brendan. He's every good romance trope rolled into a real person. Thank you. I love you.

Then there are my kids, whose audacity and silliness remind me every day how I want to live. I love you both, and I'm so proud of the people you are.

To my parents, who've always supported me. Growing up knowing I was loved was the launching pad for every big scary thing I've been able to do. And to my grandparents, who showed me how to tackle hardship with humor.

To my sister, who takes care of everyone around her and would have written a funnier book. When I describe Dawn as "honest about hard truths and loyal to a fault," that's Kari.

To the many editors and early readers who helped me carve a big pile of embarrassing words into an actual story—thank you. Especially my line and copy editor, Elyse Lyon, and my proofreader, Arianne Cruz.

And finally to my readers: thank you so much for taking a chance on a debut indie author. Your faith in my story gave me the energy I needed in the final stretch. The fact that you're reading this now is what makes it a real book.

WHAT LORE WON'T SAY OUT LOUD

Was Heron Valence's assassination just a coincidence, or was Lore targeting Holloway all along?

Does Lore hate Talia, or is he hiding something else?

And why does it have to be a Salaren?

Some answers are already there, in between the lines. Some are only in Lore's head.

ABOUT THE AUTHOR

HANNA GAARD writes character-driven romantic fantasy about messy people who think they're heroes. She has a degree in Media Studies and spent years in B2B marketing before realizing that storytelling was the best part of her job. What if it was her *only* job?

No Gods West of Here is her debut novel, self-published and proudly so. She lives on the Oregon Coast with her husband and two kids.

Connect with Hanna

Join her newsletter at:
www.hannagaard.com/subscribe

Follow on Instagram:
@hannagaard

www.ingramcontent.com/pod-product-compliance
Lightning Source LLC
LaVergne TN
LVHW091138150826
845672LV00005B/975